D0058387

ROGUE WARRIOR®

DETACHMENT BRAVO

ROGUE WARRIOR®

DETACHMENT BRAVO

Richard Marcinko
and
John Weisman

POCKET BOOKS
New York   London   Toronto   Sydney   Singapore

S

This book is a work of fiction. Names, characters, places and incidents are products of the author's imagination or are used fictitiously. Operational details have been altered so as not to betray current Spec-War techniques.

The Rogue Warrior's PDW courtesy of Heckler & Koch, Inc.

POCKET BOOKS, a division of Simon & Schuster, Inc.
1230 Avenue of the Americas, New York, NY 10020

Marcinko, Richard
    Rogue warrior—Detachment Bravo / Richard Marcinko and John Weisman.
        p. cm.
    Includes index.
    ISBN 0-671-00071-3
    1. Rogue Warrior (Fictitious character)—Fiction. 2. Special forces
    (Military science)—Fiction. 3. Terrorism—Prevention—Fiction.
    4. Commando troops—Fiction. 5. South America—
    Fiction. I. Title: Detachment Bravo. II. Weisman, John. III. Title.

PS3563.A6362 R637 2001
813'.54—dc21

                                                        2001021262

First Pocket Books hardcover printing May 2001

10 9 8 7 6 5 4 3 2 1

You lot say you want to know
the two most important things about Ireland?
Well, first of all, Cain and Abel, *they* had to be
from bloody fuckin' Belfast, didn't they?
Second, in Ireland we have our own Holy Trinity:
Death, Pain, and Sufferin'.

—PADDY COHAN OF THE IRA, HOLDING
COURT AT THE LION'S HEAD TAVERN,
NEW YORK CITY, 1962

THE ROGUE WARRIOR'S
TEN COMMANDMENTS OF SPECWAR

- I am the War Lord and the wrathful God of Combat and I will always lead you from the front, not the rear.

- I will treat you all alike—just like shit.

- Thou shalt do nothing I will not do first, and thus will you be created Warriors in My deadly image.

- I shall punish thy bodies because the more thou sweatest in training, the less thou bleedest in combat.

- Indeed, if thou hurteth in thy efforts and thou suffer painful dings, then thou art Doing It Right.

- Thou hast not to like it—thou hast just to do it.

- Thou shalt Keep It Simple, Stupid.

- Thou shalt never assume.

- Verily, thou art not paid for thy methods, but for thy results, by which meaneth thou shalt kill thine enemy by any means available before he killeth you.

- Thou shalt, in thy Warrior's Mind and Soul, always remember My ultimate and final Commandment. There Are No Rules—Thou Shalt Win at All Cost.

Contents

PART ONE
DEATH

CHAPTER

1

OH, DEAR GOD, HOW I DO LOVE PAIN. IN FACT, THOSE OF YOU WHO have read the previous eight books in this series understand all too well that I have an ongoing, enduring, even unique relationship with pain. For those of you who haven't, let me say that pain and I enjoy a symbiotic bond, a fundamental, intrinsic link, a basic and perpetual connection. The gist of this link is that whenever I endure pain, I realize I am guaranteed to still be very much, very Roguishly, *alive.* In fact, my life is the perfect articulation of an essential, Froggish precept taught to me during Hell Week by an old, grizzled pipe-smoking UDT chief boatswain's mate named John Parrish. Chief Parrish's theory goes: *no pain . . . no* pain.

And so, friends, I can report to you with no hesitation whatsoever that right now I was very much . . . alive. And where was I, you ask? Where, precisely, was I experiencing so much life?

I was flat on my back, punctured by an irregular bed of nails. Big nails. Sharp nails. Many of them antique nails—the old-fashioned, hand-wrought kind of nails. I was stuck, arms and legs akimbo, in a crawl space between the second and third floors of a Victorian-era mansion that had been turned into a series of flats (which is how the Brits refer to apartments) in Hammersmith, one of Central London's closest-in suburbs, trying not to make a sound as I made preparations to use a silent drill to install a flexible, fiber-optic cable attached to a fish-eye lens through Victorian hardwood subfloor, 1930s asphalt tile, and 1950s carpeting that sat precisely seven inches above the ol' Rogue snout.

Except—there's always a catch, isn't there?—to get to the target area, I'd had to wriggle on my back across seven feet of nail-enhanced, back-lacerating crawl space. Why were the nails there in the first place? Who the fuck knew, and who the fuck cared. I hadn't seen them at first because I hadn't used any lights as I made my way into the crawl space because light might give away my existence to the six armed and dangerous IRA splinter group tangos just above me. Oh, I had a tiny, red-lensed flashlight that would assist me once I was ready to do the drill bit, but that was it. I'd do my drilling, install the fish-eye lens, and then retreat, unspooling fiber-optic cable as I did, so it could be plugged into our TV screen, allowing us to see the bedroom of the flat above, and see what they were doing in there. We already had video of the living room and kitchen areas. But when it came to the bedroom we were blind.

Yes, I see you out there. You're saying, "Hey, what the fuck? Why not use all those techno goodies in your arsenal. Like micro thermal viewers that can pick up human beans from across the street, and state-of-the-art X-ray glasses, and all that shit. It is the twenty-first century after all."

Well, friends, "all that shit" is dandy if you are a cardboard-and-meringue Hollywood adventure hero whose action toys are made in China by slave labor. But me, I'm the old-fashioned real thing, and unfortunately the real action adventure hero doesn't get to play with gadgets that work in movies but not real life. In the movies, there are always timers on bombs to tell you how many seconds are left before the hero's gonna get blown up. In Hollywood, the good guy always manages to crack the computer password in a matter of seconds. In Hollywood, they never count the rounds they shoot.

Not us. My men and I do things the old-fashioned way. We count rounds. Why? Because most SEALs go into combat with only three hundred of 'em, and you can't fucking afford to waste a single shot. And in all the years I've ever played with explosive devices, I have never, ever, even once, seen a bomb that had a digital or analog timer courteously counting down the seconds for me so I'd know precisely when the sucker was gonna explode. No fucking way. And last, I leave all the serious computer shit to the professional hackers. Sure, I can tell you all about sniffers and protocols. I can program in COBOL. I can even write UNIX code if I have to. But these days everything computerwise changes so fast that I'd rather hire some nineteen-year-old PO3 puke who knows it all, rather than have to spend twenty hours a week trying to keep up with the latest developments in bits and bytes.

Nope, I want to save my time for what I do best: killing tangos and breaking things. To wit: I sneak and I peek, and then I hop and I pop, which I almost always follow with the ever popular shooting & looting.

The sneaking and peeking part of this particular goatfuck was long finished. We'd deployed a piece of National Security Agency eavesdropping gizmo known as a Big Ear to monitor the apartment the tangos were in. Big Ears are laser microphones with a throw of about 150 yards. But our twenty-million-dollar gizmo could not tell me whether or not the tangos inside had finished assembling the weapon they were working on. *That* called for what the military bureaucracy formally refers to as "eyes on."

After all, no piece of equipment, no matter how much it costs, can force people to talk if they're security conscious. And these tango assholes understood the rudiments of surveillance. So they never spoke to one another about what they were doing, or how it was going. Instead, they spoke in generalities. If there was anything to say about the weapons they were building, it was most certainly done by sign language and notepad. They'd obviously seen all the current action adventure movies, too, and they were taking no chances. So I was stuck here, doing my snoop & poop the old-fashioned—by which I mean painful—method: creeping, crawling, and bleeding.

Now, I'm sure you want me to explain why I, a humping, pumping, cap-crimping, deep-sea–diving SEAL, whose proper element is H_2O, was flopping around like a suffocating flounder in the first place. Hey, asshole—there's water in those copper pipes over there, and that's close enough for me. So shut the fuck up, sit the fuck down, pay some attention, and I'll give you the sit-rep—or at least as much of it as time permits.

I was here because I'd been assigned to a clandestine, patch-work, multinational, joint counterterrorist task force known as DET (for DETachment) Bravo. DET Bravo was headquartered in London. It was made up of Americans and Brits and assigned to deal proactively with the no-goodnik splinter groups who were trying to wreck the Good Friday peace accord, which was bring-ing reconciliation to Northern Ireland in fits and starts. By no-goodniks, I mean those few hard-line terrorist groups, both IRA and Unionist, that had decided the best way to bring the agree-ment to a screeching halt was to target Americans and Brits in London and in Northern Ireland.

As you probably know, one of the by-products of the Good Friday Accord was the immediate expansion of American multi-national companies into Northern Ireland to bolster the economy. Corporations—from Dell Computer, to American Express, to Intel, Cisco Systems, as well as scores of other cutting edge busi-nesses—moved some of their operations into Northern Ireland. There were enormous tax advantages for doing so, not to mention a large and well-educated labor pool.

But all of that economic expansion and growth had come to a full stop. The Good Friday Accord had come unraveled because groups of hard-line tangos were targeting American executives in Belfast, Derry, Portadown, Newry, and Ballymena in Northern Ireland, and—more to the immediate point—right here in

London. Half a dozen American businessmen had been killed in the past four months alone. The result: the corporations were shutting down offices and pulling their people out.

With the economic situation deteriorating and the political polls hitting rock bottom, our government and the Brits finally decided to form a joint task force to deal with the tangos targeting Americans. The Irish would not stand for any armed Americans on their soil—and the Brits weren't about to push the issue. But London was open turf. And so, working out of a suite of MI5's former offices on the fourth floor of Curzon Street House, a six-story office building located at the top of Curzon Street in London's fashionable Mayfair district, was DET Bravo, a unit composed of FBI and CIA counterintelligence analysts, elements from Scotland Yard and Special Branch, as well as NSA and its British equivalent, the Government Communications Head-quarters (GCHQ), based in Cheltenham. Finally, exiled to the dank, bomb-proof basement of Curzon Street House (and at the fist, or business, end of a largely analytic and bureaucratic arm), was an unwieldy patchwork of British military units, American SEALs, and a working group from SO-19, Scotland Yard's armed, special-operations unit.

Being part of DET Bravo hadn't been my idea. I was happy doing what I'd been doing: troubleshooting for General Thomas E. Crocker, Chairman of the Joint Chiefs of Staff. But after a series of misadventures in the Caucasus, and the direct intervention of a politically appointed ambassador whom I'd embarrassed, I'd been unceremoniously yanked off General Crocker's staff, assigned to a soon-to-be-defunct security program, and assigned an office sans phone in an unoccupied warehouse deep within the Washington Navy Yard. If that wasn't being put on the shelf, I don't know what is.

But I don't have a whole lot of shelf life. In fact, I don't have *any* fucking shelf life. When I'm ambushed, I do what Warriors do best: I counterattack. Just because my shirtsleeve is five inches longer than my inseam, don't think I'm just another knuckle-dragging Neanderthal. I speak five languages level four fluently. I have an MA in political science from Auburn University. I have one-on-one briefed the president of the United States. And I know how the game of hardball is played in Washington.

So, I went on the offensive. I made sure that friendly staffers on the House of Representatives and Senate Armed Services committees knew who was doing what to whom. I exposed some long-closeted skeletons inside the Pentagon's E-ring, including a 1999 tit-tweaking episode concerning one of the Army's highest-ranking female ossifers and the Air Farce's vice chief of staff. And finally, thanks to General Crocker's influence (and the balls to make politically incorrect decisions and ram 'em down the Navy's throat), I was "exiled" to London, to head the American military element of DET Bravo.

And so, here I lay in P^4 condition: pricked, pierced, punctured, and perforated. My basic black BDU shirt (the upper portion of that ever-oxymoronic battle dress uniform), was shredded. My jeans were in no better shape. My back resembled something out of one of those Freddy Krueger scarification movies. But I'd managed to make it all the way to my objective, and even—ooh, it felt so *g-o-o-o-d*—insert the drill.

Now came the hard part. All drills, even the so-called silent ones, make some noise. I flicked the "talk" switch on my radio three times to say I was in position. Then listened to the radio receiver in my ear, through which my Brit comrade in arms, brigadier[1] Mick Owen, would give me the "go." Mick, who was in overall charge of this op, had arranged for a crew of Scotland Yard's finest undercover operators masquerading as electric utility workers to jackhammer the street in front of the flat as I drilled.

---

[1] That's a Brit one-star general, equivalent in rank to our own brigadier general.

I lay silent, waiting. And waiting. And waiting. WTF.[2] I hit the switch again. Nothing. Nada. Bupkis. I reached around and tried to trace the radio wire from my ear to the miniature transceiver that sat in a pouch on my CQC vest, and discovered that the wire itself had been shredded along with the vest as I'd crawled into position.

Oh, great. But I had no time to lose. And so, jackhammers or no, I withdrew the drill (I can tell you it resembles a multispeed Dremel Tool and still not violate my security clearance) from the specially constructed pouch on my chest. C-a-r-e-f-u-l-l-y, I set it up, attached the drill head, switched the power on, and began to work.

Have I told you the subfloor above my nose was wood? I have? Good. Because minuscule shavings from the subfloor started to drop into my eyes. No, I wasn't wearing goggles. Don't ask why. Now, I really *was* working blind. I tried to shift my head but I couldn't do that if I wanted to use my miniflashlight. And so, I blinked the fucking shavings out of my eyes and just kept drilling.

The good news was that it didn't take long. I had a tiny hole in a matter of minutes. Quickly, I disassembled the drill and packed it up securely. I took the fiber-optic cable with its fish-eye lens and worked it up, up, up into the hole, then took out a pocket viewer, attached it to the cable end, and peeked.

The brightness of the image made me blink. I'd drilled the hole in an exposed position. The damn thing had to be concealed to work properly, and I'd missed the fucking couch. I focused my eyes and risked taking a peek, exposing about an inch and a half of fiber-optic cable. Shit—I was about six inches too far to the starboard. I coitus-interruptus'd the cable, reassembled the drill, shifted my body a foot to the right, and s-l-o-w-l-y started the whole process, including the fucking sawdust in my eyes, over

---

[2]What The Fuck.

again. Then I stowed the drill, reinserted the cable, attached the eyepiece, and carefully worked the lens up into position under the narrow bed, where it would not be so obvious.

Bingo. Now I saw the whole room, distorted in the two-hundred-degree wide angle lens. I disengaged the pocket viewer, screwed on a coupler, tacked the cable in position so I wouldn't pull it out as I exfiltrated, then attached the 150-foot roll of fiber optics I carried to the coupler.

Now came the fun part. I scrunched my shoulders and tried to turn around so I could make my way back, those two painful-plus yards, to where I could swing down from the crawl space and work my way into the air shaft, then drop nine feet into the apartment where we were staging our assault.

Except I couldn't move. I was hung up, like a crab in a trap, unable to get my fucking BDUs unsnagged from the goddamn nails. But time was a-wasting. The clock was ticking, and there were a dozen shooters waiting for me in the apartment below and its immediate environs. And so, I operated by the same rule by which I have lived my entire professional life: **I Didn't Have to Like It, I Just Had to Do It.** To whit: I wrenched my shoulders and back and butt and legs off the nail points and muscled my way back to the air shaft, leaving shreds of cloth and scraps of skin (or maybe it was the other way around. I was beyond caring at that point) as I did.

• • •

Exhausted and bleeding, I rolled into the air shaft, caught the toe of my Size Extra-Rogue assault boot on the wooden frame, and pulled my body off the nails. God, it felt good to be so . . . alive. Carefully, I climbed down the air shaft, unspooling cable as I went. It was only another three yards to the apartment below. I backed through the two-foot-square hole in the wall that we'd cut six hours earlier, handed off the cable reel to a Special Branch intel dweeb named Roger, and went down on my hands and knees as if I'd been gut-punched. "Shit, that hurt."

The master chief I call Boomerang, who knows that *sympathy* is the word that sits in the SEAL dictionary between *shit* and *syphilis*, reminded me that if we were going to take the fuckin' tangos down, I'd better stop wasting time, get off my hands and knees, and get into my gear. But then he brought out a couple of antiseptic swabs from the first aid kit in his fanny pack and wiped my back down. At least I'd stave off infection for a while. I'd complete the treatment later with a healthy dose of my favorite cure-all gin, Bombay Sapphire.

Besides, Boomerang was right, of course. Master chiefs most always are. So, I pulled myself to my feet and started shrugging into my CQC gear.

While I'm making ready to go over the rail (metaphorically speaking), I'll explain the dynamics of today's Murphy-wrought tactical problem. We had those six armed and dangerous tangos in the apartment. They, in turn, were in the final stages of assembling what we knew to be a trio of portable, powerful bombs. That's why we had to go in during daylight, instead of waiting until night to hit 'em. We couldn't allow even the remotest possibility that they'd slip away and set off a bomb somewhere in London.

How powerful were the bombs? Well, the tangos had somehow managed to get their hands on 550 grams of Cubanol, the U.S. military's latest generation plastic explosive. Cubanol is octanitrocubane-based,[3] which meant that with their one pound plus of plastic, they could make up to three bombs capable of blowing fifty-meter-by-fifty-meter holes in the ground. Octanitrocubane, you see, is 25 percent more powerful than C-4 plastic explosive, and twice as powerful as TNT. It is also totally shock-insensitive, which means that unlike C-4 you can smack it with a

---

[3] Octanitrocubane has a very high density—2 g/cm[3]. The denser the explosive compound, the more energy it transfers when it goes from solid to gas and energy during combustion.

hammer and it still won't explode. But most revolutionary, at least so far as the EPA tree-huggers assigned to monitor the Pentagon are concerned, Cubanol was designed to be environmentally friendly.

Yup, octanitrocubane may blow you to the well-known smithereens, but it won't release greenhouse gases or fluorocarbons into the air, or damage the ozone layer. No, I am not kidding.

The former Leader of the Free World and my ex–commander in chief, the selfsame individual I consistently refer to as Blow Job Bill, may not have given a shit about protecting our nuclear secrets from China, or our diplomatic secrets from Russia. But by God, he was going to make damn sure certain that our bombs didn't cause global warming. And so, BJB signed an executive order back in 1998, directing that all the bullets, bombs, and other ordnance developed during the remainder of his administration conform to "green" regulations laid out by a cabal of tree-hugging political appointees at the Environmental Protection Agency.

That's right, folks: you might have thought that our military was under the control of the National Command Authorities.[4] You would be wrong. I can tell you definitively that is not the case. Our military is really run by . . . the EPA. Go figure.

Digression aside, we had to hit the apartment, take down the tangos, and capture the bombs. And we had to do it all without having isolated the immediate area beforehand, because according to our intelligence assets, the tangos had already managed to assemble the first of the bombs, and they were perfectly capable and willing to set it off inside the apartment, immediately making this densely populated area a lot less densely populated (but still safe for the ozone layer).

No, we're not talking about Muslim fundamentalists here. But you're right: the thinking is very much the same. In point of fact,

---

[4] The president and the secretary of defense, or their duly deputized alternates or successors.

according to the intel squirrels at Scotland Yard, these assholes were from a small but dangerous group calling itself the True IRA, or TIRA. TIRAs were hard-liners, most of whom had served long terms in Northern Irish prisons for assassinations, car bombings, and revenge killings. For years, the True IRA had scrounged for funds: they'd robbed banks and jewel couriers, they'd stolen cars, they'd even stuck up grocery stores to finance their operations. But about nine months ago, TIRA had received an influx of cash from sources unknown that had allowed the group to expand its operations. They'd bought new explosives and arms. They'd also shifted ops to London—the belly of the British beast. And that was bad news, because the intelligence available to DET Bravo indicated that these TIRA assholes were just as willing to die for their cause as any Hamas, Hezb'allah, or Islamic Jihad martyrs were to ride the magic carpet ride to Allah for theirs. Just so long, that is, as they could take me and my DET Bravo shipmates, plus a bunch of innocent Brit victims, along with 'em. Which explains our desperate need to see inside the entire apartment, so we would know where each and every bad guy was as we hit the place. If we didn't take 'em down in one fell swoop, one of 'em might set the fucking device off, in which case a sizeable portion of Hammersmith would be vaporized.

So here we were, operating in total stealth—and worse, in daylight. Even so, we'd managed to make our preps without, apparently, sending the tangos any bad vibes. We'd made our way to the flat where we'd stage our assault in pairs and threes. We had managed to stash a four-man element from SO-19, the Scotland Yard's armed counterterrorist squad, on the roof of the apartment house, and another sextet of DET Bravo personnel—SAS shooters from 22 Regiment dressed in civvies—cached in an alley on the far side of the building, to make sure no one absquatulated out the back door. But there was no overt police presence: no Special Branch roadblocks, Metropolitan Police cars, or other signs that the authorities—that's us—were in the neighborhood.

Why? Because neither the Metropolitan Police nor SO-19 was able to say for sure whether these TIRA assholes had mounted a countersurveillance operation, watching us as we had watched them. Which meant we had to act as if that was exactly what they'd done.

So, we'd gone the covert route, which was risky, but could be effective in the long run. Our radios were ultralow frequency and secure so they wouldn't betray us either to the news media, or the bad guys.[5] We dressed in civilian clothes, and what combat gear we'd carried in had been concealed by long overcoats.

Here was the good news: Special Branch had managed to clear out the flat directly to the right of the tangos, and had planted listening devices and cameras in the walls. We'd slipped into the flat directly below courtesy of a lovely old couple who didn't mind our cutting through the wall so long as we promised to patch the hole and match the paint. Now for the bad news: instead of using us SEALs to hit the tango apartment, today's assault team was made up of one Royal Marine named Andy, two Paras—Bill and Gill—and four of us SEALs: Nod DiCarlo, Butch Wells, Boomerang, and me.

What's so bad about that you ask. I mean, aren't I talking about seven people who know how to shoot and loot and do it full-time for a living? Well, yes I am. But there's a factor about dynamic entry that must be explained right now for you to understand my considerable concern about the success of this op. Dynamic entry has to be flawless. It has to be smooth. My men and I work twenty hours a week on entry techniques. That time and energy gives us our seamless and seemingly effortless choreography, which allows us to move with the precise violence of

---

[5] Tangos often keep TV sets on in their safe houses, because TVs can be affected by UHF and VHF radio transmissions, which cause snow or horizontal lines on the screen. Many an op has been compromised because the raiders couldn't keep their radio transmissions to a minimum, and the bad guys were prepared.

action, surprise, and speed that are imperative to close-quarters-combat entries if they are to succeed.

But today, over my strenuous objections, my guys and I had been paired up with a trio of strangers. They may indeed have been the three best shooters in the world. But we'd never worked with them before. We hadn't had any opportunity to cross-train. We didn't know their moves, and they didn't know ours. There was none of the physical shorthand that goes on in all dedicated assault teams, whether they are SEALs, or Delta shooters, SWAT cops, or DEA takedown squads. And that, my friends, was so far as I was concerned, a recipe for disaster.

If I'd had my way, the assault element would have been either all Brits, or all SEALs. But despite my protests (not to mention Mick Owen's as well), this was the Labour Party administration here in Britain, and the veddy tony PM (that's the prime minister, for those of you who don't follow British politics), is slavishly Clintonesque. No, that doesn't mean he spends his afternoons getting blow jobs from the Downing Street interns. It means he likes to be politically correct at all times.

Thus, the PM gave in to the Royal Navy paper warriors and the British Army's memo-writing officers at the Ministry of Defense who demanded that elements from *their* uniform services should be able to claim a share of the glory. They threatened to go public if it didn't happen—and the PM buckled. No thought was given to unit integrity or tactical cohesion. It was politics all the way. I guess I should be happy that they hadn't assigned me a squad of Royal Air Farce runway cops in the bargain.

Now let me give you the kicker: Detachment Bravo was not even a military operation. Mick didn't report to the Ministry of Defense. DET Bravo had been placed under the command of the home secretary who, not giving a shit about what he referred to as "a bunch of armed thugs," assigned one of his junior political appointees to keep an eye on us. Which said JPA did, by second-guessing and/or countermanding every fucking move we made.

And thus, under the jurisdiction of idiots, we'd been ordered to operate with people whose techniques were unfamiliar to us, no matter what the consequences to the mission's success might be.

That, folks, is what happens when you are being governed by alleged leaders who see the military as yet another opportunity for social experimentation, or simply a bureaucratic entity. These types never understand that the only reason to have an army (or a navy) is to kill people and break things.

But like I said, I hadn't been given a vote. Neither had Mick. So, here we were: politically correct, nationality diverse, and neatly balanced by service. But we were probably going to get ourselves killed. And then guess who'd take the blame. Not the fucking prime minister, the bloody home secretary, or the idiot JPA. No: Mick and I would take the fall. It was our ears and balls they'd hold up for the crowd to see.

• • •

Roger the intel squirrel screwed the end of the fiber-optic cable into the viewer, and I was finally able to peer at a trio of screens whose fields of vision now surveyed the whole apartment except for the long hallway leading from the front door. The images were slightly fuzzy, but at least we had 'em. I picked up a grease pencil and marked the position of the bombs on the white board Mick had used to diagram the flat. The assembled bomb was in the bedroom, which made my lacerations worth the pain. The other two sat in pieces on a table in the living room.

The flat was laid out in a rough T-shape. You came in the front door and immediately hit a fifteen-foot-long hallway, off of which were two doors (one was a walk-in closet; the other led to a loo, which is how Brits call the head. As you can see, Britain and America are two friendly countries separated only by their common language). At the end of the hallway was the rectangular living room. To the left side of the living room was the bedroom. To the right sat a small kitchen, with no door. I checked the screens and understood from what I saw that these TIRAs were professionals. They had one man stationed at the front-door end of the hallway, and another behind cover at the far end. They'd put heavy drapes over the windows to preclude flashbangs coming through or surveillance catching them from the outside. This was going to be one hard, hard fucking target. And so, even though every one of us could allegedly shoot a twenty-five pence coin at fifty yards with his MP5, I understood only too well that the goat-fuck potential for this little exercise was very high, given our lack of unit integrity.

I peered at the screens and made Xs on the white board where I saw tangos, then diagrammed the moves I wanted our assault team to make. It didn't take long to come up with a game plan, because like those all-star football games, we'd have to stick to the most basic plays. So, I'd KISS this op off by keeping it simple, stu-pid: we'd blow the door, hit the hallway, wax the first two bad guys, then swarm the living room, split into three two-man groups with Butch Wells our rear safety, and take the rest of the bastards down. We'd have it AODW—all over and done with—in sixty seconds, and then it would be off to the Goat, my favorite London pub, for a half dozen rounds of the SEAL's favorite bit-ter—Courage.

I went over the plan three times. Shit. The Brits were shaking their heads up and down like the fucking toy dogs that sit in the back of car windows. But there was no choice here: the music was playing, and we had to dance with these assholes. Well, at least I'd do the leading in this little waltz. I caught a glimpse of Boomerang's expression. It told me he understood this op was as full of big, loosely basted seams as *Herr Doktor* Frankenstein's monster. But then, WTF, this was only rock and roll, right?

CHAPTER

2

THERE WAS NO USE WASTING MORE TIME, SO WE LOADED UP QUICKLY. I went over each man's gear, making sure that no matter how fast we might move, there was nothing dangling that would go tinkle-tinkle and give our presence away. One of the things that screws up assault teams time and time again is that they can be heard during their approach because they have not secured their gear properly. A magazine rattles in its pouch. Or a flashlight smacks against a piece of metal gear. Or a handcuff case that hasn't been properly closed comes open and the fucking cuffs hit the deck. Or an assault pry bar rattles in its scabbard, and the bad guy hears it—you get the picture.

And so I took the time to make sure we were all tied down and our flaps were Velcro'd shipshape. I inspected everyone's weapons. And then we slapped loaded mags into the MP5s, and smacked the bolts forward, chambering rounds. Since the HK USP's extractor does not act as a loaded-chamber indicator I thumbed the hammer on the pistol back, then eased the slide to the rear just enough to make sure I could see that a round of Federal's 147-grain HydraShok was chambered. Then I eased the slide forward and decocked the pistol by sweeping the control lever downward. Finally, we checked our comms to make sure we could all hear one another, as well as listen to Roger the Intel Squirrel's running commentary about who was where.

When I was satisfied that we'd circumvented Mister Murphy—at least for the moment—I cracked the door of the apartment and we moved out in stealth mode. Because I live by the credo of Roy Henry Boehm, the Godfather of all SEALs, who taught that all leadership can be defined by the two words *follow me,* I took point, my USP in low ready position. Boomerang, who was carrying the shaped charge that would blow the door, followed close in my wake, an MP5-PDW subgun with its lightweight stock folded, slung around his neck. Andy the Marine came third, his suppressed MP5 providing Boomerang with cover. Nod, carrying another suppressed MP5, followed Andy. Butch Wells, whose Haavaad Yaahd accent courtesy of his hometown—Reading, Massachusetts—makes him incomprehensible to most Brits, followed in the utility infielder position, his suppressed MP5 in low ready. Bill and Gill carried silenced, stockless MP5s in the Brit CQC fashion, which is to say they held them at high ready. I signaled them to bring up the rear.

We slipped out of the apartment single file, slid into the stairwell, and carefully, toe-heel, toe-heel, began to climb up one floor, staying well back from the rail.

Did my back hurt? Bet your ass it did. But I put the pain out of my head and concentrated on the business at hand. You cannot be a Warrior and complain. Cold, heat, pain, discomfort—none of these adverse conditions can be allowed to affect the success of your mission. And so I simply tuned the pain out and focused on my field of fire, remembered to scan and breathe to keep my vision from tunneling, and paid attention to the white sound in my new earpiece. If there was any untoward movement in the apartment, Roger would let us know in plenty of time to make adjustments. I concentrated. There was nothing but dead air in the hairy Rogue ear. That was good.

I moved cautiously but without hesitation, my GSG-9 boots

silent on the stair treads. I was concentrating so hard that my whole body was a sensory antenna, receiving signals and interpreting them. I heard my heart beating ga-thoomp, ga-thoomp, and felt the pulse pounding in my wrists. Adrenaline is a wonderful thing, my friends. It always happens like this just before combat. My breath goes a little shallow; my heart rate increases to full-tilt-boogie pace, and my asshole gets so tight it would be hard to work a single strand of angel-hair pasta up inside. I fucking love it.

I drew abreast of the thick fire door on the top-floor landing. I eased open a pouch on my CQC vest, withdrew a small can of Teflon lubricant, and sprayed the heavy hinges and the retaining spring to make sure there would be no squeaks when I opened the thick metal door.

I replaced the can, reached my gloved hand down, and gently pulled the fire door open. Behind me, Royal Marine Andy had moved into position, the muzzle of his subgun providing cover as I "cut the pie" around the doorway, exposing only as much of myself as I could determine was safe to do.

All clear. Boomerang wedged the door open, then we all continued, heel-toe, heel-toe, down the marble floor of the corridor toward the target doorway, hugging the wall. I could feel the vibrations of jackhammering, and the muffled, throaty growl of the air compressors as we were finally provided with audial camouflage by Scotland Yard's undercover people. And then, in my earpiece, I heard a Cockney accent stage whisper: "Straight base to assault group: scrub-scrub-scrub. You've got anuvver target 'eddin' your way."

I looked down to the far end of the narrow corridor. Fuck me: the elevator indicator light was green, and the arrow was pointing in an "up" direction. Why the hell hadn't they stopped whoever it was before they climbed into the elevator? Why the hell hadn't they grabbed him/her/it outside the building? The answer was: it didn't fucking matter, because this wasn't the time or place for any recriminations. This was an immediate problem and I'd have to fucking deal with it right now, because we were way, way past the fucking point of no return. There was no way to get back into the goddamn stairwell without making the sort of ruckus that would alert the badniks inside the target flat, jackhammering outside or no. But I would sure as shit ream someone a new fucking asshole once we were secure. What was this, amateur night?

I silent-signaled to Bill, Gill, and Andy to drop flat and stay put. Then my hands told Nod, Butch, and Boomerang what to do. I got three upturned thumbs. Shit, we'd done this sort of thing before on at least three continents. Boomerang laid the shaped charge on the deck and we headed past the target flat to the elevator double-time. Butch and I took the port side. Nod and Boomerang stacked to starboard. I pressed my ear against the cool metal door and listened to the electric hum of the motor as the car drew closer.

It stopped. I drew back. The door clicked, then it was pulled open from the inside.

I didn't wait. I swung around into the car and came face-to-face with . . . Elevator Lady. EL was a very startled young woman of about thirty, wearing a dark blue beret over her raven black tresses, and an ankle-length green Loden overcoat. Her arm supported a huge, paper grocery bag. Her eyes, which went wide with fright at the sight of me, were emerald green. "Good God," she exclaimed in perfect, upper-class English, "What in heaven's name are you doing?"

Her reaction wasn't unexpected. After all, I must have looked quite the sight: balaclava covering my face; goggles over my baby blues, suppressed submachine gun hanging off its sling; and CQC assault vest dripping with gear.

But there was no time to explain, or to tell her she had lovely eyes. Not to mention the fact that I had no way of knowing whether this demoiselle was one of *them,* or just an innocent bystander in WPWT.[6] And so, before she had a chance to react, or more to the point, to scream, I swung her around and slapped my hand over her mouth. Boomerang stepped in, grabbed the grocery bag, eased it onto the deck, and gave it a quick once over to make sure she wasn't carrying explosives or other lethal goodies. She wasn't. As he was doing his thing, I dropped EL into quick & easy unconsciousness with an LAPD sleeper hold.

She struggled, but not for more than a couple of seconds. Then she was out cold. I let her loose and she sagged to the deck. I dragged her out of the elevator car, and lay her on the floor, where Nod and Boomerang were waiting to duct-tape her arms and legs. By the time she came to, this exercise would all be over, I'd apologize for my brusque overture, and we'd sort things out. Maybe I'd even ask her out for a cuppa, or better yet, the beverage of her choice at a friendly pub. Then I radioed Mick and made it clear that I wanted one of his people to get up here and cover her while we went in. Lovely, she might have been. But I was taking no chances.

Mick's voice came back at me tersely. "Can't deal with that right now, Dick—I have a nasty *situation* here. That chap from Whitehall is on the other line and he is not making things easy for me."

The JPA no doubt. Fucking bureaucrats. They want to micromanage everything. "Tell the cockbreath to sod off."

Mick was not amused. "That comment was played on the speakerphone, Dick,"

Another coup for Roguish charm. Shit. We were fucked. But I wasn't about to leave Elevator Lady by herself. I looked at Butch. "You stay with her."

Butch's face fell. His MP5 drooped on its sling. But he obeyed. "Aye-aye, Skippah."

---

[6] Wrong Place, Wrong Time.

With the distraction under control, it was time to get back to work. We made our way down the hallway. Boomerang retrieved the shaped charge, which looked like a string of white Styrofoam sausages connected by a fifteen-foot length of high-explosive det cord, around the perimeter of the old, painted wood door. We stacked at a forty-five-degree angle to the door's hinge side. I flicked the "transmit" button on the radio three times in rapid succession to let everyone know we were going in. Only then did Boomerang rig the detonator and wiring.

I gave him an upturned thumb. He pulled the spring-loaded detonator switch back, then released it with a *thwock*.

Whaaam—the door splintered in a huge cloud of orange flame and white smoke. The hinges and locks shattered. Nod tossed the first of the flashbangs. Two figures were silhouetted in the million candlepower flash.

Whap. I was sent to my fucking knees by an elbow to the head as Andy the Royal Marine charged past me, screaming, "Get down get down get down, you Mick motherfuckers!"

Oh, fuck me. The asshole was upsetting the choreography. And then, the no-load, pencil-dicked pus-nutted cockbreath actually *stopped*. Stopped cold as he sighted his MP5, as if we were at a fucking carnival shooting gallery, not in the middle of a tactical op. That was bad fucking technique. Worse, he'd created a road-block for the rest of us, and now we were all hung up in the doorway, allowing the bad guys to regroup and pick us off one by one, or blow the fucking bomb and vaporize us.

The only answer was to get the asshole out of the way ASAP. But as I struggled to my feet so I could run right over the stupid dipshit, one of the TIRA tangos took care of the problem for me. He peeked around the wall, brought up a small-caliber, silenced automatic pistol, fired once, and Andy's head exploded. The Royal Marine went down like the proverbial sack of *merde*, his blood splattering my goggle lenses and making it hard for me to see.

I wiped the goo with my forearm and, USP up, started forward, down the narrow hallway, screaming "Target positions? Target positions?" into my radio. I wanted information from Roger, who could see where the bad guys were.

But all I heard was static. My fucking radio had gone dead again. Was it from the flashbang concussion? It didn't matter. We were all now operating blind. With at least one goddamn completed bomb on the premises.

Fuck. *Scan. Breathe.* I stepped over Andy's inert form and kept moving. *Remember to concentrate on the front sight. Scan breathe. Scanbreathe.* I picked up a target in my front sight: a human head and thick neck exposed around the end of the corridor. And then: *pistol muzzle.*

I stitched a half-mag of shots upward, shattering plaster as the rounds climbed. I finally caught him in the face with the sixth and seventh shots, and he went down in a heap. Perfect combat shooting? No way. I was a butcher, not a surgeon. But I didn't give a rusty fuck because however badly I'd shot, the rounds had done the job.

I kept moving, steadily so the rest of the team could flow down the hallway. I pointed toward the closet doorway.

Nod lapped me and took it. When I heard him shout, "Clear," I moved past it and let Boomerang lap me, so he could deal with the loo.

Bill rolled a second flashbang down the hallway into the living room. That gave Boomerang the chance he needed. He opened the loo door and tossed a flashbang. Then he went in, low. I heard one-two-three three-shot bursts rip into the tile. Then Boomerang shouted, "Clear, Boss Dude—it was empty."

Now I moved fast-fast-fast, down to the end of the hallway. I cut to my left, my back against the wall, searching for targets. Nod gave me cover. Bill and Gill flowed smoothly to the starboard side of the living room, their MP5s up and ready. Boomerang came last, sliding to the port side to give Nod and me protection.

Bill shouted, "Get down-down-down!" I heard a burst of automatic weapons fire. Shit—the sound didn't come from an MP5, but something lighter. I glanced to my right and saw that another of the Brits was on the floor.

"Boomerang—"

I hadn't had to say anything. My tall master chief had already shifted his position to reinforce the Brits, his MP5 raking the opposite side of the room.

I heard a scream, and my peripheral vision picked up Boomerang advancing on a downed target. Since I'd already committed to the port side, I kept moving left, toward the bedroom door. This op had gone completely FUBAR.

I swung up close to the wall. Nod came up behind me and slapped my shoulder to let me know he was ready to move. I nodded once to tell him I'd received loud and clear, and then, crouching low, moved around the doorframe and into the bedroom.

Surprise: *there were three of them in here, and two were pointing weapons at the doorway. Roger the intel squirrel had counted wrong.* Oh fuck, oh shit, oh doom on Dickie, which as you know means I was being fuckee-fuckeed in Vietnamese.

Except . . . these assholes were not Warriors. If they had been Warriors they would not have hesitated. They would have pulled the trigger as soon as they sensed movement. They would have shot through the goddamn wall and hit us outside. Instead, they just stood there, frozen like jacklighted deer.

Since I *am* a Warrior (in fact, since I be the one and only, singular, trademarked, copyrighted, original, accept-no-substitutes Rogue Warrior™), I *do* know how to take YES for an answer. So, I didn't hesitate. I took down the port-most target with five-six-seven quick shots in the face, chest, groin, and legs. Which is when USP's slide locked back and I realized that I had fuckee-fuckeed my own trademarked, copyrighted, all-rights-reserved Rogue Warrior® self by not counting rounds. My gun was empty, there were still bad guys left alive, and there was no time to transition to my subgun. Maybe I could commit assault with a friendly weapon and beat them all to death with my dick.

That was the bad news. The good news was that Nod, who was right behind me, carried an up-and-ready MP5, which he now brought into play, shooting over my shoulder. He took the starboard target with two quick bursts that cut the sumbitch in two pieces and slapped him against the wall, leaving a bloody Rorschach on the off-white paint as he slid onto the floor.

That left target three. Who wasn't armed. At least with a pistol. No, T-3 was holding a small, rectangular package stuffed inside a plastic container. Nod had seen what I saw, because while he'd swung the muzzle of his MP5 onto T-3, he'd taken his finger off the trigger.

Meanwhile, T-3 was fumbling with his package, groping for something he couldn't quite get his fingers around.

It is at times like this, my friends, that time moves very, very slowly, and you see every fucking detail of what is going on around you, almost as if you are drowning and scenes from your life play out before your eyes.

In this case, I clearly saw T-3's cowlick of reddish hair, and his jug ears, and his freckles, which made him look kind of like an Irish Dennis the Menace. I noted that he chewed his fingernails. I saw that he wore ultrachic, thick-soled, steel-toed, Doc Martens lace-up boots with bright red shoelaces. I realized that he had a chipped front tooth. And I saw that whatever it was he was carrying had been crammed (absurdly, I thought) into an opaque plastic Tupperware refrigerator container.

This all took about a quarter of a second. And then, I launched myself across the three yards separating us, and forearmed T-3 across the narrow bed under which I'd spent so much time and left so much skin as I installed the worthless fucking fiber-optic cable and minilens and knocked him back into the wall. Except the blow didn't separate him from his package, which he now tucked into his body like a football.

This was good news, because while T-3 was concentrating on the package, I could concentrate on him. Unmindful of the goddamn MP5 hanging off my chest I wrapped him up and rolled him away from the wall, using my knees and elbows and my bulk to smother him and relieve him of his life.

But he was a wiry little motherfucker and despite his fiddling with the package, he kicked and bit and clawed at me. He caught the barrel of my MP5 and used the sight to rake my face. He tried to stick the muzzle up my nose and then wrestled on top of me so he could straddle my chest, grab the trigger, and clear my nasal passages permanently. The fucking muzzle caught inside my nostril and ripped it as I pulled free.

Nod joined the fun. He grabbed T-3's left foot and twisted—hard. T-3 screamed. Then he regained his composure long enough to auto rotate out of Nod's grasp like a goddamn M8 NOTAR Little Bird[7] and deliver a hufuckingmongous kick to the SEAL's balls, which sent poor Nod spasming onto the floor, his knees tucked in agony.

This was no fun. I bitch-slapped T-3 with my empty pistol. That stunned him for a second. I dropped the pistol and tried to transition to the MP5 so I could put the cocksucker out of his misery— and mine. But then he came in close, grabbed the subgun barrel again, and slapped me upside the ol' Roguish head with it, catching me from cheek to ear, right alongside my eye.

Oh, that *hurt*. I tried to focus and wrap him up because he was close enough for me to bear hug him now. Don't forget, friends, I am a big, strong motherfucker who presses 455 pounds, 150 reps, every fucking day on the outdoor weight pile at Rogue Manor. But I guess T-3 didn't know that, because he was having nothing to do with my wrap-up exercises. He wriggled out of my grasp,

---

[7] The Hughes 500 minichopper NO TAil Rotor variation used by such SpecWar units as Delta Force and SEAL Team Six.

and swiveled as if to get away. Then, with sudden and renewed ferocity, he turned, grabbed my French braid with both of his hands, and cracked it like a whip, up/down, up/down, smashing my head smack-smack into the floor.

I saw fucking stars. Belay that. I saw the whole Milky fucking Way. My entire universe went white. I saw spots. And then, in between the stars and galaxies, I saw the tip of T-3's Doc Martens steel-toed boot coming toward my head. And then—*blackness.*

I awoke suddenly, shook myself into full consciousness, rolled onto my hands and knees, looked around the small bedroom, and realized that T-3 had scarpered.[8] I struggled to my feet. I tried to focus on the big dial of the watch on my left wrist. I'd been out about a minute and a half. Nod was nowhere to be seen. I staggered out of the bedroom. "Boomerang—"

"Yo, Boss Dude." Boomerang was in the far corner of the living room, beyond two head-shot tango corpses. He was kneeling over one of the Brits, his thumb pressed firmly on a large wet patch, dark with arterial blood, on the Para's chest. Gill's eyes were misted over. His skin was blue white. "Lucky shot caught the sumbitch under the armhole of his vest, Boss Dude. Nasty. I sent Nod for help—all our fucking radios are out." He looked up at me. "I don't think Gill's gonna make it."

"Where's the other Brit—Bill?"

Boomerang jerked his thumb toward the small kitchen. "Working in there to make sure those goddamn bombs don't go off, I think."

This op had really turned into a goatfuck. "What about the guy with the package?"

Boomerang's forehead wrinkled up in concern. "What guy?"

"The tango in the bedroom who kicked the shit out of me and took off."

---

[8] That's IRA jail slang for "take off."

Boomerang's eyes went wide. "I never saw anybody come out of the bedroom, Boss Dude," he said.

"Shit." I lunged down the hallway toward the corridor. I looked to starboard. The corridor was empty. I looked to port, down to where I'd left Elevator Lady unconscious.

The grocery bag was still right where Boomerang had set it down. But Elevator Lady had disappeared. All that was left were duct tape remnants, the long Loden overcoat, the beret—and a black wig. I didn't need a fucking Ph.D. to grasp the fact that Elevator Lady was now a definite part of the tactical problem. Worse: Butch Wells, whom I'd left watching her and the elevator, was missing. The elevator door was closed. Why? Because EL and T-3 had used it to make their getaway.

I pressed the transmit button on my radio. "Butch—yo, Butch." There was nothing but silence. I had a very, very bad feeling in the pit of my gut. Oh fuck, oh shit, oh doom on Dickie.

I looked at the second-hand timer on my watch. Five minutes and forty-six seconds of total clusterfuckery had elapsed since we'd come up the stairs to take down the apartment. This was probably the worst screwup I'd ever been involved in, and I knew in the depths of my Roguish heart that I was gonna be operating in payback mode for a long, long time to come.

CHAPTER

3

I THOUGHT MY DAY HAD ALREADY TURNED COMPLETELY TO SHIT. I was wrong. Things actually went from badder to worser over the next few minutes. You already sense Butch Wells was dead. And that T-3 and Elevator Lady had vanished. Worse, they'd managed to slip right through the dragnet of Scotland Yard, Metropolitan Police, and SAS shooters that had converged on the scene once our takedown began. How had they done it? I had no fucking idea. But they had simply evaporated. And we confirmed Butch's body in the elevator. He'd been shivved, bringing the total number of official corpses to three—so far.

Outside, it was chaos. Traffic was gridlocked from the Hammersmith flyover all the way to Knightsbridge; the North End Road was blocked all the way to the District Line Underground stop at West Brompton. The side streets were impossible to navigate, which kept the ambulances from being able to get close. I noticed with some bemusement that however bad the traffic was, it hadn't managed to keep the press away. Reporters were already buttonholing neighbors to ask them how they felt. The first of what I knew would be dozens of TV vans were pulling up onto the narrow sidewalks, and crews were setting up cameras and lights. Somehow, local television news crews always remind me of the vandals who come down out of the hills after a huge battle to murder the wounded and loot the corpses.

And while all the madness was going on, Mick Owen was being flayed alive by the selfsame deputy assistant home secretary under whose signature this hobbled, bobbled, and badly cobbled operation had been allowed to proceed in the first place. Before the fact, this asshole had wanted to claim every bit of the credit. Now, of course, it was all Mick's fault—and mine.

And then in the midst of all that shit, someone in the control van got a phone call from a desk assistant at CNN's London bureau, asking for a comment about the Brook Green School takeover.

The Brook Green School takeover, you say? Isn't that just a little far-fetched, you say? Far-fetched it may indeed sound. And who the hell knows how CNN even got the van's phone number in the first place. But it still fucking *happened.*

I dashed into the van just in time to hear the Metropolitan Police transmission confirming that a one-story, sixty-eight-student primary school that backs up on Brook Green, about three hundred yards north of Hammersmith Road, about a quarter mile from where I currently stood on unsteady sea legs, had indeed, about twelve minutes ago, been invaded and occupied by a trio of armed terrorists.

The cops confirmed that the principal had been immediately shot dead and her body dumped on the front steps as evidence that these tangos were serious. And CNN's London bureau had received a call from someone who claimed to be one of the participants, demanding to go live, worldwide. And CNN, journalistic paragons that they are, had put her on.

The caller was a woman who said she was an officer in the True IRA. She'd told CNN's viewers the takeover was a response for the authorities' wonton murder of TIRA soldiers. She and her companions had weapons and explosives, and they would not, she said, hesitate to use them to kill themselves, and all the children.

I listened to the tape. I'd heard the perfect upper-class English accent before: it was Elevator Lady. I should have killed the bitch when I'd had my arm around her throat, before she'd had a chance to murder one of my SEALs and escape to sing this bloodthirsty TIRA-lira-lira song. But there was no time for hand-wringing now. I had to act quickly and decisively, because I certainly wasn't about to allow myself—or anyone else—to perpetrate a second goatfucked operation in one day. After all, I'd lost one of my best people, the tango with the bomb was out and about, and now there'd been a fucking school takeover.

And so, I didn't give a shit what any deputy assistant home secretary wanted. I was through with bureaucrats and their politically correct methods. I was angry. I was white-hot angry. And when Warriors get white-hot angry, WE ACT. My immediate objective was to take charge of this charlie-foxtrotted op, hit the schoolhouse, get all the kids out alive, and make sure I brought the scumbuckets who'd decided to take innocent lives and endanger children to Roguish justice. By which I mean *they'd* get to leave the school in fucking body bags.

As the support troops rushed to get everything packed up so we could move sites, I stuck my head into the control van and invited Mick Owen outside. I wanted to palaver in private. He hauled his thick-framed body out of the captain's chair, shook himself like a wet dog shedding water, and said, "Good idea."

It had started to drizzle, the kind of misty, cold, fine late autumn drizzle that soaks through to the skin. Mick pulled on a smock in the distinctive SAS camouflage pattern, with one subdued star on each shoulder epaulette. He'd put on weight since we'd last worked together, and his thick hair, combed straight back off his forehead, was flecked through with gray. But he was still as solid as an NFL running back, with thick thighs, narrow waist, bull neck, and extralarge hands, all set on a five foot nine inch frame that weighed in somewhere in the 240-pound range.

Mick had scored a series of rapid-fire promotions since my

Green Team had worked with his SAS shooters in London back in the early 1990s. They were the result of his work in places like Northern Ireland, Bosnia, and Kosovo. But from the look on his face right now, I knew that Mick would have traded the fucking star in an instant if he could command a brick[9] from his beloved SAS Pagoda Troop and take down the fucking school himself.

But that's not the way the British military works. Generals command. They do not go over the rail to shoot and loot. And so, the shooting and looting would be ceded to others, and I wanted to make sure that when it came to delegating, Mick delegated all those responsibilities to *moi*.

I'd already been on the cellular to the rest of my DET Bravo team, and they were on their way (if they could ever make it through the gridlocked traffic). It was a small contingent—but all were capable shooters who'd worked together for a long time. I'd brought Terry Devine to London. He was now a radioman second class, and he'd proved his worth in Germany and Azerbaijan. In fact, I'd nicknamed him Timex, because he can take a licking but still keeps on kicking (ass). Rotten Randy Michaels, my E-9 former Army Ranger had made the trip, too. Rotten is precisely the kind of asshole I want around when the *merde* hits the old *ventilateur.* And since I brought Rotten, I had to add his swim buddy, Nigel, all 115 pounds of him, to the contingent, too. That was fine with me. Nigel (real name Rupert Collis) grew up not ten kliks from here, in the mean streets of London's East End, and if I was going to have a Rupert amongst my enlisted men, it might as well be Nigel.[10] DET Bravo's best sniper was a toothpick-sucking, snuff-dipping, tattoo-enriched fair-haired boy named Goober. Goober is from Georgia. And if he has a last name, no one knows what it is. Frankly, I don't give a damn what his last name might be. All I care about is the fact

---

[9] That's the Brit way of saying a platoon.
[10] That's a bad pun, friends. You say you don't get the joke? Okay, I'll explain: *Rupert* is British Army slang for *officer.* Got it now?

that Goober can hit a fucking dime at a thousand yards. Not once, either, but every time he pulls the trigger. And bringing up the rear was Digger O'Toole, real name Eddie, a swinging-dicked, big-balled, go-anywhere, do-anything kid from Hollywood, Florida, whose idea of fun (when he isn't chasing pussy) includes reducing structures to small pieces of rubble.

I pulled Mick between two police vans to keep us away from prying camera lenses and lip readers. "Mick, I can't afford another fuckup."

The look on his face told me he hadn't needed to hear that comment right now. But he still shook his head in glum agreement. "Agreed." He scuffed his thick boot sole against the pavement. "So, how do you think we should handle this new development?"

"If you don't mind taking some heat, I have five people on their way right now who can do the job and do it right."

"Your SEALs?"

"That's right."

He grimaced. "That's not going to go down well at Whitehall."

I jerked my thumb toward the apartment house. "Mick, Whitehall was just responsible for *that* fuckup; which fuckup they are right now, even as we speak, trying to hang around your neck and mine. So, screw Whitehall. Screw joint operations. I just lost a man—and fuck it I'm gonna make those bastards pay. I want to get even. So do my people. I'm going to take this one on by myself so it gets done right."

Mick looked into my eyes. "That's easy for you to say, Dick. You don't have to live with Whitehall on a permanent basis. I do."

"But you also know I'm right. SO-Nineteen can't do this as well as I can. SAS can, but it will take you three hours to bring your hostage-rescue team down from SAS Hereford. There are eight shooters from Twenty-two Regiment detailed to DET Bravo. Some of them are already on site. We both know they're not hostage rescue specialists. But there's a top-notch sniper team, and the other six blokes are capable and they're bright. My guys and I have worked with them over the past three weeks. You give SAS the perimeter to hold, and let me deploy the snipers. Then you let me go in and kill 'em all. Because that's what I do, Mick."

"You're being terribly blunt."

I tapped the receiver of my MP5. "Nobody made me an O-Six because I did well in touchy-feely. They did it because of my skill with a fucking submachine gun."

His expression softened. "Still have your sense of humor when dealing with flag officers, I see."

I saw by his face that if I pressed him, he'd let us do the job, so I went in for the kill. "Mick, you know and I know that my guys can end this before the situation gets any more out of hand." I paused to gauge his body language. It told me he was looking for a way to let me go in. "But we have to act—act *now*. Before they kill anybody else. Before they detonate the fucking Cubanol. Before Whitehall tries to take charge."

"But—"

I attacked. "I'm not gonna do any more talking. I'm just gonna go Rogue."

"Go Rogue?"

"Unless otherwise directed, I'm gonna set things up the way I want 'em set. I'm gonna move. I'm gonna attack. I'm gonna take the school down—my way. That lets you wriggle past the 'joint operation' bullshit you've been stuck with, and allows me to get the fucking job done."

Mick sighed. Then he scratched the hair just above his right ear. "I can't take another cock-up today, Dick."

He was going to bend. "I know. We won't let you down."

"Three fuckin' men are dead already—one of them yours," Mick said, his voice flat. "That's three more than I lost in eleven years of operations in Northern Ireland."

"In Northern Ireland you didn't have a dozen pinstriped assholes from Whitehall looking over your shoulder on a minute to minute basis."

"I don't mind 'em looking," Mick said vehemently. "I mind it when they try to tell me how to do my job."

He was right of course. And the situation isn't exclusive just to the British. Think about the past few "situations" in which the United States has become involved, gentle reader. In Iraq, instead of engaging in a campaign to bring down Saddam Hussein at the end of the Gulf War, the White House waffled, and Saddam has outlasted the last three American presidents. In Mogadishu, White House staffers set the rules of engagement, resulting in the deaths of more than two dozen American military people. During the Kosovo war, noncombatant politicians in the White House decided what targets to hit and what targets to leave alone, thus ensuring that NATO forces would *not* bring the war to a speedy close.

I could give you other examples, but there's no time right now. Right now, I had to assemble every piece of information I could about the school. We had to set up a perimeter and keep the press away. And I had to come up with a plan that would allow us to take the tangos down without losing a single child. If there was even one tiny corpse brought out of that school, we'd have screwed up past all redemption.

CHAPTER

4

SINCE I AM AN OPTIMIST, I WILL GIVE YOU THE GOOD NEWS FIRST. The GN was that the school site was controllable. The building itself was rectangular in shape and a single story in height. It was surrounded by half a dozen old shade trees—chestnuts, I think—on the sides, and by a huge swath of Brook Green on the rear. The street on which it sat, a cul-de-sac called Latymer Court, was L-shaped, allowing us to monitor all access, and also keep our control location out of sight of the school. Mick emptied the eight houses facing the school building and turned them into observation posts. He tapped into the phone and power lines, so we took control of them. Hammersmith Road, the six-lane avenue just to the south into which Latymer Court emptied, was shut down, too.

Mick also took care of another important detail: he set up an isolated crisis center for the parents of the kids who were being held, just as much to keep them away from the press as to make sure they received accurate updates on what was going on. Hostage parents caterwauling into cameras is no way to help solve the problem. Indeed, when politicians see parents screaming about doing something, they often react by making bad, even deadly, decisions.

As for the Brook Green School building, there were two eight-foot-high-by-four-foot-wide windows in each of the six class-rooms and the cafeteria, and narrower windows, also eight feet high, in the offices. There were no window shades, which gave us a tremendous advantage. There were two entrances: a front door and a rear door. Sniping positions were either from the houses directly across from the school, or from the green. Although the building had a basement, there was no way to get in and out through it. So the good news was that we had the tangos bottled up, and we could set up a wide perimeter, giving us a lot of lati-tude to move around. The hour also worked in our favor: it was now 1520—3:20 P.M. in civilian time—and it would be growing dark within the hour. I like darkness because it conceals my moves. I asked Mick to cumshaw a bunch of work lights so we could illuminate the school. The more we lit the place up, the less the bad guys would be able to see what we were up to.

The bad news of course was obvious. There were more than five dozen kids in that school, as well as six teachers, one janitor, two cafeteria workers, a secretary, and the assistant to the princi-pal. That made seventy-one hostages, if everyone had shown up.

Let me pause long enough here to give you a quick primer on hostage rescue in the twenty-first century. It is a lot different from what it was when I got into the hop & pop business a couple of decades ago. The first thing we used to do in a hostage situation was to control the phones. If the bad guys wanted to talk to any-body, they had to go through us. Nowadays, tangos are more than likely to have digital cell phones. They can pretty much call who they want to, and breaking into their conversations can be diffi-cult. And then, there is the Internet—with its own phone capabili-ties, E-mail and instant messaging. So controlling access to the bad guys is a lot more complicated than it was just a few years ago. So, to put it simply, the dynamics have changed, and we have had to change with them.

Now we carry scanners that allow us to monitor digital cell net-works. We can shut down the cellular repeater stations in a specific neighborhood if we have to. And we know how to hack our way into most ISPs[11] so that we can commandeer a system being used by terrorists to communicate.

But that didn't help us here and now. Now, I had to get the perimeter set up. I had to get floor plans of the school, and I had to make sure that every one of the assault team was reading from the same page of the score. There was not a lot of time. If we didn't get these kids out within a couple of hours or so, the press was going to make our job impossible. You look skeptical. Don't be. Hostage rescue and publicity are not compatible. Take my word for it: the clock was ticking.

• • •

Takeover plus 00:21:44 The perimeter was contained. There were only three tangos—we knew *that* for certain. And that fact told me they'd have to hold the hostages in tight groups to control 'em. Our audio equipment, backed up by the sniper teams, indicated that students were being kept in the two front-side classrooms on the left side of the schoolhouse as we faced it, and the sixteen adults were crowded into the principal's office in the right rear, guarded by an unknown female tango. I had my sniper team set up in the rear, and two teams from the Metropolitan Police armed assault group SO-19 set up in the front. Most of the work a sniper does is intelligence gathering, not shooting. This was certainly the case here, as we tracked the tangos' every move.

We had our first lucky break when Digger O'Toole was able to sneak and peek close enough to the school to set some listening devices close in. We were also able to lay our hands on a second laser mike, courtesy of No Such Agency. These devices can take sounds off a window at a distance of 150 yards. We use them in denied areas like Moscow and Beijing to eavesdrop on officials who think they are secure. NSA's London station had one in tran-

---

[11] Internet Service Provider.

sit out near Lakenheath Air Force Base. It was choppered in within the hour, delivered onto the playing field at St. Paul's School on the South Bank of the Thames, and rushed over Hammersmith bridge. I'd already set one Big Ear out front. The second was positioned at the rear.

00:42:21. From what I could see and hear from the communications equipment we were able to muster, Elevator Lady and her two compadres expected us to hit the doors simultaneously. And that was the way they were defending the building. The Cubanol bomb was the big question. No one had mentioned it, and from what my sniper teams could see, T-3, who was holding the students in the right-hand classroom hostage, was keeping it out of sight.

00:43:11. Mick called into the school on the phone line. I listened in as the telephone in the principal's office *brinng-brinnged* three times. Then a female voice answered.

"What do you lot want?"

Mick's voice was even and reassuring. "My name is Owen. I'm one of the people outside. We want to know that the children are all right. We'd like to stay in contact with you. And we'd like to be able to retrieve the principal's body from the front steps."

"The children are fine. Take the bitch away. But I don't want to talk to you."

"What do you in there want?"

"Independence for Northern Ireland."

"That's something I can't do for you," Mick said, "and I'm not sure that holding a bunch of children is going to help you achieve it. Let's talk about things we can agree on."

"Sod off." The phone in his hand went dead.

"Fuck," Mick said to no one in particular.

00:46:10. I let Rotten and Boomerang work on an assault plan. Like most SpecWar commanders, I believe in bottom-up planning. So I try to let my senior enlisted do the initial work. They know their people and they're usually better equipped to plan an op than I. As usual, they'd been war-gaming in their heads for almost an hour now, and what they came up with was so good it was almost the kind of plan I'd devise myself.

They'd designed a keep-it-simple-stupid operation. With only three targets to neutralize, and the main doors booby-trapped, we'd send one two-man and two three-man elements through the windows and take 'em all down in a matter of seconds. It was straightforward and it was workable. But it lacked something . . . Roguish. You see, if my men and I can think of an assault plan, it's probable that the bad guys have thought of the same possibilities. And so I always like to add a little something that no one thinks of, to make my takedown foolproof.

00:51:00. In this case, I happened to think about how a bunch of Peruvian special forces rescued a passel of hostages inside the Japanese embassy in Lima a few years back. The hostages had been taken by a group of Marxist terrorists from the Tupac Amaru Revolutionary Movement. Peruvian special forces that had been trained by my old CIA pal Jim Wink[12] tunneled their way under the embassy and then struck from three points at once, disorienting the terrorists and bringing all but one of the hostages out.

I'd noticed a sewer line running parallel to the school. In London, sewer lines are often six to eight feet in diameter, and they are used to conduit electrical cable and other materials through foundations and into buildings. I asked Mick for a street plan and discovered that one of the sewer feeders on Latymer Court ran directly under the school basement. I dispatched Nigel and Digger into the sewer to run a fast recon. The answer from my now-stinky SEALs was that we could work our way directly below the school kitchen and pantry, both of which were in the basement. My idea was to place a shaped charge there, and use the explosion to cause a diversion. And just as the tangos' atten-

---

[12] This is a pseudonym.

tion was sidetracked, we'd hit Brook Green School in three places at once.

01:09:40. Mick Owen called. "The PM's people are calling. I've been ordered to set up negotiations in the next hour, Dick."

"Stall 'em. You know and I know that if we start talking, they'll kill someone to show how serious they are."

"I know it, and you know it, but—"

I cut him off. "Mick—I'm almost set. Give me half an hour."

"Either you are a 'Go' in fifteen minutes, or I've got to stand you down."

"Roger-roger, Mick. Fucking loud and fucking clear." Shit. Time was running out. Either we were going to move now, or this fucking thing was going to drag out for a l-o-n-g time and more people would die. I pulled Goober off sniping detail. He'd go in with me as Alpha group. Rotten Randy, Nigel, and Nod would form the second team—Bravo—while Boomerang, Timex, and Digger would be the third assault group: Charlie. With his SAS snipers covering the front, Mick moved the SO-19 sniper team to the rear of the building. If either team had a clean shot, by which I mean a head shot, they would take it—but only at the precise instant we initiated.

Now, two of our tangos were women. That did nothing to make me alter my assault plan—or my resolve to take no prisoners. Many cops and soldiers have a natural hesitation about killing women. I do not. In fact, my men and I train so that we can shoot women without thinking about it at all. Because in that split second of hesitation, the woman will kill you. Besides, I am an EEO kind of Rogue, and I believe that all tangos, male and female alike, should get an equal chance to ride that magic carpet to HELL.

01:14:21. I radioed Mick that we were a GO. We split up and began our approach. The approach is the most difficult and least practiced element of dynamic entry. Most teams cannot approach their target without sounding like a herd of elephants. Moreover, they do not utilize cover, so the bad guys can see them coming. Not us. Our approach would be slow, deliberate—and silent. We would use the lengthening shadows and come from oblique angles.

I wanted Elevator Lady all for myself. So Goober and I took the port-most classroom, which would be white seven o'clock on the Colour Clock Code favored by SAS assault teams—the left front side of the building. Boomerang, Timex, and Digger took black one (rear right-hand side), and Rotten, Nigel, and Nod, who still sounded like a countertenor, would hit white six and take down T-3, to avenge their fallen shipmate.

We'd changed into black assault gear: BDUs, CQC vests, Kevlar helmets and goggles for the guys, and a black watch cap and goggles for me, because I hate the fucking helmets. I'd made sure that Rotten had brought our own Motorola radios. At least *they* worked 50 percent of the time, which gave us an advantage over Brit comms, which I'd discovered were as worthless as the electrical wiring in an MG-TC. We all carried suppressed MP5s. There was a reason for this. First, submachine guns make an awful lot of noise, and I didn't want to panic the kids or the adults. Second, maybe we'd get off the first bursts without being noticed, which would mean we'd be able to neutralize (read kill) the baddies sans problems. And third, if we heard a normal-sounding shot, it wouldn't be us shooting.

01:17:30. I led the approach, moving cautiously from the mouth of Latymer Court, keeping well out of any ambient light thrown by the work lights shining on the school. To my left was a block of three-story row houses. I used them for cover, moving from house to house, my MP5 at low ready. Behind me, Goober carried the six-foot assault ladder with padding on both rail ends. The ladder would be set just below the windowsill, allowing me to rake the window with the steel bar I carried in a scabbard, then make entry. Six feet behind Goober, Rotten Randy, Nigel, and Nod moved cautiously, Nod and Nigel carrying the ladder and Rotten Randy providing rear-guard cover.

We'd progressed not a hundred feet when I heard Mick's voice in my ear. "Fuck-fuck-fuck."

I silent-signaled a stop. "What's up?"

"Chopper," he said. "Fucking television news chopper is crossing into the no-fly zone. Get your people out of sight now."

We did not need this kind of shit. Not now. Not after the day I'd been through. If it were up to me, I would have had the police shoot the fucking thing down. But that would have been politically imprudent. It didn't matter that by trying to get pictures, these assholes, whoever they were, were putting people's lives in danger. They didn't fucking care. It was all grist for their news mills. Worse, television choppers are now commonly equipped with night vision atop their four-hundred-millimeter lenses, so we couldn't just duck into the shadows and wait 'em out.

It wasn't fifteen seconds before I heard the whomp-whomp-whomp of the chopper somewhere out there, the noise getting louder and louder. We had to disappear. I ran for the closest house and tested the door. It was, of course, locked. I smashed it with my foot just below the doorknob, busting it wide open. We'd pay the owners later. "Inside."

We crammed into the vestibule of the darkened house and waited. The chopper engine thundered closer, echoing off the neighborhood's houses. I pressed the transmit button. "WTF, Mick?"

There was silence in my ear. I didn't like the stillness because it gave me time to think about all the things that could go wrong.

- The windows might not shatter quickly and we'd get hung up silhouetted against them.
- The windows might blow in, right atop the hostages.
- T-3 might explode his device and we'd all be vaporized.
- A single hostage might be killed or injured because of something we'd forgotten to factor into our plan.

And then, the rolling thunder began to recede, and Mick's voice came back to me, breaking into my pessimistic reverie. "Solved," he said. "You can get on with it."

01:21:21. We maintained radio silence as we crept through the most dangerous segment of the approach: the thirty yards of bare ground that separated the grove of chestnut trees from the school building. The work lights had been focused into the windows, which gave us some security, as anyone staring out would be blinded by blue halogen lamps. But it didn't guarantee we wouldn't be seen.

By the time I reached the corner of the red brick schoolhouse I had sweat through my BDUs, even though the temperature had fallen into the low forties, and I was wet from the drizzle. I let Nod, Nigel, and Randy slip past Goober and me, crabbing toward their target window.

01:22:35. We began the setup. I unslung my MP5 and made sure I had a full mag loaded and a round in the chamber. I went over Goober's equipment, and he inspected mine. And then, looking down the foundation at Rotten, we began to set our ladders in tandem, bringing them up under the windowsill, and setting them firmly in the wet grass.

Except, setting them was a problem. The earth was soggy, and the ladder feet would not plant firmly. Yeah, that meant it was Doom on Dickie time again. But to be honest, language didn't matter, because whether I was being screwed in Vietnamese, or by Mother Nature, it was no fun being fuckee-fuckeed.

I let my fingers do the talking. Next to me, Goober stood, ready to KILL. But tonight he'd have another assignment. His job would be to brace the ladder by jamming his back against the wall and holding it firmly in place while I made the assault. With luck, I'd make it inside and hit Elevator Lady before she could react. Goober's face told me he wanted to be more integral to the take-down than play the buttress role. Well, that might have been the case if Butch was alive and we still had a three-man assault team. But it was impossible now.

It was almost *Show Time.* I tested the ladder. It was solid. I pulled my goggle strap tight and topped everything off with the black knit watch cap. Goober looked me over and tapped me once on the left shoulder, signifying that I was good to go.

But before we initiated, I wanted an intel dump from the sniper teams and a confirmation that all my men were ready to go over the rail. We didn't want the bad guys right in the window as we hit, even with the explosive diversion in the basement. And we had to attack simultaneously. I pressed the "transmit" button on the radio and whispered, "Sit-rep?" into the throat mike.

"Bravo go." That was Rotten Randy's basso profundo.

Boomerang's nasal voice echoed in my earpiece: "Charlie go."

"Sniper one go."

"Sniper two go."

"IED go."

I glanced up toward the light reflecting off the windowpane. My heart was thumping in my chest. I slid around and put my right foot on the bottom-most ladder rung, testing its position. Goober's eyes stared as I put my weight on the ladder and went up one rung, then another, hunching over as I climbed to keep myself well below the windowsill so as not to silhouette myself.

At the third rung I was almost doubled over to keep out of sight. Which made it . . . *Show Time.*

"Initiate!"

I hadn't even gotten the third syllable out when a huge explosion shook the schoolhouse. I felt the concussion in the soles of my assault boots. But I didn't have time to think about it. I popped up and raked the glass around the windowsill with the steel rod in my left hand, shattering it and making a path for us.

It broke into hundreds of shards and fell around me. Goober suddenly nudged up beside me and let three three-round bursts go, providing suppressive fire. Shit—he wasn't supposed to be there but the ladder didn't fucking move, so who cared. I brought my MP5 up and went through the window—goddamn frame snagged my watch cap and pulled the fucking thing off—swung my butt high to clear the sill (don't need no friggin' glass fraggin' Dickie's ass), and brought my legs up, around, and over. I vaulted. My right boot hit the floor. Then my left.

MP5 up, I was scanning and breathing just the way I should have been. I didn't tunnel, either: there was too fucking much rage in me to make any mistakes. These tangos had killed one of my people, a brother SEAL. And now they'd taken innocent children hostage, which gave them a nonappealable death sentence in the book of justice I carry in my head.

At times like this, things almost always happen as if in Slo-Mo. And so, let me describe what I saw. There were thirty or so kids on the floor, all hunkered down and facing the door. Except, almost every one of their eyes had turned toward the sound of shattering glass. Their expressions told me they were about to panic—their mouths open as if to scream. In the doorway stood Elevator Lady. Her left arm clutched a blond-haired girl—a shield against anyone attacking down the corridor. EL's extended right hand held a Czech-made Skorpion machine pistol, pointed down the corridor.

I was already inside the room by the time Elevator Lady realized she'd been snookered by the explosion downstairs. Her eyes widened when she saw me. That was when the kids began screaming. A few started to scramble to their knees. I screamed, "Down-down-down, kids. Everybody down. Everybody stay down."

Elevator Lady swiveled, scrunched her body tight behind the kid, and began to swing the machine pistol toward the children. Toward me.

But it was much too late for her. The verdict was in—and Elevator Lady had been found guilty as charged. My MP5 was already up and off safety before she'd even begun her move. I had a perfect shoulder mold with the MP5's retractable stock. I concentrated on putting the front sight between EL's eyes, six inches above her young hostage's head. I acquired a perfect sight picture, and squeezed the trigger.

At six yards, even though my heart rate may be way above 150, I always hit precisely what I aim at. A three-round burst of frangible SWAT 9-mm carbine loads caught Elevator Lady in the tiny triangle separating the bridge of her nose from her forehead. Her head literally exploded from the kinetic force of the high-energy rounds. She dropped through a cloud of her own blood, brain, and bone fragments, her left arm still clutched around the hostage.

Except—she'd had her finger on the fucking Skorpion's trigger, and the gun went off as she fell.

I launched myself at Elevator Lady's corpse, caught the barrel of the goddamn weapon just as it was coming down below horizontal, and fought to keep the muzzle angled upward, toward the ceiling and away from the huddled, screaming kids. When it was finally pointed in a safe direction, I yanked the Skorpion out of her dead hand, dropped the magazine to the floor, and thumbed the weapon's safety to the "on" position.

I ripped the little girl hostage out of EL's grasp and held her against my chest. She was okay but in such traumatic shock she was unable to talk. I tucked her under my left arm and out of the way. I rolled Elevator Lady over with my foot. She wasn't going anywhere. I turned and saw that Goober had the room covered from the window. His hands told me we were secure.

I pressed the "transmit" button and said, "Alpha clear. One tango down." Then I dropped the MP5 on its sling and swept the little girl into my arms. She was covered in blood spatter and brains. I wiped her face. "It's all right, honey—it's over. You're safe."

As I spoke I heard Rotten Randy in my ear. "Bravo clear. No casualties." I hoped he meant among the hostages.

"Where's the bomb?" I wanted to know where the hell it was.

Boomerang's high voice gave me the news I wanted to hear: "I got it, Boss Dude. It's safe—disarmed. We're clear. No one hurt."

I have been a part of these sorts of missions for a long time, my friends, and I have never before seen an operation go down so perfectly. This had been flawless. Textbook. They'd teach this one in every goddamn special operations school in the world.

Best of all, my WARRIORS had come through. They'd avenged their brother SEAL. I yanked my ballistic goggles down around my neck, and gave the little girl in my arms a bearded, ticklish kiss on the cheek. She nestled in the crook of my neck and shoulder, arms around me tight, and began to sob great gulping sobs of relief. "Honey," I said, giving her another smooch, "we took care of the bad people. Everything is gonna be just fine. You're gonna be all right."

"Oh, sir, oh, mister constable, I hope I will be," she sobbed, and then she squeezed me as tight as she could around my neck.

My friends, there is nothing so wonderful as the innocent love of a child except, perhaps, to wreak Roguish vengeance on anyone who would harm such a child. I stood among all those screaming but safe kids, feeling totally and professionally fulfilled.

And then, the moment passed, and it was time to go back to work. I shifted the little girl's weight in my arms and pressed the "transmit" button on the radio mike. "Okay, so let's call in the cavalry to disarm whatever the hell they have on the doors, so we can get these hostages out of here and back to their parents."

I gave the little girl in my arms another big hug and kiss, and watched as some small part of the ordeal she'd just been through evaporated from her eyes. Ecstatic, euphoric, exultant, elated, I hit the mike button again. "Bravo Zulus, guys. You made 'em pay for what they did to Butch. You did great work—you killed 'em all."

CHAPTER

5

ANY ELATION I MIGHT HAVE FELT LASTED ONLY AS LONG AS IT TOOK for the bulldog editions of the morning newspapers to hit the stands. Somehow, a photographer from the *Daily Herald,* one of London's less principled tabloids, had managed to infiltrate the perimeter, and he'd videotaped our assault with a digital camera equipped, it would seem, with a very effective telephoto lens. His video appeared on the paper's Web site.

One huge, graphic still photo covered the front page of the paper's bulldog edition. Above it, the headline read: "American Bullets, British Babies." Maybe it wasn't as dramatic as the shot of Elián González being snatched out of a closet by an MP5-carrying Fed, but it did the job. It caught me in profile, just as I shot Elevator Lady. The picture froze my kill-'em-all-and-let-God-sort-it-out expression, the cloud of blood as EL's head exploded, and the look of pure terror on the little hostage girl's face.

It is said that every picture tells a story. But the story pictures tell are not necessarily true. The truth, however, did not matter to the Powers That Be. Not even when there was a dead American SEAL (whose flag-draped coffin rated not a single picture in the British newspapers) to be mourned.

Of course, the powers that be didn't have time to mourn Butch

Wells. They were too busy dealing with the fifteen hundred protesters marching outside the American Embassy protesting the
fact that American military personnel were shooting British
Nationals on sovereign British soil. The fact that the TIRA terrorists had murdered two British military personnel, one U.S. Navy
SEAL, and taken a school full of children hostage appeared to be
totally irrelevant to the protesters. Go fucking figure.

Our ambassador extraordinary and plenipotentiary, a cookie
pusher from Foggy Bottom, was called to Downing Street and
read the well-known riot act by the prime minister for allowing
such undiplomatic behavior to be committed by U.S. nationals on
her watch. (Being politically correct, she never once brought up
Butch's ultimate sacrifice on behalf of the peace accords.) Mick
Owen, who reports to folks a lot less diplomatic than the prime
minister, was unceremoniously reamed a new asshole for allowing me to do the down and dirty. And I? I was summoned
posthaste, chop-chop, double-time, hup-two, hup-two, to report
to the antique-filled office suite of Admiral Eamon Joseph
Flannery, United States Navy, at 0900 the following morning.

Admiral Flannery, USNA[13] 1968, known to his subordinates as
Eamon the Demon, is currently CINCUSNAVEUR, which translates from Navyspeak as Commander IN Chief, US NAVal forces,
EURope. His offices, which face Grosvenor Square, are in the
same building on the corner of North Audley Street that once
housed the headquarters of Dwight D. Eisenhower when Ike
planned Operation Sword, the invasion of Europe in 1944.

But the similarities stop there. Ike was a Warrior. Eamon the
Demon is a wimp. Ike was willing to take responsibility for his
decisions. Eamon the Demon is known as "The Stealth CINC"
because he seldom (if ever) commits his signature to a binding
document or memo, but has his subordinates write and sign 'em

---

[13] United States Naval Academy.

instead. And, as Roy Boehm, the Godfather of all SEALs, reminded me when I told him who was running CINCUSNAVEUR, "Remember, Rotten Richard, Ike did his pissing into a urinal. From everything I've ever heard, Eamon the Demon sits down when he makes a wee-wee."

But Eamon Joseph Flannery still wears four stars, which gives him a certain amount of clout in matters of Navydom. And even though I didn't come under his chain of command, he had the political muscle to make me show up at his office. And so, after a 0430 wake-up call, and a 2.5-hour PT session with my men that included an eight-and-a-half mile run twice around Hyde Park, I showered, shit, and shaved, and dressed in a blazer and pressed gray flannels, a dress shirt, and my raincoat, trudged through the cold drizzle from our out-of-the-limelight hotel on Half Moon Street up along Curzon Street, worked my way to New Bond, and from there turned port on Brook Street. I crossed the police barriers on the northeast side of Grosvenor Square by the Marriott hotel, steered starboard on North Audley, and pushed through the glass-and-steel revolving door of CINCUSNAVEUR headquarters.

In the old days, I would have gone directly to the office of my old shipmate Command Master Chief Hans Weber, and received an intel dump that would forewarn and forearm me about what was happening at North Audley Street. But Hansie was long gone. He'd retired not six months after I left London to chase down a bunch of Russian mininukes in the Rhine Valley a couple of years back. So these days I didn't have a single intelligence source here. In fact, even the network of chiefs on which I'd relied since I'd been an E-2 tadpole was unraveling one by one, due to retirement, or just plain exhaustion from having to deal with a military that grows more dysfunctional by the day.

And so, I showed my creds to the Jarhead behind the bullet-proof, glassed-in guard post on the ground floor, took the elevator to the third floor, turned left, then hove right and sailed into the admiral's reception area on the dot of 0900 hours.

A so-young-he-was-probably-still-wearing-nappies-at-night lieutenant commander was waiting for me, t-t-tapping a government issue ballpoint pen impatiently on his knee as he sat in an uncomfortable-looking armchair. As I pushed through the door he rose.

"Captain Marcinko." It wasn't a question, and he didn't give me time to reply. Instead, he actually looked down his nose at me. "I am Lieutenant Commander Troy M. Wesley, Admiral Flannery's aide," he said, a snide tone to his voice. "The admiral has been waiting for you in his private office."

I wrinkled my brow at his behavior and replied in kind, mocking his snotty delivery. "I am Captain Richard No Middle Name Marcinko," I stated. "And I guess I should be overwhelmed that you have deigned to take the time from what must be a busy schedule to welcome me to the command."

He looked at me as if I'd stepped in something nasty. "Oh, please don't be overwhelmed, . . . sir." The kid wheeled, giving me his back. Obviously, he was performing for the attractive yeoman first class sitting behind the receptionist's desk. I winked at the yeoman, whose name tag identified her as P. Baker.

"I'll show you the way, . . . Captain," Troy M. Wesley said to the wall, the disdain in his voice echoing off the wood paneling.

I peered at Lieutenant Commander Troy M. Wesley's narrow shoulders as he prissed past the yeoman's desk toward the hidden door that led to the admiral's hideaway. Well, fuck him. He was representative of most of the young staff officers you see these days. He was no warrior. His eyes had already told me he was unprepared to die. His eyes had already told me he was more interested in making real estate investments and building stock portfolios than he was in making war and breaking things.

And so, in no mood to be screwed with by officers whose behavior had been influenced by spoiled children, I treated him like the brat he was. I caught up with him, turned him around with a big paw to his shoulder, backed him up to Yeoman Baker's desk, and wedged him there so he couldn't move. "Fuck you, Commander. I was coming in and out of this place when you were still shitting mustard in your nappies—that's Brit for diapers in case you didn't get it. So you will not fuck with me. In fact, you will pay me respect. Not because I wear a lot more stripes than you do—which I happen to—but because I've actually killed people and you haven't, and you probably won't, unless you panic and blow up a lot of innocent civilians by mistake when the assholes who run this here Navy give you command of something big and gray to play with long before you're ready to assume any real responsibility."

I paused long enough to watch him grow wide-eyed. He kind of sagged against the desk. I put my face up against his face just like old Navy chiefs like my UDT 21 platoon chief, Ev Barrett, used to do to me, or Marine drill sergeants used to do to their boot-camp Jarheads when they wanted to terrorize them. "What's the matter, sonny?" I asked, my rough beard hairs touching his cheek. "You *scared*?"

I watched with delight the effect my words were having. So, like the generations of chiefs and gunnies I knew as I came of age in the Navy, I examined his nose. Carefully. Up close.

As I did, Lieutenant Commander Troy M. Wesley started to flinch. Big mistake. I did my best Everett E. Barrett imitation. "You *will* stand at attention, you no-load, pencil-dicked, numb-nutted puke, or I will reach down your fucking throat, grab you by the sphincter, turn you fucking inside out, and drag your worthless ass into the admiral's office in that condition so he can see what a real-life, government inspected, ruby red, grade A size-one asshole really looks like."

I shifted my body so that Lieutenant Commander Troy M. Wesley couldn't see my face, and checked to make sure my performance was playing well with Yeoman Baker, who was sitting directly behind the officer's back. She had what can only be described as a shit-eating grin on her face. She gave me the thumb-and-forefinger in a circle hand sign that told me that either I was a Brazilian asshole, or everything was A-OK. I chose the latter interpretation and winked back at her.

Then it was back into character. After all, the admiral was waiting. Okay: it was time to see whether the training session had worked and the kid could be controlled off-leash.

I crooked my finger toward the young officer. "Come," I growled.

Lieutenant Commander Troy M. Wesley came.

I do so love success. "Heel," I barked, and wheeled toward the hidden door.

●　●　●

The admiral was standing posed somewhat grandly by his fireplace as I came into his hideaway office. He turned toward me and lowered his arm off the mantel. "Captain," he said, watching intently as his cowed aide followed me into the small but nicely appointed office.

I inclined my head toward him. "Admiral."

There was an awkward pause. I guess he'd expected me to appear more contrite, given the uproar over my actions.

Yeah, right. I growled, "You sent for me."

He turned away to inspect the gas fire in the fireplace. "Yes," he said.

I watched him watch the flames. "Is there something you want me to do?"

Eamon the Demon glanced over to where Lieutenant Commander Wesley stood. "Dismissed," he said to Lieutenant Commander Troy M. Wesley.

We both watched as the young officer turned and left, closing the door behind him. Then there was more silence. The admiral was a tall man, and lanky. There was a certain awkward, geeky disjointedness to him.

He veered across the room to a leather wing chair and finally settled himself into it, his long legs dropping onto the adjacent ottoman, his bony knees protruding at different angles. I could make out the joints through the material of his trouser legs. He touched his fingertips together, forming his hands into an angular little house, and then wiggled his fingers. Finally, he looked over at me. "There is a problem," the admiral said obliquely.

I really wasn't in the mood for games. "Care to tell me about it?"

He looked at me, annoyed. "You know, you are not much beloved by our British hosts," he said.

What was this, Obvious 101? As if I didn't know. As if I hadn't had to make my way through the fucking demonstration still going on in front of the embassy. But I wasn't about to give him anything. So I said simply, "Oh, really?"

He stared at me. "Do not play games with me, Captain," he said. "This is serious."

"I did my job, Admiral. I lost one of my best people. But I got the kids out. I neutralized three assholes who would have gone on to kill a lot more innocent victims, and I'm damned if I'm going to apologize for it."

"I know all of that," he said. "I'm sorry you lost that man. And you have a point: you did your job. But you also have to think about the political consequences of the situation. You cannot act without factoring in the politics."

"Oh, yes I can."

He looked at me, shocked. *"What?"*

"It is not my job to factor in the politics of what I do. That is *your* job, Admiral. It is an admiral's job to deal with the press, and the problems of political correctness, and all the public opinion pollsters. It's an admiral's job to keep the fucking politicians off my back. My job is to hunt down terrorists and kill them."

He came out of his chair like a pair of shots and lurched over to where I stood, wagging his long, bony finger all the while until it was within six inches of my oft-squashed snout. "I will not have you speak to me in that derisive tone of voice, Captain. I know that you enjoy the protection of the Chairman of the Joint Chiefs. But if you will remember, General Crocker's term is about to expire, and I do not think he will be appointed a third time. And that is why you are here, with me, right now. To deal with your problem."

I watched the admiral's lips flap. But I wasn't listening. Unfortunately, what he'd just said was absolutely true. I was in London because General Thomas E. Crocker, the JCS chairman, had insisted, over the objections of the chief of naval operations and a laundry list of other federal agencies and cabinet secretaries that I be designated as the OIC, or Officer In Charge, of the American military component of Detachment Bravo. The Navy certainly hadn't wanted me here. The State Department hadn't wanted me here—in fact they'd tried to blackball me by going behind General Crocker's back to the White House. But since General Crocker had wanted me to take on this job, and since he has balls, that is what happened.

That was all on the one hand. On the other hand, Eamon the Demon was absolutely correct: General Crocker's term was swiftly drawing to a close. He'd be gone in a matter of weeks now. And the new administration had no intention of renominating him. The heir apparent was a Marine general named Carlton "Chip" Walker. His rise within the Corps had been truly spectacular. Twelve years ago, Chip was a blockhead colonel serving as a military aide to the secretary of defense. But he also played basketball—as did the then-SECDEF. Walker's talent as a power forward got him his first star. His talent as a power brown nose got him his second and a third stars, according to the corridor RUMINT at the Pentagon.

And how did he get his fourth star? I don't want to go there—and neither do you. And besides, isn't our military governed under the policy of "Don't Ask, Don't Tell" these days? Currently, Chip was serving as the Marine Corps commandant. And his name had been floated in the press—he'd probably leaked it himself—as the "best in breed" selection for the Chairman's slot.

Except for one small fact. Chip Walker was an idiot. Okay, so that's not enough to disqualify him. You are right. There have been a fair number of idiots who have served as JCS Chairmen. But Chip Walker was a dangerous idiot, in that he had the habit of knuckling under to any—repeat, *ANY*—political pressure. And so, he had already eviscerated the Corps' rapid response capabilities. He had instituted the same kind of integrated male/female training that had brought the other uniform services to their sorry state of readiness. And he hated Warriors. Despised them as knuckle draggers and Neanderthals. He'd even said so in a speech once. He'd been invited to address the national convention of the feminist organization NOW, and there he'd actually called Warriors "a necessary evil in a postsexist democracy." No, I am not kidding.

The bottom line was that I was about to lose my one remaining rabbi at the Pentagon, the result of which was that I'd be tossed to the wolves by the long, long line of admirals, including Eamon Joseph Flannery, to whom I'd said, "Fuck you, strong message follows," one or two or three times too many.

My reverie was interrupted by Eamon the Demon's chicken-squawk voice. "And so," he clucked, "I had to take steps."

He was looking at me strangely. Oh, fuck. I'd missed at least a paragraph—maybe more.

"Come again?"

His expression was disdainful, as if I was learning-challenged. We used to call it thick-as-a-brick dumb. But that was before everything was politically correct. The admiral sighed. Have you noticed how good our alleged leaders are at sighing these days? Greta fucking Garbos, all of 'em.

"I have been handed a problem," Eamon said slowly, as if I didn't speak much English. "A previously unknown Irish terrorist group, the Green Hand Defenders."

"Never heard of them."

"Nor had anyone else," Eamon said. "Until our British cousins overheard a conversation between two of their members."

"A conversation."

"It dealt with the targeting of Americans."

"Was this recent?" If it was, I should have been told. This was obviously something that fell under Detachment Bravo's bailiwick.

"Six months—maybe more," the admiral said. "But we—that is to say, I—only found out about it three days ago."

"We?"

"I. We. Us. The United States Government."

"The Brits were holding back?"

The admiral retreated to his wing chair and turned away from me. "It seems that way."

"I'll have a word with Mick Owen."

Eamon the Demon swung toward me. "That is precisely what I do not want to happen," he said. "We did not discover about the Green Hand Defenders through the normal liaison relationship I enjoy with our British friends from the Ministry of Defense, or the Intelligence Service. We—that is to say, I—came upon them through a backchannel source who has been vastly helpful to me in the past. Therefore, I would like to keep our knowledge of this particular group compartmented."

"Compartmented."

"Private. Some of our British friends have obviously sought to deprive us of information we—that is to say I—believe they should have shared. I want you to find out why."

I thought about what the admiral had just told me. "Then why me?" I asked. "Like you said, my rep with the Brits is none too good right now."

"Precisely," the admiral smiled, as if to himself. "Precisely." He ran a hand through his thinning hair. "Let me be specific," he said. "You will report what you find to me. To no one else. When I know all there is to know about the Green Hand Defenders, I will decide upon the appropriate action, which you will implement."

"And if I decide that what you are telling me now is inappropriate and go to the Chairman?"

Eamon the Demon looked at me, his eyes narrow. "That," he said, "would not be a wise decision on your part. You are in deep trouble in Washington because of this last escapade of yours."

"I've been in trouble before."

"But this time is different," the admiral said. "This time, the Chairman can't protect you."

He paused, then fired for effect. "But *I* can protect you. And I will—if you help me."

I'd just about had enough of this asshole. "Pardon my French, Admiral, but why the fuck should I ever help you? You have no chain-of-command responsibility over Detachment Bravo. You don't write my fitreps. I don't work for you—I work for the Chairman. And until he is relieved, that's the way things are going to be."

He looked at me evenly. "I don't like you, Captain," he said. "I do not like your methods, your manner, or your style of command. But this is business—serious business. And I am willing to work in a strictly quid pro quo relationship. I want to find out about the Green Hand Defenders. Who they are. What they are up to. What their capabilities and intentions are. Whom they are targeting. You can do that for me much more easily than I can do it for myself, and with much less attention from the British authorities. In return, I will, for the time being, protect you and your men from those who would like to end your careers more abruptly and immediately than you might like."

Now he was finally beginning to make sense to me. I didn't give a shit about my career. I never have. But my men had to be shielded from the sort of political vengeance that Pentagon admirals, especially petty, spiteful, vindictive admirals like Eamon the Demon can wreak. And if this pussy-ass was willing to protect them, then I would most certainly deal with him—until I came up with something better.

"Will you put this in writing?"

"I am not a stupid man, Captain. Writing does not . . . *enhance,* shall I say, understandings such as this one." Then he grew serious. "But I know you to be a man of your word. And so, I will shake your hand, and consider the matter closed and the bargain sealed." And with that, he offered me his hand.

I took it in my own. It was soft and the nails were manicured, as befits an ossifer and a gentleman, not to mention the kind of paper-shuffling, responsibility-shirking C²CO that Eamon represents. And so, I applied a fair amount of Roguish pressure as we stood there, eyeball to eyeball, cementing the deal.

I stared directly into his baby grays, which told me I'd put him in considerable pain. But I wasn't about to let him go until I'd made him understand how I operate. I squeezed even harder. "I take my bargains very seriously, Admiral."

Wincing now, he pulled back until he managed to free his hand from mine. "So do I, Captain," he said, rubbing the injured paw as he did. "So do I. And believe me, when the timing is appropriate, you and your men can go after the Green Hand Defenders and obliterate them. As you just said, it is your job to hunt terrorists down and then kill them. That is precisely what I am giving you the opportunity to do." Reflexively, he massaged his sore hand some more, grimacing as he worked the joints. "Unless, of course, you'd like to be on a plane to Washington tonight."

• • •

If the real goal of Eamon's assignment to find out about the Green Hand Defenders was to make sure that I kept a low profile for the next week and a half or so, he achieved his objective, and then some. The protests continued. In fact, some fucking company called Globex even hired an ad agency to put anti-American posters on the sides of London's double-decker buses. The poster had been taken from one of the *Daily Herald*'s photos during the Brook Green School operation. It was a pretty good picture of me, seen in Roguish profile as I staged at the base of the assault ladder to go through the window of the school. One result of the publicity was that now a gaggle of protesters marched in front of our hotel, holding placards that declared me a murderer, and worse.

But I didn't give a shit. I was too busy. My face may have become public. But my guys, thank goodness, were still unknown. And they were neither idle, nor in hiding. In his 374 B.C. work on military philosophy, *The Li'ang Hsi-Huey,* General Tai Li'ang, the great Chinese tactician, wrote: "The straight line is not always the most direct path to victory." And so, I sent my men out to do what SEALs do best: sneak & peek & gather intelligence without leaving any trails or signs that they'd been in the neighborhood.

Since he was fluent in their native tongue, I sent Nigel off to pub-crawl with his pals in SO-19, Scotland Yards special ops and counterterrorism unit. Goober and Timex began hanging out in a couple of pubs frequented by British special forces and intel types, picking up snippets where they could. Rotten Randy kept his eyes open (and his lock-picking kits handy) around the DET Bravo offices. I wanted him to check the secure files to see if anybody was keeping secrets from us.

Digger O'Toole worked the American Embassy. Because of his charm, his flair, his conversational abilities, and most of all his long, swinging dick, he'd already managed to form what might be called a "highly meaningful relationship" with one of the communicators at the CIA station. And while one end of him was humping her, the other end of him was pumping her. Oh, yeah, even in this new century, pillow talk is still one of the most effective ways of obtaining human-generated intelligence.

While Digger was H&P, my two most computer literate shooters, Boomerang and Nod, started playing the Internet search engines. It is absolutely amazing, friends, what you can find using what's known as OSINT, or Open Source INTelligence these days.

While the men toiled at their assignments, I quietly activated my support network back in the States. First, I used the secure phone to get hold of da Pepperman (real name Bill, and he's called Pepperman because he grows ornamental bushes of fifty-thousand Scoville-unit, bright red Thai peppers in front of his three-bedroom center-hall colonial in Crofton, Maryland). Pepperman is my inside guy at No Such Agency.

I caught up with the former Noo Yawka, and after the usual FYVM[14] greetings, I begged, cajoled, and threatened until he promised to take a look at all the ZU-Messages, Whiskey-Number files, and Echelon intercepts over the past six or so months,[15] looking for anything that might in any way relate to something called the Green Hand Defenders. Da Pepperman was somehow unhappy with my request. "Goddammit, Dick, I already have a full-time job. Do you know how much fucking work this is going to be?"

I wasn't impressed. "What's your point?"

There was silence on the line. And then: "You are going to owe me. Big time."

"This won't be the first time for that, either."

I rang off and tried to call my old pal Jim Wink at Christians In Action. Wink's radio call sign is Heinz 57, since he has taught counterterrorist tactics in fifty-seven varieties of countries before they promoted him to supergrade and chained him to a desk to run Langley's CTC, or Counter Terrorism Center.

But Wink was nowhere to be found. He'd picked the locks on his shackles and escaped, his office said. He was working on some code-word project in Jordan while simultaneously trying to repair

---

[14] Fuck You Very Much.

[15] ZU-Messages (pronounced ZU) are NSA's highest-priority intercepts. They are intended for the Presiden'ts Eyes Only. Whiskey-Numbers are classsified just below ZU-Messages, and are currently seen by cabinet secretaries and top-level military commanders. And Echelon is the joint US/British intel vacuum, which sucks up every bit of commercial and military message traffic, telephonic, satellite-generated, and Internet-based, between Moscow in the east, Helsinki in the north, Tunis in the south, and Tehran, Iran, in the Middle East. And now that *you* know three of our most secret secrets, please rip this page out of the book, write a note in the margin stating that our secrets are safe with you, and send it to: Director, National Security Agency, 9800 Savage Road, Fort George G. Meade, MD 20755-6000. If they believe you, they will do nothing. If they don't, they will arrange to change the compartments and give the programs all new code designators.

the current fractured relationship between King Abdullah's intelligence service, the *Mukhabarat,* and CIA. If anybody could do that, it was Wink. Jim and Abdullah were old friends. They'd known each other so long that they were on a first name basis. By this, I mean to say that the king called Wink "Jim," and Wink called the king "Sir." He didn't spell it *cur,* either. Anyway, Wink might be back in a couple of weeks. Or he might not be back for months.

So, next I dialed up my other top-flight source when it comes to matters of intelligence, the Brooklyn-born, Bay Ridge–bred colonel at DIA I refer to as Tony Mercaldi.[16] I struck out there, too. Da Merc was on leave. In Sicily, taking a month of vacation to celebrate his twentieth wedding anniversary. This was quickly becoming Doom on Dickie time.

But as you probably know by now, we SEALs are resourceful. So I started making calls and developing new sources of information. Doing this kind of research is not easy. Indeed, gaining closely held intelligence never is. You have to be persistent, and guileful, and you have to know how far you can push people, so that they give up their info without knowing it. What works in your favor is the fact that intel people tend to stovepipe their information, not sharing it with other service branches. And so, what NSA knows is not necessarily passed on to DIA. What the Navy knows is not shared with the Army or the Air Farce.

And so I persevered. I didn't have to like it, I just had to do it. Similarly, my guys bitched and moaned, but they also came up with results. Nothing overwhelming, but enough so that this old Roguish camel was able to get his snout under the edge of the Green Hand Defenders tent, and glimpse a little bit of what was going on inside.

Like what, you ask?

---

[16] This is a pseudonym.

Okay, here's what I knew by the end of the first week. And don't skip over this stuff, because it's going to become significant later in the book.

- Digger's CIA communicator told him that right after a top-level meeting at MI6 three or four months ago, the London station chief had put in his retirement papers, taken terminal leave, and gone house hunting in Provence. It was station RUMINT that he'd been told about some new kind of Irish Hezb'allah and didn't want to get involved.

I interrupted Digger's narrative. "Hezb'allah?"

"That's what she said," Digger told me. "Not that they're Arabs. But that they're organized like Hezb'allah."

I thought about that, and part of it made sense. What made the original Hezb'allah terror organization unique was that unlike other tango groups, Hezb'allah had been built around a single clan: the Musawis. That had made it hard to infiltrate. Now, our station chief had been told by MI6 about a terrorist group that couldn't be infiltrated. He'd been asked to help, and, Digger continued, it was rumored that he'd demurred because he didn't have the resources—read agents—to do the job, and didn't want to be embarrassed by admitting it. And so, he had retired abruptly.

What did not make sense was the COS's resignation. There had to be something else in play here, and I told Digger to go back and hump & pump until he found out what it was. The shit-eating grin on his face told me what he thought about my tossing his hyperactive Brer Lizard right back into the friendly briar bush.

- Nod DiCarlo's on-line hunt-and-pecking uncovered the fact that credit for the five assassinations in which Americans had so far been killed had been taken by two obscure and heretofore largely ineffective IRA splinter groups, the Irish Brotherhood and the Irish People's Army.

"I already know that," I told him. "What's your point?"

"My point, Skipper," Nod said, "is that neither one of these fucking groups have ever been able to stage a successful hit. Not one of 'em. I went back ten years, looked at news clips, court records—everything I could get my hands on. None of 'em was ever able to get it together. The Irish Brotherhood lost more of its own people to bombs that went off prematurely than they ever killed. Two IPA guys once got in a fight outside a bar full of English soldiers over which one of 'em was badder, and they actually shot each other instead of setting up to ambush the Brits. Now, all of a sudden, these same IPA assholes are pulling off complex, intricate hits, and the Irish Brotherhood is planting sophisticated, complex IEDs.[17] It just doesn't make sense."

Nod was right, of course: it didn't make sense. But I could extrapolate one conclusion from his research that made a lot of sense—to *me*. Some smart, manipulative and above all *covert* tango was doing the research, the mission planning, and even, perhaps, the dirty work. Then he allowed the dumb, bungling, amateurish assholes from the IPA and the Irish Brotherhood to take all the credit, and—sooner or later—the whole fall, too.

- Goober and Timex became fast friends with a retired Brit EOD sergeant major named Mike, who ran the Rose and Thorn, a pub just off Piccadilly where both active and retired Brit shooters congregated. It didn't take more than a few gallons of Everards Beacon Bitter for them to develop the following info bits.

---

[17] Improvised Explosive Devices.

It seems that just about six months before we'd come to London, it was rumored that a GCHQ—that's Government Communications Headquarters, the British version of NSA—listening device in a pub somewhere in Northern Ireland picked up what appeared to be fragments of a whispered conversation between two Green Hand Defenders.

The intercept had to do with a coordinated, two-part operation against one unnamed British and one unnamed American target, culminating in a pair of simultaneous attacks in which hundreds of Americans and British nationals, many of them VIPs, would be killed in one devastating blow. The ordnance for the assault would be delivered in eight months, and it would come from a Middle Eastern source, who would also supply much of the other material needed. Once the ordnance was obtained, only three or four more steps would be necessary until the operation could be mounted.

The eight-month wait might have seemed strange to some. But not to me. The IRA has a history of carefully planning its terrorist attacks. The bomb hidden by the IRA in the Grand Hotel in the British seaside city of Brighton, which almost killed British Prime Minister Margaret Thatcher and her entire cabinet back in 1984, had been cached forty-eight days ahead of time and never discovered. That is impressive work.

There was more: according to Mike, the Brits couldn't analyze the tape because they didn't have the right voice-recognition program software. "Scuttlebutt is that the tapes were sent to that humongous NSA installation at Menithwood Hill, about twenty miles southwest of Birmingham, Skipper. After that—who knows."

- Nigel told me that according to his SO-19 contacts, there'd been a real goatfuck of an MI5 op in Northern Ireland about five months previously. The cops were still laughing about it. It seems that a town called Ballynahinch had been blanketed by MI5's top CT action group, augmented by the British spec-operators formerly known as 14th Intelligence Company,[18] as well as a laundry list of other British intelligence-gathering and Special Operations units. About 3.5 million pounds Sterling had been spent on the three-day op, with no evident results. According to SO-19 gossip, the political consequences for Sir Roger Holland, MI5's embattled director general, should have been disastrous, but despite the huge and expensive fiasco, he was still firmly in place. The single slap on the wrist MI5 had received was that it had been shut out of Det Bravo when the joint counterterrorist task force had been formed.

- Digger reported back that I'd been right: his Langley squeeze had told him that corridor gossip had the station chief resigning because he was sick and tired of being backchanneled.

"Backchanneled?"

"That's what she said," Digger repeated. "The RUMINT is, he was being cut out of all the action and he didn't like it."

"Any idea what kind of action we're talking about here, Eddie?"

Digger shook his head. "Can't say, Skipper—it's way above her pay grade."

• • •

The following afternoon I sent Goober and Timex back to Mike's pub and asked them to dig a little deeper, too. Why did I do that? I did it because if the Brits spent the equivalent of five and a half million dollars on a seventy-two-hour op, and it pro-

---

[18] As was the case in *Echo Platoon*, my contacts at MI6 have asked me not to use the current unit designator, and I plan to honor their request. This is fiction, after all. Besides, it's backstory.

duced no results, and no one's head rolled, they were either: (A) very flush with cash, or (B) hiding something. I believed it was the latter.

I believed that the op had borne fruit, and that the Brits had quietly backchanneled us and asked for a covert favor or two. The one person I knew who could verify that supposition was my old comrade in arms and reluctant information-provider, Pepperman. And so, I dialed da Pepperman on the secure phone and refined my original request by asking him to review all the liaison work our Echelon people did for the Brits roughly five months ago.

Forty-eight hours later, he called me back.

"What are you, a fucking crystal ball reader?"

"Say what?"

"You sent me to dig up that . . . info, right?"

"Yeah."

"Well, I can't get my hands on it."

"Why?"

"Because it's all blue-tabbed PEO.[19] It's all ZU-Message reporting."

"Any idea what's inside the folders?"

Pepperman paused. "Look, Dick," he said, "I could lose my job over this. And I need my pension. Believe me, I still have two kids to put through college."

"It was *that* sensitive?"

"The director sent the file to the White House. From there, so the story goes—and I can't substantiate any of it—it was taken by armed courier directly to London."

"*London?*" That was unexpected.

"Ten Downing Street."

I thought about it. "Bill, you gotta help me here. Give me some-

---

[19] President's Eyes Only.

thing I can work with. Something I can follow up. I don't have any hooks into the PM's office, and you know that as well as I do."

He started to say something, stopped himself short, and then continued. "Okay, we're talking about a conversation that took place in Northern Ireland."

That was no help. "Where?"

"Someplace called Randallstown."

The name rang a bell, but I was obviously having a Senior Moment, because I couldn't come up with what it was. "So?"

"We did some work on the intercept for our cousins," he said noncommittally.

That was when the bells rang and the whistles went off. Pepperman was obviously talking about the surveillance op in the Northern Ireland pub Goober and Timex had heard about. "Bill, you're not being very helpful here."

"I could go to Leavenworth for what I'm telling you, Dickie."

"So far you haven't told me very much."

Pepperman sighed. It was a long, deep, mournful sigh. He has spent his entire professional life at NSA, and he is devoted to the organization. "We used a new voice-recognition system to distinguish what was being said and separate it from the rest of what was going on in the pub."

"Did you say pub? My people here just picked up some bullshit about a tango plot that the Brits discovered in a pub in Northern Ireland about six months ago, but no one mentioned Randallstown. Are we talking about the same incident?"

I was greeted with silence. Then Pepperman said, "Shit."

"If you don't say something, I'll take that for a yes, Bill." I waited. There was nothing but sweet, confirming silence.

Do you see what I see here? I was starting to see a pattern emerging. And so, it was time to start connecting dots. "Bill," I said, "about a month after Randallstown, the Brits staged a huge and very expensive op in a place called Ballynahinch. Allegedly they came up dry. Did the first event have anything to do with the second one?"

More silence. And then Pepperman said, "Thing was, that because of our voice-recognition program we were able to establish for the Brits that the accents in the first conversation were from Ballynahinch, not Randallstown. Then we programmed our Echelon equipment to sweep every phone conversation in Ballynahinch until we matched one of the voices."[20]

I asked, "Wasn't that illegal?"

Bill answered, "It would have been if the Brits did it."

In case you don't get the significance of what Pepperman is saying here, let me explain it for you. Since the United States does not answer to the British rules of law, we eavesdrop on phones for them in their country, and since they are not subject to our laws, or have to report to Congressional oversight committees, they eavesdrop on phones for us within the United States.[21]

I wasn't about to get into the finer points of ethical conduct with him right then. (And besides, according to the TEN COMMANDMENTS OF SPECWAR©,[22] you do whatever you have to do to win, right?) I pressed him hard. "What do we know, Bill? This is goddamn important to me—and it may be critical to my mission."

He groaned and grunted, as if he were in pain. I waited out the

---

[20] Echelon's voice-recognition program is based to a large degree on the Berger-Liaw Neural Network Speaker Independent Speech Recognition System, whose development was partially underwritten by the U.S. Navy in the late 1990s. The system can distinguish words buried in vast amounts of random "white nose," noise with amplitude *one thousand times* the strength of the target signal. The system can pluck words from the background clutter of other voices, such as the hubbub of bus stations, lobbies, bars, and auditoriums. Then, NSA scientists at Echelon took the basic Berger-Liaw program and enhanced it to include the ability to identify regional accents, so that the system can isolate a London accent from one from Birmingham, or pick out the native New Yorker from a roomful of people born in Detroit, Chicago, Philadelphia, Los Angeles, Miami, or Boston.

[21] You think I'm kidding. I'm not. That's how No Such Agency abides by the rules set up for it by Congress, rules that forbid it from eavesdropping on Americans. NSA does not

silence. "Dick," he finally said, "if I were you, I'd start looking at a company called Globex and a kid called Kelley—that's spelled with an *e* and a *y*—who owns it."

Globex? Globex was the selfsame corporation that had paid for the ad campaign that was plastering my Roguish puss on double-decker buses and protesters' placards. And now I was being told that Globex had something to do with a five-million-dollar-plus covert op in Northern Ireland, a series of Echelon intercepts, and a Whiskey-Number message that had been sent directly from the White House to Ten Downing Street.

My friends, there is a God. And so far as I am concerned, He is the God of War. He is the fearsome, Unnamable Name of the Old Testament, who wreaks vengeance on profaners and sinners and his enemies and slays them all—every single fucking one. That's my kind of God. So if, by chance, the selfsame Globex corporation that had been gibbeting *moi* in a negative public-relations campaign had anything whatsoever to do with the death of Butch Wells, or the Brook Green School hostage-taking I'd just been flayed over, I'd wreak my own form of Old Testament, Roguish vengeance on Globex—and the people who owned it.

But that would come much later. Meanwhile, Pepperman was talking. "Look, Dick," he said. "I gotta go now. I gotta make the world safe for democracy."

---

eavesdrop on Americans. The Brits do it for us. So do the Canadians. And the Australians. Why? Because they're not breaking any of their nations' laws by doing so. And conversely, when Tony Blair wants to know what's being said on a phone in London, Woking, or Manchester, he can ask his pals at NSA to do the job for him, and then he can look the camera straight in the lens and say, with absolute honesty, that none of the British intelligence services are eavesdropping on British citizens. Of course they're not. *We're doing the dirty work for him.*

[22]© 1994, 1995, 1996, 1997, 1998, 1999, 2000, 2001 by Richard Marcinko and John Weisman.

"Bill," I said, "thanks. You have been more help than you know."

"No prob," Pepperman told me. "But, hey, Dick?"

"Yeah?"

"It's not that I don't like you. But don't call me again. Not for at least six months, okay? This one's gonna get just a little bit hot."

• • •

It took me about sixty-eight seconds to punch the word *Globex* into the Google.com search engine on my Dell Latitude. Globex, I discovered a few nanoseconds later, was a software program that takes Sun Computer Systems' Java software ten steps further in helping different types of programs communicate with one another. Globex software was a key part of many Fortune 500 computer systems. The company, which had gone public nineteen months previously, was controlled by Gerry and Gwilliam Kelley, two of Northern Ireland's most prominent software billionaires. Yeah, *billionaires.* For the past two years, Globex's annual capitalization had been well into the high twelve figures, and the Kelleys' stock options alone put them at number sixty-nine in the *Forbes* Four Hundred.

I did some more research. Gerry and Gwilliam Kelley were a pair of gregarious twentysomethings from Ballynahinch who, within the past half decade, had transmogrified themselves from a couple of hackers with desktop computers in a rented garage, into a two thousand-employee corporation of internationally known and respected software providers. According to articles in *Business Week* and *Fortune,* the Kelleys were smart, shrewd, and politically very well connected. A huge photograph of the two of them at Bayley's Hill, Gerry's sixty-acre estate just outside Sevenoaks, Kent, southeast of London, showed an attractive, even striking pair. Gwilliam was the younger Kelley—twenty-two according to the magazine clips. He had an impetuous, curled-lipped, Euro-trash look to him as he stood, his arm crooked against one of the estate's gateposts, red mud on the toe of his loafer, dressed in what looked to be a five-thousand-quid[23] suit.

Gerry Kelley was twenty-four. He was tall, and gangling, with a mop of unruly, curly, carrot red hair, and dark, passionate, fiery eyes. In the picture, he was holding a tennis racquet, the ragged jeans low around his hips revealing high-hitched patterned boxer shorts, a UCLA sweatshirt that had been cut back into a T, and old, duct-taped running shoes, looking somewhat like a tall, thin, muscular version of a college sophomore from some midwestern university. Gerry was the brains behind the company—the programmer who'd been known to closet himself for weeks of hunt and pecking on the keyboard. Gwilliam, as baby-faced as whatsisface Cappuccino from *Titanic,* was Mister Personality. He handled sales and marketing, and managed the company's considerable outside investment portfolios, which included a venture-capital fund focused on developing the economy in Northern Ireland, and Mrs. Kelley's Kitchen, a string of Irish-pub-themed, highly profitable saloon franchises in Germany, France, Argentina, and the United States.

Next, I dug up the list of franchisees for the bars and asked Digger to have his squeeze wash them through the Christians In Action database. Why did I do that? Because bars and restaurants are a great way to move a lot of cash without leaving very many tracks. In the United States, La Cosa Nostra uses bars and restaurants to launder its money. So do the cocaine cartels and the Russian *vory.*[24] I wanted to see if the Kelleys were allied with anyone in Russian organized crime, or South American drug smuggling.

I began to pass the Kelleys and Globex along to my support network of chiefs, gunnery sergeants, and grunts. If Gerry and Gwilliam were making ripples almost anywhere around the globe, I'd learn about it. And here is a piece of intelligence-

---

[23] *Quid* is slang for an English pound sterling.
[24] Organized crime syndicates.

gathering truth, my friends. When you are looking for hard information, it is more productive to know the gunny who runs an embassy's Marine security detail than it is to go to dinner with the friggin' ambassador. The ambassador's too busy passing out cookies to hear anything worthwhile. But ol' gunny has his ear to the ground. He's heard the rumors. He's got his antenna up. And so, I started casting my net—worldwide.

Finally, I pulled an all-nighter and did my own intensive research on the brothers Kelley, owners of Globex, Ltd. The company was headquartered five miles north of Ballynahinch in a compound that had obviously been modeled after the Microsoft campus in Redmond, Washington. But the Kelleys didn't live in Northern Ireland anymore. You already know that Gerry, who the *Times* rumored to be on the short list for a peerage, has his sixty acres in Sevenoaks. But I discovered he also kept a nineteenth-century carriage house on Hay's Mews, just off Berkeley (pronounced Barkley) Square, in London's Mayfair district, not six blocks from the American Embassy. I browsed the photos on the *Architectural Digest* Web site and discovered that his "carriage house" was actually two adjacent Victorian structures that had been gutted and crocheted together. The result was spectacular. Oh, yeah: Gerry (or his decorator) had discrimination. Belay that. Gerry had something better than discrimination. He had *money*.

But I wasn't looking at those photos to see Gerry's taste in art and fabric. I was looking to see where he lived. Even though the photos didn't reveal his address, I was able to figure out exactly where the house was located by analyzing the pictures and comparing them to an exceptionally detailed map of Central London streets.

Gwilliam, whose string of pubic . . . whoops, excuse me, that was *public* relationships with bulimic-looking VERBs[25] was regu-

---

[25] Vacant-Eyed Rich Bitches.

larly chronicled (and amply photographed) in the *Mirror* and the *Sun*, owned an eighteenth-century row house in Hampstead, two doors away from where the poet John Keats had once lived, as well as a hilltop villa on the French Riviera, halfway between Nice and Cap Ferrat, from which he could keep an eye on the Kelleys' 293-foot oceangoing yacht, the *Báltaí*.

I found a short picture spread on *Báltaí*, which the Kelley brothers had bought only nine months ago, in the *Observer* Sunday magazine. The interior was Keep It Simple, Stupid modern, down to the lavish use of ultramodernistic stainless steel, copper, and brass fixtures, cutting-edge communications devices and computer systems. The boat came complete with a small covered swimming pool on the aft end of the quarterdeck, a chopper pad (the chopper, an Aérospatiale *Écureuil* [squirrel] AS-350 according to the article, its rotors obviously folded, was domed over with an outsize plastic pod, giving it the look of those radome telecommunications antennas you see at Fort Meade when you visit No Such Agency), and a permanent crew of twelve.

When it wasn't anchored near Cap Ferrat, it could take Gwilliam and his VERBs on long cruises. Put the emphasis on *long*, please: *Báltaí*'s range was just over 5,100 nautical miles at its cruising speed of thirty-three knots, with slightly less range at flank speed, which was just over forty knots. She was sleek—and she was almost as fast as one of Admiral Arleigh Burke's destroyers

Indeed, Gwilliam, I read in the electronic version of the *Daily Telegraph*, was currently somewhere overseas, ostensibly checking up on the ever-expanding world of Mrs. Kelley's Kitchen franchises. But thanks to my noncom support net, I could be a lot more precise than the *Telegraph*. According to a piece of E-mail from a gunny named Jarriel, Gwilliam Kelley was currently conjugating one of his VERBs in the Argentine capital of Buenos Aires. That put Gwilliam beyond my reach—at the moment. But, according to the latest newspaper OSINT, Gerry the cherry was right here in London.

I checked the big-watch-tiny-pecker timepiece on my left wrist. 0500 hours. I debated the likely consequences of taking some direct action vis-à-vis the Kelleys for perhaps thirty seconds, then resolved to pay Gerry an early morning visit.

Now, I understood that there would be consequences to my action. Under normal circumstances one does not go a-calling on one's enemies. In fact, it is probably a good idea to keep one's enemies at arm's length, relationshipwise, so that he/she/it can be demonized in an impersonal way. It makes killing 'em so much easier. But there are times when the rules should be broken, and this was one of them. I wanted to take the measure of this man. If my instincts told me he was dirty (and my instincts seldom are wrong), I wanted to shake him up and make him act precipitously. And so, I decided that a social call was in order, even though I hadn't brought any engraved formal calling cards with me. That was okay. I always carry something far more effective than a calling card when it comes to making up-close-and-personal introductions. I pack a pistol.

CHAPTER

6

SOMETIMES, AS GENERAL TAI LI'ANG WROTE, ONE TAKES THE INDIrect path to victory. But in other cases, the straightmost course is best. That's one of the reasons flexibility in all situations is the sign of the true Warrior. Besides, it has always been my practice to take the measure of a man eyeball to eyeball, not by reading news clips, analysts' reports, magazine profiles, or bureaucratic memoranda. And so, I secured my research and made sure my men knew their assignments for the day. Then I showered, threw on a fresh suit, tucked my P7-M8 into an inside-the-pants holster, and made ready to hit the streets. (Yes, I know that handguns are completely outlawed in Britain. But I'm not British, I'm Roguish. And I also know that ever since handguns were banned, the rate of violent crime here in Britain has skyrocketed. That's because when guns are banned, only the criminals have guns. Remember that, the next time some gun-grabbing candidate is running for office and vote accordingly.)

So, here is the Rogue Warrior's First Law of Self Preservation: we of the Roguish persuasion practice on the range at least twice a week. And then, we carry our guns on the job. All the time. No matter what the rules may say.

• • •

It was just before 0630 hours when I took the fire stairs to the ground floor of the hotel, made my way through the small but cozy reception area, and pushed my way through the double doors onto Half Moon Street. It was far too early for any protesters, who tend to sleep late because their fucking work is so demanding. It had rained overnight and the streets were slick. But it wasn't too cold, and the sky was clear. I peered up the street toward Piccadilly, glancing at the sparse traffic. Then I turned left and started toward Curzon Street.

It didn't take me more than the half block between the hotel's front door and the dry cleaners on the opposite corner to realize that I wasn't alone. As I came out of the hotel, a maroon taxi that had been idling perhaps sixty yards back, growled into gear and eased onto the narrow asphalt street at a crawl. And a pair of baby-faced U2s,[26] one in a shiny ill-fitting shit brown suit and the other a greasy leather boy clad in a black leather jacket, thick wool turtleneck, and jeans, moved out of the apartment house doorway just off Piccadilly where they'd been lurking, flicked their cigarettes into the gutter, and started marching in syncopated lockstep, thirty yards behind me.

Who were they? I had no idea. More to the point, I didn't give an F-word who they were. Not right now. Right now I had other priorities. Besides, from the look of them and their lack of subtlety, they were amateurs: anti-Rogue student protesters, perhaps, hoping to buttonhole me. Or more maliciously, tango wannabes from the Irish Brotherhood, or IPA, the gangs-that-couldn't-shoot-straight groups Nod DiCarlo had been researching.

The bottom line was, it didn't matter who they were. I wasn't about to waste an hour engaging in a long and complicated cleaning route to shake this tail. Nor was I going to go offensive and take the assholes out. I didn't need trouble, or complications, this

---

[26] Ugly and Unfamilars.

morning. I had a mission to fulfill. And so I decided to KISS them off. That meant keeping it all very simple, stupid, and keeping on schedule.

KSO—KISS Step One—was to turn right, not left, when I hit Curzon Street. Half Moon Street is a one-way street, with traffic running northwest. Curzon is also one way, with traffic running southwest. So, I turned north*east,* walking against the traffic flow. That took care of the taxi. KST (if you're so dense you can't figure *that* acronym out, then you have no business buying this kind of book in the first place) was just as easy. I crossed Curzon Street and marched 250 yards, turned left, walked ninety feet up Clarges Mews, then rapped on the heavy steel-plated door to Curzon Street House. I turned and smiled at the camera that was focused on the doorway. The electronic lock clicked open. I pushed the door inward, slid through, and closed it behind me. I extracted my building pass from my pocket, and showed it to Corporal Duke, the armed guard who was sitting in the biological/chemical warfare–resistant airtight security cubicle made of space-age material. The fucking thing could take a direct RPG hit and the man inside would be just fine.

He gave me an offhand salute and logged me in, his voice metallic tinny through the intercom. "Morning, Captain. Up early today I see."

"No rest for the weary, Corporal Duke." I passed through the inner air lock and marched along the corridor toward the stairs that led to DET Bravo's area of the basement. But I didn't go into the cramped warren of offices. Instead, I continued past them, slaloming my way around the unused desks, chairs, and fine cabinets stacked in the marble-floored hallway, to one of Curzon Street House's three secret tunnel entrances.

You think I'm making this all up. But I'm not. I've already told you that Curzon Street House once served as the MI5 registry. But the six-story building with its bomb-proof glass, thick draperies, and concrete "awning" between the ground and first floors, has a long clandestine history. During the blitz in the early days of World War II, its basement sheltered the Royal Family. Later, Curzon Street House became the headquarters for MI5. Until, that is, the secret service outgrew the old building and moved, first to 140 Gower Street above the Euston Street tube station, and then to Thames House on Millbank, just south of Lambeth Bridge, where it still remains.

There is another element to Curzon Street House's architecture that I haven't told you about: its three secret tunnels. The first, which was built during the site's original construction, leads to the basement of the Lansdowne Club, which sits on Fitzmaurice Place but shares a common wall with Curzon Street House. The second goes almost due east, under Stratton Street, and comes out in the basement of an art gallery on Berkeley Street that for years was an MI5 front. The third, and deepest, tunnel burrows under Clarges Mews and runs all the way to the intersection of Charles and Farm Streets, culminating in the basement of a four-story town house, next to whose black front door is a small brass plaque that reads: "London Antiquarian Book Society—Members Only."[27]

Strangers with the temerity to ring the society's doorbell despite the notice are greeted by a middle-aged, gray-haired lady watchdog who shoos them away. Indeed, the only "members" allowed inside are employees of MI5's technical services division, who use the town house as their electronics laboratory. There they refine eavesdropping equipment to suit individual

---

[27] London is filled with so many tunnels that some of the city's landmarks are in danger of collapsing, according to a secret study done by the home secretary's office late in 1999. The longest of these passages is a Royal Post Office tunnel originally built in the 1930s, which runs from Paddington in the West to Moorgate in the East—more than four miles long. Starting in August 2000, Tony Blair expanded a secret tunnel originally built on orders from Winston Churchill. That tunnel runs from Ten Downing Street under Whitehall to the basement of the Ministry of Defense. Blair's improvements include the building of new subterranean offices shielded from microwaves, satellite eavesdropping, and radiation.

cases, and hone the black arts of surreptitious entry. I made my way to the Farm Street tunnel, passed through the manned security door, and headed down the long, damp, chilly concrete passageway.

The end of the tunnel was blocked by a checkpoint. I was vetted by a pair of armed security men, and then allowed to proceed through an air lock and into a small vestibule. I pushed the button to call the elevator and waited until the electric motor stopped whirring, slid the door open and then opened the inside grate, stepped inside, closed the outer door and the inner grate, and pushed the top button.

The fifty-year-old elevator car, which was about the size of a coffin, lurched upward, motor humming. Sixteen seconds later it stopped abruptly. I did the grate-and-door routine, and stepped out, to find myself in an ornate foyer. To my right was a beautiful staircase, arching gracefully up to the town house's first floor. Straight ahead was the thick front door. To the right of it, out of the draft, was a small Regency desk, behind which sat the omnipresent, gray-haired watchdog-lady. Her eyes flicked toward the elevator as I disembarked. From her expression, it was obvious that I didn't pass muster. She stared at me, taking in the French braid and the thick beard in contemptuous silence.

"G'morning," I finally said.

"Good morning, . . . sir," she growled, spelling the greeting (and I use that term very loosely here) with a *c* and a *u*. "May I 'elp you?"

"Just passing through," I said.

"That'll be fine, then. Just step to the door, please." She came around her small desk, glanced at the security camera picture to double-check that no malefactors were lurking outside, then unlatched a trio of dead bolts and cracked the door open to allow my rapid absquatulation. "Have a nice day, . . . sir."

• • •

The door closed behind me with an audible click, followed by the solid latching of the three dead bolts. Farm Street was deserted. I saw no one on Charles Street either. I stood quietly for some seconds, listening for footfalls, or car motors, but heard nothing but my own breathing. And so, having KISSed off the opposition, I turned left and walked thirty yards to Hay's Mews, turned left again, and meandered down the center of the narrow roadway. On my right, I passed the boxy, two-story carriage house with a green rectangular, wooden front door where the late William Colby, the former Director of Central Intelligence, lived when he was a young OSS lieutenant during World War II. I recognized Gerry Kelley's house—or to be more accurate, his two houses—as I approached the intersection of the Mews and Chesterfield Gardens. From what I'd read in *Architectural Digest*, the common wall between the two adjoining Victorian red brick structures had been demolished when Kelley'd done his renovations. But the outer shells remained unchanged, giving the structure an unbalanced look. I peeked around the corner. An eight-foot brick garden wall fronting on Chesterfield Gardens was topped by two strands of electrified wire, and a pair of security cameras on gimbals.

Yes, I was probably being provocative with this Roguish social call. That was the point. Like I said, we Warriors don't usually meet our adversaries face-to-face. I will never get to bitch-slap Saddam Hussein (although I'd sure like to get the opportunity). And I will probably never get my hands around Usama Bin Laden's scrawny neck—although I'd love to break it . . . slowly. I wouldn't mind giving Muammar Qaddafi a swift boot in the balls, either (and once I almost got the opportunity). But that was the exception to the rule. And the rule is that villains like Saddam and Muammar and Usama are usually well insulated from folks at my operational level.

But let me be honest: I've been lucky. Over the past decade I've had the fortune to take down a number of cockbreaths who caused the deaths of innocent people—and do it up close and personal. And if Gerry Kelley turned out to have anything to do with the death of my shipmate Butch Wells, I'd deliver *his* death sentence face to face, too.

I retraced my steps and stopped in front of the arched, glossy black enamel front door adorned with a massive brass lion's head door knocker. I lifted the heavy ring and brought it down hard on the striker knob three times. When I got no response, I repeated my action. After the ninth blow, I heard something above my head stir.

I looked upward, to see a security camera swivel on its gimbal and abruptly tilt down to peruse me. I waved and said, "Good morning," just in case there was a microphone attached to the apparatus. There was a pause perhaps forty-five seconds in length. And then a single bolt was thrown on the inside of the door, I heard the ratcheting of a lock being turned, and the door itself swung inward.

Gerry Kelley, his thick red hair a mess, his long, angular body wrapped inside a thick, quilted silk robe done in subtle green, brown, burgundy, and burnished gold ancient madder, towered in the low, arched doorway and beckoned me inside. He was a good actor, as seemingly insouciant as if he'd been expecting me.

"Good morning to you, Captain Marcinko. Up betimes, I see." He glanced skyward into the clear, cool London air. "And a lovely morning it is to be up betimes, if I don't say so myself."

He extended his hand. "Welcome, Captain. Please come in." I took it. His grip was strong, and—much to my surprise—his hand was as rough as eighty grit sandpaper. This Gerry Kelley was someone who did manual labor. He exerted a considerable amount of pressure on my paw. I squeezed back, ounce for ounce, smiling as I did.

We played macho man for about ten seconds. I won—I could see it in his eyes. The young Irishman released his grip, extracted his hand, and shook it twice. "I like a man with a firm grip," he said as he stepped aside to let me pass.

I crossed the threshold into the carriage house. Kelley eased the door shut until the latch clicked audibly. Next to the frame, a light nodule on the control panel for a sophisticated security system blinked green. Then Gerry Kelley turned, and led me forward. "This way, Captain."

I had to admit his place was impressive. The entire space, all two and a half stories of it, had been gutted, so that I was greeted by a single, huge, high-ceilinged room, whose space was defined by a trio of six-panel, nineteenth-century coromandel screens, ten-foot-high walls of books, and huge, ornately framed antique mirrors. The cooking space was delineated by floating walls made of alternating stainless steel, copper, and brass panels.

The artwork was eclectic. A huge Andy Warhol portrait of Lenin dominated the foyer. To my left, I spotted a pair of early Lichtensteins and a large Mark Rothko oil, counterpointed by a trio of sixteenth-century, school of Botticelli, Virgin Marys. The floors were made of wide, antique heart-of-pine slab boards and covered with Persian carpets. Area-defining spotlights hung from the vaulted ceilings. It was all totally unexpected, and quite spectacular.

I stopped long enough to take it all in. Kelley watched me absorb the details. "What do you think?"

The Rogue's First Rule of Conversation is, Don't Give Anything Up. "Nice enough for a crash pad."

The Irishman cracked a smile, and his knuckles. "Coffee, Captain?" he asked. "I just brewed a pot."

I was here to take the man's measure, not palaver over beverages. "No thank you."

He nodded. "Fine, then," he said. "It'll be business, then. What brings you here this fine, clear autumn morning?"

I faced him. "Your ads," I said. "The posters on the sides of the buses."

His hands dropped to hip level. "You don't like them."

"That's right."

His eyes went hard. "Too bad," he said. "You'll have to live with them. Until, that is, the government does the right thing and you and your people leave."

"It was British kids we saved."

"Captain," he said, "the British are fully capable of saving their own children. But that is beside the point." His round face screwed into a concerned look. He reached into the pocket of his robe and extracted a small pager, looked at the readout, and then said, "Excuse me for just a moment, Captain, but I must deal with something."

He turned and disappeared behind the Rothko. Three minutes later, he was back. "Pardon the interruption," Gerry Kelley said. "One of the problems with running a business is that you can never, ever, be out of touch with your people."

Now, my friends, let me stop things long enough to give you a little Roguish insight. The man who reappeared was not the same one who'd left to make a call. His entire demeanor had changed. His stance was a lot more hostile. His body language had shifted, ratcheting from "neutral" to "aggressive." That piqued my curiosity. But I didn't bring it up. I let him continue his monologue.

"The fact," Kelley said, "is that you Americans seem to believe that you can insert yourselves into the middle of a problem, solve it with a few words or a piece of paper, then leave—and everything will turn out all right. But that is not the case. Not here, or anywhere else. In fact, you Americans leave the situation worse than it was when you insinuated yourselves into the crisis in the first place."

I would never admit it to him, of course, but he had a valid point there. Look back over the past decade or so and think about the times we have used our armed forces to try to fix an internal problem in a sovereign nation. America's record is not good. We failed in Somalia. We failed in Haiti. We failed in Bosnia. And we failed in Kosovo.

A few years ago, I would simply have reamed Gerry Kelley a

new asshole, or given him the ol' Roguish wake-up call, and be done with it. But this was a new century, a new millennium. And so, I spent the next hour in earnest conversation, giving myself an ample opportunity to take the measure of the man.

It isn't necessary to re-create all the dialogue here and now. Suffice it to say that Gerry Kelley disagreed—vehemently—with the way the British government and ours was dealing with the Irish problem. He resented the American companies who were setting up shop on his turf and getting tax advantages that he— that is to say Globex—did not enjoy. He was passionately opposed to the military cooperation between us and the Brits. He believed that Echelon, the joint SIGINT project, was actually a cover for a huge domestic spying operation in Britain and Ireland (and I have to admit that he wasn't far off the mark there, although I certainly didn't confirm it for him). And most of all, he resented the way Her Majesty's government had allowed the Americans to become an equal player in Northern Ireland. That was where things got interesting.

"It is my country to win or to lose, Captain—not yours."

"You'd rather see it remain the way it is; rather see your people killing one another, than have us try to help create an environment that nurtures peace."

"I believe that we Irish have to solve internal problems on our own," he said obliquely.

"Do you believe Northern Ireland should be reunited with the Republic?"

"I believe," Gerry Kelley said, "in one nation, indivisible, with liberty and justice for all." He gave me a grim smile. "Sound familiar, Captain?"

It did, and I told him so. "It's a noble sentiment."

"It is that," he agreed. "But we Irish have to bring it about ourselves. Not because you Americans impose your values or your agreements on us, either through economic blackmail, or through force of arms."

I am no politician, and I told Gerry Kelley that. "Politics aside," I said, "what about the Americans who have been killed? I had a man who died recently, fighting for peace in Ireland. He came here with the best of intentions. There are other Americans, businessmen, who have been killed in the past months. Didn't they deserve some protection?"

There was a pause. And then, Gerry Kelley said, "You Americans deserve whatever you get."

"Including getting murdered."

His eyes were now full of hate. "Including anything. You Americans are plagued by a national arrogance coupled with a naïveté of character that makes you inviting targets for every democratic and revolutionary liberation movement in the world."

Democratic and revolutionary liberation movement? Where was this asshole coming from?

And then I realized precisely where he was coming from. Gerry Kelley was twenty-four. He'd been born in 1977. To him the British campaign to free the Falkland Islands in 1982 was something he'd read about in history books. Ditto Lady Margaret Thatcher, whose Tory government had brought Britain out of forty years of economic and social doldrums and made it into the vibrant, multicultural society it was today. To children like Gerry Kelley who came into their teens in the late 1990s, the Cold War is ancient history. To them, NATO, whose members include former Warsaw Pact nations like Poland and the Czech Republic, is a toothless bureaucracy. To them, the Euro is official currency. There had always been desktop and laptop computers equipped with modems, and they'd always had color screens. Pentium was a way of life. Televisions all came with remote control units, and there had always been a Sky Channel on which you could watch CNN. To Gerry Kelley, the Vietnam War (if he'd ever read about it at all), was as distant as World War II, or the Hundred Years War.

What I'm saying here, is that Gerry Kelley, for all of his billions of pounds, or punts, or dollars, or Euros, was nothing more than a wet-behind-the-balls *kid*. A *child*. Worse, he was a spoiled child. A spoiled child of a new millennium who had no idea what REAL LIFE was all about. He'd grown up during the two greatest decades of economic growth in the history of mankind. He'd become a dot-com billionaire long before his twenty-fifth birthday. But like many generations of spoiled children who'd gone before him, he had, for whatever reasons, decided that instead of devoting his life to doing positive things, he'd go negative. And so he'd adopted the aggressive vocabulary of privileged, dilettante revolutionaries very similar to the bogus liberation pseudophilosophy disgorged by the mostly upper-middle-class members of 1970s and 1980s terrorist groups like the Baader-Meinhof gang in Germany, Italy's Red Brigades, or America's own United Freedom Front or Students for a Democratic Society.

My friends, this was nothing more than bullshit. This carrot-topped cockbreath was spewing the same specious bullshit I've heard for years, about us Americans deserving what we get; he was justifying Americans being killed because we were trying to impose values like democracy and freedom and equality like a ruthless bunch of imperialist, colonialist, hegemonists. What a huge pile of horse manure. What a truck load of cow pies.

No: worse. Billionaire or not, computer genius or not, this numb nuts twentysomething had just crossed over the line I keep in my head. He didn't mind that Butch Wells was dead fighting for peace in Ireland. Well, okay, I could maybe live with that without killing him, because Butch was a Warrior who knew the risks of what he did. But Gerry hadn't stopped there. Now he was advocating the murder of innocent victims. He was promoting the sorts of cowardly acts I have spent my whole career fighting against. The sorts of acts we'd gone into the Brook Green School to prevent. "I can't allow—"

He broke into my words. "You see? *You see?* Just listen to yourself, Captain. *'I can't allow . . .'* Don't you know how arrogant that sounds to people like me? Don't you understand how off-putting those words are to those of us who come from sovereign nations other than yours. *'I can't allow . . .'* That is gunboat diplomacy, Captain Marcinko. That is hubris. It is absolute conceit."

Gerry Kelley paused. And then he said something else he shouldn't have. "Conduct like yours," he said, "invites retribution. Indeed, Captain, conduct like yours *deserves* retribution."

Invites retribution? Deserves retribution? Oh, I'd show him some old-fucking-fashioned Roguish God-of-War retribution. I didn't wait. I didn't say "May I?" I was simply jump-his-bones *on him* all of a sudden. Like stink on shit.

Oh, yeah, his hands may have been rough from manual labor. And oh, yeah, he was a wiry, strong, feisty youngster who from the way he handled himself obviously liked a bar fight every now and then. And he'd no doubt hired himself a personal trainer who knew a few moves. But that and a one-pound coin would get him a ticket on the fuckin' Jubilee Tube Line, so far as I was concerned.

You see, my friends, I have decades of real-world experience handling and mishandling assholes like this one. And so, I let him make his moves, running the gamut all the way from *a* to *b*. And then, when he'd run out of said moves, I feinted left and popped him open-handed, *slaaap* across the cheek. *"This* is retribution, Gerry," I said, keeping a safe distance between us as his hands judo-flailed and kung-fucked up. I feinted left again, smiled nasty through my War Face, and caught him with my other hand, *slaaap,* leaving a red welt on his freckled skin. "This is Old Testament–style retribution."

He forgot both *a* and *b* and simply bull-in-china-shop charged. I stepped out of the way and caught him with an elbow blow to the back that staggered him. And then, when he did the bull-charge thing again, I let him get close, wrapped him up in my big, strong arms, popped him with my forehead, and when his eyes unfocused I caught him with a knee to the balls that crossed his eyes the right way and sucked every bit of breath out of him. And as he stood there, gagging, bent over, and in full-tilt agony, I smacked him with a smart jab to the nose, which broke the damn thing (I heard the cartilage splatter), and put him plop onto his back, atop the nineteenth-century red, blue, and mustard Turkish Kirshehir graveyard carpet upon which we were so fittingly standing.

I watched for a few seconds as he lay writhing in agony, the blood running down his upper lip. "Gerry," I said, "there are some things youth and money can't buy." I reached down and grabbed him by the lapels of his quilted robe and stood him up so that I could look him in the eyes. "Real life experience is one"—I smacked him—"and Old Testament retribution is another." I smacked him again. Then I held him up close to me so he'd never, ever, forget what I was telling him. That's the way it is with kids these days. You have to be very explicit, so they understand what you are saying.

"Y'see," I told Gerry Kelley, "*retribution* is an Old Testament kind of word, and you are not an Old Testament kind of guy." I searched his face to make sure he was getting the message. "*I* am an Old Testament kind of guy, Gerry." He wasn't getting the message as well as I would have liked, and so I kneed him in the balls again.

When his eyes uncrossed, I resumed my monologue. "Gerry, you have to listen in order to learn. So listen, and listen good." I peered into his eyes to stare into his soul. I have to tell you I didn't much like what I saw.

"Okay. We were talking about retribution," I said. "Retribution is what people like *me* do to people like *you*, when we discover that people like *you* have been doing something naughty." I gave him a few seconds to absorb the concept. "Got it?"

But from the look on his face, he obviously didn't Got It. Not yet. And so, I popped him one more time. After all, proper inculcation takes real effort. And, just as I hoped he would, Gerry Kelley finally Got It.

I dropped him back on his carpet and headed for the front door. As I opened it, I could hear him retching onto his antique graveyard carpet. "Be a good kid, Gerry. Stick to computer programming. Leave all the retribution stuff to us Old Testament people."

CHAPTER

7

MY MOOD NOW CONSIDERABLY IMPROVED, I MARCHED TO THE TOP of Hay's Mews, crossed Berkeley—pronounced Barkley—Square, and walked north on Davies Street, one of Mayfair's major north-south arteries, heading toward Oxford Street and Remo, my favorite eggs-and-bacon coffee shop in the world, to grab some breakfast. Davies Street was not yet rush-hour crowded. But knots of pedestrians were beginning to throng the narrow sidewalk, making their way to work in Mayfair's exclusive shops and high-rent offices. Traffic was heavy, but moving. The morning air was still cool and Roguishly perfumed with diesel fumes.

As I walked, I thought about what I'd just learned. And every-thing in my long experience in dealing with terrorists, psychos, and other felonious malefactors all over the globe told me that like them, Gerry Kelley was up to no good. None at all. More to the point was that Gerry came from Ballynahinch, the same loca-tion of the unique Irish accent that NSA's voice recognition pro-gram had tied to a member of the Green Hand Defenders.

That could be just a coincidence, you say. In my line of work, friends, there are no coincidences.

And think about this. All perps can be identified by three ele-ments: motive, means, and opportunity. Gerry Kelley satisfied elements one and two. He'd just told me that we Americans deserve whatever we get. And he had the financial resources to pay established tangos to do his dirty work. That left element three: opportunity. Once I was able to establish that part of the triad, Gerry's ass would be *mine.*

Which is why I decided that, after my breakfast and well fortified by Remo's strong coffee, I'd head back to Curzon Street House to find Mick Owen and fill him in about Gerry Kelley, Brother Gwilliam, the Green Hand Defenders, and my week's worth of research. Yes, I remember that Eamon the Demon had specifically ordered me to keep my investigation to myself—and to him. But frankly, I didn't give a rusty F-word what Admiral Eamon Joseph Flannery wanted. I knew the sonofabitch would sell me out sooner or later, whenever it would benefit his career the most. That had always been his usual modus operandi.

Besides, to be perfectly frank, if you're working in a foreign country, you'd better have a local rabbi or sea daddy who can cut through the red tape for you and make your work easier. But you don't get unless you give. In Japan, I've always traded information with my pal Toshiro Okinaga, whom I first met when he was a sergeant in the National Police. Now he's a high-ranking officer in Kunika, Japan's counterterrorist police unit. In Germany, General Fred Kohler, who runs Berlin's newest CT unit, the Kommando Spezialkräfte, or KSK, has pulled the ol' Rogue dick out of the fire more than once. In the Middle East, a diminutive Warrior named Avi Ben Gal has always been there to put his Israeli back up against my American shoulders during the tough times. But the key to working with these Warriors has always been that we work together, as a TEAM. To Eamon, the concept of TEAM is foreign. To Eamon, loyalty goes only one way: it worms up the chain of command until it reaches him. I follow the precept set down long ago by Roy Boehm, godfather of all SEALs, who always preached to us tadpoles that loyalty is a two-way thing. It ascends the chain of command, but it also goes the other way. I demand loyalty from my men. But I return it molecule for molecule. That, my friends, is how you encourage and promote unit integrity and the TEAM concept. And it is how I have always worked with my foreign counterparts.

I also understood that Mick was in a tough spot politically. Mick's rank had changed. And with that star, so had his responsibilities. But Mick's personality hadn't changed—not one iota. And when you have operated balls-to-the-wall with someone, and they've always come through for you in the past, there's no reason to believe they'll let you down in the present. Bottom line: there was a lot to talk to Mick about.

And I guess I was concentrating on that, rather than keeping my eyes open. Because I can honestly report that the protective radar system that sits in my brain behind the pussy detector, which is usually operational 24-slash-7, was either malfunctioning or unmanned. Because I certainly did not notice the old VIQ, or Van In Question, as it cruised past, and then drifted to curbside sixty feet ahead of where I was walking.

I'd just passed abreast of an antique store specializing in Greco-Roman sculptures. I glanced toward the shop window to admire a small section of frieze featuring the goddess Diana, then continued at flank speed toward the low, Victorian wrought iron fence that sits around the red brick of Clarridge's Hotel. Then, in passing, I noticed three men in dark, anonymous coveralls pile out of the van. They walked to the rear, threw open the tailgate doors, and began to pull out a huge, rolled-up Persian carpet.

Mister In Front grabbed the front end of the rug and yanked it. Mister Middle took up the bowed-down middle as it cleared the van, and Mister Rear End grabbed (what else?) the rear end. They hoisted the carpet onto their shoulders and began to cross the sidewalk, heading for Clarridge's service entrance. Their action now effectively blocked the sidewalk a mere eight feet ahead of me, causing me to slow down. And *that*, friends, was when the hair on the back of my neck stood straight up. Why this happens I

RICHARD MARCINKO and JOHN WEISMAN

have no idea. But there it was: another example of this instinctual, primordial, primeval act that has saved my life scores of times over the past decades.

It is said that when you are about to die, your life flashes before your eyes in slow motion. And so, here is a complete list of what I suddenly became conscious of, in the few milliseconds after the hair on the back of my neck stood straight up.

- I realized I was virtually alone on the sidewalk: one-two-three-four pedestrians six yards ahead of me, two about ten yards to the rear, and one, in a black leather jacket, uncomfortably close in the blind spot off my left shoulder.
- I recognized the van's driver. It was Mister Shit Brown Suit from earlier in the day. And guess what: Mr. SBS had not moved from his seat behind the wheel and the van was still in gear. I knew that because he was tromping the brake lights and looking back in my direction somewhat nervously.
- I saw that the three rug carriers were not paying attention to the rug, or looking toward the service entrance of Clarridge's. Like the van driver, they were all focused on me.
- I saw a small, curved black plastic box with two metal contact points on one end in the hand of the man holding the middle of the rug.
- I saw that there was no advertising on the side of the van—that, in fact, the vehicle had been recently repainted, judging from the dark color of the inside of the rear doors.
- I realized that the yellow and black license plate on the rear was covered in insects—a strong sign that it had been removed from the front of another vehicle.

And *that* was when all the alarms finally went off and the klaxon horn in my brain went *oougah-oougah,* dive, dive, dive.

Oh, this was sweet. A professional snatch op in broad daylight, right in the fucking center of the city. And it was *moi* these tangos were after. It's simple, really: you knock the target into Mister Middle, who zaps him with the stun gun. And then, as the target collapses you load him into the truck and off you go. If anyone protests you say the poor asshole's had a heart attack and you're taking him to the hospital. It is a classic snatch move, first used by the Corsicans who work for DST, which stands for Directorate for Surveillance of the Territory, the French domestic intelligence, counterespionage, and counterterrorist service. I once watched a team of my old pal Jacques Lillis's Corsican thugs snatch an Algerian tango on the crowded, upper-crust Rue de Rivoli not half a block from the Ritz Hotel. They were so smooth that the tourists and shoppers never noticed as they grabbed their target, smacked him unconscious, tossed him into a van, and drove off.

That's impossible, you say. No it's not. Believe me. A good team can make it appear easy. Effortless. You can be walking ten feet behind the target, they can snatch him right in front of your nose, and you'll never notice. The fact is, daylight snatches are tough, complicated, intricate maneuvers, and you'd better use professionals who've rehearsed the moves hundreds of times. But these assholes were nervous. Downright jittery. If I'd been paying attention, I would have seen 'em the proverbial mile away. But even now, even this late in the game, I could take active and effective countermeasures. When you are ambushed, after all, your best defense is a furious, aggressive, uncompromising counterattack.

That is precisely what I did. Instinctively, I whirled toward the curb side of the street just as a leather shoulder lurched into the space where the center of my back had just been. I ducked away from the blow, turned, and struck back toward where it had come from, gratified when my forearm made contact with a young kid in a black leather jacket and jeans. To no one's surprise (especially mine) it was the same Greasy Leather Boy who'd shadowed me from the hotel earlier in the day. He twisted away. No chance. I grabbed him by the sleeve, spun him around, and smacked him hard upside his head.

But obviously not hard enough. From out of nowhere, a fucking sap in his off-side hand whipped around and caught me *whap* in the face. To be precise, it caught me right on my much-broken Slovak snout.

Broad daylight be damned—I saw fucking stars. In fact, I saw most of the whole fucking Milky Way. But I had no time to appreciate the view because I was engaged in demonstrating the Rogue's First Law of Physics. I sidestepped, grabbed at the hand, wrist, and arm attached to the sap, then swiveled and hyperextended the aforementioned arm, causing the rest of Greasy Leather Boy's body to follow.

That was the good news. The bad news was that my movement carried me toward the rolled-up rug. That, of course, was when Mister Middle brought up the stun gun and tried to apply it to my body so I'd stop making such a fuss and come along like a good chap. His arms went wide to corral my path, the stun gun in his right hand, its business end pointed toward my midsection.

I lurched to my left, dragging Greasy Leather Boy with me as I pulled away from the stun gun.

Mister Middle slashed at me, his face contorted, eyes narrowed. All he fucking needed to do was hit me once with the fucking thing, a fact I realized that he knew just as well as I did.

But here's what he did not know. He did not know that I am a big strong motherfucker who presses 450 pounds, 155 reps, 365 days a year at the outdoor weight pile at Rogue Manor. And so, I held on to Greasy Leather Boy, one-handing him as he struggled to simultaneously fight me off and not get stung by his pal's stun gun electrodes. Oh, he was serious about not getting zapped. But not as serious as I was. So struggle be damned, I put Greasy Leather Boy between the stun gun and me, holding him with both my arms now and using the kid as my own human shield.

Mister Middle thrust at me once-twice-thrice. I parried by using GLB. The fourth time he came at me, he zapped it right into Greasy Leather Boy's thigh. That, too, was GNBN. Good news because it wasn't me who'd been electrocuted. Bad news because I was now holding on to 160 pounds of dead weight.

It was time to lose the shield. But instead of simply dropping Greasy Leather Boy I took the kid by the belt and the scruff of the neck and threw him at Middle Man, whose hands (and stun gun) instinctively went out in front of him, which of course applied a second huge jolt of electricity to Greasy Leather Boy.

"Aw, shit," Middle Man said aloud. His eyes followed the kid's body to the ground. "Shit," he said again.

Mister Middle's eyes were on Greasy Leather Boy. That meant he wasn't looking at me. I reached out and grabbed his right wrist to ensure that the stun gun would come nowhere near *moi*. Then, I—

Okay, okay, okay. I've got to interrupt myself to provide you with unshakable evidence that these assholes were absolute fucking amateurs.

It is this: the two guys holding the ends of the rug didn't react. They just stood there holding the rug.

Back to real time. Mister Middle, however, *was* moving. And his actions didn't bode well for me. He dropped the stun gun (onto Greasy Leather Boy, who got yet a third heavy jolt), reached into his pocket, and extracted a hufuckingmongous combat folder.

My friends, I hate edged weapons. They are dangerous. They are nasty. You almost always get cut. And so, I didn't wait for Middle Man to take the initiative and do a quick slice 'n' dice on the ol' Rogue man. He brought the blade around, business side out, as if to slap me.

I jumped back, beyond his reach. As his arm went past, I trapped his wrist with both my hands, stepped in toward him so that I could use my bulk, then took his wrist and bent it back-

back-backward over the top of his arm until I heard it snap. He screamed. His fingers released the knife, which went clattering.

Too fucking bad. I released his broken wrist, grabbed him by the shoulders, and head-butted the sumbitch, which sent him reeling backward. I went after him. That's when Mister Murphy decided to stick his ugly puss into my business. Mister Middle grabbed me with his good arm and pulled me with him, ripping my blazer and jerking me rudely enough to make me trip over Greasy Leather Boy's inert body. Now that I was off balance, Mister Middle kicked out at my legs. He missed the direct blow but smacked me good upside the right knee.

Oh fuck oh shit that hurt. I went down—hard—onto the sidewalk, dislodging the P7-M8 from its inside-the-waistband holster, and sending it skittering across the sidewalk.

Pistols in London are a bad idea if you are a foreigner—even a military foreigner like me. And so, I went scrambling after the gun, which gave Mister Middle the opportunity he needed. He launched a wicked kick at my head. I saw it coming in enough time to deflect the blow.

I grabbed his foot, twisted, and yanked. That took the cock-breath right off his feet—and gave me enough time to tackle the pistol and jam it back into its holster. Then I returned all of my Roguish attention to Mister Middle.

I rolled toward him, grabbing at the combat folder as I went, heedless of the holes I was tearing in my trouser legs. He backpedaled. I just kept coming at him. Finally, he was able to scramble to his feet, which was more than I could do, and he headed, his broken wing flapping, for the van. His pals dropped the rug and exeunted, stage right, to join him. They pulled him inside, jumped in themselves, and yanked the rear doors slam shut. Mr. Shit Brown Suit floored the vehicle and peeled away from the curb, leaving an ugly set of rubber tracks behind. And *moi*? *Moi* was left kneeling on the sidewalk, panting, with the knife, the stun gun, Greasy Leather Boy's inert body, and the fucking rolled-up rug.

Well, I didn't want the goddamn rug. But I wasn't about to leave the stun gun, the knife, or the real evidence—Greasy Leather Boy—behind.

I scooped up the stun gun, gave GLB another 300,000-volt shot for good measure, found the on/off switch, rendered the thing safe, and slipped it into my pocket. Ditto the knife. Then I pulled myself to my feet, got my arm around Greasy Leather Boy's waist, leveraged him to *his* feet, took him by the collar of his black leather jacket, and dragged him the 150 feet to the corner of Brook Street, where three taxicabs were sitting, engines idling, outside Clarridge's front doors.

I managed to open a cab door and tossed Greasy Leather Boy inside, climbed in myself, shut the door behind me, and wiped the trickle of blood coming from my nose onto the ruined cuff of my ruined custom-made shirt. The driver looked back and said, with amazing, British stiff-upper-lip insouciance, "And where to for you and your . . . friend, sir?"

"Curzon Street House, please. And quickly."

The driver mumbled to himself, then swiveled, hunched himself behind the wheel, and we pulled away from the curb.

"What was that you said, driver?"

He peered into the rearview mirror as he steered a right-hand turn on New Bond Street. " 'I should 'ave known,' is what I said, sir. I should 'ave known that it was Curzon Street House you'd be going to. I should 'ave bloody known."

•   •   •

Greasy Leather Boy's name was actually Sean Maloney, he was twenty years old, he was a self-professed corporal in the Irish People's Army, and his passport number was JH-214266. That's all he gave us: the old NRS[28] bit. He was still giving us the NRS bit (actually, he was just asking us to *"póg mo thón,"* which translates

---

[28] Name, Rank & Serial Number.

somewhere in the area of "kiss my arse" in Gaelic) when a pair of ragged-at-the-fringes counterintelligence minions from MI5 showed up unannounced, displayed a sheaf of papers stamped MOST SECRET, and took the poor sod away to give him a proper interrogation.

GLB gave us a lot more, of course, except he just didn't know it—and we certainly didn't pass anything on to MI5. First of all, the kid was carrying both a cell phone and a pager, neither of which Mick handed over or even mentioned. I thought that a bit strange on his part, but then Mick has his own way of operating.

And operate is what he did. After GLB had been taken away, it didn't take Mick Owen more than six minutes to come up with a printout of all the calls and messages young Sean Maloney had made and/or received in the last seventy-two hours. It took another sixty-eight minutes to put names to the numbers. As I pored over the list I found two to be significant. I noted that young Sean had called the number of a pager that had been leased to the Mrs. Kelley's Kitchen Irish Pub headquarters. That call had been made at 0652 this morning. Three minutes later—0655—he had received a one-minute phone call from a cellular phone owned by the Globex Corporation, LTD.

I put a pair of pencil ticks by the pertinent phone numbers, looked across Mick's desk at him, and slapped my palm on the gray metal surface. "That's enough for me," I said.

"What is?"

I turned the readout so he could see the numbers I'd checked. "This. See these phone numbers?"

He gave them a once-over. "I do."

I gave him an SAS (Short And Sweet) version of my face-to-face with Gerry Kelley. Then I explained the significance of the telephone and pager numbers I'd put pencil ticks next to.

Then I told him I believed that Gerry had hired the IPA—and maybe other splinter groups of tangos, too—to take the credit for his own dirty work. "I want Gerry Kelley's ass, and I want it now, Mick."

I'd never seen it happen before, but every bit of colour actually drained out of Mick's face. "Hold it, Dick," he said. "Don't you say another bloody word."

"I—"

His expression revealed absolute fury. "Not another bleedin' word I said." He stood up, and grabbed the readout in his meaty hand.

I started to protest, but the look on Mick's face cut me off in midbreath. Silent and brooding, he stalked to the office door and curtly beckoned me to follow.

We made our way down the long, dingy corridor to a fire door, climbed one flight, pushed open a thick steel door and exited into a carpeted hallway. Mick opened the second door on the left-hand side and indicated that I was to follow him. I closed the door behind me and found myself in a small chamber that resembled an air lock. Mick was working the cipher key on a heavy, insulated door.

When it opened, he pointed me inside. I went through the foot-thick opening into a room that was about ten by sixteen feet, with fabric-covered walls, no windows, and a drop ceiling. There were ten plastic chairs placed around a simple wood table. Mick eased the door closed behind us, waited until it sealed and the lock had clicked securely.

We were now obviously inside a bug-proof room; a bubble; a SCIF.[29] Mick tossed the readout onto the table. Then he turned to face me. "*Gerry fuckin' Kelley,*" he said, his voice betraying shock and disbelief. "What the hell do you know about Gerry fuckin' Kelley?"

---

[29] Sensitive, Compartmented Information Facility.

CHAPTER

8

I TOLD HIM, OF COURSE. JUST AS I'D PLANNED TO. HE SAT THERE, his expression somewhere just past shell-shocked. When I'd finished my recitation, he shook his head and said, simply, "The Bastards."

"Who?"

Mick's big, scarred, calloused palms went up. "It doesn't matter," he said. "Not to you, at least."

"I think it does."

"Gerry Kelley is my problem, Dick, not yours."

He was talking to himself, and I didn't much like it. And Gerry certainly wasn't just his problem. The on-again, off-again peace process, of which we Americans had been an integral part for more than half a decade now, was unraveling as if by the hour. Five American executives were already dead. Half a dozen others had been injured, some of them seriously.

An Echelon intercept of a conversation between two unknown people from Ballynahinch, the same Northern Irish town in which Gerry's company was headquartered, dealt with the killing, sometime in the near future, of hundreds of innocent American and British victims in one deadly blow. My gut, which is seldom wrong, was telling me loud and clear that Gerry was involved right up to his nasty eyeballs. And now Mick was looking at me and saying it was none of my business.

Well, it *was* my business. It was the business of the United States, which I represented. I do not believe that we Americans should send our troops off to places like Haiti, Kosovo, or Somalia. That is a waste of our resources. More important, it diminishes our military readiness, overextends our shrinking military's capabilities, and employs Soldiers as cops and social workers, instead of Warriors. I've always said that if you want to be a Warrior and kill the enemy, become a SEAL. If you want to help poor countries recover from disasters, join the Boy Scouts or the Peace Corps.

But there are two areas in which the United States can use its position as the world's one remaining superpower. First, when American lives are taken, we can strike back quickly, effectively, and ruthlessly against those who have committed murder. Second, we can be an honest broker and negotiate differences between enemies. Not by buying their cooperation, as we have historically done in the Middle East, but through sheer force of will, our own commitment to democracy, and (given a decent administration) some vigorous, persuasive diplomatic skill.

The United States was currently an integral part of the Irish peace process. We had a stake *not* because of any president or secretary of state's ego, but because innocent American blood had been spilled in the cause of peace. I'd said that to Gerry Kelley and now I told the same thing to Mick Owen. The difference between 'em (you already know there are a lot of differences) was that Mick understood what I was saying.

And so we sat in that SCIF for three hours and talked. I don't want to recount the whole conversation, but here's some of the gist. During the first hour, I told Mick what I'd been up to for the past week. It was then we discovered that Mick had been assigned the same problem as I had. Except he had been told that some of the supergrades in the Home Office—I interpreted that as

MI5—believed the *Americans* were holding back intelligence about the Green Hand Defenders. It had been further explained to him that because of MI6's close and continuing liaison relationship with the CIA, it would be impossible for the British secret intelligence service to work the GHD problem without the Americans knowing what was going on.

And so, the GHD "problem" had been turned over to Mick Owen by the Home Office. Mick had been ordered to target the Green Hand Defenders, then report whatever he discovered to Sir Roger Holland, MI5's director general, through an MI5 cutout, an anonymous civil-servant type whom he'd meet once a week at White's, one of the venerable gentlemen's clubs on St. James's Street.

"Shit," I said. "Mick, they were mirror-imaging us."

"Precisely." His face was grim. Both of us had been ordered to target the GHD. The only difference was that Mick had been forbidden from taking any action at all. At least Eamon had promised that my men and I would be allowed to go after the scumbags at some point in the future.

I have to tell you, the whole mess gave me pause. Outwardly, there was no obvious connection between Eamon and MI5. I mean, what does the fucking CINCUSNAVEUR have to do with the British domestic-security agency. But stowed in the back of my mind was the factoid Digger O'Toole had humped and pumped so hard to obtain. Digger's punch had whispered that one reason for the CIA London COS taking his abrupt powder was that he was sick and tired of being backchanneled in the CT (for CounterTerrorism) area.

It hadn't made sense at the time. It had been a piece of the puzzle that just did not fit. But now it made perfect sense. Perfect, that is, if you like convoluted, intricate, labyrinthine, Machiavellian politics.

What the fuck is all that noise? Hold on a minute, will you? There's a huge commotion outside the locked door of this here

SCIF. Let me go and take a look. Holy shit. It's a fucking APE.[30]
He just showed up waving his blue pencil and whining that I've
committed an editorial faux pas; the logical jump here is just too
big, and you readers out there will never accept it.

No, you dweeb, it's not too big a jump. Not at all. And here is
why.

- Item. The CIA station chief complained about being
  cut out of the CT loop because of a backchannel relationship an American had with the Brits.
- Item. Eamon had received his GHD information from
  a backchannel.
- Item. Then there was the info about the alleged
  humongous MI5 goatfuck op in Northern Ireland
  five months ago—except no one's head had rolled.
- Item. Remember what Eamon the Demon had told
  me? *Eamon knew about the Echelon intercept.* Eamon
  knew that the pair of GHDs caught on tape in Randallstown had been talking about targeting Americans. No, he hadn't mentioned Randallstown itself,
  but *he'd known about the intercept.*
- Item. The subject of the intercept in question was a
  huge terrorist operation in which hundreds of Americans and Brits would be killed at once.
- Item. Remember Pepperman's whispered warning?
  He'd told me that the ZU-Messages about that very
  Green Hand Defenders operation had been passed
  straight from the White House to Downing Street.

On the one hand, that info-pass now made sense, because
Gerry Kelley was about to be knighted, something that would not

---

[30] All-Powerful Editor.

do the PM a lot of good if Gerry turned out to be a murdering tango.

On the other hand, if *I* were the prime minister, I'd deal with Gerry very, very quietly and efficiently, but leave no trail that led to Ten Downing Street. First, I'd cut MI5 out of the DET Bravo loop, which would create resentment in the domestic spy agency. Then I'd let MI5's director backchannel his information flow through an ambitious American—Admiral Eamon the Demon— and take MI6 out of the picture.

Then, I'd subcontract someone like Mick and let him do the dirty work. Or better still, if I were the current prime minister, I'd use MI5 as a cutout and Mick Owen as a decoy, and use Sir Roger Holland's cozy relationship with Eamon the Demon to drop the Gerry Kelley/Green Hand Defender problem on the Americans and let *them* take all the heat. In fact, if I were the prime minister I could think of one American—that Roguish SEAL fellow, i.e., *moi*—who'd already taken a lot of heat.

And if the ol' Rogue Warrior® got singed to a crisp by the Green Hand Defenders problem, well, then, hard cheese for the ol' Rogue Warrior®.

So, you big APE, if you take all that information, and you shuffle it, and you deal it out, no matter how many times you cut the cards, or how many times you shuffle the deck, the hand you're going to have in front of you will be the same.

And that hand reads like this: Eamon and MI5's director general were doing business together. Why they had originally joined in cahoots, as they used to say in the old Roy Rogers westerns, I had no fucking idea. Maybe Eamon was trying his hand at power politics—and given his sorry history, he was being eaten alive. Whatever had caused him to toss in with MI5 and be used by the prime minister didn't matter to me. All that mattered to me was that Eamon had sold out his American troops. Moreover, it was also obvious that he and MI5's director general were up to no good.

No good? That's right. They were planning to set me on the GHD. But I'd been forbidden from taking action against the tangos without permission. And yet, the GHD was about to set in motion a dual-pronged attack that would cause the deaths of hundreds of innocent victims.

Now, if I were cynical, I'd tell you that Eamon the Demon and Sir Roger Holland didn't give a shit about victims. Eamon's kind never does. To Eamon, who missed the Vietnam War, the Gulf War, and every "police action" in between, spending his entire career as a paper-pushing bureaucrat, they're simply numbers on a page. And at least twice in the 1990s, MI5 had stood by and allowed IRA bombers to hit targets in London, because the agency was engaged in an internal, bureaucratic turf war over its counterterrorism programs with Scotland Yard's Special Branch, and the London Metropolitan Police's SpecOps counterterrorist center. While the MI5 bureaucrats wrote their memos defining their turf, and stabbed one another in the back over CT budget allocations, five people had died; more than sixty had been injured.

That's what I'd say if I were cynical. But then, you already know I'm no cynic. I'm simply a SEAL. A SEAL who hates to see innocent blood spilled so admirals or directors general can play "gotcha" politics, or wage turf wars.

And Mick? Despite the star on his collar, Mick's a simple shooter who thinks like me. Mick doesn't give a shit about anything but getting the job done. Like me, Mick detests the paper warriors, office politicians and apparatchik managers who run today's military. Like me, he thinks that Warriors should break things and kill people.

And so, we sat there in that bug-proof room, and we plotted and we schemed and we played out scenarios, and after another couple of hours, we came up with something so nasty it was virtually guaranteed to piss off both Washington *and* Ten Downing Street. Which sounded pretty fucking good to us.

I wanted to mount an op against Gerry Kelley right away. We

were up against a ticking clock here. The Echelon intercepts were almost six months old. They'd caught a conversation that dealt with an operation that was to take place within half a year. Half a year was *now*. My goal therefore was to shake Gerry up and make him do something impulsive and stupid. After all, that tactic has worked for me in the past. But Mick convinced me to take a more wait-and-see approach. I'd already shaken Gerry up, he argued. The abortive snatch op against me was evidence of that. For the moment, he suggested, we'd be better off gathering more intelligence. There was nothing we could do, after all, unless we knew exactly what Gerry and the GHD had planned. This guy was a SUC—Smart, Unpredictable, and Cunning. It made no sense to take him on unless we were absolutely confident we'd be able to prevent his operation from succeeding. So until our ducks were in a row, Mick counseled against any premature hopping & popping.

Despite the ticking clock factor, Mick made a lot of sense. We had no idea what the GHD was planning, except that it was a huge, complicated op and that the Echelon intercept led me, for one, toward the belief that the explosives were coming from somewhere in the Middle East. Well, we could start there. Mick got on the horn to his contacts in the Gulf. I called Avi Ben Gal in Tel Aviv and asked him to check his sources in Israel, Lebanon, and Jordan. Avi called back in less than an hour. He'd run my info through "Springs," the supercomputer used by AMAN, Israel's military intelligence organization, but said he couldn't detect a single ripple about arms from his neck of the woods being moved to any Irish tango splinter group. Mick's Mukhabarat contact in Qatar wasn't any help either.

But it didn't take long for something else to turn up. I'd passed Gunny Jarriel's sit-rep that Gwilliam Kelley was conjugating one of his VERBs in Buenos Aires to Mick. Mick said that the son of one of his old Army mates—a guy who was now a successful investment banker based in Paris—had a kid named Robert who was working for MI6 under embassy cover in BA. He called

Argentina in the hope that his former mate's kid would be happy to repay dad's two-hundred-quid bar chit at the Ritz Hotel in Paris on an off-the-record basis. Twenty-nine hours after Mick's query, we received GNBN from young Robert of MI6. The GN was that he'd been willing to do some spade work on our behalf. The bad news was that the Mrs. Kelley's franchisee in Buenos Aires was a fellow named Brendan O'Donnell.

I didn't recognize the name but Mick did. He pulled the file from our DET Bravo database. O'Donnell was a TIRA killer who had served sixteen years in a British prison for murder, arms dealing, and bomb making. He'd been freed during one of the many Tony Blair amnesties of the late 1990s, renounced the IRA for being soft, and made his way to Argentina, where he raised money for IRA splinter groups like the TIRA tangos who'd taken over the Brook Green School. In fact, when Mick and I cross-checked, we discovered that four suspected TIRA tango assholes were currently in BA. They all worked for the Mrs. Kelley's Kitchen franchise, too. Like I said, in my profession there are no coincidences.

More to the point was this: Argentina is a hotbed of radical Islamic fundamentalism. No, I am being serious. There is more to Argentina than red wine, great steaks, and tango dancers. But tango dancers aren't the only sorts of tangos in Argentina. There are tangos there who have nothing to do with dancing. For example, Hezb'allah is active. So is the Islamic Jihad Organization. So is Hamas. There are large Palestinian and Iraqi communities in Misiones Province in the north of the country. Misiones is a kind of landlocked peninsula between Paraguay and Brazil. And according to Mick, Misiones was the figurative headwaters for a huge river of black market weapons, which flowed from Brazil and Paraguay, ending hundreds of miles later in the smuggler's paradise of the Tigre delta, about twenty miles northwest of downtown Buenos Aires. From Tigre, Argentina's fundamentalist Islamic community could move the arms through Argentina, shipping them out of the big port of Buenos Aires, or take them across the Rio de la Plata to the more loosely controlled Uruguayan cities of Colonia or Montevideo, from where they could easily be shipped anywhere in the world.

The intel we'd originally received indicated that the arms the GHD planned to use against their target would come from the Middle East. I had always assumed—so had Mick—that meant *originating* in a Middle Eastern country. But that's because I'd forgotten Everett Emerson Barrett's credo, which he repeated more times than I care to remember, to us fledgling tadpoles. "Never ASSUME," Chief Barrett would tell us. "Because ASSUME makes an ASS of U and ME."

So, what if the *arms dealers* were of Middle Eastern origin— Palestinians, or Lebanese from Hamas, Hezb'allah, or the IJO— but they actually *lived* in Argentina, Paraguay, or Brazil?

A lot of the pieces for an op in that part of the world were in place, so far as I was concerned. Brendan O'Donnell was a bonafide no-goodnik. He was a stone-cold killer, an arms dealer, and most important, a bomb maker. He managed Gwilliam Kelley's bar franchise in Buenos Aires.

Four TIRA tangos were also on scene, and there was a convenient arms and ordnance market available to them. Both Britain and the United States maintained sizeable diplomatic communities in Argentina. We already knew that Brendan O'Donnell had motive. But we also now realized that he had the *means* to kill large numbers of victims, as well as the opportunity—a large number of potential targets. To me, there was only one possible reaction, and it included making reservations to Buenos Aires.

I told Mick what I was thinking, and he immediately agreed. That just floored me. I mean, the guy was putting his star— indeed, his whole career—on the line for me. Not one general in a hundred would do that these days. I looked across the table at Mick. "You don't have to do this," I said. "I don't give a shit about my career. I'm never gonna get another stripe. But you have an incredible future in front of you."

"Oh, hell, man," Mick said, his face serious, "the only thing that really matters is getting our friggin' jobs done, by which I mean making sure these assholes don't get *their* friggin' job done." But, he counseled, anything we did would have to be done stealthily. We'd have to leave a crew behind to make waves in London in order to keep Eamon the Demon off my back and Sir Roger, MI5's director general, off his.

That made perfect sense. Moreover, I wanted to keep an eye on Gerry Kelley. If I had *hocked Gerry's choinik*,[31] as Avi Ben Gal is fond of saying, then he'd be speeding up his schedule. I wanted to blanket him with surveillance: follow his every move, tap his phones, slip beacons on his vehicles—the whole full-court press.

But that kind of surveillance is labor intensive. And neither Mick nor I had huge crews of people available to us. But lack of numbers has never hampered SEALs. Boomerang, Rotten Randy, and Timex were each level-four fluent in Spanish. They'd make the trip with me. The remainder, Nod, Goober, Nigel, and Digger O'Toole, would work the streets in London in a joint CT op with Mick's SAS shooters. They'd handle any DET Bravo problems, and keep Gerry Kelley under close surveillance. It would be demanding, time-consuming work that would cut into the usual pub crawling and pussy chasing. But they'd do it.

Mick wouldn't travel alone, either. He'd bring an Arabic speaking SAS trooper named Hugo, just in case we had to ask up-close-and-personal questions to any IJO scumbags we might come across.

One serious question was how we'd get to Buenos Aires in combat-ready mode without attracting any attention. It is hard to move heavy locked boxes of arms and explosives across international borders when you are trying to travel in mufti. It is even more

---

[31] In Yiddish, literally "rattled his teacup."

difficult when your own government has to be kept in the dark.

Actually, the keeping-our-government-in-the-dark aspect of this stealth op was the easiest problem to deal with. We simply dropped off everyone's radar screens. First, I waited until 1735 hours, five minutes past the scheduled workday, to make sure that Eamon, who never worked a minute beyond his allotted eight hours (which includes his two-hour lunch) had left North Audley Street. Then I called his office and asked his secretary ("Oh, he's just left? I'm *soooo* disappointed . . .") to pass the admiral a UNODIR[32] message that I was doing some in-depth research and would be out of touch for a few days—maybe a week or so, maybe more. By the time Eamon learned anything, I'd be long gone.

Meanwhile, Mick met his MI5 cutout over a double whiskey at White's on St. James's Street and said much the same thing. Then we went out and bought a few warm-weather items (it was going to be late spring in BA). Mick, who'd been to Argentina operating covertly during the Falklands War, handled the hotel accommodations. I took care of making airline reservations, and that was that.

You want to know how we smuggled all our stuff on commercial flights. The answer is that we didn't. We left it all—CQC gear, diving equipment, weapons, ammo, and explosives— behind, and traveled like weekend tourists, with carry-ons and dressed in civilian clothes. We went singly and in pairs, too—not as a group. Half a dozen large, muscular, young men tend to stand out when they travel together, and standing out was something I did not want us to do. Moreover, when we fly on commercial aircraft, my men and I may carry military documents and burgundy "official" passports, but we travel with blue-jacketed civilian U.S. passports. That way we do not attract

---

[32] UNless Otherwise DIRected.

a lot of undue attention as we pass through airports or cross international borders. Mick's people follow a similar operational mode. It was all a lot less complicated than you might think. And so, we made our way to Buenos Aires with just our tourist passports. No guns, no gear, and no idea where to begin our search.

PART TWO
PAIN

CHAPTER

9

So, here's the bottom line: I set up communications lines so I could stay in contact with Nod. Then I took the Chunnel train to Paris, where I caught an Aerolíneas Argentinas nonstop flight from Charles de Gaulle Airport. Thirteen hours later I wheeled down at BA's Ezeiza International Airport, and passed through customs and immigration without any problems. I hired one of the local *Remises* (prepay taxis) from the airport and headed into the city.

As I'm going, there are a few things you might want to know about Argentina, and about Buenos Aires. The most basic is that in Argentina, dollars and pesos are interchangeable. The exchange rate is one to one. And so, we'd pay our way in greenbacks with no *problemas*. Second, Buenos Aires is huge. The city encompasses hundreds of square miles. The population is just over twelve million people. Indeed, more than a third of the Argentine population lives in Buenos Aires. Third, every single one of those twelve million people thinks he or she is Mario fucking Andretti. Put an Argentine in a car, and you have an instant formula one race driver. And so, the trip into town reminded me of the cut-to-the-chase training sessions we used to have at BSR raceway in West Virginia, where we honed our tactical driving skills by playing bumper tag at 130 miles an hour. Lemme tell you: riding in a

Remise can be a white-knuckle experience even to those of us of the Roguish persuasion.

I clambered unsteadily out of the taxi on a small, cobblestone plaza in Recoleta, right in the center of town. I looked around. I'd always been told that BA is like Paris. Actually, at first glance it was nicer than Paris. The weather was better, and the people were certainly more friendly. Parisians almost never smile. *Porteños,* which translates roughly as "port people" and is how the Buenos Aires natives are called, had a Latin sparkle in their eyes. And the *Porteñas*—you make your own translation here—*Hoo Yah!* Lemme tell you right now, having only been on the ground for an hour or so, the women in Argentina were something wondrous to behold.

I did a quick recon. Directly in front of me were the thick, unimposing double glass doors of the Hotel Étoile. Off to one side of the entrance were two bright red public phone booths, exact copies of what they had in 1950s London. At my back was a small, triangular park filled with a dozen young men and women, each holding eight, nine, ten happy, smiling, tail-wagging dogs on leashes. Couples sat on benches under the shade trees. Roller-bladers cruised the narrow, winding paths, slaloming among the pedestrians. Directly behind the park, loomed the huge, ornate gate of the Cementerio de la Recoleta, the huge, nineteenth-century necropolis where Eva Perón, among others, lies in her mausoleum. And off to my port and my starboard were a series of bustling outdoor cafés, filled with a boisterous, lunchtime crowd. White-jacketed waiters carried trays of steaks, salads, omelets, and sandwiches. There were mugs of foam-topped draft beer and carafes of red and white wine. It was like a fucking midday carnival.

I paused long enough to do a quick look-see. The tables were filled with an eclectic mix. There were suit-and-tie businessmen working cellular phones in pursuit of profit. There were tables of VERBs in Chanel and Lanvin, sipping bottled water and picking at endive salads as their cigarettes, marked with thin rims of lipstick, sent narrow columns of smoke skyward in the still spring air.

A pair of lovers sitting side by side stroked each other's faces, shoulders, and arms, their omelets untouched. Two casually dressed men in their twenties sitting opposite one another worked feverishly on laptops connected to cellular modems.

From somewhere off to my port side, I caught a shrill whistle. I turned and looked. Fifty yards away, at the largest of the cafés, protected from the adjacent street by a six-foot hedge of green, Mick Owen was standing, a smile on his face, beckoning to me. He was with Hugo, Boomerang, Rotten Randy Michaels, Timex, and a stranger in a suit and tie, who were in animated conversation seated around a small, white table under the shade of a huge, white beach umbrella that alternately bore the logo of Old Smuggler Scotch whiskey and ornate script spelling out the words *La Biela*.

I slung my bag strap over my shoulder, threaded my way through the maze of crowded tables, snagging a vacant black plastic armchair as I went, and dragged it toward them.

Boomerang looked past the Art Deco, obviously Paris-influenced streetlamp, squinting vaguely in my direction as I approached. He was wearing a loud Hawaiian print shirt, jeans, and sandals. The former surfer had been on the ground for less than a day but he'd already managed to pick up a fair amount of color. He raised his Oakleys onto his high forehead and his face took on a huge grin as I hove up to the tableside. *"Buenos días, Pibe.*[33] *¿Como está usted?"*

"Todo bien, gracias. ¿Y usted?" I dropped my carry-on next to Timex, who was eagerly working his way through a bottle of Quilmes, the local beer, and plunked myself down.

Boomerang sipped his pastel-colored *jugo. "Piola."*[34] He jerked his thumb toward the thin stranger sitting with the group and said, "This is Robert Evers, Boss Dude. He's Mick's friend from the embassy."

---

[33] *Lunfardo* (Buenos Aires street slang) for *Dude.*
[34] It means *cool* in *Lunfardo.* I told you Boomerange spoke fluent Spanish.

From the way Robert Evers looked he was an indubitable Robert. Let me explain. Before I became a complicated, complex, multifaceted Richard, I was just a simple Dick. Not this guy. He'd never been a Bob—always a Robert. He wore the same sort of embassy uniform common to senior American and Brit diplomats worldwide: a gray pinstriped suit, starched white shirt, and a green tie that told me he was a member of the Naval and Military Club of London. He was younger than Mick or me—late twenties or perhaps early thirties— with flecks of prematurely gray hair around the temples and the kind of unremarkable face that you don't ever quite remember. In other words, he was an archetypal spook.

I reached across the glass-topped table and extended my hand. "Dick Marcinko, Robert. Good to meet you."

His grip was firm and dry. "Robert Evers, Mr. Marcinko. Good to meet you, too."

Mick jumped in. "Robert's a political officer at our embassy. Been here just over a year."

"You must like it."

Evers looked at me. "It has its moments," he said cryptically.

The formalities over, I waved at a waiter, ordered a double espresso, then looked back at Robert Evers. "So, here we are—a group of average tourists. What are the best sights for us to see?"

"Oh, I gather you won't be staying in BA long enough to visit very many of the sights," Evers said.

I decided to follow his lead. "Oh?"

"No," Evers continued. "From what Mr. Owen told me, you chaps are anxious to take a trip up-country and get out in the bush. Just as you arrived, I was suggesting to Mr. Owen and your chaps that you visit Misiones Province and do a little camping."

I know all about Misiones Province—and so do you. Remember? That's where Palestinian and Lebanese arms dealers smuggle weapons across the loosely watched Brazilian and Paraguayan borders, so they can be brought by truck or boat down the network of roads and rivers that finally lead to the Delta del Parana, near the town of Tigre, where they're cached in the thousand-plus square miles of swamp and grassland that extends from the federal capital region into Entre Ríos province. I grinned at Robert Evers. I do so like it when you can speak in code right out in the open. "That sounds about right," I said. "I'm a big believer in Outward Bound sorts of activities. They're good for building character." I paused. "Of course, I'd like to do a little hunting, too, if that's possible."

"Oh, the hunting is very good in Misiones these days," Robert Evers said. "But you'll have to be quick about it because the game moves very fast, and can be tremendously difficult to track unless you're proficient."

"We always try to be good when it comes to tracking game. In fact, the challenge is in the tracking." I waited until a waiter slid my coffee in front of me, said *"gracias,"* and then continued once he'd withdrawn "I'd like to get going within a few days."

"I'd suggest that you move even sooner than 'a few days,'" Evers said. "The hunting season in Misiones is actually quite short."

"So, we should leave by when?"

"I would recommend that you depart by tomorrow evening at the latest," Evers said.

I looked at Mick. "How does that sound to you, Mick?"

Mick's face was impassive. "From everything I've heard, I'd have to say Robert's suggestions seem to be right on the money, Richard."

"Well, that still gives us a full day for sightseeing, doesn't it?" I asked. I looked past Evers. Two young men, each with about a dozen dogs, made their way down the sidewalk toward the corner, a four-lane thoroughfare crammed with taxis and cars gunning their motors as the drivers waited for the lights to change.

"Hey, Robert," I said, pointing, "what's with all the dogs?"

He followed my finger. "Ah," he said. "Those are a staple of the Buenos Aires lifestyle. We call them *pasaperros*. It means professional dog-walkers." He gestured at the high-rise apartment houses crammed close together on the streets that bordered the small park. "There are, so the story goes, three million dogs in this city. And *Porteños* love their dogs. They pamper their dogs. So, the people who live in flats hire professional dog-walkers—*pasaperros*—to take the dogs out two or three or even four times a day and exercise them. It's quite a sight, isn't it?"

I nodded. "Does this happen all over the city?"

"Wherever there are high-end flats," Evers said. "In the poor neighborhoods the dogs run free. In the neighborhoods where there are villas, the dogs get exercise in their own private back-yards. Mostly, you see it here in Recoleta and the Barrio Norte, or in the upper-class *barrios*—that's how they refer to neighbor-hoods here—of apartment flats like Belgrano, San Telmo, or the Microcentro."

Live and learn. "I guess there's a lot to see here."

"I'm still a neophyte," Evers said. "And I've been roaming the city on a serious basis for a year."

I'll bet he had been doing his roaming on a serious basis. Lemme tell you, if you want to get to know a city well, go out with a seasoned, gifted intelligence officer. Good case officers know every back alley, every side street, and every nook and cranny of a city, because when they go out to meet with their agents, they can't ever get lost or become confused about where they are. They have to be able to ACT, because they must always consider themselves under surveillance. And so, they take the time to learn the cities in which they operate.

"We probably don't have any time for sightseeing," I said. "But we'll need dinner tonight, and I think it would be nice to find a place where we could have a few brewskis. Any suggestions?"

"Well," Evers said, a wry smile on his thin lips, "you'll want to eat some great steak while you're in Argentina." His expression grew conspiratorial. "As a British diplomat I'm probably not sup-posed to say this, but it's a fact that Argentine beef make the finest steaks in the world—better even than the angus that comes from

Scotland—and one of the best places for it is a German restaurant called the Zum Edelweiss. It's near the Colon Theater—an easy walk from your hotel. Afterward, as you said, you'd probably like to do a bit of pub crawling. The one place I recommend you stay away from is an Irish bar called Mrs. Kelley's Kitchen." He jerked his chin past me, indicating the crowded sidewalk to my right. "It's about two or three blocks in that direction."

"Good advice." As much as I might want to visit the Mrs. Kelley's Kitchen franchise, I was going to stay away. I didn't want Gwilliam Kelley's antennae up. I looked over at Mick Owen, who was in charge of procuring weapons. "Has Mick told you that we're interested in getting our hands on some hunting gear for our visit to Misiones Province?"

Evers's head bobbed up and down. "I've been looking through my sources," he said. "But your request could pose a problem."

"Nothing serious I hope."

"I don't know yet. I have a couple of leads," he said, his face showing concern. "I may be able to have something for you by early tomorrow morning."

I was puzzled. The request was not all that tough to handle. Then I looked into Mick's face and realized what the real story was. We'd probably put Robert Evers between a rock and a hard place. Brits do not like weapons. They leave weapons to folks like Mick and me.

Nevertheless, I pressed the Brit spook. "Do you think you'll be able to help us out?"

Robert Evers ran a hand through his thick hair, displaying, for the first time since I'd laid eyes on him, a bit of nervousness. "I believe so," he finally said. "I think so."

Well, that was at least potential good news. If Evers could secure weapons and ammo, we could put the rest of our equipment together in a few hours at camping supply or army surplus stores.

The Brit polished off his coffee and stood up. "I have to go," he said. "Organizational meeting at the embassy. Keep the ambassador happy and off our backs, y'know." He shook hands all around. "Good to meet you chaps," he said. "Enjoy the city." He winked at Mick. "*Chau*, Mr. Owen. I'll be in touch."

• • •

I gave some thought to calling Gunny Jarriel at our embassy but decided against it. He'd already been helpful, and since we were here in mufti, if my presence became known, it might get him in hot water. And so I checked into the Étoile. Even before I unpacked, Mick turned the cable TV on. Once we'd taken that step, which would ensure that our conversation would remain private, Mick explained that Robert Evers had put his ass on the line for us. MI6's activities in Buenos Aires, he said, were highly restricted by the political bosses in London, who for reasons unknown to anyone did not want to offend the Argentine government with operations that entailed the recruiting and running of Argentine nationals.

You say that kind of thinking doesn't make sense. I guess Robert Evers agrees with you, because he bent the rules from the git-go. Bent 'em, hell. According to Mick he paid 'em no attention whatsoever. He had aggressively recruited Argentine nationals as agents from the day he'd arrived, and now he was using his networks to gather intel for Mick and me.

Which is why we knew that Gwilliam Kelley was still in Buenos Aires, checked into a five-room suite on the top floor of the Grand Hyatt, the huge luxury hotel sitting next to the French Embassy, at the southern terminus of the twenty-four-lane wide, traffic-intensive, pedestrian nightmare, Avenida de 9 Julio. The 9 Julio is Buenos Aires's equivalent of Paris's Champs Élysées, Rome's Via Nazionale, or London's Pall Mall—or, more accurately, all of them rolled into one huge, two-mile-long thoroughfare, flanked by towering office buildings and apartment houses, many topped with huge neon signs that give it a Times Square–like, almost carnival atmosphere.

Robert Evers had an agent on the Hyatt's concierge staff, and so Gwilliam's comings and going were being roughly covered. Evers's man had even managed to insert one of his subagents into the hotel's regular rotation of limo drivers, which gave him the opportunity to drive Gwilliam and his VERB occasionally. Gwilliam's schedule was irregularly regular. His day began at 1800 and stretched until the early morning hours. He jumped from club to club, ending every night at his own saloon, where he held court from three in the morning until about 0630. Then, three days ago, he and his VERB had gotten up early—it was just after noon when they called for a limo—and, joined by a local attorney and a sleazy-looking Colombian in an ice cream suit, they'd driven out to the northwestern town of Tigre, where the Colombian paid a suitcase full of cash to buy a huge, walled villa with an adjacent dock, on the Arroyo Gambado, one of more than three dozen hundred-foot-wide tributaries that empty into one of the delta's main water-ways, the Río Lujan. The place was now guarded, Evers had said, by what he described as an eclectic group of South Americans.

"Eclectic?" I asked.

"Colombians, Panamanians, and Nicaraguans," Evers said. "They were probably trained by Israelis or Cubans and got their experience guarding *narcotraficantes*."

That made sense. A whole generation of Latin American body-guards has been trained by renegade Israelis, former East German and Cuban security officers, to work for the Colombian drug car-tels. Now, many of them hired out elsewhere in the world.

Twenty hours later, according to another of Evers's agents, Brendan O'Donnell and two of his four TIRA comrades from Mrs. Kelley's Kitchen had caught a commercial flight from BA's down-town Aeroparque to Posadas airport, about ten miles south of the Paraguayan/Argentine border in Misiones Province. They'd left BA not even a full day before we'd arrived—no wonder Robert Evers had emphasized that we'd have to move fast.

Moving fast was something we were good at. Boomerang and

Timex were already scouring the city for web gear. Rotten Randy was out shopping for edged weapons. Hugo had a list of the clothes we'd need, and the addresses of half a dozen stores where he'd find 'em. Money was no problem. DET Bravo's covert nature lent itself to keeping huge amounts of operational cash in the fire-proof safe next to my desk in the basement of Curzon Street House. Mick and I had each packed five hundred one-hundred-dollar bills in our carry-ons. I figured we'd be able to deal with the bean counters later.

The only out-of-the-ordinary request Robert Evers had made was that each of us go to one of the many five-shots-for-five-dollars instant photo machines scattered throughout the city, and provide him with a strip of portraits. "Humor me," he said. "They're for my scrapbook."

It was a strange thing to ask for, but as Robert was tossing so many favors in our direction I didn't give it a second thought. "You want pictures, you got 'em," I said, and six hours later, Mick handed the young spook six strips of quick-and-dirty color portraits. We'd made sure that in at least one of the photographs on each strip, each of us showed young Robert Evers that he was number one so far as we were concerned.

Mick reported that Robert Evers's face had cracked a smile. "He said, 'Oh, *those* are the ones I'll put on display,' and slipped the photos into the breast pocket of his jacket."

I shrugged. "To each his own." And then I got on with my work. I checked in with Nod DiCarlo, who reported in pre-arranged code that things on the Gerry Kelley front were all quiet. He told me that the local soccer team had scored a goal. That meant one of Mick's techs had managed to slip a tap onto the phone line at Gerry's Hay's Mews home. He added that Nigel had gone sightseeing. That meant he'd snuck into the garage of Kelley's office building and planted a beacon on the frame of Gerry's Mercedes.

And he told me that Digger's energetically active social life

ROGUE WARRIOR: *DETACHMENT BRAVO*

looked as if it had just taken a turn toward the positive. That translated into the fact that O'Toole's embassy squeeze had given him a line on obtaining one of NSA's new handheld cell phone monitors. "I think he'll score within a few hours," Nod reported. Good: that told me they'd have one in hand soon. I told Nod to pass bravo Zulus to the men, then rang off. I had work to do.

● ● ●

I'd assigned myself as transportation officer and was pulling up to the terminal at Aeroparque Jorge Newbery, the single-runway airport that sits on the banks of the Río de la Plata a mere ten minutes from downtown, when I realized I was going at things ass-backward.

Item: flying up to Misiones Province wasn't going to solve anything. Brendan O'Donnell and his TIRA-lira-liras were long gone, and picking up their trail was going to be difficult, if not impossible. Locating them might take days—and days were something I didn't have.

Item: the action was going to be here in Buenos Aires. That's where one of Gwilliam's pals had just bought a big, private villa that was convenient to hundreds of miles of anonymous waterways. It was where Britain and the United States maintained two huge embassy compounds, where hundreds of Brits and Americans could be killed simultaneously. Similar ops had been done before. In 1998 Usama Bin Laden attacked our embassies in Kenya and Tanzania at the same time. In 1985, Abu Nidal had staged dual attacks on airports in Rome and Vienna during the peak Christmas-travel season.

"Only by watching the enemy and learning his intentions," General Tai Li'ang wrote in his treatise on strategy *The Li'ang Hsi-Huey,* *"can you learn what steps you must take to control the events that will dictate the outcome of the struggle."*

That couldn't happen if I was up in Misiones Province chasing Brendan O'Donnell. It would only happen if I remained in Buenos Aires and prepared myself and my men for the battle ahead. I wanted to see what was going on behind the walls of that villa—it would help determine whether Gwilliam and his people were planning an attack on the American embassy.

And so, instead of buying airline tickets, I jumped back in the cab and told the driver to take me to the Plaza Italia, which is a short walk from the American Embassy. Yes, I realize that I told you not so long ago that I was wary about making my presence known to anybody at the embassy. But I wasn't planning to pay a visit or make any social calls. I wanted to do a quick threat assessment, and see if the embassy was vulnerable.

How could I make that sort of judgment in a matter of minutes or hours, you want to know. Well, in point of fact, it's a simple matter of knowing what to look for, and what sorts of questions to ask. And I've been looking and asking for a couple of decades now. And so, I took myself for a walk. I started at the bus stop 150 yards from the heavily fortified gate that led to the consular section, and walked all the way around the perimeter of the nine-foot, RPG-resistant, mesh and steel post fence that surrounds the huge, modernistic compound.

AMEMBASSY Buenos Aires (as it's called in State Department–speak) is one of our newer facilities. It was designed under guidelines established by a commission on embassy security headed by former National Security Adviser Brent Scowcroft, in the wake of embassy attacks on American diplomatic facilities in Beirut, Khartoum, and Islamabad, among other places. The building sits facing northwest on a five-acre triangle of land bordered by three wide avenues. The embassy grounds are contiguous on one side to a secure Argentine government site. Directly across from the building's facade is a large, fenced open park. The closest structures—a large block of five-story commercial office buildings—are more than five hundred yards away, across Boulevard John F. Kennedy.

The embassy itself is constructed of reinforced concrete, with explosion-resistant windows, heavy, terrorist-proof metal doors, and interior "safe rooms" in case of invasion. It is set back from the street by a minimum of one hundred feet. The entryway is protected by a four-foot-high concrete barrier that conceals, behind it, a trench deep and wide enough to prevent the heaviest cement truck—the new millennium's terrorist vehicles of choice because they can ram through most antiterrorist barriers—from crashing through and propelling itself under the embassy portico.

Access to the embassy is closely monitored by cameras and also by roving patrols of local police, supplied by the Argentine authorities, who patrol the perimeter of the compound. Inside the fence line, security is handled by special agents from DS (State's Bureau of Diplomatic Security) and the Marine Security contingent, which was currently headed by my old safety-net *compadre,* Gunny Jarriel. To gain access, you had to pass through a primary checkpoint, where your identity was established by an FSN (it stands for Foreign Service National, which is Statespeak for a local employee), who then allowed you to proceed into a small, bomb-resistant chamber containing a one-person-at-a-time metal detector.

If you were carrying no weapons, you'd be cleared to proceed into a second chamber, which contained a remote-controlled, ever-so-slow-moving revolving door whose sections and ceiling were all made of thick, bulletproof, bomb-resistant steel. The reason for the revolving door was that it was equipped with explosives-detection devices. If the sniffer warning light went off, the security guard could freeze the door in place and isolate you until reinforcements arrived, and in any case you'd be confined 150 feet from the embassy itself.

From the revolving door, you went through a second metal detector, this one manned by a DS agent. After this checkpoint, you were admitted to the compound. If you weren't carrying a State Department, DOD, or federal law enforcement ID, you would have to be escorted to your destination. Automobiles, including the ambassador's limo, went through similar procedures as they threaded their way through a series of narrow Sturns that precluded any suicide bomber accessing the embassy garage at high speed. Staff parking was all outside, beyond the perimeter fence, and was patrolled by both local security guards and Buenos Aires cops. In other words, the place was being run according to the commission rules. Security was tight. Everything was done by the numbers.

Which is why it took me less than half an hour of seemingly aimless meandering to spot the flaws. But spotting flaws wasn't going to be enough. I wanted to know whether the place was under active surveillance—whether Brendan O'Donnell and his people had been able to identify the same chinks in the embassy's armor that I had. And the only way to do that would be to mount what's known in the trade as a countersurveillance. Now, in most Hollywood movies (*Beverly Hills Cop* comes to mind), surveillance is a couple of bad guys sitting in a car across the street from their target, and countersurveillance is a pair of cops sitting in their car watching the bad guys, who never seem to notice 'em. In real life, that kind of shit doesn't work.

In real life, surveillance is often sophisticated and hard to spot, and mounting countersurveillance is difficult, tedious, and boring. It is hard to stay unnoticed for long. It is even harder to remain alert. It is in many ways like sentry duty: you have to overcome boredom, monotony, and ennui. You have to remain finely tuned so that you can pick up even the slightest ripple that might give the opposition away. You also have to be continually innovative and constantly unconventional. You have to be able to change your appearance at the literal drop of a hat. I am talking about hard work. It is no fun.

• • •

It was late afternoon when Boomerang and I took the first shift. I sent Rotten Randy Michaels over to Mrs. Kelley's Kitchen to get a look at the people running the place and scope the location. Yes, I know that we'd previously decided not to go near the place so as not to spook the tangos. But if anyone could get in and out without causing any ripples it was the former Ranger, Rotten Randy.

Meanwhile, I hired a pair of taxis—two of the thousands of anonymous yellow and black Renaults that cruised the streets. Then I gave the drivers three hundred dollars each to let me or Boomerang (or the second shift of Timex and Randy) drive the cabs while they rode in the backseat like passengers. Given the thick wad of greenbacks we were waving it wasn't hard to convince 'em. Then I had the drivers take us to a clothing store where I bought eight different patterned short-sleeved shirts and eight one-size-fits-all hats. Timex bought us a pair of off-the-shelf bright yellow Motorola Talkabout radios and five dozen double-A Energizers. We made sure we had fully charged the batteries in our global-capable cellular phones. Then it was time to go to work.

1613. I cruised the neighborhood around the embassy looking for static surveillance: parked cars with someone inside, or people loitering in the street. Except for a few delivery trucks, a Federal Express van, one lone *pasaperro* with a trio of unruly dogs making his way around the intersection of John F. Kennedy and Avenida Colombia, I came up dry.

1656. I parked at a cab stand on Kennedy and scanned the windows of the office buildings. I saw nothing untoward. I wheeled the cab onto an anonymous side street and switched vehicles with Boomerang, then headed out again.

1715. The dog walker meandered down Colombia, pulled along by the same three unruly pups. He stopped to joke with the rent-a-cop walking post by the long line of parked cars belonging to the embassy staff. The guard played with one of the dogs, a friendly, hyperactive Airedale who kept trying to do backflips.

1724. The dog walker made his second go-round just as most of the embassy employees left work, Some headed toward the Plaza Italia; others climbed into their vehicles and drove off. None of them checked beneath their cars before they climbed inside. Not one checked the trunk, or under the hood. I tell you, these naïve diplo-dinks are as unobservant as that Australian singer Oblivious Newton John.

Boomerang and I remained in the neighborhood until well after dark, without noting any suspicious activity. Well, that was to be expected. If I were a tango and I were going to hit an embassy, I'd hit it when it was full of people, not after working hours. But when you're mounting a countersurveillance operation you cannot assume anything. And so, at midnight, Boomerang and I were relieved by Rotten Randy and Timex, who lingered on station to watch, look, and listen all night, even though it cut considerably into their eating and—most important—their beer-drinking and pussy-chasing plans. Those would have to wait until after Boomerang and I took over the duty at 0600.

0215. While Boomerang dropped onto his bed for a combat nap, I turned on the television to mask the sound, picked up the cell phone, dialed London, and got a coded sit-rep from Nod. Things were quiet, he reported. Gerry Kelley had been keeping to a regular schedule. He hadn't communicated with Gwilliam, so far as my guys could tell. There had been no further attacks or bombings. DET Bravo's intel squirrels had all their antennae up— but hadn't picked up any ripples of TIRA or other IRA splinter group activity.

I asked if there'd been any further news about Leather Boy, the kid I'd rolled up on Davies Street. Nod said he didn't know, but he'd do some snooping and give me an update the next time I called. What about Eamon the Demon, I asked. "Not a peep from North Audley Street, Skipper," Nod reported.

"Well, you know how to find me if the *merde* hits the *ventilateur*."

"Aye, aye, boss-man."

"Good." I rang off, rolled over, and racked up. It had been one long, fucking day, and the schedule wasn't going to improve much in the foreseeable future.

CHAPTER

10

0617. I STRETCHED, YAWNED, AND REACHED OVER TO OPEN THE passenger-side window, because Enrique, the driver, who lay snoozing on the backseat of his cab, had just released a huge, wet balloon of a fart. Timex had parked in a cab stand most of the night, lights and engine off, watching the well-lit embassy from half a klik away, until I relieved him at 0545. At 0605, the municipal water truck had sprayed the street in front of the embassy clean. At 0610, the security lights were switched off. At 0615, the rent-a-cops began to show up for the morning shift. That's right, friends, the perimeter wasn't guarded twenty-four hours a day. I told you things were being done by the numbers.

0629. The city was slowly coming to life. It would be rush hour soon. From somewhere off to the southeast, I heard the growl of a truck, approaching from the direction of the Plaza Italia.

I tapped the "transmit" button on the bright yellow walkie-talkie. "Radio check."

Boomerang's distinctive high-pitched voice came back at me five by five. "*Buenos días, Pibe.*"

"Anything?"

"Nada." The walkie-talkie squawked feedback and I adjusted the volume knob. "It's been all quiet by the office complex."

"Then let's cruise, and take a look-see anyway." I dropped the radio onto the seat, woke Enrique so he could play the passenger, switched on the ignition, threw the cab into gear, and eased away from the curb. I drove slowly around the embassy perimeter. Just as Boomerang had said, it was all quiet. As I turned right, from Cruz onto Avenida Cervino, Boomerang wheeled his cab in the opposite direction, covering the ground I'd just left behind. All clear.

0656. I was back in position to cover the entire front side of the embassy compound. The *pasaperro*, with his three dogs pulling ahead, began his first slow march of the day past the gate area. There were still only two of the eight-man rent-a-cop shift walking their beats. I flicked the button on the Motorola. "Geezus—he's up and working before the fucking rent-a-cops."

Boomerang's voice came back at me immediately. "Maybe we should talk to *him* about doing some security work, Boss Dude."

0728. Dog walker's second go-round. By now, the rest of the fucking rent-a-cops had finally shown up. Embassy staff began to trickle in.

0801. The ambassador's car pulled into the protected driveway. The antiterrorist barriers were dropped, and the limo proceeded into the underground garage. But no one mirrored the undercarriage. No one opened the trunk or the hood. Over the next eighteen minutes, six other senior staff arrived, all of them driving their own cars directly into the garage. None was checked for explosives. This was a fucking accident waiting to happen.

0829. Dog walker's third go-round. He paused to chat with the rent-a-cops. The FedEx panel truck pulled past the main gate, slowed, then moved on. The visa line was starting to form around the consulate entrance. I could see action inside the embassy itself—staff scurrying around; people coming and going.

1006. I changed clothes and did a brief walk-around to stretch my legs and see what was happening on the far side of the compound. All clear.

1131. The *pasaperro* was back, taking the dogs on their mid-morning jaunt. His walkabout was disturbed by a fracas at the visa section. A team of Gunny Jarriel's Marines escorted a trio of nylon-restraint-sporting troublemakers to the gates. Outside, the instant their restraints were removed, they began beating on the rent-a-cops. It took only four and a half minutes for a tactical team of Buenos Aires cops to arrive in their SWAT truck, subdue the perps, and drive 'em off to jail or wherever.

1142. In the midst of this goatfuck, the FedEx truck pulled up on the far side of the road and parked about three hundred yards from the main gate. The rear of the truck faced the embassy. That certainly raised a "caution" flag in my head. I shifted position so that I could ease my binoculars over the dash and focus them on the truck's cab. When I made out the driver inside, I saw he was frantically punching the keys of his electronic package-tracker. Then he disappeared into the rear of the truck for five minutes. Then he reappeared, picked up a cellular phone, spoke on it for a few seconds, and then settled himself behind the wheel, strapped his seat belt tight, threw the vehicle into gear, and drove off in a big hurry. You had to hand it to him: the area around the American Embassy was one of the few places in Buenos Aires that he could park to do his paperwork without getting hassled.

1200. Timex and Rotten Randy relieved Boomerang and me. I headed back to the Étoile for a well-deserved shower, shit, and shave. Boomerang went in search of *Porteña* pussy. Ah, the unquenchable, testosterone-enhanced energy of the young.

• • •

Day Three. 0600. I told you this was boring. In fact, we'd almost begun to settle into a routine: the dog walker in the morning, noon, and evening, the visa line, the unprotected cars, the rent-a-cops showing up late, the FedEx truck on his appointed rounds, and the cruising taxis. We'd accepted them all as a part of our daily schedule, which was not good. One of the most important elements of countersurveillance is keeping yourself and your team right at the edge of the observational envelope. You are a sponge, soaking up information and processing it, noting minute changes that could become significant once you understand the whole picture.

And so, instead of remaining static, I decided that today we'd conduct a rolling surveillance of the embassy and its grounds. That would shake us up and, I hoped, force us to detect something or other we hadn't picked up on before.

0612. I wheeled the cab in a U-turn, then continued around the compound in a clockwise direction, circled the Plaza Italia once, twice, thrice, and then cruised in a more or less northerly direction, up the Avenida Sarmiento, took a left onto Colombia, and another on Cervino, and cruised back past the embassy once again. I picked up no bad vibes; nothing unexpected. In the intervening four minutes, half a dozen cars had pulled into the most convenient parking spots. As usual, the rent-a-cops were nowhere to be found. I saw that Boomerang's cab had slid into a convenient spot from where he could watch the comings and goings at the front of the embassy. "Move," I told him. "Keep your eyes open." I watched as he drove off.

0627. I continued around the perimeter back onto Avenida Santa Fe, the six-lane artery that ran all the way downtown. Two blocks ahead, workers were setting up barricades for a construction site, and reducing the avenue's six wide lanes to two narrow ones. I wasn't about to get stuck, so I reversed course by swerving to starboard.

Shit. I'd turned into a literal canyon: a narrow, unmarked, one-way residential street lined with tall, slender apartment houses set cheek-by-jowl behind a thin ribbon of sidewalk. To park and still allow a single lane for traffic, residents had set their cars half on the sidewalk, and half in the street.

0636. I eased the cab along, scanning the high-rises. It was obviously as crowded here as it is in Tokyo—with living space at a similar premium. The architecture was eclectic. Modern, concrete housing was juxtaposed, contrapuntally, with Art Deco apartment houses that would have looked right at home in the Paris of the 1920s. I cruised slowly up to an intersection: a two-lane street called Guemes. When the light changed, I turned left so I could head back toward the embassy compound without having to go through the roadblock on Santa Fe.

That's when I saw my old pal, the *pasaperro*. I wouldn't have noticed him except for the fact that he was having a hell of a time trying to unload the hyperactive Airedale from a beat-up, chocolate-colored Peugeot van while his other two dogs—a Heinz-57 variety mutt and a nice-looking female Rottweiler, strained at their leashes. I slowed down to take a closer look at his vehicle, which was parked, right-side wheels up on the sidewalk, at the corner of Guemes and another unmarked street, diagonally across from a small vegetable store that was just opening up for business.

Now, my friends, the *pasaperro*'s arrival struck me as odd. Does it do something similar to you? I mean, we've both been told by Robert Evers that *pasaperros* normally work specific *neighborhoods*. That means, they show up every morning and pick up their dogs from the apartment houses, then walk them, then return 'em, and so on and so forth all day. That's what I'd assumed this guy was doing.

But we all know that assuming makes an ASS of U and ME. So, I should have remembered not to assume. Because this here professional dog walker, this here particular *pasaperro*, he brought his *own* dogs with him to this specific neighborhood. The very neighborhood, you'll remember, that adjoined the embassy compound. And it didn't look as if he was going to pick up any other *perros*, either.

I grabbed one of the hats I'd bought and jammed it on my head to conceal my French braid, pulled the visor low across my eyes, and then cruised past the sumbitch as he locked his van, eased a leather satchel on a long strap across his chest, and started up the unmarked street, toward Avenida Santa Fe—and the eastern side of the embassy complex, the three dogs leading the way.

I kept going, turned right at the next corner, then turned right again at the first street I could, drove until I could make a right turn, then made my way back onto Guemes. I pulled slowly past the van, this time making a note of the license plate on the palm of my hand. Then I got on the radio and told Boomerang to keep an eye out for the dog walker and to take careful note of what he did. Me, I had other things to do.

I drove up the street and pulled over in front of a small café. Just like Rome, every residential neighborhood in Buenos Aires has half a dozen or so small, mom-and-pop cafés, where *Porteños* go for their morning dose of caffeine and sugar, which translates into espresso laced with lots of *azúcar*, and plates of sweet buns or croissants. Like cafés in Paris or Rome, you can sit for hours, reading the newspaper and sipping excellent espresso. First, I switched my hat and my shirt. Then I ordered Enrique to go around the block and park. I told him to sit far enough down Guemes so he wouldn't be *prominente*, or be noticed by the dog walker, but close enough so he could see me if I came out of the café and waved at him to come and pick me up *rápidamente*.

I grabbed the Motorola, jammed it into a back pocket, and slid out of the cab. Enrique pulled away and I jogged over to the café. It was on the opposite side of Guemes, perhaps sixty yards up the street—southwest—of the dog walker's van. He couldn't leave, except by passing my position; in other words, it was a perfect surveillance location. I took a table next to the window, ordered a double espresso, and paid for it. You don't want to have to leave quickly only to discover that your waiter's taking a cigarette break out back. Then I dug in my pocket, came up with the cellular, flipped it open, and called the hotel. I asked in Spanish for Mick's room.

He answered on the third ring. "Owen."

"It's me. Can you get hold of your pal? The guy we had lunch with yesterday?"

A pause. Then: "Sure, but at this hour?"

"Yeah, right now. I have a local license plate I'd like checked."

"I hope he'll be able to do that for us."

"So do I." I squinted down at my hairy palm and read the number off for Mick. He repeated it to make sure he had it right. "I'm on it," he said.

"Good. I'll get back to you in an hour or so."

"It's okay, mate, I'll call you."

Brigadier or not, that was a bad tactical idea. You don't want a phone ringing when you're on a surveillance unless it is a matter of absolute life or death. I insisted: "Negative-negative. I'll call *you*."

I guess Mick got the message loud and clear, because he said, "Righty-o," and the receiver went dead.

• • •

0856. I was on my fourth double espresso and second croissant when I saw the *pasaperro* and his three dogs making their way up the street. The *pasaperro* was in a hurry. He had all three leashes wrapped around his right wrist and he was almost dragging the poor dogs. He switched hands and dug in his pocket, found his keys, unlocked the van, swung the rear gates open wide, and impatiently slapped his palm on the cargo area decking. The dogs took the cue and jumped in. He slapped the doors shut, went round to the driver's side and clambered in, turned the motor, and without bothering to check the rush-hour traffic flow, pulled into Guemes and headed west.

As you know, I'd already paid the bill. I sauntered outside, looked left and right as if searching for something—which of course I was—and then held up my hand as if hailing a cab. In fact, I could see the taxi. Enrique had wedged it up on the sidewalk half a short block behind the van. But there was no fucking Enrique behind the wheel. There was no fucking Enrique anywhere.

WTF? Had he gone to drain his lizard? Had he fallen asleep? Had he been taken out by the opposition? The answer was: it didn't fucking matter. All that fucking mattered was that Señor Murphy had managed to sneak aboard my flight and was here in Buenos Aires creating his usual havoc. So what time is it, kids? *It's Doom on Dickie time.*

I watched the van creep slowly up the jam-packed street. I moved back around the corner and yanked the yellow Motorola Talkabout out of my back pocket.

"Boomerang—"

The response was immediate. "Yo, *Pibe.*"

"Lost my transportation. I'm on foot following our friend."

"Gimme the coordinates, *Pibe*, and I'll be there."

Coordinates? I didn't have any fucking coordinates. So far as I was concerned, I was at the corner of Walk and Don't Walk. "Shit, I don't know where the fuck I am. I'm on a street called Guemes, but I don't have a clue about the cross street." I looked up and down the street helplessly. "I think I'm somewhere close to the Plaza Italia."

"On my way, *Pibe.*"

On his way was no good. Not now. I peeked around the corner. The van was already two and a half blocks ahead of where I stood. I took one last futile look toward Enrique's taxi, and then I started jogging after the van.

Here is the good news. It was rush hour, and traffic was moving in fits and starts. Here is the bad news. It was rush hour, and drivers in Buenos Aires don't give a shit about pedestrian welfare. I felt like a goddamn matador, dodging bumpers and rearview mirrors as I tried to navigate the frantic stop-and-go traffic. There was something else, too: when you're running after a car, you tend to draw attention to yourself. The human eye is a complex mechanism. It tends to instinctively pick out any motion that is dissimilar from its surroundings. That's why your eye is drawn to the flashing of a deer's flicking white tail in the woods when you're hunting. Or toward the one asshole who's running in a crowd of walkers.

Not only did I have to chase the cocksucker in the van down, I had to do it while keeping myself in his blind spot. And so, I had to slalom from side to side, as he wove in and out of traffic. And let me be honest about this: I wasn't gaining on him. Yes, I am in top physical condition. Yes, I can run a mile in less than five minutes and thirty seconds. Yes, I can do six hundred fingertip push-ups, and a thousand sit-ups without breaking a sweat. But all of that doesn't mean shit when you're out and about and trying to navigate your way through rush-hour traffic and follow a target vehicle without being noticed.

Well, guess what: stealth wasn't getting me anywhere, except left behind. So what if he saw me. He didn't have any idea who I was—or whether I was after him, or just some anonymous asshole out running. I vaulted the fender of a Mercedes and just flat-out sprinted up Guemes after the van. I was gaining on the sumbitch, too—when a fucking Fiat convertible driven by one of your Argentine Dale Earnhardts or Jeff Gordons or whoever the fuck gunned his car right through one of the side-street intersections heedless of what was in his way.

I almost didn't see him coming. At the very last minute I caught the flash of sunlight on his bumper. And then, I was flipped straight into the air.

I knew enough not to tense my body, so I relaxed and just took the blow. But shit, I came down hard. My shoulders cracked the Fiat's windshield. The back of my head smacked the top of the windshield frame. My butt and feet smashed into the hood, leaving a Rogue-size indentation. I rolled off the car seeing double. There was going to be a fucking nut the size of a tennis ball on the back of my head.

And what about the goddamn brown van? I looked up Guemes and saw two of 'em. They were fuzzy. And then, both of the fuzzy vans made a swerving right turn and disappeared from view.

I stood there, my head pounding, my body sore as hell. At which point Mario fucking Andretti, or more properly, Maria fucking Andretti, pulled herself out of the Fiat and started point-ing to the bumps and lumps on her convertible, and beating me with her purse while she screamed abuse.

Frankly, I didn't think ladies were supposed to know the sorts of words she was using. Nor would it have been possible for me to do to myself the acts she was suggesting I perform. But then, maybe she wasn't a lady, and perhaps she'd never taken a course in the laws of physics.

0909. My vision was clearing up by the time the cops arrived. I saw Boomerang on the periphery of the crowd, but waved him off with a glance. I didn't want to attract any more attention to myself than I already had. Since I was wearing running shoes, I explained that I'd simply been out for a morning jog when Maria cut through the intersection sans waiting for her turn.

On the plus side, there were witnesses who backed me up. It was Maria Andretti who received the citation, not me. On the minus side, the cops took down my name. Why was that *mala suerte?*[35] Fact is, they have computer databases in Argentina, too, and sooner of later, one of 'em would spit out just who Richard (NMN) Marcinko was, and the Argentine authorities would come looking for me to see just why I was visiting. Lemme tell ya: it's not easy being Richard Marcinko, Rogue Warrior®. I sometimes think I was happier as an anonymous Dick in the teams.

But that's neither here nor there. What's here and now is that I knew the clock would be ticking once the cops filed their report. Was it guaranteed I'd be identified? The answer is no, because Mister Murphy is an equal-opportunity asshole, and he affects Argentines just as much as he screws with *yanquis* like me. But I'd have to operate as if I'd been ID'd. Which meant ratcheting up the speed of our ops. Which would, of course, be more difficult, now that I'd managed to lose track of the *pasaperro's* van.

---

[35] Bad luck.

1012. We went back to the Étoile and regrouped. At least Mick had news, even though it wasn't positive. Bob Evers had called one of his agents—no doubt a cop, although he hadn't elaborated to Mick—to check on the license plate. Bottom line: it had been reported stolen eight months ago. That made sense. If I were a tango and reconnoitering a target, I'd change my license plates at least once a day—maybe more. And how do you get those plates? You steal 'em and cache 'em until you need 'em. That's easier in places like Europe and South America, where license plates do not have expiration stickers on 'em.

All my instincts told me that the embassy was being staked out so it could be hit sometime in the near future. And so, as much as I didn't want to, I felt it was my duty to talk to the RSO—that's the State Department's Regional Security Officer—and let him know what I was thinking. I picked up the phone and called Gunny Jarriel, told him I was in town, said I'd like to meet with the RSO or any of the embassy's security officers, and that I'd be at the embassy at noon.

• • •

I was fifteen minutes early. The gunny was not on duty. I could see that because he was wearing a pair of dark suit trousers held up by fashionable silk braces, a white button-down shirt, and a diplomatic blue patterned tie, standing behind the spit-and-polish E-5 (sergeant) who checked my ID and issued me a GO ANYWHERE UNESCORTED laminated badge, which I clipped to my lapel under his unrelenting gaze. When he'd ascertained that I was PROP-ERLY IDENTIFIED, the sergeant buzzed me through the Class-III bulletproof door. Gunny Jarriel was waiting in the narrow vestibule.

"Rotten Richard, you hairy-palmed sumbitch. Welcome to BA." He wrapped me up in a big *abrazo.*

I returned the *abrazo,* then held him at arm's length and looked at him critically. He'd matured in the half dozen years since I'd seen him last—a tinge of gray meandered around the temples of his flattop. But he was still a lean, mean fighting machine. He wasn't big, but he was wiry, and strong, and he knew how to use his strength. I'd seen it: when we'd met, he was an E-6 (staff sergeant) teaching Close Quarters Combat and hostage rescue at the U.S. Marine Corps school for embassy security guards down at Quantico. I'd brought a squad of my Red Cell shooters down to give a demonstration, and we'd all bonded over copious amounts of Coors Light after we'd done our demonstrating. Now he was an E-9 master gunnery sergeant, which in the Marine Corps hierarchy, put him at the Right Hand of God. Buenos Aires was his last tour. The Gunny was going to retire after BA, after twenty-five years in the Corps—eighteen of those years overseas.

He led me down a narrow corridor lined with lockers containing BDUs, gas masks, shields, Monadnock batons, bulletproof vests, and helmets toward the Marine security office, propelled me through the steel door ahead of him, then shut it securely behind us.

His face was serious. "So, what's up, Dick? Is my post in trouble?"

I raised my hands in mock protest. "What, no preliminaries? No makee nice-nice before fuckee-fuckee? No . . . foreplay, Gunny?"

The Gunny's eyes crinkled in a smile. "Hey, it's not me. First, you send me an off-the-books query about that asshole Irishman named something or other Kelley. Next thing I know you turn up here in BA and call. You tell me you want to see the RSO and you want to see him like, *right now.* So, I figure you know something we don't, and it has to do with the Irish fella you were asking about."

"Got some coffee?"

"Sure." The Gunny's thumb hooked toward an industrial strength BrewMaster sitting on a file cabinet. "But be careful. That stuff'll put hair on your tongue."

"Hell, you know how much I like official-issue Uncle Sam's Misguided Children coffee." I strode over, found a reasonably clean mug, and poured eight or so ounces of the black stuff—and "stuff" it most certainly was—then gulped. Shit—I almost spat it back through my nose. That fucking batch of coffee was strong enough to wake up someone from under fucking heart-transplant anesthesia. I blinked as the burnt caffeine taste hit my palate. "Interesting . . . beverage," I wheezed as the Gunny grinned. "*You* going to have any of this?"

"Not on your life," he said. "Shit, Dick, I'm the guy that made it."

Mug in hand, I leaned my butt on a desk across from where the Gunny stood and gave him a Roguish no-shitter. I told him about the Mrs. Kelley's franchise, and who was running it. I didn't have anything definite—no schedule, no method, except that any attack would probably be using explosives, or RPGs. I told him about the bogus dog walker and—double-checking my notes— that the *pasaperro* had been on scene through the whole scuffle outside the visa section.

Gunny immediately realized the significance of that. "He knows exactly what the cops' response time is," he said.

"Right on."

"So, how's it gonna go down, Dick?"

I was honest with him. I couldn't be sure how they'd play things. But I told the Gunny what I'd seen, and I told him what I thought. My bottom line: there was going to be an attack.

Gunny Jarriel perched on the edge of his desk, occasionally scratching at his cheek while I spoke. But he didn't interrupt. When I'd done, he remained silent.

"So, what do you think, Gunny?"

His lean face hardened. "I think we have some serious work to do, and not a lot of time to get it done."

"Look—what I just gave you is the result of less than four days of work. I certainly saw things I didn't like, Gunny. But you know as well as I do, these things aren't always done deals."

The concern in Gunny Jarriel's face was apparent. "If it was just you, Dick, I might agree. But what you came up with is all part of a bigger pattern of probes," he said. He paused. "A fucking dog walker," he said, as if to himself. "I should have picked that one up."

In the next fifteen minutes, the situation became a lot clearer, both to the Gunny, and to me. Because Gunny *was* a Gunny, he'd been working overtime. And he'd noticed things over the past few weeks that he hadn't liked. The same cars sitting across from the embassy compound day after day. After spending long hours poring over the surveillance videos, he'd seen them. And there had been a couple of break-in attempts on the staff cars parked outside the fence line. Even worse, three suspicious packages had been delivered in the past four weeks. Before that, there hadn't been three suspicious packages delivered in a year's time.

"Someone out there is probing us," the Gunny said. "I don't like it when somebody tries to stick his finger up my asshole without any KY."

"Agreed." I took another swallow of coffee and winced. "So, why not take your opinions to the RSO and work with him to harden the target?"

"I've already hardened the target as much as I can. But we don't have an RSO."

"How come?"

"Embassy politics, Dick, embassy fuckin' politics." He swiveled off the desk and began to pace. "We had a good RSO here until three and a half weeks ago. Guy named Olshaker."

I remembered the name. "Tall drink of water. Prematurely gray. A real pussy-hound. I met him in Rome a few years back when I escorted Chairman Crocker to a NATO conference."

"That's him—same guy. Same M.O. with the women, too. We got him the tour after Rome."

"So?"

"Olshaker was too aggressive for the ambassador. In case you didn't already know, our ambassador here is a professional diplomat. Which means he doesn't like agressive RSOs like Olshaker. Kept telling him he was offending the Argentines because he was being 'provocative,' as he kept calling it. You know the routine. 'They are our hosts and we cannot offend them by telling them how to do their jobs.' Or, 'We cannot offend our hosts by trying to keep tabs on foreign nationals who happen to live here, or by requesting that our Argentine hosts do it for us.' Well, Olshaker didn't give a shit. He knew what his job was, and his job was to protect this place—even protect assholes like the friggin' ambassador. And so he just kept on keepin' on."

"What happened?"

"Ambassador had him shit-canned. Sent him home early. No replacement on the horizon, either."

That was too bad. When we'd operated together in Rome, I'd liked Olshaker's moves. He understood the security beez-i-ness. I suffered through another swallow of the Gunny's coffee. "So, who's taken over the security duty until Olshaker's replaced?"

"That's the real bad news. The ambassador decided to turn all matters of embassy security policy over to the Christians In Action station chief."

Now I was shocked. "Isn't that impossible?"

Gunny Jarriel's body language told me it wasn't impossible at all.

I'd heard of clusterfucks but this was unprecedented. "WTF, Gunny? We both know embassy security isn't anywhere in the Agency's portfolio. And the ambassador—"

The Gunny cut me off. "That may all be true enough in most embassies, Dick. But we have sort of a special case here." He glanced over at the door to the office to make sure it was closed securely. "Lemme give you the no-shitter. What we've got here is a power-hungry chief of station who has, from the day he arrived, described himself as a world-renown expert in counterterrorism, manipulating an ambassador whose brain-activity level is about equal to a block of wood. I'm telling you, Dick, our ambassador's complete understanding of what the Central Intelligence Agency can and cannot do is so off base, it has got to come entirely from reading Tom Clancy novels."

There is a Naval Special Warfare technical term for situations like this one. It is, "Holy shit."

Gunny Jarriel paused. "And that's the good news."

If that was the good news I could hardly wait for the other *zapata*[36] to drop. "Okay, so now give me the rest of it."

Gunny Jarriel's face took on an I-just-sucked-a-lemon expression. "Mel Potts is the station chief here, Dick. Melvin fucking Potts."

Oh shit, oh fuck, oh Doom on Dickie.

Let me explain. Melvin Potts was a lieutenant (j.g.), when he went through BUD/S. I never knew how he made it. He was one of those short, plumpish, four-eyed officer types who never appeared to be comfortable doing anything physical. But somehow Lieutenant (j.g.) Melvin finished, and he was ultimately assigned to a platoon at SEAL Team Two. That's when I first met him. I was commuting to Little Creek in those days, selecting the crème de la crème of Naval SpecWar roguery for the original seventy-two billets at SEAL Team Six.

Mel elbowed his way into the office I was working out of and offered me his services as a self-proclaimed expert in counterterrorist tactics and theory. Offered doesn't quite do his performance justice. He told me he was a world-class expert in CT, and that without his help, SEAL Team Six would never get off the ground. It didn't take more than five minutes for me to understand he had no idea what he was talking about. I told the lieutenant I'd give him a call if I ever needed his unique capabilities, eased his fat ass out the door, and made sure that the entire command knew it.

Which infuriated Mel so much that he tried to go behind my

---

[36] Shoe.

back and get appointed to a slot without my having chopped[37] his name. When I learned what he'd done, I took the sumbitch out behind the obstacle course, where I gave him a Roguish attitude adjustment during which I broke his nose. I lost track of Mel for a while, although I heard he'd somehow lateralled to the CIA, where he disappeared into the Wilderness of Mirrors, mercifully never to be heard of again.

That "never to be heard of again" stuff isn't quite true. For years now the SpecWar community has heard horror stories about the former Lieutenant Putz that proved once and for all that the Peter Principle was alive, well, and flourishing at the Central Intelligence Agency. In the 1990s, working the Somalia desk, he botched the tactical intel about the location of a notorious Somali warlord in Mogadishu, resulting in the deaths of eighteen American Army Rangers and Delta Force shooters.

There's more: during the 1998 Kosovo bombing campaign, Mel Potts was the man ultimately responsible for intelligence regarding Belgrade's targeting assessments. That's right: *he* was the guy who misplaced the Chinese Embassy, which we then bombed by mistake. But did Mel get fired for screwing up? The answer is that he did not: the Teflon Putz managed to slip away unscratched while another less fortunate officer was fired and six others disciplined for his screwup. In fact, every time he fucked up, he'd been *promoted*. Three years in Buenos Aires was his reward for Belgrade. And if that's not enough to make you puke, listen to this: currently Mel was an SIS (Senior Intelligence Service) officer with the equivalent rank of a two-star general, which, incredible as it may seem, made him the number-two ranking diplomat at AMEMBASSY Buenos Aires. Doesn't *that* give you a shitload of confidence about the alleged "leaders" running our intelligence-gathering apparatus?

---

[37] Approved.

Gunny Jarriel's sour expression told me the whole story. "Dick, I can't even get cleared into his office. He treats my men like dirt. From the way he looks at us, he probably thinks we should be swabbing out the embassy's heads. There's no way I can take you up there."

"Hey, if it has to be done, it has to be done." I drained the Gunny's coffee. "You and I can backchannel on this one. I'll keep you sit-repped; you do the same for me."

Gunny Jarriel snapped to attention. "Aye-aye, sir." And he wasn't spelling it with a *c* and a *u*, either.

I cracked a smile. "Hell, Gunny, there's one good thing about all this crap."

"What's that, Dick?"

I tapped the empty mug. "That shitty coffee of yours put me in the perfect fucking frame of mind to see the former Lieutenant Putz."

CHAPTER

11

THE FORMER LIEUTENANT PUTZ KEPT ME WAITING FOR AN HOUR AND fifteen minutes, no doubt just to demonstrate how important he was. He finally buzzed his executive secretary, who buzzed her assistant—I heard the whole process—who came out into the corridor where I'd been provided with a hard steel chair, and beckoned me forward, allowing me to finally enter sanctified ground.

I had to admit that his office was, well, palatial. It was as big as most ambassador's offices. On one wall, Mel displayed several dozen awards and citations. The credenza, an antique job, held framed photographs, some of them inscribed, of Mel with three American presidents, the president of France, the German chancellor, the king of Jordan, and four directors of central intelligence.

Mel was nowhere near as palatial as his office. He'd put on a fair amount of weight over the years. The red blotches on his face were evidence of a bad skin problem. His hair, thick when I'd known him, was now styled in one of the most incredible combovers I'd ever seen. Under the right atmospheric conditions, it probably caught the wind, standing straight up like the fucking flying jib on a thirty-meter boat. His nose, which I'd broken so many years ago, hadn't ever healed properly, giving him the look of a fat, bald, four-eyed English bulldog. He wore an ill-fitting suit of diplomatic blue pinstripes, a white shirt, and a red, white, and blue tie, held in place by a gold SEAL Budweiser tie tack. He stood safely behind his desk and waited until I approached him, then reached his hand tentatively across the tooled leather surface. "Long time no see, Dick."

There was no reason at all to be nice. I kept my hands where they were. I looked him up and down in the contemptuous manner the old Team chiefs had taught me. "Hey, Putz-man, still working out every day, I see."

My greeting was followed by a fifteen-second interval of what the radio talk-show hosts describe as "dead air." Then the Putz withdrew his hand. The expression on his chubby face grew cold. "You called and asked to see me," he said. His eyes narrowed. "And by the way, how'd you get that pass? I usually approve those personally."

That sounded like Mel's idea of a coherent embassy security policy, i.e., personally approving the visitors' passes. But I'd already committed myself and so there was no reason to beat around the bush. "Look, Mel, I understand that you're the guy in charge of making the embassy's security decisions these days," I said.

Mel's chest puffed up like a little bird's. "I am."

"Well, I have good reason to think your embassy is going to be attacked in the near future by a splinter group from the IRA hoping to shatter what's left of the Northern Irish peace agreement we helped work out. They will probably use some kind of explosive device—maybe an RPG or an antitank missile."

Mel remained standing. "That's preposterous," he said flatly.

I looked straight back at him and said, "I don't think so."

"Frankly," the Putz said, "I don't care what you think, Dick." He retreated a step and plunked himself into his chair, tilted it back, and placed his loafers on the tooled leather surface of the desk. He didn't invite me to sit down. "What you *think* is simply opinion, and I don't respect your opinions."

This asshole was being as petulant as a spoiled child. But I wasn't in the mood for petulant right now, because there were lives at stake. Even so, instead of coming around the desk and bitch-slapping the shit out of him, I pressed on. "Look, Mel, we've had our differences in the past. But this is serious. I have come upon some intelligence indicating that you will be hit."

"Intelligence."

"Yes."

"Well, Dick, let me give you what you always liked to call a 'no-shitter.' There are two of us in this office, and one of us—me— is an intelligence professional. So, you tell *me* what you have, and I'll tell *you* whether or not it is intelligence."

No, I did not throttle the conceited little motherfucker, although I gave it serious thought. I stood my ground and I gave him the same kind of concise, succinct, direct, and factual briefing I have given to the president of the United States, the secretary of defense, the secretary of the Navy, and other high government officials. I never take a lot of time. But what time I do take is filled with unassailable fact. And that, despite any professional misgivings I might have had about him, is what I did for Mel.

The monologue took six minutes. When I was done, he took his feet off the desk, scrunched closer to it, and played a silent arpeggio on the leather surface. Then he looked up at me and said, "Dick, what you have told me is not intelligence. It is nothing but bullshit, complete and utter horse puckey." He paused so he could see my reaction and then, satisfied with what he was provoking, he continued.

"Let me do something for you, Dick, that no one has probably ever done before. And that is, to define intelligence. What is intelligence? It is *product*, Dick, product which results from the collection and processing of information concerning activities and situations both actual and potential, and relating to activities and situations both foreign and domestic. That product is of great potential value to policy makers, because it allows those at the highest levels of our government to understand both the capabilities and the intentions of America's friends and its adversaries." He paused. "That," he said, "is what intelligence is."

His palm slapped the surface of his desk. *"You,* Dick, have not satisfied my definition of intelligence. And therefore, what you have told me is not intelligence. Why? Because it is not product. It has not been processed, or analyzed. It has not been categorized, or assessed. It has not been appraised, or evaluated. It has not been weighed, or deliberated. It is simply . . . your opinion. And your opinion, Dick, no matter how experienced you may be at— how do you refer to it? Ah, yes: 'hopping and popping,' and 'shooting and looting,' isn't it? Anyway, no matter how proficient you think you are in those areas, you are not an intelligence professional. And what you have told me, while marginally interesting as crude, raw, unvetted, unsubstantiated *in-for-ma-shun,* is inapplicable, unsuitable, and probably irrelevant to the current security operation at this embassy."

I'll tell you, this prissy motherfucker sure had learned how to use twenty-dollar words, hadn't he? No wonder he was in the Senior Intelligence Service with the equivalent rank of a two-star general. He certainly *talked* just like most fucking two-star generals. Frankly, friends, I'd had it with the Putz, and with his fancy vocabulary. I'd come here to help. I'd broken out of stealth mode and come over here because I knew American lives were at risk. And now I was about to be shut down by this pompous, arrogant, self-important bureaucrat.

I looked down at the Putz. "Y'know, I've heard most of that shit before, Mel."

He looked up at me, surprised. "Oh?" he said, "You have? When?"

"I heard it from intelligence professionals just like you just before Prince Khaled Bin Abdullah's people killed nineteen Americans at Khobar Towers in Saudi," I said. "And I heard it again from assholes just like you in the weeks before our embassies in Kenya and Tanzania were blown up," I said.

And because I was speaking reassuringly, I was able to draw

closer. When I'd approached where I wanted to be, I reached across the desk, took hold of Mel's tie, and then slowly reeled it in around my extra-Rogue-size hand, and pulled it up close, so that I could examine it, and him. Now, my friends, here is a variation on the Rogue Warrior®'s First Law of Physics:[38] grab a stupid asshole by his tie and the rest of his body will follow wherever you take the tie.

And that is precisely what happened here. As I yanked, Mel's round face followed the big double-Windsor under his double chin, until I had him right where I wanted him—right up against my own hairy, Roguish face.

I looked at this quivering piece of jelly and was sickened. "Y'know, Mel," I said, "Americans always seem to die because stupid motherfuckers like you refuse to see the clear and present danger."

He wasn't getting it. So I continued. "You assholes set idiotic rules of engagement, and then after it's all over, you blame some fucking sergeant for not manning his post." Mel's eyes started to wander. I pulled on his tie.

"You will be attacked," I said. "It is simply a question of how, and when."

I shook the tie in my hand and watched as his reddened face mirrored every movement of my hand. I turned my head and gave him a nose-to-nose War Face. "Got that message loud and clear, Mel?"

His head shook up and down, wattles wobbling in the affirmative.

That's what he signaled. But here is what I knew: I saw in his eyes that he didn't believe me. I saw in his eyes that he would probably never believe me.

And the result of his skepticism would be inevitable: once again, Americans would die. And Mel would weasel out of any responsibility.

---

[38] The Rogue Warrior®'s First Law of Physics © 1999, Richard Marcinko and John Weisman.

I looked down at the wide striped tie wrapped around my hairy fist. The gold Budweiser tie tack was atop my right index-finger knuckle. I unrolled the tie just enough so that I could release the tie tack's pin from its holder, then held the miniature gold Budweiser in my hand by its five-eighths-of-an-inch-long pin, and examined it carefully.

Let me stop here long enough to tell you that I am always moved by the sight of the SEAL trident. It is the symbol of a brotherhood. I come from an unbroken line that descends from the first volunteers who braved the cold waters off Fort Pierce, Florida, in the early days of World War II. Scouts, Raiders, NCDUs,[39] UDTs,[40] and SEALs—we are all a band of Froggish brothers. The Scouts and Raiders and NDCUs sometimes took 70, 80, 90 percent casualties—but they always PERFORMED THEIR MISSIONS. UDTs never refused an assignment, no matter how demanding it might have been. My brother SEALs have never left a wounded or dead teammate in the field. All my brother Frogs have been forged on the same anvil of pain, hammered and tempered until they realize in the depths of their souls that THERE IS ABSOLUTELY NOTHING THEY CANNOT DO.

That is why I become so emotional whenever I see our sacred Trident. *MY* sacred trident. And it is why I am offended when I see pimple-ass wannabes wearing SEAL T-shirts with tridents, or come upon no-loads sporting SEAL Team trident patches at *Soldier of Fortune* conventions. It is why I want to commit mayhem and violence when I look at the current avalanche of Trident-intense fake SEAL equipment sold in gun magazines or military-equipment catalogues. It is why I want to beat the crap out of former SEALs who encourage the wannabes by marketing ersatz SEAL shit.

Hey, you pencil-dicked, shithead, can't-cunt marketing-slash-

---

[39] Naval Combat Demolition Units.
[40] Underwater Demolition Teams.

sales assholes, YOU ARE MESSING WITH MY HISTORY, AND I DO NOT LIKE IT.

Anyway, that was what ran through my brain in the few seconds during which I was looking at Mel Potts's Budweiser tie tack.

Now, let me make myself perfectly fucking clear: I was not upset that Mel was wearing the sacred Trident. He had, in point of fact, earned it. Just as I earned it. Mel Potts was a brother SEAL. The sorry fact of life was, that even though I hated Mel the Putz's guts, if we were in battle together I'd die for him, because those were the rules of the Froggish bond between us.

Of course, just because he wore the Trident didn't mean he was necessarily a good guy. There are good SEALs and there are assholes. There are Warrior SEALs and there are, well, putzes, just like Mel. And just because Mel was entitled to wear the Trident didn't mean I had to like the *way* he was wearing it. I mean, he should have worn his Trident proudly. On his chest. Not like some piece of fucking costume jewelry.

The more I thought about that, the more I knew I was right—and what I had to do. And so, I opened up his pinstripe suit coat with my left hand, then took the Trident, and placed it on his shirt, my left hand holding it steady on his greater pectoral muscle, two inches above his left nipple, which is where I wear the sacred Trident on my own uniform.

Mel watched what I was doing with a sort of dumbstruck, bemused detachment, as if he couldn't believe what he was seeing. He watched in silence right up until the instant that, having let go his tie, I *Hoo Ya, motherfucker!* hammered the Trident *smack* through the muscle and cartilage of his pec and stuck it straight onto his chest. And since he didn't work out, and didn't have very much in the way of pecs, the blow was hard enough to spike the tip of that five-eighths-inch pin right down into one of his fucking ribs.

Boy did *that* ever bring the cockbreath to life. "*Geeeeezus!*" he screamed in pain. And immediately, a small but expanding circle of blood formed around the Budweiser. *"Geeeeezus H. Christ,"* he caterwauled.

Now blooding, as what I'd just done to him is called, is a serious offense in today's politically correct armed forces. Blooding has always been controversial. In some circles (the Rocks and Shoals Navy of World War II for example), blooding was frowned upon because it wasn't part of Old Navy lore. In some of today's elite forces—certain SpecOps units of the Army and the Marine Corps come to mind—blooding is tacitly accepted by the troops as a rite of passage, even though it is an offense that can get an officer or non-com court-martialed if said rite gets made public. But here is not the time or the place to debate the rights and wrongs of blooding. Besides, since Mel and I weren't engaged in an official U.S. Navy ceremony, I didn't think anyone would object if I used the sacred Trident to remind Mel that he was still a part of an elite organization of WARRIORS, and that he should always wear his Trident with PRIDE, DIGNITY, AND HONOR, not as a fucking piece of accent jewelry.

Of course, this is Mel Putz I'm talking about, and as I just said, just because he was once a SEAL didn't make him any less of a cockbreath. Tears in his eyes, Mel grabbed at his tit and tried to yank the Trident out from where I'd hammered it. But I'd smashed it down pretty hard, and he was not successful. From the look on his face it was painful going.

But he kept at it, screaming all the while. "You *stuck* me," he brayed, sounding like a fucking barnyard animal. "You *wounded* me." Finally (I told you SEALs always complete their missions) he managed to pry the Trident from his chest. He held it between trembling, pudgy fingers and shook his hand in my direction, flicking blood. "You . . . you . . . you *assaulted* me."

I looked over the desk at him. Here was the sorry fucking truth: Mel Potts may have made it through BUD/S but he didn't have the heart or the soul of a SEAL Warrior. He was more akin to my former nemesis, the currently retired Rear Admiral Pinkney

162

Prescott III. Mel and Pinky represented all the pussy-assed, can't-cunt commanding officers who'd made it through BUD/S but lacked the essential heart, soul, and GUTS to become true WARRIORS. Just because he wore the Trident didn't mean that Mel Potts was worth anything more than a turd floating in the toilet, a fucking piece of *merde*.

I turned on my heel but stopped long enough to say, "Look, Mel, I told you that the embassy is gonna be attacked. Either take steps or suffer the consequences."

The Putz's expression told me he didn't give a rusty F-word what happened to the embassy. It was me he wanted to take action against. "I am a goddamn CIA chief of station," he screamed. "I am a senior American diplomat. I am the number-two ranking American in Buenos Aires. Believe me, you frigging animal, Washington is going to hear about this unprovoked physical attack on me." He gulped for air, then continued. "I will be on the phone to the chief of naval operations within the hour. If your career isn't already in the sewer, it will be when I get done with you."

I was on him like stink on shit. I shoved him back into his chair so hard that he crashed into his credenza and knocked over most of his "ain't I great" photographs. "Fuck you, Mel," I said, over the sound of shattering glass. "Fuck you very, very much indeed, because it ain't over till it's over."

● ● ●

I was delighted with my performance. Mick's review was not so positive. "You know he's already probably gotten Washington on the line."

Playfully, I flipped Mick the finger. "So, I'll call Chairman Crocker and fix things."

Actually, that wasn't such a bad idea. I mean, the embassy was vulnerable, and I didn't want people killed. Sure, I'd already told Gunny Jarriel to ratchet up the security, but it wouldn't hurt to let the Chairman know, too.

I tried the Chairman's private number. But the phone in his

hideaway had been disconnected. I called the JCS staff office and asked to be patched through to the Chairman, only to be informed by an eager-beaver O-4 named Hurley that the Chairman was taking his terminal leave and could not be contacted.

But, Lieutenant Commander Hurley continued, she could and would connect me to the office of the chief of Naval operations, whose executive assistant had just E-mailed the entire joint staff that if I called, I was to be put through immediately.

This was obviously Mel's doing. It was Doom on Dickie time.

Mick's face reflected the seriousness of the problem. "If this Mel chap pushes it, you're going to be recalled, Dick."

"Fuck him, Mick—we'll survive." I wiggled my eyebrows in a halfway decent Groucho imitation. "Hey, they gotta find us first, right?"

"And where do you propose hiding out?"

"I actually thought about that on my way back to the Hotel Étoile, Mick." I pulled the drapes, cutting off the view of the Cementerio Recoleta and turned up the volume on the cable TV, just in case there was anyone with a set of NSA-style Big Ears out there. "I'm willing to bet that your pal Robert Evers has a safe house or two that he's not using right now."

"You've already got him supplying us weapons—something for which he could be cashiered, I should add."

"So, what's your point, then, Mick? If he's gonna get shit-canned for slipping us a few guns, what the fuck's a safe house or two?"

Mick looked at me, incredulous. "I have to admit, Dick, you have the biggest bloody pair of solid brass balls I've ever come across."

I gave him the trademark Rogue Warrior® grin. "Yeah—but they come in handy."

I guess he took me seriously, because that's the way he looked. "Oh?"

"Hell, yes. I can dive without ever having to use a fucking weight belt. What about you, asshole?"

CHAPTER

12

MICK AND I *treffed*[41] WITH ROBERT EVERS, AS THE GERMANS MIGHT say, at the Gran Café Tortoni, a fin-de-siècle restaurant on the Avenida de Mayo a few blocks from the Casa Rosada—Argentina's presidential residence. We left the Étoile and walked past La Biela, pausing just long enough to admire the *Porteñas*, then walked down to the Avenida del Libertador, took a circuitous route that passed through the Bullrich shopping center to make sure we weren't being followed, ambled around the Casa Rosada and meandered through the Parque Colon, wandered past the majestic Estado Mayor and Ministry of Defense, cut back across the Plaza de Mayo, walked down into and up out of the subway station across from the presidential palace, and finally marched three long blocks to the rococo entrance of the Gran Café Tortoni.

It was like walking into a time warp. Outside, it was the twenty-first century. Inside, it was Toulouse-Lautrec's Paris. The Tortoni had dark walls chockablock filled with paintings that ranged from Degas-style cartoons in ornate gilt frames, to large

---

[41] Kraut spook-talk for a covert rendezvous.

abstractionist oils. The floors were marble, polished and worn by more than a century of *Porteño* shoes coming and going. A huge, ornately carved service bar dominated the port side of the long, narrow restaurant. There were impressive, rectangular Tiffany glass skylights and brass-and-glass chandeliers from which golden light emanated. The conversation level was loud enough so that, despite the fact that the café had opened up its front windows and expanded onto the sidewalk, by the time you got fifteen feet inside, the street sounds had been completely overwhelmed by cross-talk.

The place was an eavesdropper's nightmare. It was packed to the gills, and the decibel level was somewhere between vacuum cleaner and lawn mower. Small, round, or rectangular marble-topped tables were crowded with groups of animated Argentines. White-aproned waiters carrying small black trays slalomed heedlessly to and fro. There were clumps of earnest dot.com businessmen working the cellular phones. There were groups of nattily clad politicians cutting into steaks and sipping *vino tinto*. Ink-stained wretches—old-fashioned journalists—worked their sources, taking notes as they leaned across the table in order to hear anything, nonwriting hand cupped to their ear as they tried to make out over the din what they were being told. Over by the service bar a pair of paint-speckled artists shook their fists in each other's faces as they loudly argued aesthetics. A single elderly man dressed in a 1940s three-piece suit, boiled shirt, narrow black necktie, and gray flannel spats was a solitary note of calm in this chaotic cosmos. Sparse silver hair pomaded flat against his skull, he pored, lips moving as he read, over a carefully folded newspaper, a single, half-finished cup of espresso on the table in front of him.

Mick and I progressed down the narrow, bustling aisle between tables. Finally I saw Robert Evers waving at us from a corner table in the rear. We joined him at a two-foot, round marble table with a wrought iron pedestal base, adjacent to the wall separating the main dining room from an area containing six billiard tables and more than two dozen boisterous players. Evers had a Campari soda sitting in front of him in a tall glass. It looked so good I ordered one myself. Mick, ever the Brit, ordered a pair of draft beers.

Evers wore a variation on the diplomatic uniform once again. This time it was gray houndstooth, a white Turnbull and Asser shirt, and a *blue* tie that told me he was a member of the Naval and Military Club of London. He inclined his glass in Mick's and my direction and said, "Cheers."

We returned the greeting. Evers waited until the waiter serving our drinks had come and gone. Then he leaned toward Mick and me.

"You're lucky you didn't visit Misiones Province," he said.

"Oh?"

"The very people you were interested in finding returned to Buenos Aires last night." The Brit sipped his Campari, then returned it to the table. "They flew into a small private airport in the delta. Six hours later, they rendezvoused with a small river boat, the *Patricia Desens.*"

"Small?"

"Sixty, maybe seventy feet," Evers said. "There are hundreds and hundred of these little craft on the rivers. They carry fruit or vegetables, and they're rumored to make extra money by smuggling."

"Rumored."

"That's what they say."

"Where's the *Patricia Desens* now?"

"It tied up to the dock at that villa Gwilliam's Colombian friend bought for about eight hours. Then it disappeared into the delta."

"How do you know all of this," I asked.

Robert Evers's body language told me loud and clear not to proceed any further.

I shrugged. Hell, I can take yes for an answer as well as anybody.

There was a momentary silence. Then Evers blurted, "The political situation where I work is not very good." He sipped his drink and continued in a low voice. "I am virtually prevented from doing my job. My chief tells me continually he does not want me poking my nose in areas that could prove, as he calls them, embarrassing for Her Majesty's government. But you see, there are areas of concern that I believe should be addressed. Since I cannot deal with these problems, I was hoping that perhaps you would get the job done."

What Evers was telling me made perfect sense. After all, over the past two decades, MI6 has become as toothless as the CIA. Like the CIA's Directorate of Operations, or DO, MI6 now eschews risk-taking and audacity. Just like the Agency considers political correctness when it collects information for the president, MI6 now skews its information to the political views of the prime minister. Like the CIA, it has been corrupted. And Evers didn't like that, so he was helping us out.

Abruptly, the British spook changed the subject. "By the by," he said, "the license plate Mister Owen called about earlier was stolen just over two weeks ago."

If I'd needed formal confirmation that the *pasaperro* eyeballing the embassy was a tango, the fact that he had a stolen license plate on his van made it official. I rapped the table with my knuckles. "I'd be willing to bet that the Mrs. Kelley's franchise owns a brown van."

"You'd be right," Evers said. "Very similar to the one you described to Mr. Owen, too."

In my book, friends, one and one equals two.

I looked at Evers. "I owe you a big one, Robert."

He looked at me with his gray eyes, trying to read where I was going. "I'll just hold the chit for now, Mister Marcinko," he said warily.

"That's a good idea, Robert, because you're going to be holding a lot more of 'em by the end of this lunch."

• • •

Young Robert Evers could have been a SEAL, because he may not have liked it, but he did it anyway. Later in the afternoon we checked out of the Étoile, and after we ran an SDR, or Surveillance Detection Route and came up clean, he installed us in a safe house in the Belgrano district, about fifteen minutes by car northwest of the American Embassy.

It was a comfortable place—four bedrooms, a big living room, and a decent kitchen—on the fifth floor of a narrow, eight-story apartment house. It had a huge terrace that looked out southeast across the huge Palermo golf club and beyond it, the Río de la Plata. Four blocks away, Evers said, drawing us a map, was an MI6 car with local plates, parked in a locked garage. He looked at the happy expression on my face and then pointedly handed the keys to Mick.

But best of all, the safe house came . . . furnished. There were six Glock Model 19, 9-mm pistols, each with two fifteen-round magazines, sitting on the couch, along with four Heckler & Koch machine pistols and twelve twenty-round magazines of a type I'd never seen before, and two detachable Gem-Tech suppressors. Robert Evers explained that the machine pistols had been delivered to the embassy for evaluation as side arms for the military drivers and bodyguards, and he'd managed to get his hands on them because no one in the mil-group office had the time to take 'em out and do any field testing, so they'd been sitting gathering dust. On each receiver was stamped the letters PDW—for Personal Defense Weapon.

I picked up one of the machine pistols. It was very light—less than four pounds, including a permanently illuminated holographic Trijicon sight. I made sure the weapon was empty by dropping the flush-fit, double-stack magazine out of the grip handle, locking the ambidextrous bolt back, and then doing a visual and physical examination of the receiver and chamber. Then I pulled the retractable stock out, locked it in place, and fitted the weapon to my shoulder. It was a wee bit small, but still comfortable. The iron sights were big and clear—and so was the holographic sight. I liked the fact that I could use either one. The trigger was smooth. I hefted the pistol in my hand. It was actually only a couple of inches longer in length—and a shitload lighter in weight—than the .45-cal MK-23 SOCOM (Special Operations COMmand) pistol built for SEAL and Special Forces clandestine ops.

"What the hell do these things shoot?" I asked Evers.

"Four point six by thirty-millimeter rounds." he said.

I don't like peashooters, and 4.6 x 30 falls under that category. "What are the ballistics?"

"I'm not altogether sure," he said. "The bullet weight is 29 grains. From what the armorer told me, the muzzle velocity is just over twenty-three hundred feet per second." He paused. "Whatever that means."

What that meant was that the PDW was only a couple of hundred feet of velocity behind the current M4 carbine carried by most SpecOps troops. And the machine pistol in my hand weighed about one-third of what an M4 weighs. "Let's see the ammo."

The MI6 officer eased a trio of cardboard cartons from under the couch. "Take a look."

There was one carton labeled 115-grain NATO ball 9-mm, and two with no markings whatsoever except a stamp that read: MADE IN THE UK. I slit the first of the anonymous containers, pulled a box of cartridges out, and opened it up. The round was made of solid copper, with a classic hollowpoint tip. The second carton was filled with ball ammo: hardened copper-projectiles. The spec sheet said the ball ammo would penetrate a NATO-spec (trauma) plate at two hundred meters. That's impressive ballistics for such a tiny round.

I looked at Evers. "I guess shooting this is kind of like firing a twenty-two caliber on steroids, right?"

Robert Evers shrugged. "I wouldn't know," he said. "I've never fired a handgun in my life. My experience is limited to shotgunning at partridge and pheasant on the weekends."

I closed the stock, flipped the front hand grip back, and hefted the PDW as if it were a pistol. It was a little ungainly, but far more balanced than the MK-23 SOCOM handgun. I fitted one of the suppressors to the end of the stubby barrel and dry-fired the weapon. It handled nicely.

Let me phrase that in a slightly different way. It handled nicely in the living room of a safe house with no ammunition and Mister Murphy kept at a safe distance. How it would handle in the field, under sphincter-puckering conditions when the adrenaline was pumping and the weapon had been carried underwater in the muddy delta, I had no idea. Because those were the approximate conditions under which the PDW would have to prove itself.

Normally, I would have preferred a battle-proven MP5, or a CAR-16, to this new, untested gun. And I would have liked USPs, not Glocks. But I was the supplicant here, and beggars can't be choosers. Besides, let me tell you a truth about Warriors: Warriors consider weapons as their tools. And frankly, it really doesn't matter what kind of hammer you use to drive a nail—just so long as you know the proper technique for nail driving. The same theory goes for weapons, too. I may prefer HKs. But I will use whatever I come across to get the job done.

Finally, Robert Evers provided us with a few nuggets of tactical intelligence before he left. Gwilliam Kelley and his VERB had checked out of the Hyatt and moved into the villa near Tigre. The *Patricia Desens*, the shallow-draft riverboat that Robert's agents had lost track of, had been spotted a few hours ago, making its way back up the river toward the house where Gwilliam was now staying.

Evers flattened out a detailed commercial map of the Tigre delta and marked the location of Gwilliam's villa with a Montblanc ballpoint. It certainly was isolated. A narrow dirt road, no doubt built on a berm above the brackish water, led from the house about half a mile northeast, ending on the two-lane highway that meandered from west to east traversing the delta.

The rear of the house backed up on a wide tributary that ran roughly north/south. I knew that we had to insert quietly and take a look-see. I wanted to know what, if anything, was aboard the *Patricia Desens*. I wanted to discover what Gwilliam might be hiding in his villa. So, I stared at the map, war-gaming insertions and extractions. It didn't take long for me to put a couple of scenarios together.

After the MI6 officer departed, Mick closed the door and threw the bolt. "So," he said, "what's on your mind?"

I studied the map of the delta some more, then pointed toward the weapons on the couch. "I think they need a little practical field evaluation. Robert claims that the suppressors work wet and dry, and that the PDWs won't jam even if you swim 'em in to a target. I say we make sure he's right."

• • •

We left shortly after dark. Mick went and got the car; Boomerang, Rotten Randy, Hugo, Timex, and I waited just inside the tiny, sweltering lobby, each of us holding a bag of equipment. The load-in didn't take very long—although by the time we squeezed the six of us into the fucking vehicle it probably looked like one of those tiny circus cars out of which twenty clowns tumble. Within a few minutes, we were moving northeast on a wide boulevard lined with tall apartment buildings, heading toward the six-lane expressway that would carry us through the bedroom suburbs of San Isidro and the outer suburb of San Fernando, all the way to Tigre.

The car, an ancient four-door Fiat, had more than local plates. It had the kind of Latin American, Third World air-conditioning known as four-seventy air. That means you open four windows and go seventy miles an hour and maybe you get cool. I hoped that would be the case, because even with the sun down, it was still in the eighties, with the kind of pervasive humidity common to tropical climates.

We sat in silence, staring out the window as Mick drove. I realized that as we progressed from the center of the city, the gestalt of the landscape changed. The suburb of San Isidro resembled in many ways the upper-class suburbs of Paris or Madrid. But as we moved farther north, the First World gave way to the Second, and then the Third. The roads grew narrow. By the northern end of San Fernando, concrete had been replaced by asphalt. By the time we were nine kliks past Tigre's *mercado de frutos,* the asphalt gave way to dark, pocked macadam. And by the time we left the old two-lane highway and turned north onto a rough, gravel track that ran parallel to the Río Lujan, we were in a place that more closely resembled the Fourth World fringes of San Salvador or San José, Costa Rica, than the suburbs of Paris or Madrid.

The gravel road dead-ended in a T-shaped intersection. I used a red-lensed waterproof flashlight to chart our position on the map Robert Evers had given me. I tapped Mick on the shoulder and pointed left, toward a narrow one-lane dirt road that I hoped ran parallel to the river. "We should be able to drive about a mile—maybe just a little more—in that direction."

"And then?"

"And then we walk."

Mick grunted. He eased the Fiat to port. He switched the headlights off so we wouldn't be seen. "Done and done."

It was just after 2100 when Mick pulled into a ragged clearing half a mile from the end of any road, and—we hoped—roughly two hundred yards from the riverbank. Mick turned off the ignition and we sat in the damn car for fifteen minutes in absolute silence, so that we got used to the sounds of our new environment, and our environment got used to us.

Then—slowly and silently and not before we'd made sure that the interior dome light had been turned off—we exited the car, opened the trunk, and started to pull out our equipment. Only Boomerang, Rotten, Timex, and I would make the river crossing. Mick and Hugo would stake out this bank of the Lujan, protecting our six with two of the PDWs, and sweeping the area with the one set of commercial-grade night-vision goggles Hugo had found at a sporting goods store.

I have to admit that our assault was pretty sparse. We'd managed to buy masks and fins, but we had no SEAL vests or CQC load-bearing equipment. We had thick nylon belts, on which we'd hung the diving knives Boomerang had bought us. Tonight, we'd forgo the fins—no need for 'em on an op like this one, although each two-man team would pack masks, just in case. I've been on too many ops where you just know you'll never need a certain item, and then guess what—the one thing you left behind is the one thing you need the most. And so, we'd pack the masks. Rotten Randy and I would do the swim with the suppressed PDWs strapped to our backs. The Glock pistols, all the spare magazines, and everything else we might need would travel in nylon knapsacks carried by Boomerang and Timex.

The situation was far from ideal. We had no wet suits, or coral booties either. Instead, we'd swim in jeans and dark sweatshirts. You say that sounds cumbersome; bulky; unwieldy, and therefore dangerous. You are 100 percent correct. But it would be even more dangerous for us to try to make our assault at night—in this bright moonlight—while exposing large areas of our, how-can-I-put-this-succinctly . . . lily white skin. To complete our sneak & peek outfits, my guys would swim in tennis shoes. Yes, they'd probably be squishy once they reached the opposite shoreline. But that was the hand we'd been dealt, and that was the hand we were gonna play. Me, I'd go barefoot. Those of you who know me know that the soles of my size extra-extra-Rogue feet are just as hard as any fucking Vibram hiking boot sole. They got that way when I was in prison, because I ran two miles barefoot every day on the six-laps-to-the-mile cinder track at the Petersburg, Virginia, Federal Boys' Camp and Mayoral Blow-Job facility. Sure, my feet bled the first month. But I just ran through the pain and the soles finally toughened up. That's the Warrior's Way, my friends.

We took our own damn time making preparations. First of all, there was no requirement to be in and out by any specific hour, although I certainly wanted to be long gone by the time the sun came up. And second, we were operating blind tonight. We had no up-to-the-minute tactical intel, except the nugget or two Robert Evers had told us about the crew of imported gunsels guarding the villa, and the lack of cameras. Let me tell you, gentle reader, that operating under such conditions often leads to what we SEALs refer in Naval Special Warfare technical terms as a C2, or clusterfuck condition.

Huh? What's that? You say you think ops like this are POCs.[42]

Hey, fuck you: strong message follows. I am the Rogue Warrior®. I know about this shit and you do not. Now sit the fuck down, shut the fuck up, and let me explain the C2 possibilities.

C2-1. The body of water that must be crossed is infested with alligators, who tend to think of SEALs as a basic food group.

C2-2. The opposition has night-vision equipment, and they see you coming before you see them.

C2-3. The opposition has taken precautions against maritime ops and strung up a series of nasty booby traps in the water.

C2-4. There are animals and/or other protection devices loose around your target. For example, there could be dogs in the compound. Worse, there could be geese. Geese are among the most effective protection devices known to man. They raise a horrendous ruckus whenever any strange creature approaches. More than a quarter century ago, the VC used geese as early warning systems when SEALs were staging snatch ops in Vietnam. The geese were more effective than guard dogs, because they sensed the SEALs approaching at a greater distance and were much harder to silence.

---

[42] Pieces Of Cake.

C2-5. Mister Murphy could show his ugly puss by ensuring that just as we made it to the dock, one of the local guards decided it was time to wander down the dock and drain the old *lagarto*[43] in the lagoon, or flick his *cigarillo* into the water.

C2-6. Oh, fuck—you get the idea. Besides, it's actually getting late, which means it's time to move out already.

• • •

We made our way about 180 yards from the clearing down to the riverbank. Mick swept the opposite bank with his night vision, then looked south, then frowned. He offered me the glasses. "Take a look."

I peered downstream. I didn't need his night-vision glasses, either. That's because less than a quarter mile downriver of where we lurked, and not more than a hundred yards below the tributary where we'd pass in order to get to Gwilliam's villa, was a fucking guest house cum restaurant cum bed & breakfast. They were currently serving dinner on the veranda, which was strung with festive lights and which, of course, overlooked the tributary's waters. Right past where we would be swimming. There is an old SEAL rule of thumb that says, "If they can see you then you are fucked." Well, they *would* see us, if we made any kind of a disturbance while making our infiltration. They'd see us because we would have to swim directly under the brightly lit veranda on our way in, and also during our exfiltration. It was yet another C2 factor to consider.

As they used to say at SAS, buggers can't be choosers. And so, Mick shrugged, gave me an upturned thumb and mouthed, "Happy landings, mate."

I tapped his shoulder. "Oh, and fuck you very much, too, Mick." Then, parting the saw grass, I eased down the bank and

---

[43] Spanish for *lizard.*

slid into the water. Oh, fuck me. The water was only about sixty-eight or so. That was a lot cooler than I'd expected. In fact, you can get hypothermia in sixty-eight-degree water if you remain in it long enough and the air temperature drops. But that didn't bother me. SEALs do not approach the water and test it with their tippy-toes. SEALs do not complain about cold water. SEALs JUST DO IT. And so, I eased down the bank and slipped into the river, my nuts shriveling appropriately as I went.

The bottom was soft mud. Soft, oozy mud. Nasty, soft, oozy mud. I pushed off as best I could and started moving across the dark water with a slow, steady sidestroke, my head low and my eyes on the opposite shoreline. Boomerang, Timex, and Randy followed me into the water and swam behind in a ragged formation.

There wasn't much of a current—only a half a knot or so. But given the fact that we were all being weighted down by what we carried and what we wore, swimming across any kind of current was a chore. I let the water carry me downstream, cutting against it to take me to the far side of the Lujan, so I'd be as far away as possible from the diners on the hotel veranda.

2142. I swam slowly and deliberately, keeping my right arm under the surface of the water as much as I could. It wasn't as effective as a real sidestroke, but it kept the water movement to a minimum. We would pass within eighty or ninety feet of the hotel. I could already make out the pinpoint lights of the candles on the tables, and hear the music.

2149. I stroked carefully past the veranda. The lanterns were festive. I could hear the murmur of conversation—or thought I could. Oh, yeah: the tables were filled with couples and four-somes, all of them drinking wine, eating good food, and looking forward to a late night that would culminate in endless nookie.

And then there was me. Cold, wet, and suffering from terminal lack o'pussy. My friends, there is no fairness in life.

2156. A hundred yards past the hotel, I increased the pace of my stroke and made good time as I swam up the tributary. I slowed once to check up on the rest of my crew. Once I saw them strung out behind me, I resumed my steady sidestroking.

2212. About a half klik of swimming later, I pulled up and treaded water. Perhaps a 150 yards ahead, on the port-side bank, I could make out a long wooden dock rising out of the water. Above it ambient light from Gwilliam's villa punctuated the darkness. The villa was the only structure on the tributary.

I'd already decided that we would attempt a two-pronged approach tonight. Boomerang and I would swim to the dock and probe the house from there. Rotten and Timex would swim past the dock and check things out from the far—which is to say the eastern—side. Now I waited for the rest of the team. We formed up and continued our infil, keeping close to the riverbank so that we could use the thorn brush, marsh grass, palmettos, and mangrove to conceal our approach.

2218. Eighty yards upstream, the dock lay ahead of me. But there was more. Just as promised, a riverboat was berthed to the far side of the long wooden structure. It looked like one of the hundreds of small craft that plied the Río Parana all the way north past the city of Rosario, eight hundred miles north to Misiones Province, or churned the waters between Argentina and Uruguay on the Río de la Plata. The boat was about sixty-five, maybe seventy feet long, and from the look of its silhouette, it pulled a draft of no more than a yard. The small, raised wheelhouse was aft, connected to a kind of shack, which is probably where the captain slept and ate. The rest of the bargelike deck was reserved for cargo—and cargo there was: even in the dark I could see a tarp covering a pile of something. I swam closer so I could make things out more clearly. Three small hatch covers lay atop the shallow hold. Atop two of them, a pair of tarps had been laid over something, then tied down tightly.

The running lights—one atop the small single mast, another atop the wheelhouse, and two more to port and starboard about amidships—were all extinguished. There was no glow emanating from the single window of the shack behind the wheelhouse. I listened carefully for the sound of a generator. I heard nothing. This craft was unoccupied.

2221. Fifteen yards in front of my Roguish snout I sensed movement. I froze in the water. A lone security guard, a pistol jammed in his belt and an Uzi on a sling over his shoulder, walked down to the edge of the dock and flicked a cigarette into the water. As it hit, the hiss was surprisingly loud. But then, all sounds seem to be amplified at night. I watched as the guard checked the boat, then ambled back up the dock and disappeared from sight through a curtain of vegetation.

Thank God for ambient light, and for unprofessional security assholes who wear light-colored clothes at night. At least for the moment, Mister Murphy was screwing with the opposition instead of fucking with me.

2223. Boomerang and I treaded water under the dock while Rowdy and Timex swam behind the riverboat and kept moving upstream. We would link up in two hours under the dock, and exfil as a unit. I let them have three minutes to work their way toward their positions, then I began my own evening's fun & games.

I slid my arm into Boomerang's knapsack, grabbed my diving mask, washed the silt out of it, and snapped the rubber band tight under my French braid. Then I retrieved the waterproof flashlight and looped its lanyard around my wrist. First things first: I dove under the riverboat and examined its hull, to see if there was anything attached. It's an old UDT caching trick to build a small watertight compartment on the outside of a boat's hull and use it to carry contraband or anything else you don't want most folks knowing about. This was not fun. It was painstaking work, especially in the dark; especially because noise discipline had to be maintained. Even so, it took me less than five minutes to resolve that this riverboat's hull was clean.

Well, "clean" is an overstatement. The boat appeared to be in fair overall shape at best. The cabin siding was rotted in places, there were rust spots on the metal, and the exterior wood needed a lot of attention. I surfaced, took in fresh air, then went under again and used the waterproof flashlight to check the prop and rudder area. The prop had recently been replaced. It, and what I could see of the shaft, were well maintained. That, too, is an old Warrior's trick: you keep your craft in shitty cosmetic shape, and the world underestimates you.

I silent-signaled Boomerang to start a pattern search on the downstream side of the dock. While he did that, I swam to the stern, pulled myself up on the old tire that partially obscured the boat's name—it was indeed the *Patricia Desens*, and its home port was Santa Elena—and eased my way over the low railing onto the stern, just behind the shack's narrow louvered wood door.

What I wanted to do was to check the wheelhouse. I wanted to see if the *Patricia Desens* had any state-of-the-art communications or global positioning equipment. I wanted to check its charts and see if I could determine where it had been and where it might be going. Then I'd creep forward and examine whatever was concealed beneath the tarps. But between me and everything else was that ramshackle ramshack, and it is a hard-and-fast rule that one does not go past an unsecured area without checking it first.

So, first things first. From the position of the hinges, the door opened outward, pulling from starboard to port. I tested the doorknob. It was not locked. I eased the door open c-a-r-e-f-u-l-l-y, and maneuvered myself inside.

The space was tight, and it smelled of stale sweat, old beer, and piss. To my left, I could make out a dim shape in the darkness—a bunk, maybe, or a low cabinet. I hit the switch on the red-lensed flashlight to take a closer look.

Which, of course, is when the captain of the *Patricia Desens* awoke because he'd sensed someone invading his space. He lurched into a sitting position with a confused *"¿Que pasa?"*

I wouldn't want to take bets on which one of us was the more startled. But the difference between *el capitán* and *mí*, was that my reaction time was a lot faster than his, no doubt because he'd recently polished off the empty rum bottle that lay beside his dirty pillow.

Instinctively, I snapped my right arm out and hit him— *whaaap!*—with a jab that caught him right on the point of his jaw. The blow sent his head slapping back against the bulkhead of the shack, and my fucking fist waving lamely in the stale air like that old Italian guy going *"Mama mia* thatsa spicy meatball" in the Alka-Seltzer® commercial. Geezus H. Keerist, I'd jammed my hand against the asshole's jaw, and the pain shot from wrist through elbow and shoulder, right up behind my now-crossed eyes.

But pain be damned, it was a perfect punch. *El capitán* dropped neatly back onto his bunk, unconscious. It had all gone perfectly. Except, of course, for the fact that my left hand was now sending distinct SOS signals to my brain. Oh shit oh damn oh fuck that *hurt.* And why the hell hadn't I just smacked him with the flash-light? Hey, if you don't ask, I won't tell.

But I wasn't about to spend precious seconds hurting. I looked around for something to secure him with. I cut a length of rope from a coil at the stern and tied him down. I ripped a square of fabric off his pillowcase and stuffed it into his mouth, and then used more strips of the pillowcase to secure the gag in place. All of which took longer than you might think because I basically didn't have the use of my left hand.

2229. I searched the wheelhouse. There was a state-of-the-art radio transceiver, as well as a pair of global-capable satellite cellular phones. I checked the chart locker but came up with nothing. On a small oilcloth-covered table was a chart the captain had been working on. I gave it a QOO.[44] It was a pilotage chart of the Río de la Plata and the Uruguayan coast. I directed my flashlight onto

---

[44] (Pronounced *KOO*): Quick Once-Over.

the sheet of waterproofed paper. A course had been set—a thick line of red grease pencil zigged and zagged toward the little port town of Punta del Este, which sat on the tip of a peninsula about thirty miles east of Montevideo, Uruguay. I knew about the place: it was a high-class beach resort. The kind of thousand-buck-a-day hotel where you find Eurotrash like Gwilliam and his VERBs. I folded the chart and stuck it in the rear left pocket of my soggy jeans. I took everything else I could lay my hands on and stashed the booty in a blue plastic pail, which I left on the *Patricia Desens*'s stern, to be picked up later. Then I began a systematic search for cargo.

It didn't take long. Oh, sure, I went below, checked the coffer-dams for explosives, and found nothing. And I made a cursory search of the small cargo area in the forecastle. And I checked the line locker and found nothing but line. No, what I was looking for was right in plain sight: resting atop the hatch covers under that pair of old tarps.

How did I know what I was looking for? It is because I am a professional, and I know bad shit when I see it. And in this case, the bad shit was a pair of sealed cylinders, each about twenty feet long and two feet in diameter, and each marked with the same two Arabic numerals—38—painted in white on the dark plastic.

I can't read much Arabic, but I can understand Arabic numerals. 38 stands for *Talateen tamanya*. Thirty-eight.

And even though I've never taken the DIA's crateology course I knew damn well what I was looking at: a pair of missiles. Precisely what kind of missiles they might be, I didn't know—the number thirty-eight sounded familiar, but for the life of me I couldn't put a missile designation to it. That's right: even the Rogue Warrior® isn't omniscient all the time. Besides, I wasn't about to take the time to find out.

Later, after we'd checked the villa, come back aboard, hijacked the boat, and had the *Patricia Desens* all to ourselves, we'd open up the cylinders and see what specific model missile Gwilliam had bought. We'd spend some time interrogating the captain, too.

2239. But there was no time to ponder hypotheticals. I was already way behind the schedule I kept in my head. So, I slipped back over the side to see if Boomerang had come up with anything else.

The answer is that he hadn't. I gave him the flashlight, then pulled a lightweight, twenty-four-foot line from the bag on his back and started my own pattern search on the upstream side, using the pilings and the *Patricia Desens* as my reference points.

2234. Nothing. I unhitched my guideline, surfaced, moved a dozen feet toward the shoreline, attached the line to another piling, and started all over again from ground zero. Again, I found nothing.

2250. I struck gold on my third pattern search. Tied to the base of the piling, beneath three inches of mud, was a hefty piece of line. I tested it and discovered resistance on the other end. I untied my own lightweight search line, then used the taut line, covered with delta goo and muck, to guide myself upstream, feeling gingerly as I went. I didn't want to hit a trip wire or a booby trap, so I proceeded inch by inch up the line until I finally felt a knot. I ran my fingers over the knot and then, carefully, beyond it—and discovered that the line had been tied to a heavy plastic crate that was half buried in the muck and goo of the river bottom. I surfaced, and grabbed some air. Forty feet away, I saw Boomerang's narrow face in the ambient moonlight. I waved him over to my position.

We spoke using our hands. Boomerang had discovered two more waterproof crates tied to one of the pilings on the downstream side of the dock. I silent-signaled about what I'd found. I added that I was going back to take another look-see. He slipped the red-lensed diving light's lanyard over my wrist.

We both dove into the ten-foot-deep water of the channel. When I reached the crate, I hit the switch on the light. I used the flashlight so he could see my hand signals. He lifted the crate off the bottom, and the two of us swam it back toward the dock.

I muscled my way back onto the stern of the *Patricia Desens*. Then Boomerang handed me the crate we'd carried back and I carefully laid it on the deck. He retrieved the other two crates he'd found, handed them up to me, and I laid them gently on the decking.

Why not open 'em up now? Because later, I'd have all the time in the world—something I didn't have now. Remember: once we'd finished our recon at the villa, we'd slip back aboard, untie the mooring lines, and drift downstream. Then, once we'd put some distance between us and the dock, I'd start the engine and we'd make off with all of Gwilliam's goodies—and doom on him.

I checked my watch again. 2320. Shit—sore wrist or no, it really *was* time for us to go to work.

CHAPTER

13

BOOMERANG AND I MADE OUR WAY ALONG THE PILINGS AND WORKED our way onto the shoreline, progressing slowly and deliberately, searching for sensors or trip wires and careful to leave no trail. Even though the night air was warm, we were thoroughly chilled through by almost an hour and a half in the water. Well, guess what: cold is just a sensation, and like all sensations, it, too, would pass. And if not, it didn't fucking matter—we'd finish our work no matter how cold we were.

It was time to DAC,[45] so we split up. I melted into the underbrush on the port, or western, side of the path, while Boomerang worked his way up the eastern—starboard—edge. I made my way slowly, a few inches at a time, careful to stay well away from the wide gravel swath that led toward the walled villa fifty yards away. I hadn't progressed eight yards from the dock when it hit me: a thick, sweet scent, wafting down along the ground toward the water. I stopped moving and waited, all my senses keened, trying to identify the perfumed smell.

---

[45] Divide And Conquer.

And then I realized what it was: it was men's cologne. Sickly sweet men's cologne. And there was a *señor*, nearby, who was wearing it. It was immediately obvious to me that his name was Señor Brut, and he was somewhere very, very close by, waiting to ambush me.

Now, you might ask why someone who was about to spring an ambush would ever douse himself with cologne in the first place. That is a good question, but it betrays a certain cultural naïveté on your part. I will explain. In some societies, and the populations of many countries in South America are among them, cologne is worn by some men all the time. The group in question includes even soldiers in combat and cops on duty. Maybe they don't realize that the opposition can actually smell 'em coming. Maybe they don't give a shit. Maybe, since everyone is wearing cologne, they realize that all those smells just merge, and no one knows if the odor he's sniffing is friendly or unfriendly.

But let me assure you, it is always easy for *moi* to locate a platoon of Venezuelan commandos hidden in ambush, or a SWAT team of Brazilian cops setting up a stealthy, clandestine approach to take down a house of no-goodniks, even in the thickest part of the upper Amazon basin or the nastiest stretch of São Paulo's urban jungle. Why? The answer is, because so many shooters are wearing Canoe, Habit Rouge, Obsession, or similar potent scents. And those . . . odors precede them by some eight or nine yards, or sometimes even greater distances than that.

It's actually quite self-defeating: the teams use camouflage to make themselves invisible; they darken their faces so they won't reflect light at night; they wear the ever-popular jungle camouflage, or ninja black, BDUs so they will blend in with their surroundings. And then they douse themselves with fucking perfume.

I think it is dangerous. I believe it is a grooming habit that can get you killed. Which is why I do not allow my men to wear any kind of scent whatsoever. Ever. In the units under my command, all perfumed soaps, fragrant unguents, aromatic aftershaves, and other senseless perfumery are *Zutritt verboten*.[46] So much for the Rogue's theory of scent-based warfare. And now, let's get back to real time.

2324. I froze exactly where I was, and listened. It took half a minute, but then I heard Señor Brut breathing. He was obviously a heavy smoker who therefore couldn't draw a lot of air into his lungs noiselessly. He wheezed. And that—along with his cologne—is how I was able to find him.

I followed my nose and my ears, moving grass blade by grass blade as silent as a jaguar or Bengal tiger in hunting mode. Yes, I am a big man. But I can move my rippled muscle mass without making a sound, and that is what I did. Stalked the sonofabitch in the darkness just like a big, stealthy cat, until I was close enough to see him.

It was indeed the cigarette smoker I'd seen on the dock earlier. Now, he was kneeling in a kind of low, *camuflaje*[47] duck blind affair, with his suppressed Uzi muzzle pointed over the top of it directed toward the path, giving him a wide and relatively unobstructed field of fire. But he wasn't alert. He wasn't in Condition Red. Hell—he wasn't even in condition yellow. The gun was still slung over his left shoulder. His right hand and arm rested lazily over the wooden stock of the weapon, his finger indexed along the trigger guard.

But he obviously had heard something: his attention was directed toward the opposite side of the path. That, of course, was where Boomerang was working his way toward the villa.

I watched. Señor Brut shifted his position slightly to give himself a better view over the top of his blind. That gave me the opportunity to move another two feet closer. Then, finally, he

---

[46] Off limits.
[47] I think you can figure out this Spanish word for yourself.

upped his threatcon from alpha to bravo, raising the Uzi, bringing it up toward his shoulder. But he was now doing what so many unschooled gunsels do: he was tunneling. His cone of vision, indeed, all of his audio/visual concentration was completely focused on Boomerang—a spread of no more than twenty degrees. Which meant, of course, that he was excluding every iota of sensory perception from the other 340 degrees around him. He was paying no attention at all to *moi*. So, of course Señor Brut didn't sense my presence until it was far too late for him to do much about it. He kind of turned, wide-eyed and surprised, but by that time I was on him.

First things first: I wrestled the Uzi out of his grasp. Suppressed or not, I didn't want his fingers impulsively squeezing the damn thing's trigger and sending a burst of full-auto who-knew-where. I twisted, and the subgun came loose from his grip. But I couldn't get the sling from around his neck. Why? Because Señor Brut was in reality a brute Señor, a wiry little man who was all muscle and no body fat at all, and despite the fact that I outweighed him by a hundred pounds or so he fought hard and he was determined to do me as much damage as I was about to do him.

We rolled around, which jammed the PDW strapped to my back directly into my kidneys and didn't do me much good at all. So I popped him in the face, breaking his nose. He snorted blood at me and tried to make a snack of my left ear. I returned the favor. Then, from somewhere out of left field, the edge of his right hand came up and caught me like a hammer right in the Adam's apple. I choked and couldn't get any air. And he took advantage: he bit and clawed and kicked and kneed as best he could. And then, he started to open his mouth. I knew what he was up to: he was going to call for reinforcements.

I couldn't let that happen. I slapped my hand over his lips— which is when the cockbreath bit me. Bit me good. I was gonna have to get a goddamn rabies shot after this evening's festivities.

Fuck. Enough was enough. I rolled atop him and smashed his

larynx with my forearm. His eyes went wide when he realized he was about to die, and he struggled even harder against the pressure of my body and my momentum. But it was too little, too late. I kept crushing until I'd choked off all his air. Then I took his head and gave it the Roguish three-sixty, listening with some satisfaction as I heard the bones separate and finally give way.

I laid him back on the ground, rolled onto my own back, and caught my breath. I thought I'd lay there for no more than a second or two, but obviously I'd been there longer—and unconscious for some of the time—because when I opened my eyes I saw Boomerang's face looking down at me.

His expression was the kind of who-gives-a-shit look caregivers bestow on the drooling, dementia-ridden denizens of nursing homes when they've just shit in their Depends.

"Had a nice nap, *Pibe*," he mouthed.

I looked up at him and let him read my lips: "Fuck you." Then I rolled over and began to frisk the corpse. I stowed Señor Brut's wallet—the name I read off his Colombian driver's license was Luis Garcia—and his pistol in Boomerang's knapsack, and handed the Uzi over, too. Then I started to move the body. I didn't want to leave him where he was. I wanted to put him under water, where he'd be harder to find.

Yes, this probably meant I wouldn't get to prowl and growl through the villa grounds as much as I'd hoped to. But I couldn't leave such obvious evidence that we'd been here. If the asshole just disappeared, there was a chance Gwilliam's people might think he'd drowned. Not much of a chance, to be sure. But it was certainly a better option than leaving Señor Brut's corpse in the bushes, where he'd most certainly be found by his *compañeros*.

0002. We went through Señor Brut's duck blind. He had it very well stocked, which told me he'd pulled all-night sentry duty and he wasn't expecting a replacement. There were binoculars, and cigarettes, and a package of sweet buns, two extra magazines for the Uzi, and two thermos jugs of sweet coffee, all set neatly by a folding canvas stool. I decided to leave everything untouched—except for the binoculars, the Uzi, and the spare mags, all of which I could certainly put to good use tonight. I handed them off, and then Boomerang helped me heft Señor Brut's corpse onto my shoulders. Carefully and, most important, quietly, I made my way down to the bank. I retrieved a five-meter length of chain from the *Patricia Desens* and wrapped Señor Brut's body in it. Then I dragged him into the water, muscled him out into midstream, and let him ease out of sight in the slow current. Then I stroked back to where Boomerang was waiting for me.

0012. We worked our way around the western side of the villa wall. The wall itself was pretty classic South American Villa: it was ten feet high, probably concrete block core reinforced by steel rebar, and faced with hand-applied stucco. At each corner, a post atop the wall held a pair of halogen floodlights focused down into the courtyard. The structure was topped with concertina wire, and shards of broken glass had been cemented into the crown of the wall to make an assault even more difficult. But not for folks like me. I simply scampered up a convenient tree, two of whose heavy limbs overhung the wall by five feet, to get a panoramic view of the compound.

Okay, okay: since this book is a novel, I don't feel bad about admitting to you that what I just said was total fiction. So, let me be completely honest. I didn't scamper. I far from scampered. I used every tired, aching muscle in my much-abused body and fought my way, foot by foot, inch by inch, centimeter by centimeter, up five or so yards of smooth bark, through thickets of unfriendly, thorny branches and razor-sharp-edged leaves.

Climbing a tree is not easy when your wrist is throbbing painfully. Nor is it easy if you do not have the right equipment, like a set of crampons, or a wide leather climbing belt and a soft rope to help you hold your position on the trunk. Climbing a tree in Argentina—where the leaves of the species of tree I happened to be climbing burned my skin every time I brushed against one of them, where the branches were filled with two-inch-long thorns that were as tough and as sharp as eight-penny nails, and where the bark was as slick as deer guts—was ANF2A, which, as you can probably guess, stands for Absofuckinglutely No Fun At All. Not to mention that my C2[48] was compounded by the fact that I was operating in hostile territory and couldn't make any noise that might lead to my discovery.

By the time I settled my weight in the tree crotch, I was fucking shaking. My face and neck were on fire from the goddamn leaves and thorns. My sweatshirt was shredded. My right hand felt like I'd just picked up a handful of white phosphorus. And my left leg? Holy shit, my left leg hurt more than my fucking right hand. I fought the nausea and the burning, and worked to get my body under control, by which I mean I forced my brain to wall off the pain and injuries, and concentrate on GETTING THE FUCKING JOB DONE.

I did a Zen breathing exercise to slow my respiration. And then I checked the rest of me, because I still had an extreme, throbbing pain in my right thigh. I ran my hands over the fabric of the jeans, found the problem, reached down, and used my right thumb and forefinger to wrench a good-size thorn out of the meat of my sartorius muscle. Oh, *that* really felt good. By which I mean I was very much alive right then.

But there was no time to celebrate life. I peered over the wall into the compound. To be honest, there wasn't much to see, but there was a lot to see. Let me explain. The rear courtyard was deserted except for three vehicles: a shiny, black Land Rover, a fifteen-foot white FedEx delivery truck, and an all-too-familiar-looking, beat-up van that was anonymously dark in the dim light, but was probably painted chocolate brown. I recognized two of those three vehicles—and so, I hope, do you.

---

[48] Remember that? It stands for Clusterfuck Condition.

Gotcha, Gwilliam.

Remember what I told you about countersurveillance? You don't? Then you are a shit-for-brains who needs to take one of those reading retention courses. But since you actually paid good money for this book I guess I'll have to repeat myself. Okay: I told you that the core of countersurveillance is a matter of staying on the edge of the observational envelope. In a nutshell, that means remembering details and never becoming complacent. Complacency is at the root of every successful terrorist operation.

I saw what Gwilliam had in mind—and so should you, by now. Every day at the same time, a FedEx truck pulled up three hundred or so yards from the front of the embassy while the driver did his paperwork. The first time that had happened, the guards probably took notice of him. And the second and third and fourth times, too. But by the third week or so, he was just another part of the scenery around the embassy grounds. The FedEx truck was simply one more element factored into the embassy's daily schedule. He had become, in fact, invisible.

That, my friends, is how real-life terrorists—the sorts of terrorists who really know their business—work. They do not act impulsively or run seat-of-the-pants ops. They understand how operations work. They gather intelligence. They do their homework. They lull you into indolence, apathy, and laziness. And then, when your guard is down, they strike. Remember: I'd told Gunny Jarriel all about the dog walker. I hadn't mentioned the Federal Express truck, because I, too, had accepted it as just another regular element of the daily grind. I had broken my own SpecWar Commandment. Even I, whose understanding of counterterrorism is second to no man's, had committed the sin of assuming.

The only thing I didn't know is how they'd hit the embassy. Even if the fucking FedEx truck was filled to the brim with explosives, it would do only minimal damage to the embassy building because of the way the place was set back from the street. Even the most powerful truck bomb does no good if you can't use the target building itself to increase the power of the explosion, and the embassy was a hundred yards from the curbside—which made it almost four hundred yards from where the truck parked every day. And I knew that they'd never shift the truck's position for the attack, because shifting it just might give the attack away to the embassy's security personnel.

Here is another factor I didn't know: was the truck in this here courtyard the same truck I'd seen at the embassy, which made the driver an accessory or a participant, or was this a substitute truck that Gwilliam and his people would use only once.

0019. There was only one way to find out. And it involved a considerable amount of pain. But first, I wanted reinforcements. I silent-signaled Boomerang, talking with my hands until he understood what I wanted and what I needed. He answered with a single up/down nod, and then disappeared into the bush. I concentrated on scoping out the villa and the rear courtyard. I didn't want us to be caught on video, or trip any motion detectors.

0024. I interrupted my eval, looked down, and saw Randy and Timex patiently standing at the base of the tree. I hadn't heard them approach, which gives you some idea about their tradecraft. I let my fingers do the talking for a few seconds. Randy nodded, then removed the lightweight line out of his knapsack, worked on it for about a minute, coiled it up, tied off the ends, and tossed the line up to me. I caught it on the second pitch. Then, the line around my neck, I inched my way out onto the thick limb, balancing myself as best I could as the springy wood moved under my weight. As I inched out, Boomerang, with Randy's PDW on his back, worked his way up the slick bark of the trunk a lot faster than I had, eased past the thorns, and settled into the crotch of the tree.

He was there by the time I'd just moved past the top of the wall and its nasty, sharp obstacles. Once clear of the razor wire and broken glass, I attached the line to the limb, tested the hitch to make sure it would hold, and then swung my body out, and down, my weight transferring to the line, on which Randy had improvised a series of climbing knots.

I lowered myself hand over hand until I stood on what the Kennedy clan of Massachusetts calls "terror firmer." As Boomerang covered me I unslung the suppressed PDW from its stowed position on my back, and adjusted the sling so the weapon could hang in a CQC position around my shoulders. I dropped to one knee, extended and locked the folding stock, and put the subgun to my shoulder in low ready position to cover Boomerang's insertion.

The courtyard was paved in patterned tile. It was perhaps seventy feet square. On the far side was a driveway, also of tile, that no doubt led to the front of the villa, the main gate, and the road. I say "no doubt" because there was no way any of these vehicles had been brought up from the dock. The path and the gate were too narrow, and the dock wouldn't support the weight of the truck.

Boomerang lowered himself onto the tile and made his PDW ready. I looked up. Rotten Randy had pulled the climbing rope back up out of sight. He was sitting in the crotch of the tree, at the base of the limb we'd dropped from, Señor Brut's silenced Uzi scanning the courtyard to give us suppressive firepower should we need it.

0028. *Show Time.* The villa was designed in the classic Spanish hacienda style. In other words, it looked something like a block-style capital letter *U,* all surrounded by a wall. There would be a front courtyard, probably gated. As you faced the *U,* straight ahead would be the house's public areas: the living room, the dining room, and maybe a library or den. The kitchen and staff quarters would be in one of the vertical members of the *U,* in the front part of the house. On the opposite side would lie the private living quarters. In haciendas, the wide, formal corridor that joins the two wings generally contains a huge foyer and a small inner courtyard, as well as the living room and dining room.

I moved quickly along the port-side of the villa, making sure not to cast any shadows, because the lights were still on in that part of the house. I made my way to a shuttered window. The lights inside were bright, but I could see nothing. I paused and listened. A group of men were talking sports and listening to a radio.

Hostiles be damned, I retreated the way I'd come, made my way past the Land Rover and all the way across the dark courtyard. In some haciendas, the rear courtyard holds a swimming pool. In this one, it was obviously where the vehicles were kept out of sight.

That meant the master suite was adjacent to the driveway. I checked, inching along foot by foot. There was a huge, double window, protected by a wrought iron grille. Behind the grille, I could see burglar-alarm sensors on the double panes. That, too, was normal for haciendas: the private wing can be completely sealed off from the rest of the house, giving the owners a secure area to retreat to. The private area is often alarmed, and entry is through a heavy steel door.

Okay, now that I had the layout in my mind, it was time to see whether I could break-and-enter. I snuck back along the driveway, made my way along the rear of the villa, and gingerly checked the French doors that led to the main corridor. The crenellated locks were all secured. I examined the locks and decided it wouldn't take much to pick 'em. Quickly and silently, I moved away from the glass doors.

Boomerang handed me his PDW, then squirmed flat on his back, checking underneath the vehicles for booby traps with the red-lensed flashlight. He pulled himself out from under the dark van, gave me an all-clear signal, and wriggled beneath the Land Rover.

Fifteen seconds later he was moving under the FedEx truck. He emerged from the far side of the vehicle, and just like Yeoman Baker in Admiral Eamon's office had done, he signaled that I was a Brazilian asshole.[49] I thanked him by returning his weapon.

---

[49] That's the old thumb-and-forefinger in a circle.

0029. The van was unlocked. So was the Land Rover. And one important question was answered as soon as I hit the courtyard. The FedEx truck turned out to be a fake. It was an old panel truck that had been painted white. The orange and purple FedEx colors and lettering had been applied in all the right places. But the paint job was recent. The truck had originally been a dark color. That was obvious the minute I got a close look at the damn thing. But real or fake, the fucking thing was locked up tight. The doors were sealed, and the rear, roll-up gate was secured by an interior lock.

Meanwhile, we checked the unsecured vehicles to make sure there were no alarm systems in place, and then searched them one by one. We opened up the Land Rover first. I went to the driver's side door, cracked it, reached inside, and turned off the interior light. Then Boomerang opened the passenger-side door and we went to work.

I slipped my hand under the driver's seat and felt around. My fingers found cold metal. I retrieved a stubby Browning double-action .380. I dropped the magazine and then ran my fingertip across the loaded-chamber indicator just aft of the ejection port. I thumbed the pistol's safety up, into the "fire" position, eased the hammer back, quietly slid the slide to the rear, ejected the chambered round, then pressed it into the magazine.

I slid the mag back up into the butt of the pistol with the heel of my palm until it seated with a *click* that was loud enough in the silence to bring a disapproving glance from Boomerang. Then I eased the slide back and chambered the first round in the mag. Holding tight, I eased the slide back just far enough to visually inspect the chambered round. Finally, careful to keep my right index finger indexed on the frame of the weapon, I held the hammer with the wounded web of my right thumb, dropped the safety with my left thumb, eased the hammer down, then manipulated the safety back up into the "fire" position. Satisfied with my efforts, I slipped the pistol into the back pocket of my jeans—it would make a nice souvenir of the night's activities—and continued my search.

Which turned out to be basically fruitless. The Land Rover contained nothing but a *plano*[50] of the Capital Federal. I was just about to ease its door shut when I felt the pistol in my pocket. I took an instant and gave the matter some thought. Then I retrieved the piece, dropped the mag, unchambered the cartridge, emptied the mag, dropped the rounds in my pocket, replaced the magazine, and set the pistol back where I'd found it.

Why did I do that? I did it because all operations are like chess games: you have to think eight, nine, ten moves ahead or you may be a dead motherfucker before your time. I did it because, on the one hand, I didn't want some fucking asshole busting out onto the patio in the middle of the night because he'd forgotten his pistol in the car, and when he found it missing he'd get suspicious. And I pocketed the cartridges because, on the other hand, if a Colombian actually *did* come bursting out onto the patio looking for his *pistola*, I didn't want the damn thing loaded and lethal to *mí* when he found it.

0032. I pressed on the Land Rover's door until the latch clicked audibly. Then Boomerang and I progressed to the van. Just as we did, a bunch of lights in the bedroom wing of the hacienda came on.

Okay, who the fuck out there just kicked the trash can over and awakened Mister Murphy? Boomerang looked at me for further instructions. My expression told him to keep on keepin' on, because it was probably just Gwilliam or his VERB taking a midnight piss-call (I hoped).

Boomerang followed the instructions I'd given him. He opened the driver's side door, turned the interior light switch off, climbed

---

[50] Spanish for *street plan.*

behind the wheel, clicked the door closed, then began his search. I cracked the rear right-hand door, pulled myself inside, and shut the door behind me. The van smelled of dogs, sweat, oil, and dust. There was a three-foot high pile of old rags—towels, mats, and other fabric detritus—through which I was rooting when the courtyard lights came on.

CHAPTER

14

WTF—HAD I MISSED ALL KINDS OF WARNING SIGNS? I GUESS I HAD, because all of a sudden it was like fucking DAYLIGHT, and yet, not a single hair had stood up on the back of my neck; no red light had gone off in my brain; no klaxon horn went *ougaa-ougaa*. Talk about having a Senior Moment (well, here in Argentina, I guess it's called a *Señor* Moment).

Looking through the grimy windshield, I could see lights coming on all over the house. And then, the French doors opened up. I ducked under a foul-smelling remnant of furniture pad. I heard machine-gun Spanish—two voices with Colombian accents told me the boss and his VERB had finally finished fucking and so it was time to move. I hoped that the travel they were talking about didn't include the van.

Boomerang snaked his long torso through the space between the front seats and just like me, burrowed into the pile of old mats. We tried like hell not to wobble the van as we worked to make ourselves invisible. Well, *almost* invisible. Our PDWs, butts collapsed, were in our hands, business end pointed outward, safeties off. No way was anyone going to get into this fucking van without being vaporized. I knew that unless we'd set off some kind of sensor—and I doubted that, because I hadn't seen anything suspicious—we still had the upper hand: we controlled the element of surprise. And I also knew that we had supporting fire from Rotten Randy, who was invisible up in that fucking tree, because to see him the bad guys would have to stare directly into their own halogen floodlights.

But in truth, I didn't want to make a ruckus. I wanted to take a look inside the FedEx truck, then get the hell out of Dodge. And no, I wasn't anxious to kill anybody either, because I didn't want any of these folks to know I'd even been here.

So, what about the boat I was about to steal, you ask? Well, I hoped Gwilliam would believe that the captain of the *Patricia Desens* had made off with his missiles and whatever else was in the waterproof crates—a case of simple smuggler's greed.

I worked on slowing my breathing and heartbeat, because my fucking heart was pumping at about 180. I settled my back up against Boomerang's, and thought about all the possibilities. It is the anticipation, my friends, that gets to you. The inoculation itself isn't so bad—it's watching the fucking doctor approach with the goddamn needle in his hand.

My field of vision was severely limited. I could see a narrow swath through the windshield. From the sounds of the voices, there were only two of 'em. And they were headed for the Land Rover. One of 'em complained about having to take the long way into town. The other said it didn't fucking matter because Gwilliam would spend the whole trip finger-fucking, which made both the Colombians laugh. I heard the heels of their shoes clatter on the courtyard tiles. Then a vehicle door opened and slammed shut. A second door did the same. And then the vehicle's engine started. It was revved violently once, twice, thrice, and then the fucking thing screeched out of the courtyard.

I chanced a quick peek and watched the Land Rover's bright taillights disappear down the narrow driveway alongside the house. And then the courtyard lights went off, and we were plunged into semidarkness again.

But the lights in the house were still on, so Boomerang and I just sat tight. At least they hadn't been coming for us. That was the good news. The bad news was that we had to sit in the van until things got quiet.

0047. Twelve minutes is a fucking lifetime when you are in a vulnerable position. It is amazing, however, to realize how sensitive one's senses become when you are deprived of outside stimuli. Your senses compensate for deprivation. For example, we couldn't see very much at all. But we could certainly hear. And there was nothing our ears didn't pick up. Including, after eight minutes of silence, the sound of light and stealthy footfalls approaching the van.

I pressed my back tight against Boomerang's. How many Colombian assholes were in the house? We had no idea. Had someone seen something when they came for the Land Rover? Had I left a wet footprint or some other form of pecker track and now the security force was coming back to double-check the situation? Had someone missed Señor Brut and decided to recon the area?

I didn't have to answer any of the above questions, because the next thing I heard was muffled tapping on the van's rear-door panel. The tapping was in Morse code, and the signal meant all clear.

The van's rear door cracked and Rotten Randy's shaved head appeared in the crack. "Olly-olly oxen-free," he stage-whispered. "You pussies can come out and play now."

I got a quick sit-rep as soon as I emerged. Timex had gone around to the front of the villa to recon. Gwilliam and his VERB had piled into the back of the Land Rover with two of the Colombians and driven off, down the single lane of gravel that led to the road to BA.

"For a night on the town?"

"Timex said it didn't look that way, Skipper. The stooges tossed a pair of suitcases into the back of the Land Rover."

That left a bunch of Colombians in the house. Randy said that Timex had managed to get "eyes on" on half a dozen armed and dangerous Colombians. He'd snuck a look through the window off the service pantry and discovered that as soon as Gwilliam and the VERB had left, one pair of well-armed, housebound *pelotudos*[51] headed for the well-stocked bar. He watched as another quartet pulled a double-X-rated video out of a yard-long shelf of S&M porn pix, then dropped their Uzis on the sofa and settled down for a long evening of *la paja con ron.*[52] Timex even heard them laughing about all the fun someone named Luis was missing.

That sit-rep, plus the fact that I'd gone through Señor Brut's wallet and already knew his name was Luis Garcia, told me these assholes weren't going to check up on their teammate. Not tonight. Not when they could spend the next six hours watching *bajar al pozo*[53] in living color and surround sound on a six-foot-wide-screen TV.

I looked up into the tree. Timex took his right hand off the Uzi and waved, somewhat forlornly I thought, from the limb. He was now our entire rear guard.

0052. Time to go to work. Boomerang and Rotten Randy checked the FedEx truck stem to stern to make sure there were no passive security devices in place. While they did, I pulled myself underneath the chassis and double-checked the frame for booby traps. The only unexpected things I came across were the bright heads of three heavy carriage bolts that had been recently sunk upward, through the cargo area decking. Recent? Yes, recent: the bolts themselves showed no signs of weathering. I rolled over and examined the ground. There were fresh shavings from the truck's wood decking lying on the tiles. No—this trio of bolts had been installed since the FedEx truck had been parked here.

---

[51] *Dumbasses,* in South American Spanish slang.
[52] That's jerking off, accompanied by large quanities of rum.
[53] Pussy-eating.

Okay, that meant breaking into the truck had gone from crucial to critical. But breaking in surreptitiously was going to be harder than it might appear, since we didn't have such car-boosting implements as a slim-jim, the long, flexible piece of steel that professional car thieves, spies, and SEALs use to run between the window and the frame to jimmy the lock, or the set of skeleton keys bought from a willing locksmith or crooked car dealer. And then, I thought about it for a second, and decided that subtlety was something I didn't need. I mean, what the fuck. If the goddamn truck was loaded with explosives, we were going to have to make some noise anyway because there was no way I was going to leave it around for the bad guys to use.

And so, to hell with tact. I jammed my knife blade into the passenger's side door lock and simply muscled the fucking door open. I pulled myself into the cab, broke the hasp on the lightweight door panel that hid the cargo compartment from prying eyes, turned the red-lensed flashlight on, and stepped through into the truck's cargo hold.

Where I just about shit. Now I saw the reason for the carriage bolts. All but two of the package racks had been removed. One remaining shelf held a twenty-or-so-pound charge of Semtex plastic explosive, a pencil detonator, and an M1 spring-tripped firing device; the other rack held four dark fiberglass cylinders. The rest of the rear compartment of the truck contained a heavyweight tripod bolted to the truck bed, and a three-container system package for what's known in my trade as the M220A1 TOW (for *T*ube-launched, *O*ptically guided, *W*ire-command link) missile system. Yeah: we're talkin' TOW antitank missiles.

TOWs were introduced in the early 1970s. They have a range of almost four thousand meters, and the latest versions of these wire-guided missiles are so-called fire and forget weapons that can penetrate thirty inches of the most advanced reactive armor plating. Those of you old enough to remember the Iran-Contra scandal during President Reagan's second term will recall that it was TOW missiles that the U.S. government sent to Iran as *bak-sheesh*[54] to induce the mullahs in Tehran to release the American prisoners that their allies, Hezb'allah (or, the Party of God), and the Islamic Jihad Organization, or IJO, were holding hostage in Beirut. The Iranians wanted TOWs back then because the wire-guided missiles were devastatingly effective against the Soviet armor used by the Iraqi Army, and this took place during the Iran-Iraq war.

Later, during the Gulf War, when a U.S. Army thermal imager picked up Iraqi armor waiting in ambush behind a two-yard-thick sand berm, a TOW gunner shot right through the six-foot berm and decimated the armored personnel carrier behind it. In another Desert Storm incident, a TOW passed through one Iraqi tank, pierced the armor of a second tank, and only then detonated.

What I had here was a basic TOW system, circa mid-1980s or early 1990s. Total weight for the launcher, the guidance set package, and three missiles was less than five hundred pounds. Broken down it could be carried by a single platoon. Not far—but it still came under the category of "man-portable." I was just about to take a closer look at the missile containers when Mister Murphy siphoned off all the energy in the rechargeable battery, the red-lensed flashlight died, and I was left in total darkness. Shit. I felt my way to the stern end of the truck, pried the hasp off, released the interior rear gate security lock, then oh, so q-u-i-e-t-l-y slid the door up until it retracted into the roof, so I could see what model TOW Gwilliam had laid his hands on.

The missiles in their containers weren't the most advanced. These were A1s, which had been replaced in the mid-1990s by the TOW A2 and the TOW 2B. Still, unlike the 1970s version TOW, whose reload time was slow, this upgraded model was probably

---

[54] Arabic slang for *bribery.*

capable of firing three missiles in less than ninety seconds. And even without the 2B's stand-off probe, the TOW A1 is no pussy-ass weapon. It can penetrate about two feet of armor (or concrete) before the seven pounds of high explosive detonate. All you have to do is keep the target in the launcher's crosshairs, and the missile does the rest. We are talking about a portable, effective, and reliable weapon here.

You didn't have to be a rocket scientist to put this deadly scenario together. There are countermeasures available for TOW attacks, but the embassy didn't have any of them. So it would be easy: the real FedEx truck would be waylaid. This fake one would be substituted. It would pull into its accustomed parking spot, four hundred yards from the embassy. The tangos would raise the rear gate. And then, a TOW would be fired—probably right at the ambassador's office on the second floor. The missile would defeat the bulletproof glass and the anti-rocket-propelled-grenade netting, penetrate the office itself, and then explode. Seven pounds of high explosive isn't a lot—but it would be more than enough to make rubble of anything within the ambassador's suite.

By the time the folks at the embassy realized what was happening, a second round would be already away, maybe heading for the fourth floor, where the embassy had all its communications facilities. That round would damage equipment and kill communicators and code clerks. The third round could be put anywhere. It really didn't matter. And then, using the Semtex and the M1 trip wire detonator, the tangos would booby-trap the fucking truck and haul ass. After all, they'd fired three rounds in a minute and a half, and they knew that the fucking cops wouldn't arrive for another two and a half minutes because they'd been there to gauge the response time. And when the cops did arrive, and tried to open up the fucking truck, it would go boom, destroying the evidence and also killing any cops, security people, Marines, or rubberneckers who'd been stupid enough to get close.

The more I thought about it, the hotter I got. Frankly, I'm fucking tired of assholes like Gwilliam and his brother. I'm even more tired of political pukes who keep people like me from going proactive and doing it to the bad guys before the bad guys do it to us. It makes no fucking sense at all. I mean, why do we always have to wait for innocent people to get killed so that we can *react?* I'd rather go proactive and save lives.

But we don't work that way. One reason, I guess, has to do with America's preoccupation with fairness. I call it the Lone Ranger syndrome. It seems to me that we Americans always believe we have to wear a white hat and only fight fair. Like in all those 1930s and 1940s western B movies starring cowboy heroes like Ken Maynard and Hoot Gibson and Bob Steele and Roy Rogers. You remember 'em: when the bad guy pulled a knife, the hero threw away his gun and fought him with a knife. If the bad guy lost his knife, the hero tossed his knife away, too, and used his bare fists to subdue the black-hatted villain.

Well, pardon me, but screw that philosophy. If some mother-fucker comes at me with a knife I'm gonna shoot the cocksucker. And if he loses the knife and attacks me with his fists I'm still gonna shoot the cocksucker. I dòn't fight fair. I fight to WIN. And that is how we should conduct ourselves in this big and mostly unfriendly world: we should fight like we want to win, not like we're some prissy, pussy-assed, holier-than-thou Goodie Two-shoes.

I've already told how well sound carries at night. A human whisper can be heard sixty yards away. So just imagine how loud the throaty growl of the *Patricia Desens*'s diesel engine was as it sputtered to life, coughed twice, and then growled to full throttle.

Oh fuck oh damn oh Doom on Dickie. Had I patted the god-damn captain down? Obviously I had not, because he'd been able to cut his bonds, slip his moorings, start his boat, take whatever the fuck the cargo was—not to mention the crates we'd retrieved and stowed on deck—and head off into the night. Timex reacted as if he were about to jump and run toward the dock. I cut him off with a hand signal. I needed him—and his firepower—right where he was.

Why? Because it didn't take more than fifteen seconds for the courtyard lights to come on, and the *pelotudos* to come-a-running is why.

PNU—*Pelotudo Numero Uno*—came through the doorway, an Uzi slung over his shoulder, a huge, 45-Cal. Glock 21 in his hand, its red-dot laser sight sweeping the area in front of him. It didn't take more than half a second for him to see that the rear gate of the FedEx truck was open and his TOW was showing.

He stopped. He froze. He swung the *pistola* to port, and then to starboard, the red beam of the laser seeking a target. Sure, it was a Bad Move to stand there in the open. But then, that's why he was a *pelotudo,* and I am the Rogue Warrior®.

Because by the time he'd arrived, Boomerang, Randy, and I had already dropped behind cover, careful not to cast any shadows that would give us away. Notice, by the way, that I did not say we had *concealed* ourselves.

There is a big difference between *cover* and *concealment.* In Hollywood movies, you always see the hero conceal himself behind a wall, or a doorway, or something similar when there's a gunfight. Concealment is good, because people can't hit what they can't see. But guess what friends: in these days of cheap drywall and hollow-frame construction, bullets can and do go right through walls, and doors, and even cars. Moreover, out here in the real world, where most bad guys are of the "spray and pray" school of firearms, they'll let a whole mag go at a door or a wall or a car. And it's probable that one of those rounds, aided by Mister Murphy, is gonna hit you either directly or because of a ricochet.

So the best thing you can do is to find the sort of cover through which a hostile round will not penetrate. Boomerang, for example, had flattened himself against the rear end of the van. To hit him, a round—even one of PNU's big, fat, 230-grain .45 rounds— would have had to pierce the van's front end, travel through the front firewall, penetrate the engine block, and continue all the way through the rear doors.

Randy slipped out of my line of sight and dropped flat behind the far side of the FedEx truck, where he might have been vulnerable to ricochets off the courtyard tile, but impervious to direct fire from the house.

And I? Well, I guess I'm a "do what I say and not what I do" kind of Rogue, because I was stuck in the FedEx truck, hunkered down behind the TOW tripod, with no cover except for the three missile launch package, a three-foot by four-foot waterproof plastic container.

But by that point I was in *sight-acquire-fire* mode, while he was still trying to identify any possible hostiles. I had my front sight centered on his upper torso and a perfect cheek weld on the collapsible stock of my PDW. The center body mass shot was how I'd inculcated the shooters when I ran SEAL Team Six. These days, when most of the bad guys wear body armor, you take head or groin shots. But PNU was dressed in a short-sleeved shirt open to the middle of his chest and I saw nothing but skin. So, with both eyes open, I centered the PDW's bright orange holographic dot on PNU's center mass—the region covered by his pecs, below which the arch of aorta and superior vena cava pumped blood in and out of the heart, let out half a breath, squeezed the trigger, and loosed a triple tap.

The first two sounds were a trio of rapid clicks as the PDW's hammer fell and the ping of shell casings. PNU's chest exploded. The Glock fell out of his hand and clattered onto the courtyard tiles. His mouth dropped open. I sight-acquire-fired again with another three-round burst, this time in the head (I can report that the fucking PDW handled like a dream), and what was left of him fell backward and collapsed in the doorway.

Someone inside the hacienda shouted, "*¿Conjo, Hector—que pasa?*"

Hector, of course, was not about to answer. So the shouted

question was followed by what you might call a conspicuous silence.

Obviously, the other *pelotudos* weren't as dumbass as their defunct *compañero*, because they didn't stick their *hocicos*[55] outside to check.

No, instead, they spray-and-prayed. Full auto. It was like fucking D day—or the big shoot-'em-up downtown Los Angeles bank robbery scene in the Robert De Niro movie *Heat*. The French doors disintegrated. The windshield of the fucking van exploded into a million pieces.

And let me tell you: it was LOUD out there. Something no one ever tells you about CQC is how loud it is. These guys were firing unsuppressed weapons—from the sound of 'em they were Uzis— in full auto mode. Think of the sound a big, outlaw Harley hog makes. Multiply it by a decibel factor of two. And if the sound wasn't bad enough, they were shooting real goddamn rounds. This was no fucking movie. There was high explosive in the fucking truck. A Rogue could get killed out here. My arm caught a shard of something. I wiped blood from it and flattened onto the truck bed, trying to make myself invisible.

A pause in the firing; no doubt a momentary lull as the *pelotudos* reloaded. But we took advantage of the pause. I heard the distinctive chatter of Timex's Uzi as he fired two-shot bursts. One by one the halogen spotlights exploded, and the courtyard was plunged into welcome darkness. Then the frigging spray-and-pray began all over again and I caught another fragment—this one a splinter of wood that stuck me in the forehead giving me a very Unicorny look.

Shit, maybe they weren't such *pelotudos* after all. Face it: from the way they were shooting, they had unlimited supplies of ammo. Me? I had a pocket full of useless .380, and fourteen rounds of

---

[55] *Noses.*

hollowpoint left in the PDW. Boomerang still had all twenty rounds in his mag. I had no idea how many rounds Timex had left in Señor Brut's Uzi, but at least he had a spare pair of loaded mags.

I pulled the wood sliver out. I rolled onto my side and poked the PDW's muzzle out, searching for targets. *Nada.* The assholes were staying put behind the cover the villa provided.

"Boomerang—"

"Yo, *Pibe?*"

"What's going on?"

"Hunkered, *Pibe.* No targets."

I heard Randy's basso from behind the van: "I shoulda packed some fuckin' frags."

He was right, of course, but this wasn't the time for woulda-shoulda-coulda, and besides, we didn't have any frags to bring. We had to act—and do it NOW. I rolled back behind cover, reached up, and released the quartet of clamps on one of the heavy wood crates I was hiding behind. I slipped the goddamn cover off and peered. Inside was cradled another, smaller box, with two handles. I yanked it out and opened it up, too. It was a battery/control unit. Better: it was the battery assembly package that supplied the TOW system's main power to the launch package and its MGS—Main Guidance System.

That was the good news. The BN was that it has been years since I've assembled and fired one of these fucking things. But assembling TOWs is like fucking. Once you learn how to do it right it's hard to forget. I ran my hands over the tripod unit to see what was there and what wasn't. The answer was that they were waiting to assemble the unit just before they'd use it.

Okay let's do this by the numbers. Step one: I rooted around until I found the traversing unit, took it out of its case, and secured it to the apex of the tripod base. I dug out the big, square, main guidance system box that was the brains of the whole system, unlatched the box top, and set the MGS by the base of the tripod. Next, I found the coil of guidance cable, took the J1 connector, and plugged it into the M1 receptacle on the MGS box. Shit—I hoped that the yellow lines were aligned, otherwise the fucking thing wouldn't fire. But there was no way to know, since I was working purely by feel. Well, just like fucking, it felt good to me.

My efforts were interrupted by another spray-and-pray session from the house. Can I admit something to you? It is difficult to concentrate when a bunch of A&D[56] *pelotudos* are trying to wax one's ass.

But guess what: real Warriors don't succumb to such distractions. REAL WARRIORS PREVAIL under any and all conditions. That's what Hell Week was all about. That's what the old chiefs drummed into our tadpoles' heads when they forced us to do things we didn't want to do. To a Frog, or a SEAL, failure is always unacceptable.

Indeed, the biblical-sounding phrase THOU SHALT NOT FAIL is the philosophical nucleus of what being in the Teams has always been about. And so, indifferent to the unfriendly fire, I went to work. I unhitched the four clasps on the launch tube box lid, retrieved the tube assembly, dropped it onto the traversing unit, and secured it with the launch tube latch. Now the fucking thing was starting to look like a TOW.

There was another fusillade from the villa. "Timex, goddammit—gimme some fucking protection."

There was welcome suppressive fire from my port side. As I heard it, I found the daylight tracking device, installed it in its bracket on the left side of the traversing unit, and locked it into place. I followed that by bracketing the night sight into its bracket. Next, I took the TVPC power cable, and attached the P1 connector just as another burst of Uzi fire from the tree shut down the spray-and-pray from inside the villa.

I took the opportunity to install the battery assembly to the

---

[56]Armed & Dangerous.

MGS, then ran my hands over the connections. It seemed that I'd got everything right. But who knew. If I'd been doing this purely by the book I would have run the self-test program right then. But there was no time for any self-test program. So I said a fervent prayer to the God of WAR, then turned the system on.

And the God of WAR said, "Let there be light."

And when I saw the lights come on, where lights should have been, I knew that there is a God and that HE is indeed the GOD OF WAR, and that he loveth Rogues like me.

And the GOD OF WAR spoke to me in voices. And He said, "Loadeth thine fucking missile, thou worthless cockbreath."

And yea and verily, it was indeed time to lose the fucking Epiphany and load the fucking missile.

I jumped up and pulled a TOW in its cylindrical fiberglass tube off the truck shelf and rolled it into my arms. Which, of course, was precisely when the God of WAR decided I was having too easy a time of it, and caused the *pelotudos* to loose another barrage of full-auto in my direction.

But I wasn't about to be thwarted. My rage was so fucking white hot by now that a round straight to my brain wouldn't have stopped me. I rolled onto my side, eased the tube onto the deck, ran my hands over the fiberglass, and discovered two bullet holes a third of the way down the tube.

Oh, shit. Oh, fuck. Oh, Doom on Dickie. I was now holding a potential time bomb. The midsection of a TOW missile contains thermal batteries that provide both heat and electricity. They are powered up by an explosive squib that is set off when the TOW's trigger mechanism is depressed. The squib is also vulnerable to gunfire, or anything else that might produce a spark.

I wasn't about to take any fucking chances. I took the missile container into my arms, crawled to the aft end of the truck, rolled it out, then crawled back to the tripod, and raised myself off the deck so I could pull another missile container off the shelf, and began all over again.

The *pelotudos* must have sensed something, because there was another burst of Uzi fire. The bullets splintered the deck six inches in front of my nose and sent a wood splinter through my jeans into my upper thigh.

Oh, fuck me. This was getting old fast. I pulled myself up and grabbed a second cylinder, just as another wave of Uzi fire shattered the metal shelving three inches above my head. But this time I'd learned from my mistake. I brought the whole fifty-six-pound cylinder down onto the deck and waited until they'd finished before proceeding.

Silence from the villa. I pulled myself to my feet, dropped the launch tube about eight degrees, then cradled the missile container in my arms, keeping the aft end higher than the nose, and eased it into the launch tube. By feel, I made sure that the indexing lugs were aligned. I dropped the rear end of the bridge clamp that sat on the traversing unit and pushed down. I pulled the bridge clamp locking handle down and back, which locked the missile in the launch tube.

Was it ready to fire? Fuck, I certainly hoped it was. I dropped behind the optical sight and centered the crosshairs on the farthest wall of the hacienda's living room area. The fucking image was fuzzy because it was so damn close—we're talking somewhere in the sixty-yard range at the most. That was a potential fucking problem. Why? The TOW A1's minimum range is about sixty-five yards, because it takes sixty-five yards for the missile to arm itself. But frankly, friends, at that point in time I really didn't give a shit about fine-focus or a yard or two of range. I just wanted to blow the cocksuckers into next fucking week.

My right arm swiveled the launcher up and level. My left hand settled down onto the firing mechanism. I raised the arming lever, unlatched the trigger cover, and pressed the trigger down. Firmly.

Nothing happened.

And then I realized *why* nothing happened. Nothing happened because it takes the TOW system one and a half seconds to send the prefire sequence to the missile, starting the chemical reaction in the internal thermal batteries, blowing the explosive squib off the nitrogen bottle, and spinning the missile's gyroscope.

That was when I thought I heard an audible series of clicks and pops in the missile tube. At which point, the fucking launch motor fired up and the missile launched.

Here is a Roguish rule of physics: fire a missile from an enclosed area, and the blast will hurt you. As if to prove the point, the concussion knocked me face first into the wall. But I was lucky: the fucking afterblast demolished the driver's compartment, not me.

According to a set of unclassified specs, the TOW A1 covers just under three hundred meters in the first two seconds of flight. This missile exploded with an incredible explosive concussion just over half a second (to be absolutely precise, fifty-three hundredths of a second) after I'd launched it.

That, friends, is why the missile needed a full sixty-five yards of flight. At eighteen hundredths of a second after launch, the arming device unlocks. At 0.53 seconds, the safety and arming clock rotates and aligns the detonator with the warhead.

And that's when things got interesting. See, there's just a little over five pounds of explosive filler in a first-generation TOW missile warhead. That's not a lot. So, from the size of the explosion—which was huge—I figured the missile made it into the kitchen and hit one of the hundred-gallon propane tanks they use for powering cooking stoves in this part of the world. Why? Because the blast was big enough to lift the fucking roof off the goddamn hacienda.

That was only part of the good news. The rest now ensues: said hufuckingmongous explosion was followed by lots of *pelotudo* screams. I guess that meant I'd finally gotten their attention in the manner I like to get attention.

Show Time. I grabbed my PDW, jumped out of the FedEx truck, and charged into the smoke, Boomerang and Rotten Randy following on my heels. There was an immediate acrid smell: a mélange of high explosive, burning plastic, charred human flesh, and blood. It was the smell of WAR, and I love it. I crossed the threshold, my PDW at low ready, my trigger finger indexed alongside the frame of the weapon, advancing steadily, foot by foot, forcing myself to keep going so my guys wouldn't bunch up behind me, talking to myself all the while so I'd remember the basics. *Scan, and breathe. Don't tunnel. Keep your fuckin' eyes moving. Scan and breathe.*

Scan-and-breathe. Scanandbreathe. Scanbreathe. Scanbreathe. Scanbreathe. There was motion to my port side. The PDW came up-up-up and my front sight found a target. I squeezed the trigger and stitched one of the Colombians diagonally—nine shots from thigh to shoulder. He went down behind a burning couch. I jumped the couch, singeing my beard as I did, and put a three-round burst into his head to make sure he'd stay where he was.

"Going right." That was Boomerang's high-pitched voice. I turned just in time to watch as he and Randy disappeared into thick smoke, heading toward the master-suite area.

I heard noise to my left, turned, fired two shots as I whirled, instinctively inhaling a huge breath—of dense brown smoke from the fucking couch. It burnt like hell as it went down into my lungs—as nasty a sensation as if I'd just taken a Rogue-size swallow of battery acid. But a guy's gotta breathe. I tried dropping down to the deck where the air was better. But it didn't make much difference: all the smoke was beginning to make me woozy and sick. But, so what? *FIDO,*[57] right?

I drove on, moving toward what was left of the arched doorway leading toward the kitchen and staff quarters. From the extent of the damage and the fire that was burning out of control in that part of the house, I was heading toward the area where the TOW had exploded.

---

[57]FIDO is Army Rangerspeak for "Fuck It—Drive On."

Scan and breathe; scan-and-breathe. I made my way into what must have been the den, past the shards of what had just a few minutes ago been a big-screen TV set into a huge wooden entertainment center. I stepped over the bottom half of a Colombian. The *pelotudo* had obviously been blown in two by the explosion. Six feet away, through the thickening smoke, I could see what was left of his torso. His guts splattered the wall ahead of me.

Then I saw something moving off to my right, and instinctively I fired at the motion.

Dear readers, have I ever made the point about how important it is to count rounds?

I have indeed made that point many times, you say. It is a lesson you have taken to heart, you assert. Well, okay: how many rounds have I expended so far?

There's a deafening silence from all you assholes out there. Ah—finally, one squeaky little voice admitting that you're not quite sure how many rounds I've fired tonight.

Well, here's the point of this short, Socratic dialogue: I didn't know, either. I got that one shot off and then the fucking PDW's bolt locked back. *That's* when I realized I was out of ammo. Empty. Dry. And we all know I wasn't carrying a spare mag.

I guess the look on my face must have given me away. Because the *pelotudo* I'd been shooting at had a shit-eating grin on his as he stood up, raised the muzzle of his Uzi in my direction, and pulled the trigger.

Nothing happened. Guess what: the *pelotudo's* weapon was also empty. He'd been as good at counting his rounds as I had at counting mine.

But that didn't deter the sumbitch. He tossed the subgun aside and came at me through the smoke, a two-inch, serrated blade folding knife in his right hand held in what's known as a ninja grip: blade tip pointing up his arm and parallel to it, cutting side out. That way he could rake the blade tip at my face, whirl, and stab if I gave him an opening, or he could slash at me with the cutting edge, punching and jabbing like a boxer.

You're saying something. You want my attention. *Now?* With an armed-and-dangerous asshole coming at me? You want to know why I'm afraid of a *pelotudo* with a tiny-bladed knife.

Hey, lemme tell you something very basic about knives. Ninety-nine percent of those testosterone-intensive six-inch drop point special steel self-proclaimed badass-designed high-dollar fighting blades are so much bullshit. *Any* knife is a lethal tool if you know how to use it. All you need to do fatal damage to the human body is a ten-dollar imitation Spyderco with a one-and-three-quarter-inch blade. It will sever all the important arteries; it will cause terminal damage; it will do proper mayhem. The best folding combat knife I've ever used, the Emerson CQC-7 (in the old days Ernie Emerson used to put serial numbers on his knives; mine is number 007; fitting, huh?), has a blade that's just under three inches in length, and even Ernie will tell you some folks think that's slightly oversize for an efficient folder blade.

Okay, let me get back to work, will ya? The PIQ (if you don't know it stands for *Pelotudo* In Question you're a bigger dumbass than he is) came at me, fists raised like a boxer's. He jabbed with his right hand—the one in which he held the knife. He turned his wrist out, the blade edge slashed in my direction—and I stepped back, heel first, to move out of range.

Big mistake. My heel caught on something, and I went down, the back of my head slapping the floor with a *thwock* that made my eyes cross.

"*¡Oye! ¡Tu madre!*" He was not only calling me a motherfucker, he was on me like stink on shit. This PIQ knew how to take advantage of a guy. He switched his grip now, put the tip of the blade forward, as his knife hand came wide and then sliced down, stabbing toward my face and neck.

But stabbing left him vulnerable to counterattack. I parried with the muzzle of the PDW, knocked his knife arm aside, and then thrust up, hard, straight into the PIQ's throat.

Here is what: my arms were longer than his, and the suppressed muzzle of the machine pistol added eight more inches. Plus, I have world-class hand-eye coordination. So, the fucking suppressor caught him hard in the Adam's apple.

He had a surprised look on his face as he absorbed the blow. It may have knocked some of the wind out of him, and I'd bet you it did serious damage to his windpipe. But not enough to stop the little cocksucker. Oh, no. He shook the pain off and threw himself on top of me, flailing, kicking, and screaming sweet nothings about my parentage while he tried to imitate Mike Tyson and bite my ear off while bringing the knife blade up into my brisket.

First things first. And in situations like this one, you have to deal with the threat first. So, I tried to use both my hands to grab the arm with the knife.

That was harder than you might think. Yes, I am a strong motherfucker. But he was, too. And he was wiry, and determined not to be killed. Plus, my right arm was tangled up in the sling of my PDW, which as you'll recall, was suspended across my chest.

I knocked his knife arm upward. The blade flashed past my ear—almost close enough to make a Van Gogh wannabe out of me. I tried to roll over, but I couldn't get my fucking arm out of the sling fast enough.

Which gave him the opening he'd been waiting for, and he managed to slash me a Z pattern once-twice-thrice on the left arm. Fuck—who the hell did he think he was, Zorro?

Shit, I was gonna probably need stitches. But there was nothing to be done about it now, except to keep on pressing him.

He slashed again. This time, I managed to deflect the blow, knock his arm away, and then catch his knife hand with my left paw. I twisted it away from my body, just far enough for me to free my right arm, bring my right hand up, up, up, and grab him by the wrist.

Big mistake. I'd trapped the blade right beneath my fingers. He twisted his wrist, and the business end of the folder took off about an eighth of an inch of my right index fingertip. I bled like hell.

But frankly, Scarlett, I didn't give a damn. By now I was getting angry. I had him with both hands. I rolled to my right and caught the side of his face—*Contact!!*—with a left elbow blow directly to the zygomatic arch, the thin shell of bone on the outside of his left eye. That stunned him. He gave me another opening, and I hit him again, harder, sending zygomatic bone fragments into his skull. The PIQ screamed. He dropped the knife. It fell past my left ear. Now, all he wanted to do was escape. He panicked. He tried to roll off me, his knees scrambling, his legs pumping.

Bad decision. Because now, both he knew and I knew that he was mine, and that it was time for him to die. He was bleeding internally. I could see it from the blood seeping from the corner of his left eye. Too bad.

I rolled out from underneath him and swatted at his face again. He cowered, shrinking away from me. My peripheral vision saw the knife and I grabbed for it.

He saw what I was doing, and he didn't like it at all.

But there was very little he could do. I had the knife in my hand now, held in the same ninja grip he'd had it. I smacked his face with my left forearm, bouncing his head off the tile floor. As his head went back, I punched at his neck with the knife.

It didn't take much. I don't think the blade tip went in more than a half inch. But it was enough to sever both his external jugular vein on the left side, and the big subclavian artery on the right. I don't have to get technical to tell you that there was a lot of blood in a very short time.

The life went out of him fast because his heart was probably pumping at a rate of about 180. And with every b-beat, came another gush of blood. Some of it washed back into his lungs, and he began to drown.

Finish him off, you say? I *had* finished him off. He was dead. He just didn't quite know it yet.

I rolled onto my knees, my lungs burning from the smoke and the physical effort. The fire was getting worse. Time to move. I backed out of the den and ran into Randy Michaels, who emerged through the smoke from the kitchen.

"Three down in there," he said matter-of-factly. "I got all the paper they were carrying."

Boomerang's slim form emerged from the bedroom wing of the villa, the only part of the house that was relatively unscathed. "It's all clear back there, *Pibe.*"

"You find any documents?"

Boomerang's head shook side to side. "Nothing but a few credit card receipts, *Pibe.*"

"How many tangos are down?" I was fucking dizzy now. The smoke was really getting to me, and the fire was burning out of control.

Rotten Randy thought about it for a few seconds, counting on his fingers. "Eight," he said. "Nine counting the one you waxed outside the wall."

"Any survivors?" It would have been nice to be able to interrogate a *pelotudo* or two.

It wasn't going to happen: Boomerang shook his head. "Negatory, *Pibe.*"

In that case it was long past time to move on with our lives. "Boomerang, you and Rotten take the Semtex and blow the fucking FedEx truck—I don't want anything left of the TOW. I'm gonna make sure we haven't left any pecker tracks in the house. Then let's haul our asses the hell out of here before anybody else shows up."

CHAPTER

15

WE WERE BACK AT THE SAFE HOUSE BY 0315. MICK GOT ON THE PHONE to young Robert Evers and made sure he understood the importance of meeting with us immediately so that we could give him a sit-rep about the evening's events. I went through the papers that we'd taken from the villa. The most significant of those was a set of diagrams—street maps highlighted with vehicle escape routes, an eight-by-ten photo of the American Embassy with TOW targets circled in marking pencil, and copious notes in *Español*— all of which convinced me *sin sombra de duda*—beyond the ol' shadow of a doubt—that Gwilliam and his Green Hand Defenders pals had no intention of running the op against the American Embassy themselves.

Just like the ops in Britain and Northern Ireland that had used members of TIRA, the Irish Brotherhood, and the Irish People's Army as surrogates, Gwilliam and Gerry Kelley had hired a band of narcoterrorist *pelotudos* to do their dirty work in Buenos Aires. Other diagrams and notes showed the *pelotudos* where to set the truck, how to set up the TOW, and just where to set the plastique explosive booby trap charges.

Except, the way the booby traps were diagrammed on the sheet of paper I held in my hands, any poor asshole who slid tab "A" into slot "B" was going to blow himself up. Nice: first you hire a bunch of assholes to kill a lot of Americans, and then you double-cross them and make sure they kill themselves before they can be captured and interrogated.

The schedule Gwilliam had left behind told me that the *pelotudos* were to keep the embassy under observation for the next fifteen days by using the dog walker. They were to stage the TOW hit on the sixteenth day. Señor Gwilliam, one scrawled *pelotudo* note read, would not check in with them again. They were to act without fail or hesitation on Day Sixteen. That sealed it: the damning evidence was finally right in front of my nose. Both Kelley brothers were as guilty as I'd thought they were. And so, Gerry's and Gwilliam's names went onto the death penalty list I carry in my head.

The paperwork also convinced me that even though the clock was ticking, we now had a ballpark guesstimate of when the second shoe would drop: two weeks and two days. That, too, made sense: if Gwilliam was bringing the missiles from the *Patricia Desens* back on the Kelley yacht, nothing would happen until *Báltai* reached wherever it was they'd use the missiles against a British/American objective, a target—we knew from the pub conversation intercept I'd discovered early on—that would result in large numbers of Brit and Yankee casualties.

While I perused the intel and levied punishment, Boomerang, Rotten Randy, Timex, and I cleaned up and dealt with their assorted dings, bumps, and bruises. I dealt with my own only after they'd cleaned up and patched up. I looked at my reflection in the small, steamed-up bathroom mirror when I came out of the shower. Talk about black-and-blue (and purple, and green, and mustard, and red). I resembled a goddamn human punching bag. And felt like one, too, I might add.

But there was no time to appreciate the pain. There was too much work to do. And, as it turned out, not a lot of time in which to complete it.

Even before I dealt with my lumps and bumps I hit the phone to check in with Nod. It wasn't easy: it took more than an hour before his Froggish voice rumbled back at me on the long-distance line. "Yo, Skipper . . ."

"WTF, Nodster?"

"We're on the move, Skipper—scrambling. Our boy picked up six hours ago and amscrayed."

"Got a location for him?"

"Negatory."

That certainly threw a wrench into my neat scenario. "Fuck."

"Amen to that, Skipper. Ger—"

I cut him off. "No names. No names."

"Gotcha. Our guy drove himself to the airport at Northolt."

"Northolt. Where the hell's that?

"West of the city. Near Uxbridge."

That didn't help me either. Frankly, I didn't give a rusty F-word where the frigging airport was. "C'mon, Nod. Sit-rep. Fill me in on the important stuff."

I heard Nod breathe deeply to focus himself on the mission at hand. Then he gathered his thoughts and continued in simple declarative. "We followed. No trouble. Digger leapfrogged on a bike and beat him there by fifteen minutes. That way he was bracketed. But the sumbitch didn't have a plane waiting. He jumped a private chopper instead. One of the brigadier's guys got into the tower. They told him our target was flying to Stansted."

Stansted. I knew all about Stansted. It was the third largest airport in the London region. It was due north of the city, right off the M-11 highway. And it was where Gerry Kelley housed his private Learjet. "And?"

"We followed, but we played it wrong. I'd put Nigel at Stansted to keep an eye on the plane our guy keeps here. But he didn't use his own plane. He had a chartered Gulfstream III waiting, engines hot. The flight plan the pilot filed was to Orly—Paris."

"And?"

"He got out before we could do anything. I checked with the French. I called your old friend Jacques Lillis at DST. He told me they never arrived."

I relayed Nod's sit-rep to Mick. He reached for the phone and gave Nod a name and telephone number in Hereford, the home base of 22 SAS Regiment. "You call him. Tell him I told you to make contact. He'll ask you for single-word substantiation. Say the word, *Blackguard,* and ask for his response. He will answer, *Ferrous.* That's the recognition code. He'll help you track the bastard down."

Mick handed the receiver back to me. Nod said, "There's more bad news, Skipper."

I told Nod I didn't need any more bad news. Obviously he wasn't listening: "Admiral Flannery's office has been trying to reach you for a day and a half."

Eamon the fucking Demon. "Do you know what he wants?"

"Negatory, except he got on the phone himself the third time. Said for me to tell you you'd broken your agreement with him. He told me he knew you were off the reservation and there'd be hell to pay when you got back. Then he reamed me a new asshole for not being able to locate you because he said he was taking heat and it wasn't his fault."

Oh, this was not a good thing. Now, you and I both know that Eamon and MI5 had set *moi* up for a fall on the Green Hand Defenders issue, because Mick and I worked that scenario out some seven chapters ago. But I'd hoped to be back in London by now, with enough dirt on the Green Hand Defenders and the Kelley brothers to cause Eamon the Demon and Sir Roger Holland a sack full of nasty political problems if they didn't consent to my going after Gerry and Gwilliam sans any consequences. After all, I could cause both Whitehall and Washington a ton of political embarrassment by going public with what I already knew, and often that makes for enough political leverage to get the job done.

But because I was indeed off the reservation right now—remember, I was in the Argentine computers as fugitive—Eamon was on the upside of this situation. Which meant that he could spin my behavior any way he wanted to Washington, and Washington would go along.

Let me give you some political truth here: an O-6 can trump an admiral, an ambassador or a chief of station if he has political leverage. I know that because I have done it lots of times in the past. Right now, I had neither pry bar nor fulcrum, which left me pretty much out of the picture, leveragewise.

But all of that was *my* problem, not Nod's. And Eamon was an asshole for screaming at Nod. But he was even worse—a no-load, dumb-fuck shithead—for whining about his situation. You think I'm being facetious here. Well, I'm not. What COMMAND is all about is taking charge, and making decisions, and living by those decisions, win or lose. Today's COs—from the president on down—tend to whine and blame everyone around them when things go wrong, instead of saying, "You're right: I fucked up."

Look at how former Secretary of Energy Bill Richardson dealt with the long string of fuckups at our nuclear labs at Los Alamos, New Mexico, where the Chinese ran a series of espionage operations and stole our nuclear secrets and warhead designs, and where the DOE counterterrorist team's computer disks were misplaced or stolen and copied. Instead of shouldering the responsibility by saying, "This happened on my watch, and I am taking responsibility," he tried to foist the blame on his subordinates.

Well, fuck Bill Richardson and all the can't-cunt commanders like him. We don't need assholes like them in charge. We need leaders who make decisions and stand by 'em.

So, I told Nod I'd handle the admiral. I also ordered him to keep the bloody cell phone at hand, because I didn't want to be operating in a vacuum. Then I rang off.

"Okay, assholes, listen up: both Kelleys are on the move. Now we know their goddamn op is under way."

Mick nodded in agreement. "They have the missiles. And they've selected their second target."

Boomerang said: "But we still have no idea what the target is, *Pibe.*"

The glum look the men gave me told me they thought we were totally fucked.

•   •   •

It turned out that my guys weren't quite accurate. We became *totally* fucked at 0440, when Robert Evers arrived at the safe house, looking uncharacteristically disheveled. "I can tell you, Mr. Marcinko," he said, playing with the collar of his wrinkled shirt, "that one of the most senior people at your embassy doesn't like you at all."

"You probably mean the CIA station chief, Mel Putz," I said. "We've had our disagreements."

"I have no doubts at all you've had disagreements. Because he's convinced the Argentines to arrest you," Robert Evers reported.

What horseshit. "On what grounds?"

"Assault on a diplomat with intent to commit murder," Evers said. He looked at me. "What the hell did you do to the man?"

"I stabbed him with a tie tack."

The look on Robert Evers's face told me he had no idea at all whether I was being serious or not. He shook his head, confused, and then continued. "At first, the Argentines were reticent, because the alleged . . . act had taken place on sovereign American soil—that is to say, inside your embassy compound."

"What convinced them otherwise?"

"I'm sorry to tell you it was our embassy. Because of the strong liaison relationship your ambassador has with my ambassador, my ambassador suggested to the Argentines that they honor his request because you are a part of a rogue operation that both London and Washington believe has gone terribly wrong."

Evers looked at Mick Owen. "Mister Marcinko is to be turned

over to the American authorities and sent back to the United States under guard."

Mick Owen groaned audibly. "Is that all, Robert?"

"That's only the half of it. MI5 knows that you are here as well, Mr. Owen," he added. Evers looked completely helpless. "Mr. Owen has been declared persona non grata by the Argentine government," he blurted.

Mick scowled. "That's pretty hard to do, since I'm not traveling on a diplomatic passport."

Robert Evers's expression told us that it hadn't been all *that* hard to do. "Mr. Owen, you have been summoned back to London immediately."

"By whom?"

"By the Ministry of Defense."

There was an awkward silence. I decided to be Roguishly direct. "Robert," I said, "you will have to help us get out of the country without being stopped."

"I will *what?*" The young Brit's face took on a stony expression. But I didn't let that stop me. I showed Robert Evers the materials we'd taken from Gwilliam's villa, and explained how the Kelley brothers had planned to use narcoterrorist surrogates to attack the American Embassy. Then I spent about ten minutes giving him some background on what DET Bravo had discovered about Gwilliam and Gerry Kelley, and told him about the Green Hand Defenders, and their modus operandi. I also explained about the backchannel between Eamon the Demon and MI5, and our contention that MI6 had been shut out of all Green Hand Defender ops because of some idiotic internecine political feud between intelligence agencies.

Then I connected the dots, explaining the significance of what Mick and I had discovered so far, and what the consequences could be, should we not succeed. And then I told Robert Evers flat out there was no way I was going to fail, whether I received his help or not.

"There is too much at stake here, Robert. Too many people have already died because of these assholes. And if we let Washington and London determine how this is played out, a lot more people will get killed. Now, that may be a politically acceptable decision for a bunch of cynical politicians. But allowing innocent people to die needlessly makes no fucking sense to me. So, I'm asking for your help."

There was a pause. Then he looked at me evenly. "Mr. Marcinko, please write out the Arabic on those missile cylinders you discovered aboard the *Patricia Desens* and show me the chart you took from the pilothouse."

I wrote the Arabic numerals out for Robert Evers on a sheet of paper towel. Then I retrieved the damn chart, unfolded it, and laid it out on the coffee table. The water had smudged the thick, red grease-pencil lines, but not obliterated them.

The Brit spook tapped the paper towel. "Thirty-eight."

I said, "Correct."

"That makes them Exocet missiles," he said. "Ship-launched." He paused. "They stopped making the MM—for *missile marin*— thirty-eight in the mid-1970s. As I recall it was replaced by the MM forty, which went into service in 1993."

Yeah—when Robert Evers was probably still in high school. He was on the money, of course—and I was an idiot for not having remembered the designator numbers.

For those of you too young to know about these things, Exocets are French manufactured, subsonic, sea-skimming missiles designed to attack large warships. They look a little bit like cruise missiles. With perfect hits—meaning right at the waterline—two Exocets would be sufficient to sink most of the ships in service today.

And Gwilliam had two of them. I unfolded the chart from the *Patricia Desens* and laid it atop the paper towel. My interpretation of the course depicted was that the smuggler's boat was to rendezvous with Gwilliam's yacht somewhere off the coast of the

Punte del Este. That's why the captain had that state-of-the-art cellular satellite phone with him.

Robert Evers listened and then looked closely at the chart. Then he drummed his fingers on the tabletop for a few seconds.

"I believe you are correct in your interpretation," he said, somewhat formally.

"Robert," I said, "can you use your influence with the Argentines to keep what happened at the villa quiet?"

The young Brit thought about it for a few seconds. "I believe I can do that without causing any suspicions," he said. "After all, if your supposition about who was involved is correct, the people involved will have police records. The incident can then be portrayed as a turf fight over drugs, or as a robbery gone sour."

"Can you do it now?"

"You mean right now?"

I shook my head in the affirmative. "It's important."

Robert Evers shrugged. "I suppose." He picked up the telephone and dialed a number from memory, then had a three-minute conversation with someone he called "Jorge," explaining the scenario I'd asked him to plant with the authorities. *"Sí, Jorge—claro. Chau."*

Robert Evers hung up the phone. "It's done," he said. He looked at me. His expression told me loud and clear that I'd better not ask for any more favors.

But I wasn't about to let him off the hook. Like I said, there was too much at stake. "Robert," I said, "you've done a lot for us. Now, you have to help us get out of the country. We don't have the time to play games here."

He went silent once more. Finally, he spoke. "If it were ever to be discovered that I helped you escape," he said to Mick, "my career would be over immediately."

"I understand that, my boy," Mick said. "And you've already done a lot for us. Despite what Dick has just said, I can't ask you to do any more. We'll have to deal with this situation on our own."

"I realize that you are trying to make things easier for me, Mr. Owen," Robert Evers said. "But you have to appreciate my position."

"I do," Mick said. "We all do."

"I do not think so," Robert Evers said, a formal tone creeping into his voice.

Mick started to say something. But there was something about the young man's body language that made me put my hand on Mick's arm to rein him in. "I think Robert wants to tell us something," I said. "I think we should let him say his piece."

The young Brit's expression told me how grateful he was. "As I have intimated," he began, "it gets harder and harder to do one's job properly, given the political climate in which we work at the embassy. One is forbidden, for example, from keeping track of such people as Brendan O'Donnell. Why? Because the ambassador has specifically forbidden us from taking any actions that might cause even the vaguest possibility of any diplomatic flaps here in Buenos Aires. And one is forbidden from keeping tabs on cells of active terrorists because the ambassador has decided that neither violent Islamic fundamentalism nor narcoterrorism is a British problem. He does not want to hear that IRA splinter groups are being supplied with weapons and ordnance by Iran or the South American drug cartels; indeed, he does not want us to look into the possibility that *drogistas* operating in Argentina might adversely affect the Good Friday Accord.

"Frankly," he continued, "one is not able to operate effectively given those sorts of strictures. And so, one breaks the rules, every now and then."

I understood that. Operating UNODIR has been my way of getting around the aparatchiks who control the Navy. I've done it for years now. It was good to see that my way of doing business was being carried on by the next generation of Warriors.

The young Brit continued: "I am able to go after the Green Hand Defender people here in Argentina," he said resolutely. "I will make sure that they fail to achieve their goals—and also make sure that once they are arrested, my Argentine allies will manage to, shall we say, 'lose' them somewhere within the criminal justice system."

"That could be dangerous," Mick said. "There could be dire consequences."

The look on Robert Evers's face told us that he had thought about the consequences, and he was willing to live with them. "As I explained," he said, "sometimes one has to break the rules." Robert Evers ran a hand through his unruly hair to move it out of his eyes. "That is why I decided to assist you during your time here in Argentina. If I could not operate properly, perhaps you could. It was worth the risk. So will this be."

"We're grateful, Robert," I said. "You've helped us considerably."

"And now," Evers said, "you want me to do even more rule breaking."

There was no way of getting around it. "That's right. If what you say is correct, my men and I will have to smuggle ourselves out of Argentina. We can't do it without your help."

Robert Evers said, "I know that."

"And?"

"And I have already decided to help you. It is a blood debt that has to be paid—and I am happy to pay it."

"A blood debt?"

Robert Evers looked past me. "Mister Owen," he said, "if it wasn't for you, my father would be dead."

I turned toward Mick. "I thought you told me his father was an investment banker you knew in the army who owed you a huge bar tab at the Ritz Hotel in Paris."

"He does," Mick said indignantly. "He owes me two hundred quid, and I plan to collect."

"He owes Mr. Owen a lot more than that," Robert Evers said. "My father and Mr. Owen served together in Twenty-Two Regiment back in the 1970s. Mr. Owen saved my father's life."

"It was in Mirbat, on the south coast of Oman," Mick Owen

said by way of explanation. "In 1976 Colin—that's Robert's dad—and I were part of what we called a British Army Training Team. Ten of us—Colin and me, who were just barely lieutenants, and eight enlisteds. What Colin was doing in SAS I didn't know. He was Harrow and Cambridge and all that rot. Already had a wife and a kid—young Robert here—in nappies."

I looked at Mick, impressed. "I never knew you served in Oman."

"It was a few years before we met, Dick," the Welshman explained. "I was a kid—unblooded and naive. I'd just been badged. It was my first overseas tour."

He stretched his big arms, then jerked his thumb toward Robert. "His dad and I were in our kips when all hell broke loose. Hundreds of Commie buggers came whooping down out of the hills. They had mortars and heavy machine guns." He paused. "They'd stolen two Omani armored vehicles, too. Shit—we had three jeeps, two of which were blown to bits in the first three minutes. Anyway, his dad came out of his sleeping bag like a shot, grabbed his sandals and a thirty-cal Browning machine gun and headed for the roof. I followed him along with one of our local irregulars—*firqas* we called 'em; they were former guerrillas who'd come over to our side from the Commies—because we'd set up a light mortar up there, preranged toward the most probable point of attack."

Robert Evers nodded. "Dad's told me," he said.

"We were both scared shitless—has he told you that?"

The young Englishman nodded. "He said it could have gotten pretty rough."

Mick looked back in my direction. "Could have, hell. If the Commies caught us, they'd been known to skin prisoners as an example to the populace. And they didn't like us bastard infidels much."

Randy asked, "Howja handle it?"

"There was no doubt our position would be overrun," Mick said. But half a klik away, he continued, there was an old fort manned by Omani troops that would give the Brits a lot more effective cover than the ramshackle mud brick and straw structure they were in. They broke the mortar down, carried it off the roof, grabbed their weapons, and started down a long wadi toward the fort, covering their retreat with suppressive fire as best they could. Which is when Mister Murphy kicked in and Colin Evers took a bullet through the throat. "Severed a fuckin' artery, it did," Mick said, his face grim.

Robert Evers broke in. "My dad passed out. But Mr. Owen carried him the whole way, keeping pressure on the wound, which kept him alive."

"Your dad wasn't all that heavy," Mick said. He cracked a wry smile. "But that damn mortar got real tiresome after the first half hour."

Now, I am second to no man when it comes to listening to war stories, but there had to be a point to all of this history, and I asked what it might have been. After all, we had tangos to go after, a situation that was being compounded by the fact that the authorities were out and about looking for us.

Robert Evers greeted my interruption with obvious impatience. "There is significant history here, Captain," he said. "It has to be understood."

"I realize what you're saying, Robert. But frankly, we have to get moving—and soon."

"And you will, Captain. But you must first understand the relationship that my assistance is based on. Mister Owen saved my father's life—and the fact that he did something so selfless has always been very significant and motivating to me—"

"Dick." Mick interrupted the young Brit. "Robert here," he explained, "has never been in the military. Colin and Jane sent him to the good public schools. He went to Harrow and Cambridge, y'know, just like his dad. Robert's quite the toff. Always knows which knife and fork to use. These days, he works on his own most of the time—out and about all alone. So he never got to understand how tight you can become to someone in a brick, or when you're sharing a kip and a shit in some Fifth World Garden of Eden."

Message received. Mick was right, of course. Young men like Robert Evers don't understand that there is no experience in the world that brings people closer than having been under fire together as a part of a military unit in combat. The concept of dying for your buddy is quite foreign to most young people today. Today's kids seldom get to meet people who are actually willing to lay down their lives for their teammates. But this isn't the time or place to start a monologue on the sorry state of our national condition.

"Mr. Owen, I simply want you to understand my motivation," Robert Evers said.

"Your motivation?" Mick was now obviously confused.

"I can't ever fight alongside you the way my father did," Robert Evers said. "But I can fight alongside you in my own way."

Now, it was all becoming clear. Mick's expression softened. "I understand, boy—believe me, I do."

Robert Evers sighed in relief. "Good. Then please take these— with my father's and my compliments—and use them well." Evers removed half a dozen French passports from the inside pockets of his suit coat and laid the documents on the table.

I picked the top one up and examined it carefully. It was made out in the name of Martin Troisgros. Boomerang's color portrait— one of the five-bucks-for-five-pictures photographs Evers had asked us to give him—was professionally laminated and stamped with a holographic *Republique Française* seal that was as close to the real thing as I'd ever seen. Whoever'd done the work was as good at his work as our own CIA document maven, Freddie the Forger, because it was an excellent job, right down to the computerized European Community scanner code bar laminated inside the passport's front cover, and the magnetic strip that allowed the passport to be read like a credit card. I was speechless. I flipped through the pile until I found my own passport. I'd become a Frog named Max Bertaud. Mick Owen was Serge Iver. The rest of the men were also under alias. There were valid Argentine tourist cards in each passport.

"My dad said to tell you the champagne's on him the next time you're passing through Paris."

Mick was actually caught speechless. Finally, he found his tongue. "*Colin* did this? How could he have done it in such a short time?"

Robert Evers's eyes crinkled. "I guess you could call that a family secret," he said cryptically. "My dad said for me to tell you, quote, 'Just take yes for an answer you tatty old sod.'" Immediately, the young man's face flushed. "Those were *his* words, Mister Owen, not mine—and he instructed me to—"

"I understand, Robert, I understand," Mick said, the passport in his hand, his head still wagging in disbelief at the enormity of what had just been done for us. And then his expression changed. He'd just realized that his old mate Colin Evers was not simply a high-living investment banker with a big flat off the Champs Élysées, but was probably a very senior-grade NOC (for Non-Official Cover) intelligence officer in SIS, the British Secret Intelligence Service also known as MI6; and that Robert had followed his father into the family's chosen profession.

But no one was going to say a word about it. Not here and not now and not ever. No one's cover would be compromised by us.

Robert Evers broke the silence. "My suggestion to you all," he said, "is that you catch the hydrofoil to Montevideo. You can pick up Uruguayan visas when you land. KLM flies to Amsterdam through Brazil. Plunca, which is Uruguay's national carrier, flies to Madrid with a stop in Rio de Janeiro. Either way, you'll be back in London in sixty hours or less, without anyone knowing a thing. From there on, Mr. Owen, you're on your own."

PART THREE
SUFFERING

CHAPTER

16

0919. WE GOT TO MONTEVIDEO AND PASSED THROUGH CUSTOMS and Immigration sans incident. So we knew the documents worked. But I didn't want to head for London immediately, because there was still some unfinished business to attend to in this part of the world. The first thing we did was check into a hotel called La Cima in the old section of the city. It was a run-down, two-star place with hot and cold running hookers in the lobby, sticky carpets, rooms that stank from cigarette smoke, and old-fashioned rotary dial telephones, circa 1966. I tried to reach Nod on his cell phone. But obviously, Mister Murphy had managed to stay with us, because I wasn't able to make contact. All I heard in my ear was a fuzzy recorded message that the cell phone user I was calling either had his phone turned off or was in a dead zone and unable to receive a call. I hung up and dialed Gunny Jarriel.

The Gunny was relieved to hear I'd made it out of Argentina safely. But he warned me I'd better keep my head down, even in Montevideo. "There are a lot of folks out there looking for you right now, Dick, and I don't think they'll stop at the border."

I understood that. But it didn't matter—not with Gwilliam and Gerry on the loose and the fucking clock ticking so loudly in my head. So, I thanked the Gunny for his care and his concern, and got on with the business at hand. First, I sit-repped him on what we'd found at Gwilliam's villa, and what we'd done to make sure it would never be used against AMEMBASSY Buenos Aires. Since I couldn't discount a second attempt on the embassy, I wanted the Gunny to take active countermeasures to secure the place against possible missile attacks—and keep his eyes open for Colombians and other narcoterrorists.

"I'll order TOW screens," Gunny Jarriel said. He was talking about something that looks like a two-layer chain-link fence. The TOW can penetrate the fencing material, but the missiles guidance wires get hung up and torn by the broken chain links. It is effective, keep-it-simple-stupid protection.

And why hadn't it been deployed before? I'll let the Gunny explain.

"I was hampered making those sorts of plans," he told me. "The ambassador and your old friend Mel didn't want me putting up anything that might make it appear as if we'd gone into fortress mode. But I'll be able to go proactive now." And, the Gunny added, because of the information I'd given him, he'd be able to work quietly with his counterparts in the Argentine government to put a new security op plan together—quicken the reaction time and provide a less structured, formulaic security strategy—without having to go through the ambassador or Mel Putz.

Finally, Gunny said he'd also use a backchannel to reach out to the professionals at the Bureau of Diplomatic Security, and request an MST—an eight-man unit of DS shoot-and-looters known as a Mobile Security Team—to retrain the locals, carry out a new threat assessment, and then implement an upgraded embassy security plan. A formal MST eval would take both el Putz and the ambassador out of the loop for a while, and allow the Gunny and his people to make changes for the better.

When Gunny asked if there was any way he could repay the favor, I told him I needed some logistical help finding a small riverboat that was somewhere inside the territorial waters of the country in which I was currently sitting, and checking up on a pair of individuals who might have left Buenos Aires. He put me on hold for three minutes. Then he came back on line, gave me a name, and a Montevideo phone number, and told me to identify myself as Mister John Jones from Newark, New Jersey.

"That's original," I said.

"Hey, it'll work—and that's all that counts," Gunny Jarriel told me. "Semper Fi, Dick. Keep an eye on your six."

"I always do. Semper Fi, Gunny. Hoo Ya."

• • •

The name of the guy Gunny passed to me was Ray Lloyd. He turned out to be the U.S. Customs rep at AMEMBASSY Montevideo—or at least that's how his office phone was answered. I identified myself to the secretary as Mister John Jones from Newark, New Jersey, and asked for Ray Lloyd. She put me through immediately.

A friendly female voice came on the line. *"Heeey,* Jonesie, *que pasa?"*

Whoa, that was no guy's voice. *"Ray?* That you?"

"Yo, Jonesie, it's me—*Ramona."*

Point taken. Another example of never assume. I hope she didn't label me as part of the YAA-YAA brotherhood, YAA-YAA standing for Yet Another Asshole Times Two. "I'm just *pasa*-ing through, Ramona. Our mutual friend across the river suggested that we get together."

"Heeey, just call me Rae—that's with an R-A-E," she said in a North Joyzey accent that was pretty similar to the one I had as a ute. "We Joyzey kids gotta stick togedda."

"You got that right." I asked if she had time to see me, like right now, as my schedule was pretty tight.

"Heeey, can do." I heard her rustling paper. "It's twelve-twenty now. Meet me in twenty minutes in front of the Iglisia Matriz. It's on the west side of the Plaza Constitución."

I checked to make sure my watch read the same as Rae's, then glanced down at the tourist map under the scratched sheet of glass covering the top of the rickety-legged desk and found the PIQ.[58] It was no more than a six- to seven-minute walk away. That would give me time to try and track down Nod and see what Gerry Kelley was up to. "Will do." I paused. "How will I recognize you?"

"Don't worry, Jonesie," Rae Lloyd said, her voice suddenly all-business. "I'll know *you*."

1224. Nod was still unavailable. I had no idea WTF was going on but didn't have time to do any checking, as my *treff* with Mizz Rae Lloyd was less than seventeen minutes away.

What's that? You say I just told you that the plaza was only a six- to seven-minute walk away. You are correct. But I never ever go straight to a meeting. Not when there's the possibility of hostiles in the neighborhood. Did I know I'd be followed, or that Ramona might be shadowed? No, I did not. But I wasn't about to take any chances. And to make sure, I planned to run a short SDR[59] to see whether our presence had been noted by the local authorities—or the American Embassy.

1227. I managed to make my way through the lobby without contracting a social disease. Then I pushed through the front door into the bright sunlight and started toward my meeting with Ramona, walking slowly. But I wasn't alone. Thirty seconds after I left, Rotten Randy followed me out the door, playing the counter-surveillance role, just to make sure I wasn't taking any unwanted company to my rendezvous.

• • •

Most of the streets and avenues of Montevideo are laid out in neat rectangles. So, I came out of LaCima, turned left, and made

---

[58] Obviously it stands for Plaza-In-Question.
[59] Surveillance Detection Route.

my way along Avenida Washington, walking east, toward the Plaza Zabala. I cut through the wide plaza and walked north. So far as I could tell I was alone, but then Rotten would be able to see things much more clearly than I from his vantage point a hundred yards behind me. I ambled onto Avenida 25 de Mayo, and walked into the coolness of a convenient museum, that was housed in an old *palacio*. I peered at half a dozen eighteenth-century paintings without really noticing any of them, then came out and continued my saunter. Three blocks later I turned right, walked past a bank that was closed for lunch. (Yes, in South America, the banks close from noon to three so that the employees can take a long lunch, followed by a short siesta or, if they're lucky, a long nooner.)

1235. From the bank I continued east on 25 de Mayo, then turned right and walked along a shopping street that had a line of restaurants resembling French *bistrots,* or Italian trattorias—complete with sidewalk tables under awnings and umbrellas, surly waiters dressed like penguins, and what looked like terrific food. Then I crossed back over Avenida Washington and walked into the huge Plaza Constitución. On one side, vendors sold ice cream from carts. The benches were filled with lunchtime sunbathers. I crossed the plaza heading south, then turned to look behind me.

1238. I spotted Randy on the edge of the crowded plaza. He was roughly a hundred yards away. His body language told me I was in the clear. And so, I swung west, crossed through the heavy traffic on Avenida Ituzaingo, then strolled down the crowded sidewalk, passing directly in front of the old cathedral. The watch on my wrist read precisely 1240.

No contact. I slowed down. I stopped and admired the old church's architecture. Still no contact. I stared upward for a few more seconds, then moved on, feeling conspicuously conspicuous. I marched to the corner of Avenida Sarandí, then stood in the knot of people waiting for the light to change. Since Ramona hadn't identified herself, it was time to improvise. I'd keep going, cross the wide avenue, then turn around and sweep past the church one more time. Maybe she'd been held up. Maybe she wasn't as good a friend as Gunny had thought. Maybe—well, who knew. I was mulling my options when an arm pushed into the small of my back. It's an old pickpocket's ploy.

But before I could react, a smallish woman in a neat silk blouse, designer jeans, and sandals looked up at me and said, *"Heeey,* Jonesie—it's me, Rae. Imagine running into you here, of all places."

She was right: I never would have picked her out. She was indistinguishable from any of the other hundreds of Latin females within a hundred yards. Her arm tucked tightly under mine, I allowed myself to be guided across Avenida Sarandí. There, we wheeled to the left, waited for the light to change, and then crossed back across Ituzaingo, walking in an easterly direction parallel to the plaza.

She was about five foot five, maybe five six, with the classic olive skin of Italy—probably Sicily. She was about forty, with prominent cheekbones, dark hair cut short, and the sort of hourglass figure that Latin males find hugely attractive. She knew it too—because she swung her hips as we walked, taking in the sidelong glances with the panache of a pro. And a pro she was: we hadn't gone a hundred yards, when Ramona looked up at me and said, matter-of-factly, "Y'know there's some big bad ugly asshole following us."

"Oh?"

"Yeah. Big bald guy. Fu Manchu mustache. Ranger tattoo. I guess that makes him one of yours, huh?"

I had to smile. Ramona was observant.

I nodded. "Yeah—he's mine."

"Figured." We walked another fifty feet in silence, her arm still tucked tightly in mine. "Well, either you can send him back to wherever it is you're staying, or he's gonna have to stand around in the sun for about half an hour, and I hope he's wearing sunscreen, because this sun is brutal."

"How come?"

"How come? Cause I'm hungry, an' I wanna talk to you, not to him."

I used my left hand to tell Rotten that things were okay. Then Rae wheeled to the right, reached for the glass door to a *confitería* that was almost as traditional as the Café Tortoni in Buenos Aires, and beckoned for me to precede her inside.

I demurred. I'm old-fashioned about these things. "Ladies first, please."

She smiled a warm smile that made her dark eyes sparkle, nodded graciously, and allowed me to hold the door for her. "This place is called La Pasiva. Nice, huh?"

I looked around. It was classic South American café: marble-topped tables, marble floor, rococo design, and Art Deco fixtures. The walls, which were covered with an eclectic selection of oil paintings, had probably not been cleaned in fifty years—they were almost amber from the cigarette and cigar smoke. The only element that stood out like the proverbial sore thumb was a huge, computer-generated digital menu suspended in a four-by-six-foot frame on the back wall.

"What a mood killer."

Rae nodded in agreement. "A concession to the twenty-first century."

"Too bad."

"I thought so, too," Ramona said, her voice raised to combat the hubbub. She waved to the maître d' and we were shown to a table against the side wall about halfway to the digital menu, and handed menus. Ramona looked up at the waiter and ordered a coffee. I asked for a Heineken.

She looked impressed. "You speak good Spanish."

"Thanks."

"But I think we're better off in English." The waiter returned with our drinks. While I poured my beer, Rae ordered an *hamburguesa punto, con papas fritas.*[60] I did the same. "I like this place

---

[60] A medium-rare hamburger and French fries.

because the burgers remind me of the food I used to get at the shore when I was a kid."

"Where'ja go?"

"Ocean City and Avalon."

"It must have been fun."

"Yeah—those were the days before syringes started washing ashore. You could actually swim." She sipped at her coffee.

I toasted Ramona with my glass. "Thanks for seeing me on such short notice."

She shrugged. *"Heeey,* you're a celebrity."

"Oh?"

"You should see the cable traffic . . . Jonesie."

"You don't say."

"Oh, but I definitely do say. A lot of people with stars on their collars want your behind. Bad, too."

"Then why did you agree to meet?"

She shrugged. *"Heeey,* it's a Jarhead thing. I've known Gunny Jarriel since he was my ex-husband's platoon sergeant. Even after we split up he kept in touch. He nagged me until I went to college. He kept track and made sure I did well. And after I got my degree, he bitched and moaned until I took the civil service exam and made it into Customs. So, when Gunny Jarriel calls, I always pick up the phone. When he asks for a favor, I deliver." She sipped at her coffee, then put the cup down.

Ramona looked at me piercingly, her dark eyes searching for exactly who I was and why I was in so much trouble. "Tell you what, Jonesie boy, let's start with the truth. You tell me the story—*toda la verdad; la pura verdad*[61]—and I'll try to help if I can."

There are times when straightforward is the only way to go. And this was one of 'em. Since both Ramona and I had total trust in Gunny Jarriel, it was time for me to put my cards on the table.

_____

[61] The whole truth; the pure truth.

Which is what I did for the next half hour, my head inclined toward hers, so we wouldn't be overheard.

And at the end of it, when I'd finished, Rae Lloyd looked down at her untouched *hamburguesa* and fries, and emitted a long, low whistle. She looked at me with an expression that combined incredulity with respect and said, simply, *"Conjo*—No shit."

I picked up my own untouched burger, took a bite, and chewed. It was like eating sawdust. I swallowed it anyway and washed it down with the last of my beer. *"Es toda la verdad, Señora Ramona."*

"Tell you what," she said. "I'm gonna go back to my office and do some checking. Where are you staying?"

"The Cima."

She looked at me incredulously. "The *Semen,* you mean. That's what we call that fleabag."

"It's quiet. It's friendly."

"Friendly, oh yeah—you could say that again." She took a single bite of cold hamburger, made a face, and put the damn thing back on its plate. "They're much better when they're hot. Anyway, it'll take me about five, six hours to dig up the kind of info you're looking for." She tore the corner off the paper place mat and wrote a telephone number down. "This is my pager number. If something comes up, use that to get in touch. Otherwise, I'll call you in about six hours and we'll set up a meeting."

I slipped the paper fragment into my pocket. "Will do."

Ramona looked at me quizzically. "You gonna be okay?"

"I will be as soon as I can get moving."

"I get it. All you wanna do is get back to shooting and looting, right?" The Customs special agent read my expression. "Thought so." She reached across the table and offered me her hand. *"Heeey,* good luck, Jonesie."

I clasped her hand in my own. "Thanks, Rae."

"De nada." She stood and threw a trio of bills on the table.

I started to protest, but Ramona would have none of it. "This has nothing to do with etiquette," she said, a formidable edge creeping into her voice. "Today, lunch is on the taxpayers. Let's let Uncle pay—after all, we've been discussing business, haven't we, Jonesie?"

• • •

Lemme tell you something: if you're in law enforcement, or counterterrorism, and you want good information, get to know someone in the U.S. Customs Service. Customs does more than check your bags and collect duty when you come back from a vacation overseas. The Customs Service tracks everything from software piracy to organized crime to bank fraud. They confiscate more drugs than the DEA; they know more about the Russian Mafiya than the FBI; they have better informants than the CIA; and they have better relations with foreign law-enforcement than the State Department.

And so, Ramona Lloyd was as good as her word. Six hours after we'd abandoned our uneaten *hamburguesas* at the *confitería* La Pasiva, I had the information I was looking for. The news wasn't especially good, or encouraging. But it made me absolutely certain that a clock was ticking. Where the hell the clock was, or what the time frame might have been, I didn't know. But it was ticking. I could fucking hear it in my brain.

You say you want to know what Rae told me. Okay, I'm happy to give you the gist.

First, Gwilliam's VERB had flown alone to Paris. Gwilliam had seen her off at Ezeiza, then departed for destinations unknown. Second, *Báltai* had anchored off Punte del Este for the past nine days. It had topped off its tanks and abruptly pulled out thirty-six hours ago, destination unknown.

The crew was non-European. The captain and first mate were German. Three of the others had Iranian names. Rae had learned that particular factoid because the Iranians had been arrested in the red-light district. That certainly fit the Kelley pattern of hiring outsiders for the down-and-dirty work. Iranians made sense, too, because Iran's navy used Exocets. And Germans? I asked Ramona to wash their names through the Customs database.

There was more. At eight this morning, the *Patricia Desens* had docked at Colonia, the old port city just west of Montevideo, to take on fuel and water. Its deck was bare. The riverboat had sailed for Argentina at about the time Rae and I were having lunch. So much for running over to Colonia and interviewing *el capitán*.

Now, as you will recall from my research back in London, *Báltaí* had a five-thousand-nautical-mile range and a cruising speed of thirty-three knots—its top speed was forty-one knots.

So here's what I knew by doing some simple math. First, *Báltaí* couldn't get back to the North Atlantic (or even the Caribbean) without refueling. The most logical place for it to do that was Recife, a deepwater port on the northeast coast of Brazil. From there, the yacht could easily make the Canary Islands. And from the Canaries, they could go anywhere: Tangier, Lisbon, Genoa, Monaco, Southampton.

Second, it would be impossible to track *Báltaí*'s course without doing something like diverting a satellite to do the job. And as both you and I know, diverting a satellite was not in the cards.

So, how was I going to follow *Báltaí*'s progress? I was going to do it the old-fashioned way. I was going to use a network of port-watchers. You remember port watchers, don't you?

You don't? Well, then let me give you a nutshell explanation. Right up through World War II, the U.S. Navy had a network of paid wharf rats in just about every deepwater port in the world. These informants would pass along information about the ships that came and went. But after the war, the Warriors who ran the Navy were replaced by administrators and managers. And those apparatchiks decreed that the port-watcher system was unwieldy and impractical. Let Naval Intelligence handle things, they said, forgetting that Naval Intelligence is an oxymoron.

And so the port watchers were let go. And since then, the Navy hasn't had any decent intelligence about what's going on any-where in the world.

That's the bad news. Now there is the good news: the U.S. Customs Service has its own network of port watchers. So, if *Báltaí* put in at Recife, we'd find out about it. And with any luck, we'd be able to get a lead on the yacht's next port of call.

I gave Ramona the number of my cell phone and asked her to call the moment she had any hint of a lead on *Báltaí*'s where-abouts, or an ID on its German crew members. Then it was time to move our base of operations.

1800. The KLM flights to Amsterdam were all booked solid for the next three days. There were seats only as far as Rio. But with the help of a carefully folded hundred-dollar bill I managed to secure us all business class tickets to Madrid on Plunca. The twenty-hour, one-stopover flight was bumpy but uneventful. And, once we'd been plunked down in Spain, the guys sat in the transit lounge tapas bar quaffing good Spanish wine and munch-ing on braised octopus in garlic, stewed beef heart, cracked green olives, and hard cheese while Mick and I went off to book tickets to London and work the phones.

Mick called a pair of his former SAS mates in Hereford to elicit some intelligence about our situation. From the way they dealt with him it was obvious that he and I were neck deep in *merde*. Then he tried his office at DET Bravo and discovered that his extension had been disconnected. He dialed the phone that sat on my desk and allowed me to listen in to the recording that told us that we'd reached a nonworking telephone number in the Home Office and please to dial the main number for assis-tance.

Mick shook his head. "We are now officially declared as non-persons," he said gravely.

"So, fuck 'em."

"Easy to say. Hard to do."

• • •

Day Three: 0140. Mick wanted to get back to London and straighten out the situation. I didn't want to commit until I'd made contact with Nod. "Once Eamon or your people know where we are, we'd be operating at a disadvantage," I argued. "We'd be on the defensive, which we both know is tactically unsound. Besides, with Gwilliam and Gerry both out of the country, I don't see any reason to hurry back."

Mick thought about what I'd said, and finally saw the light. So we settled into the anonymity of the transit lounge. Let me tell you folks that if you want to real-life play hide-and-seek, one of the best places to do it is the transit lounge of a major international airport. There's food and drink, and creature comforts—if you don't mind hard chairs and squalling children. And best of all, since you haven't passed through Customs and Immigration, the government of whatever country you happen to be in doesn't know you're there.

0300. On my sixth try, I finally made contact with Nod on the cellular.

"I'm in Lisbon, Skipper."

"What the hell—"

"You don't wanna know, Skipper. And besides, I ain't got a lot of time."

"Okay, Nod: sit-rep."

"Our boy's with Brendan O'Donnell. They're cooped up in a place called the York House—it's a small hotel overlooking the port. I thought that might be significant because of that boat of theirs—the whatchamacallit."

"*Báltaí.*"

"Yeah, whatever. We tracked 'em thanks to Mick's pals. They have a car and a driver and a bodyguard and they're playing tourist: hitting the *Fado* clubs all night and the museums during the day. We've had to keep way back, because these guys are good. But we have 'em covered."

I knew that there are regular flights from Madrid to Lisbon.

"We can be there in a couple of hours. You want us to come help?"

"Negatory, Skipper. Mick's friends told me our lads are gonna pull out in five days. They have reservations on a commercial flight to the Azores."

I thought about it. And all of a sudden what Nod was telling me made perfect sense. It made sense because we were in day three of a sixteen-day cycle. That meant, for the next twelve days at least, nothing was going to happen. I say "nothing," because if the Kelleys were smart, they were going to maintain low profiles and radio silence until they staged their simultaneous two-part hit on those American and British targets.

Except, as you and I know, one element of that operation had already been canceled, by *moi*. And, if Robert Evers was as good as his word, and I had no reason at all to doubt him, given his past performance, all of the Kelleys' Green Hand Defender allies in BA were being quietly scooped up by the Argentines, and—in Robert's words—"lost within the legal system," which I certainly hoped was a metaphor for being dropped out of a plane sans parachute, ten thousand feet over the South Atlantic.

So, with part one of the Kelley op canceled, there was only part two for me to deal with.

And now that I'd made contact with Nod I didn't give a shit whether the *Báltaí* refueled in Recife, Brazil, or not. Why? Because now, I knew where the Kelleys' yacht was going to make its final refueling stop before it went on to do whatever it was going to do: the Azores.

"You stay with our boy. We'll go straight to the Azores and preposition there."

• • •

There were two flights from Madrid to the Azores in the next eight hours. One went through Lisbon to Terceira; the other stopped in Porto and then flew into Ponta Delgada. I chose the latter destination. The Terceira flight landed at Lajes Field, which is a joint civilian/military airport, and home to some four hundred U.S. NAVAIR and eighteen hundred U.S. Air Farce military personnel. I knew that, given Mister Murphy's proclivity for WPWT,[62] we'd run into someone I knew at Lajes.

And so, using our French passports, we flew into Ponta Delgado, the largest city on the island of São Miguel, the largest of the Azores nine islands. As the 737 banked in from the sea over the craggy, grass-covered volcanic hills on its final approach, Mick peered out the window and said, "Shit, it's greener than bloody England here."

He was right, too. Vegetation in the Azores, unspoiled by industrial pollution, is emerald green twelve months of the year. The islands are largely rural and unspoiled. The climate is temperate, the fish is always fresh, and the people are friendly. Since we were traveling with carry-ons only, it didn't take long to clear what passed for Customs and Immigration. Then we convoyed into the city in a pair of ancient Citröen taxis, found a modern, nine-story beachfront hotel, checked in, and hit the bar.

• • •

Day Four: 0500. I was up betimes, as that olde English diarist Sam Pepys liked to say. I pulled on a pair of shorts and a cutoff sweatshirt, and ran ten miles barefoot through the chilly surf and cold wet volcanic sand of the beach. After the summer temperatures of the Southern Hemisphere it was probably considered downright cool here in the North Atlantic—temperatures only in the low fifties. But I welcomed the chill. It reminded me of my Underwater Demolition Team Replacement Training at Little Creek, Virginia, during the fall. Hell, I am an amphibian. I am drawn to water. It doesn't matter whether the water's tropical warm or nut-shriveling cold. Just so long as it's water.

The long run cleared my head and gave me time to think. By

---

[62] That's Wrong Place; Wrong Time. Remember?

the time I'd covered five miles, I knew precisely where things stood, and what I had to do.

I knew that the time frame from when Gwilliam left the villa until the simultaneous hits were to be staged was sixteen days. We had so far used up four of those days. Gerry Kelley would arrive on Day Eight. If my pencil work on fuel consumption, cruising speed, and the North Atlantic weather conditions were correct, the *Báltaí* would arrive late on Day Eleven. The yacht would refuel and take on supplies, and then continue in a northerly direction, where it would locate and strike its oceangoing target from over the horizon, and then disappear.

Wait just a fucking second, will you? Who the hell is out here on this beach making all that racket at such an early hour?

Holy shit. Would you believe it's the big APE[63] again. He's wearing a god-awful pair of baggy plaid swim trunks and a prissy Vassar College sweatshirt, he's shivering like some pussy-ass Air Farce pilot during SERE[64] training, he's waving his fucking blue pencil in my face, and he's demanding to know how *I* know that the *Báltaí* will be heading into the north central Atlantic to hit a target in the open seas, and not steering a landward course to stage a missile attack on Buckingham Palace or the Houses of Parliament or some other potential target in Britain itself.

Hey, APE, fuck you. Stop shivering and I'll answer your question in exactly one word. And that one word is: Exocet.

See, the Exocet missile is not a multiuse weapon. It was designed specifically for one act only: skimming along the water at wave-top level and then blowing a hole in the side of a ship. The MM 38 is a two-stage, solid propellant missile. Before you fire it, the Exocet's control system determines the range and bearing of the target. In its first stage after firing, the Exocet's performance is much like that of a Cruise missile. Then, at a range of about six

---

[63] All-Powerful Editor.
[64] Survival, Evasion, Resistance, Escape.

miles, the Exocet's unique radar system automatically switches on. At that point, the missile locks on to its target, and descends to one of three preset skimming altitudes, depending on the sea conditions and the damage requirements. Exocets, therefore, do not shoot down planes like SAM-7s, or target structures and hit them from above like Tomahawks do. Exocets work solely against maritime targets.

Hey, the all-powerful editor must be happy with my explanation, because he just performed a well-executed, single-handed absquatulation. So, let's pick up where I left off, okay?

I left off in the middle of telling you that *Báltaí* would arrive on Day Eleven, to take on fuel, and supplies—and no doubt Gerry Kelley and his henchman Brendan O'Donnell, whose fellow TIRA-lira-lira tangos were responsible for the death of Butch Wells—before it headed out to sea to stalk its prey and make its kill.

And I? I would be waiting for *Báltaí*. So I could head out to sea to stalk *my* prey and make *my* kill, too.

CHAPTER

17

Day Four: 0900. There were preparations to make of course. You've heard the phrase "naked warriors" used to describe the World War II generation of what has come to be known as Naval Special Warfare? Well, we were currently very much akin to our Froggish forbears. We had our swim trunks, and the face masks, and the diving knives we'd bought in Buenos Aires, but that was it. We had no weapons or ordnance. We had no comms, except for the cell phones. We had no wet suits or fast boats, or any of the other supplies SEALs use to stage what's known in the trade as a clandestine, sea-borne tactical assault.

I mean, sea-borne tactical assaults aren't put together by chance or happenstance. You just don't go out and willy-nilly take down a vessel. In fact, let me detail for you how a squad of SEALs is usually equipped in order to assault a ship under way. Because we're talking about hundreds of pounds of equipment, much of it sophisticated and very, very specialized.

You need a fast boat like a Boston Whaler, or a RIB—a Rigid Inflatable Boat—so you and your people can get close to the target ship undetected. You need titanium-hooked steel-and-cable caving ladders atop painter's poles, so that you can snag a rail or a scupper and make the long, muscle-burning climb without being seen. You've got to wear neoprene wet suits to keep you from going hypothermic in the chilly water, and above the wet suit, fire-retardant BDUs or a one-piece Nomex flight suit to make sure you don't catch fire. You wear an inflatable SEAL combat vest and a CQC assault harness that supports the thirty to forty pounds of equipment you're carrying: the flashbangs, the flares, the radios, waterproof earpieces and throat mikes; the door wedges, the flexible nylon handcuffs, the spare magazines, the first aid kits, the water canteens, the CS gas grenades, and the climbing ropes, to give you a partial list.

You have weapons and ordnance: a suppressed MP5 submachine gun in 9-mm and six extra magazines, a suppressed 9-mm pistol and three extra mags at the very least. Suppressed because CQC in the enclosed areas of a ship is a very loud affair, and you want to keep noise at a minimum. Your breach man has a Remington 870 or Benelli shotgun and two dozen rounds of 12-gauge in assorted flavors that run the gamut from powdered zinc breaching rounds to double-ought buckshot. To scuttle ships we carry a range of explosives from blocks of C-4 or Semtex, to shaped or ribbon charges, to the new Cubane-based explosives, plus an assortment of newfangled electronic detonators and old-fashioned analog timers. To scuttle people there are frag and high explosive grenades.

Obviously, that's not the complete list, either. You wear Nomex flight gloves and a balaclava and even perhaps a knit watch cap. You carry safety equipment like flares, and chem-lights, those luminescent plastic tubes that you squeeze to make 'em light up. Many SEALs carry waterproof pencil flares and a pocket-size flare gun, as well as a couple of MK-13 smoke flares in visibility orange, red, or yellow so they can attract choppers or rescue craft if the need arises.

Now for the BNGN. The bad news first. Out of all that equipment, we currently had . . . none. And the GN? The good news was that we had more than a week to assemble enough of the inventory to make our mission achievable.

Yes, I hear you out there. You say you are dubious. Okay, Mr. Dubious, I am the Rogue Warrior®, whaddya want?

You want to know how I can assemble enough assault gear to take down a vessel under way, when I'm sitting on a small, pastoral, volcanic island group in the middle of the Atlantic Ocean, eight hundred miles from Lisbon and twenty-five hundred miles from Norfolk.

The answer to that, Mr. Dubious, is a mélange, a combination, an intermingling, of Roguish ingenuity, as well as my profound knowledge of the dynamics of SpecWar and the capabilities of SpecWarriors, with a deep understanding about the environment in which I must work. When you combine all of the above with my SpecWar credo, which is: I WILL NOT FAIL, you can come up with only one conclusion. And that sole conclusion is, that I WILL OVERCOME THE FUCKING ODDS, I WILL FULFILL THE FUCKING MISSION, AND I WILL BRING ALL MY MEN HOME SAFELY.

Let us first take the problem of transportation. As I just mentioned, we would need a fast boat or a RIB to stage our assault. Well, it so happens (the truth often being stranger and more incredible than fiction), that the Azores are one of the world's best places for whale and dolphin watching. Almost two dozen species of cetaceans—that's the fifty-dollar word for *marine mammals*—can be found in the waters off the Azores during the summer months, running the gamut from sperm whales to Atlantic spotted dolphins.

Two of the five central islands, Pico and its smaller neighbor, Faial, are each home to a handful of whale-watching companies. Some of those firms take the tourists out on fishing boats. But three of them—the companies hired by Outward Bound–type, high-excitement vacation tours based in the States—use Zodiacs, so that customers can actually run with the whale and dolphin pods, keeping up with the creatures as they race through the choppy seas.

How do I know all these details? I know them because I am educated, perceptive, and observant. I know them because, as an unconventional Warrior, a SEAL, it is my business to know essentials like these so that I can operate comfortably anywhere in the world. But most important, I know these details because, on my way back through the hotel lobby this morning after my run, I picked up every one of the whale-sighting company brochures I could find, leafed through them, and zeroed in on the one from something called Azores Whales Unlimited, which displayed pictures of satisfied customers bouncing through the Atlantic chop in Zodiac rigid inflatable boats. To be precise, bouncing through the Atlantic chop in fire-engine red, seventeen-foot-eleven-inch long, Zodiac Pro-II 550 "Thoroughbreds."

The Pro-II 550 has a top speed of fifty miles an hour, which translates to about forty-seven knots. That meant it could outrun the *Báltaí* over short distances. It has a deep V-shaped bow and deeply fashioned fin rails, which give the craft excellent handling capabilities in choppy seas, as well as the ability to plane easily and turn tightly. When fitted with a couple of supplementary twenty-gallon gas tanks, the Pro-II's range could run well over 250 nautical miles.

Day Four: 1321. While Boomerang, Randy, Hugo, and Timex spread out over São Miguel looking for useful supplies, Mick and I and a briefcase full of cash caught one of the island-hopping SATA commuter planes to Pico. We never met the pilot, but his name was probably Murphy, because instead of flying direct from São Miguel as scheduled, he diverted to Terceira, then stopped on São Jorge, and finally, two and a half hours after the posted arrival time, flew in over the crest of the huge, dominating volcanic cone for which Pico is named.

We grabbed a cab for the five-mile ride into Madalena, climbed out on the main square, paid the fare, asked directions toward the address stamped on the brochure, and, having been pointed in the right direction, started marching up a winding, one-lane, cobblestone street.

Six minutes later we stood in front of a whitewashed, two-story, tile-roofed house. There were two doors. The first was glass and led into what could have been a small travel agency or tour office: a couple of desks and lots of maps of the Azores and posters of whales were on the wall. Above the grimy office window were two hooks three feet apart. The color of the whitewash between the hooks told me that a sign must have hung there. But there was nothing to identify the place now. Mick tried the door. Nada. I stuck my nose up against the glass and peered inside. From the look of things, no one had been around for some time. But leaning up against a desk was a sign that read AZORES WHALES UNLIMITED.

Well, obviously not literally unlimited. But the fact that the place was shut down made sense: it was, in fact, three months past prime whale-watching season.

Maybe they'd be at home. The second door was made of wood, and led upstairs to what were obviously living quarters. I tried the handle. It was firmly locked. There was no doorbell, so I rapped on the heavy, painted wood. No answer. I tried again—pounding harder—without result.

Then, the door to the neighboring two-story house opened and a woman in black, age about sixty, peered out quizzically, and machine-gunned some rapid Portuguese in our direction. She had the tanned, weathered look of people who live all their lives close to the sea, or on it. You see 'em in fishing villages all over the world. She rattled on for about ten seconds, gesturing as she spoke.

But since my Portuguese is virtually nonexistent, I had no idea what she was saying. Mick held a hand out to her, palm up. "*Desculpe*—excuse me, *fala Inglês*—do you speak English?"

"*Inglês?*" Her lined face brightened.

Mick, whose Portuguese was even less fluent than mine, continued his tourist guidebook phrase conversation. "*Sim, Inglês*—yes, English."

"*Não Inglês.*"

He looked at me. "She doesn't speak English."

"I knew that." I looked at the woman and smiled. *"Desculpe— fala Espanhol?"*

"Espanhol?"

"Sim, Espanhol."

"Não Espanhol."

I tried the *fala Francês* route, but had to take *não* for an answer there, too Okay, we had reached the ol' Dead End.

No, we hadn't. I pulled the brochure from my pocket and pointed to the pictures of the whale expeditions.

"Ah," she said, and launched into another impenetrable monologue.

I interrupted her tirade. *"Não compreendo Portuguès*—I don't understand Portuguese."

"Aah," she said. She reached over and took the brochure out of my hand, unfolded it, found the map of the island, and pointed at the harbor. *"Aqui, aqui,"* she said, her gnarled index finger tapping at the port area.

• • •

Thirty-eight minutes later we stood at the edge of the small but busy port area. To my right was a tidy plaza, lined with cafés and restaurants and a trio of small, inexpensive hotels. To our left was the main harbor, with its wooden piers and fishing boats moored alongside. Directly in front of us were a series of stowage sheds, most of them weather-beaten, two-story wood structures, whose rear doors, now closed, cantilevered out over the water. The third shed in the line was painted blue and white, with the cartoonish figure of a frolicking whale. The wide front doors were wide open, so I walked inside, followed by Mick.

And immediately felt right at home. This place was as shipshape as any stowage locker in the Old Navy—the Navy run by chiefs and men o'warsmen, not bureaucrats and managers. The lines were all coiled in perfect symmetry. Racks of bright orange life jackets, sitting straight up like sailors at attention, lined one wall. The other wall held immense shelves on which sat four bright red and gray Zodiac Pro-IIs. In stands below the shelves, four 120-horsepower Yamaha long-shaft engines, polished and waxed, rested in custom-made racks.

I heard rustling in the rafters and looked up. Mick started to say something but I cut him off. "My turn." Then I called out: "*Monsieur? 'allo? Excusez-moi?*"

There was a slight pause, and then a small, mustached man in blue coveralls, a tool belt cinched around his waist, swung out from one of the Zodiac shelves and stared down at us.

"May I help you, monsieurs," he said in accented but obviously fluent French.

"We're here to rent a boat," I said in my best Parisian accent.

"Ah," he said, "but it is not the season for watching the whales."

"We know that," I called up to him. "But we are still interested in renting a boat, Monsieur . . ."

"Pereira, Pereira, Frederico Pereira. Wait—I am coming down." With the agility of a square-rigger deckhand, he swung himself over the edge and easily lowered himself by his fingertips to the shelf below, his feet catching the lip of the thick wood before his hands released their grip on the shelf above. Then he turned and made his way down a crude ladder nailed (somewhat precariously, I thought) to the warehouse's interior framing.

He dropped the last five feet to the wooden-plank deck of the warehouse, brushed his palms together half a dozen times to take any detritus from them, and offered us his hand. "Frederico Pereira," he said, "at your service, monsieurs."

Mick took his hand and shook it, in the European manner— once up, and once down. I did the same. Pereira's grip was firm. His hands had the toughness acquired by years of hard work. I gestured at the Zodiacs and the well-maintained accessories. "You keep everything very shipshape, Mr. Pereira."

He gave me a grateful smile. "I am proud you noticed, monsieur. I work hard to make sure that I have the safest, and best, boats on the island."

"And we are sure that you do, Mr. Pereira." I put my arm around the little man's shoulder. "My name is Max Bertaud. I am an oceanographer by trade. I work at l'École de la Océanographie de Paris, and my colleague, Serge, and I wonder if you would be able to rent us one of your excellent Zodiacs so that we can perform some studies on the currents surrounding the islands."[65]

"It sounds like interesting work," the little man said. "Of course, I would have to see how capable you are at handling the boat, as we do not normally rent our boats to customers. I always serve as the coxswain."

"I appreciate your concern, Monsieur Pereira, and I would be happy to demonstrate for you that I am more than capable of handling your fine craft." I smiled at Mick. "And we will be happy to pay you a supplement for the use of your Zodiac, since you will not be around to keep an eye on it."

• • •

Day Five: 0655. Nod checked in. Gerry Kelley and Brendan O'Donnell were maintaining their tourist schedule. That troubled me. "Keep your eyes open. Seems to me what they're doing is performing a long, long SDR."

"That's what I think, too, Skipper."

"Good. So make absofuckinglutely sure that you don't spook 'em, Nod. Otherwise they'll bolt, and change their plans, and we'll be fucked."

---

[65] What I am doing here is called, in the intel trade, a false flag operation. By (aptly, I think) passing myself off as a Frog, I am concealing my true intentions and objectives from Frederico Pereira. Thus, if something should go wrong, he will only be able to report to the authorities that a Frenchman named Max Bertaud, from l'École de la Océanographie de Paris, rented one of his Zodiacs to do some work charting the currents around the islands. And, of course, there will be no record of any Max Bertaud in the French government's files.

"I recognized the signs already, Skipper. We're at Threatcon Delta, but we stay out of sight."

Like all good senior chiefs, Nod had the situation already covered. "Bravo Zulu, Nod." I went on to ask Nod to detail as many of the men as he could to pick up the items we'd be needing— especially a battery-powered Magellan GPS, so we could navigate on open seas. "If you can't lay your hands on one, let me know right away."

"Will do, Skipper."

• • •

Day 5: 1000. Using my French passport, I'd rented a hotel room on the island of Pico when Mick and I flew there to secure the Zodiac. That way, we had a permanent forward base just in case the *Báltaí* docked there, instead of São Miguel. The room also came in handy for the toughest part of the supply detail: weapons procurement. We had to have at least two pistols to make our assault. Four would be even better. I wanted a pair of shotguns for the takedown, too.

The shotguns turned out to be easy to obtain: bird hunting is commonplace in Portugal, and all Nod had to do was march into a store, where he showed his military ID, and was able to legally purchase a nice Beretta over-and-under 12-gauge. Six hours later, Digger O'Toole did the same at a second hunting-supply store. Once they arrived on the Azores, we'd cut the barrels and stocks down, giving us a pair of concealable and lethal sawed-offs.

The pistols were another story. Handguns are impossible to come by in most of Europe. So we'd have to obtain 'em the old-fashioned way: thievery.

Boomerang and Rotten flew to Pico using their French passports to buy the tickets. From there, they took the ferry to Terceira, and thence jumped a bus that took them to Lajes Field, known to MILPERS (that's MILitary PERSonnel for all you non-MILPERS out there) as "Crossroads of the Atlantic, Home of the U.S. Forces, Azores, and the 65th Air Base Wing."

Using their military IDs, Boomerang and Rotten Randy simply meandered right through the main gate just as the evening shift was settling in. The white-gloved, bereted, COD (Cop On Duty) never smelled anything fishy. It didn't take my pair of merry marauders more than half an hour to locate the Crossroads of the Atlantic's weapons locker. They made sure no one was around, quietly picked the lock on the door, snuck inside, removed four Beretta 9-mm pistols, twelve magazines, and two hundred rounds of 115-grain, full-metal-jacket ammunition, all of which they stowed in their knapsacks. Then they snuck out, relocked the door, meandered into the night, and—having waited for the guard shift to change—marched back through the main gate and caught a zero-dark hundred ferry back to Pico, stowed the weapons in the hotel room I'd rented, then caught the first plane available back to São Miguel.

I know, I know. You're about to tell me that it was all much too easy. Where, you ask, was Mister Murphy? How come nobody paid Randy and Boomerang any attention? How come there weren't any guards around to stop 'em, or ask who the hell they were and what the hell they were doing on the base.

The fact is, most of our military bases are wide open and vulnerable as hell to terrorism, or just plain mayhem. That's nothing new: I proved that back in the late 1980s with Red Cell, when I was able to wreak havoc on Naval installations worldwide, "sinking" an aircraft carrier in the Philippines, taking the base commander hostage in Norfolk, placing explosives aboard a nuclear submarine in Groton, and even "blowing up" *Air Force One* in a simulation.

Well, as the Frogs say, *Plus ça change, plus c'est la même chose.* Or, as Yogi Berra would translate that, "It's déjà vu all over again." Hell, in an environment where the State Department allows a Russkie intelligence officer to plant a listening device in a conference room, or creates the atmosphere in which laptop computers containing highly classified counterterrorist files are kept in an unlocked office and therefore are stolen by parties unknown, how surprising is it to you that two of my talented, capable, highly trained rogues can bluff their way onto an Air Farce base and make off with a bunch of guns? It shouldn't surprise you at all.

Day Eight: 1200. By now we were in better shape than you might expect. I'd assigned Timex to stay at the hotel on Pico, so he could keep an eye on the weapons, buy containers to hold the extra fuel we'd need to carry in the Zodiac, and also watch the harbor just in case the *Báltaí* showed up. I'd rented a third hotel room, this one on Terceira, so we could maintain a discrete surveillance on the port. Hugo and Mick Owen manned that observation post. Yes, I was taking a risk by deploying people to separate islands, because given the erratic schedule of ferries and puddle jumpers, there was no way I could guarantee that we could assemble quickly if we had to MOVE. But I had no idea where Gerry would go—or which of the deepwater harbors *Báltaí* would choose for its refueling stop. And so I had to take the risk of dividing my forces to make sure all my bases were covered.

Which left Boomerang, Rotten Randy Michaels, and me to finish up the supplies. We wouldn't need a caving ladder, as the *Báltaí*'s rails were low enough so that if we snagged her with a rope ladder, we could pull ourselves aboard. Boomerang constructed one out of a fifty-foot length of soft, woven nylon climbing rope that he discovered in São Miguel's only camping goods store. We fashioned a hook from a twelve-inch spike, and wrapped it in a pillowcase to muffle undue sounds. I improvised half a dozen assault harnesses from the carpenter's tool-carrying belts—the ones with all the pouches.

Rotten Randy found us a ten-foot-by-ten-foot piece of fishnet at a street market. It was strong enough to support even my Roguish weight, and light enough so that carrying it wouldn't be a burden. We jury-rigged it so we could use it to climb if necessary. As for wet suits, Boomerang managed to scrounge eight commercial short-sleeved, short-pants surfer's suits. Not what I would have wanted, but anything is better than nothing when you're out on the water and hypothermia is a real risk.

• • •

1325. Gerry Kelley knew what I looked like. So there was no way I was going anywhere near any of the Azores airports today. I sent Boomerang and Rotten Randy to Ponta Delgada while I stayed in the hotel room, monitoring the phones and waiting for Nod to call and tell me where Gerry was.

1331. The cell phone in my breast pocket vibrated. "Yo."

"Yo, Jonesie."

"Yo, Rae. Whassup?"

Her voice crackled back at me. "Got some info for ya, man."

"Shoot."

"That boat—it went where you thought it would."

"Cool. Anything else?"

"Yeah: the Krauts are dirty. Not fugitives or anything, but they're into some nasty shit. Be careful out there, huh?"

"Will do. I owe you, Rae."

"*Heeey,* we north Joyzey kids gotta stick togedda, right?" She laughed, then the phone went dead.

1640. Nod's chipper voice on the cell phone. "*Boa tarde,* Skipper. We're feet dry and good to go."

But I wasn't in a playful mood. I'd been in a fucking vacuum for days. "Where're our targets?"

I guess he picked up on my tone, because he came back all-business. "They're clearing Customs here at Ponta Delgada," Nod said. "There's a car outside waiting—I figure they'll book themselves into some hotel. Me and Digger caught the flight with 'em. The rest of the guys are on the next plane."

"You have a couple of friends waiting outside."

He chuckled. "You mean Gonorrhea and Diarrhea loitering in the no-parking zone? I already saw 'em out there. We'll hand the targets off so Digger and I can come see you."

"Good man. Did you bring me any . . . presents?"

268

"You're gonna think it's effing Christmas, Skipper. I got all the goodies, including the Portuguese navigator you wanted so bad."

He'd brought me my very own Magellan. My tone softened. "You're a good boy, Nodster. *A bientôt*—see you very soon."

• • •

2225. "Very soon" turned out to be a vast overstatement. Why? Because Gerry Kelley didn't stay on São Miguel. He and Brendan O'Donnell left their car and driver waiting and impetuously caught the last SATA puddle jumper to Pico. Then they caught the evening ferry from Madalena to Horta, Faial's main port city. Had they been spooked? Who knew. Were they going to signal the Báltaí to come and pick 'em up ahead of schedule? I had no idea. All I did know was that it was way too late in the day to make any moves now.

Here was the good news: Timex was sitting on Pico. I'd called him (I don't know how we operated in the days before cell phones) and he managed to ID our two targets as they transferred onto the ferry and followed 'em to Faial. If they made any further moves, Timex would know about them.

I checked the schedules. The first flight we could catch to Pico was at 1100 the next morning. Once we'd reached Madalena, Boomerang and I would take the Zodiac and cross the strait to Faial. Rotten Randy would use the ferry, so he could transport all the gear we'd assembled. I checked in with Timex. Our boys had taken rooms at the best hotel on the island, the Estalagem Santa Cruz, built inside a sixteenth-century fort overlooking the harbor. Timex booked us six less ritzy rooms at the Fayal, a big hotel in the center of town but still convenient to the marina. "I love it here, Skipper," he reported with the exuberance of youth. "There's a buffet breakfast—all you can eat!"

2230. I called the SATA office to make reservations. Oh, yeah—right. This was the Azores, after all. And even though I don't speak Portuguese, I knew what the scratchy message on the answering machine was telling me: "Call back during normal business hours, you asshole—*beep.*"

Fuck. I called Mick Owen in Terceira and gave him a brief sit-rep. There was a direct flight from Lajes to Faial at 1400. He said he and Hugo would be on it, no matter what it might take.

• • •

Day Nine: 0700. I started calling the SATA office. It was 0940 before anyone picked up the phone. But I was able to get three seats on the eleven o'clock flight. I called the front desk and told the manager to get our bill in order.

1322. I gunned the Zodiac out of Madalena harbor and turned south, running parallel to the coastline, until I'd cleared the town. Roughly two kliks later, I turned toward the coast and guided the tough little craft through the breakers, beaching it in a small, protected cove that Mick and I had discovered the day we'd arranged to rent the boat from Frederico Pereira.

Boomerang was waiting. Piled next to him were a half dozen bright red plastic jerry cans. They looked just like the six-gallon gas containers you can find at Wal-Mart back in the States. Which is precisely what they turned out to be. Don't look surprised, friends. This is the twenty-first century and the economy is totally global.

I did some fast math in my head. With the extracapacity tanks that Frederico had already installed on the Zodiac for his whale-watching expeditions, we'd have an operational range of just over two hundred miles. We could go even farther if we siphoned fuel from *Báltaí* once we'd boarded her.

Yes, I hear you carping out there; complaining that *Báltaí* has diesel engines, and that we won't be able to use her fuel in our outboard. You are correct. But all ships the size of *Báltaí* carry Zodiacs or other small craft as launches. And those launches are generally gas powered. In any case, the matter is moot. We'd get a chance to eyeball *Báltaí* when she berthed in the Azores, so we'd learn whether or not we would be able to refuel from her supplies long before I'd committed us to following *Báltaí* beyond the point of no return.

It didn't take more than a couple of minutes to stow the empty fuel cans and strap them down. Then we eased the Zodiac into the surf, turned her around, clambered aboard, started the engine, and headed back the way I'd come for the five-mile cruise across the strait between Pico and Faial. The water was clear and cool. The chop was mild. I opened her up. The little RIB stood on its hind legs and kicked forward, and I felt the wonderful sensation of sea spray in my beard.

Two and a half kliks out, I turned the con over to Boomerang. Then I sat back on the padded double seat and allowed my body to relax. When I did, a wondrous thing happened. The little boat became a part of me, and I became a part of it, my big frame adapting to the Zodiac's aggressive attack on the water the way a cowboy and a great quarter horse meld into one being when they work cattle together.

I swiveled around. Behind us was the towering, mile-and-a-half-high volcano that dominates Pico. I dropped my head back. Above us, high, puffy cumulous clouds stood stark white against the blue sky. It was a perfect day, so flawless that the only thing it needed was a big logo in the sky that read "THE END: A Walt Disney Production." It is at times like this, my friends, that I know deep in my heart that the Old Testament God of War is a great and a noble and a beneficent God, because He allows me to see wonders like this before I am privileged to serve His will, go into battle, and kill mine enemy in His name.

CHAPTER

18

DAY TEN: 0410. *BÁLTAÍ* EASED INTO THE HARBOR AT HORTA, APPEAR-
ing ghostlike out of the night, her running lights dimmed by thin
strands of early morning fog that sat atop the water's surface. I'd
been there from midnight, watching from the cover of a blocked-
off alley facing the marina, unmindful of the chill and the damp,
sweeping the horizon with the night-vision monocle that Mick
had stowed in his hand luggage. Yes, by my own estimates of
time, speed, and distance, *Báltaí* hadn't been expected until Day
Eleven. But here on Faial I chose to follow the Roguish SpecWar
Commandment not to assume anything. And so, we'd watched
for *Báltaí* around the clock from the time we'd arrived.

I'd assigned myself the worst shift: 2200 to 0600 hours. And I
can tell you sans reservation that it had been six hours of misery
so far. But as I explained back in Buenos Aires, misery is what surveillance is all about. You cannot slacken, or tire, or relax. Your
mind must remain alert—to your surroundings, and to the job at
hand. Sure, I was stiff, and cold, and bored. But then, in that
instant as *Báltaí* emerged into my field of vision, both my patience
and the cramps in my legs, neck, and back were rewarded.

Out of the dark she came, silent as a specter, almost as large as
a destroyer escort—and no doubt just about as fast. The only

sounds I heard were the lapping of the water against the pilings, and the slap of an occasional wave on the breakwater. My excitement was palpable: the hair on the back of my neck stood up as the big boat moved into the marina—my Roguish instincts telling me there was danger aboard. *Báltaí* was barely moving as it passed the far end of the breakwater. Two hundred yards from the largest of the piers, it reversed its engines, deployed its bow thrusters, and eased gently to a complete stop. I hunkered down behind the damp concrete, my night vision poking around the end of the barricade just in case there was a clandestine counter-surveillance lookout aboard.

Atop the wheelhouse, a radar dish revolved. Behind the radar was a short, streamlined antenna mast, attached to which I made out a series of UHF and VHF antennas. Behind the mast, partially sheltered, was a pair of four-foot-high white spheres—no doubt telecom antennas. I heard the metallic crunch of anchor chain as it paid out six fathoms to the bottom of the harbor. Then—all was silence once more.

I swept the ship with my night vision, searching for any sign of the missiles. I saw nothing explicit. The *Écureuil's* forty-foot, dome-shaped cover sat bulbous on the upper deck above the main cabin, five or six yards aft of the low funnel. That, obviously, was the only location large enough to conceal a pair of Exocets and their launcher. They'd probably off-loaded the chopper and hidden the missiles there.

I shifted my gaze. There was a pair of crewmen just aft of the chopper pod, dressed for lookout duties. I swung my monocular forward. I could make out three crewmen in the wheelhouse, their silhouettes illuminated in my night vision by ambient light from the ship's instrumentation pods. I picked up movement on the port-side aft quarterdeck, below the wheelhouse and main saloon with its indoor swimming pool. Two more crewmen lowered an accommodation ladder and float off the inboard side of the vessel. Four more worked the stern davits and lowered a small launch, which was towed forward and tethered to the float attached to the accommodation ladder. But that was all the crew did. Once the launch had been lashed securely to a cleat, the crew disappeared.

That made sense to me. There were no tenders at Horta. And so, *Báltaí* would have to tie up to the pier—which she would dwarf—in order for its fuel tanks to be topped off, to take on fresh water, and load other supplies. But that would be done only after 0600, when the marina opened. Until then, the boat would rest at anchor.

• • •

0955. I remained out of sight. There was no need for Gerry to see me. Not yet. I sent Boomerang, Nigel, and Hugo on the morning recon. They ambled down to the marina, and Boomerang and Hugo struck up a conversation with one of the dockworkers helping to refuel *Báltaí*. It didn't take more than a couple of minutes' worth of oohing and ahhing about the luxurious craft to learn that Gerry Kelley and Brendan O'Donnell had already moved aboard. Nigel stayed in the background, quietly making sketches and taking notes. By 1025, Boomerang heard that *Báltaí* was due to leave at zero dark hundred the following morning. Zero three hundred to be precise. The harbormaster was already complaining publicly about having to work additional hours. By 1100, Nigel was able to finish his diagrams, which would help us find our way during our attack. He also noted that *Báltaí* had a small diving platform attached to her stern. That would make our initial assault much easier to accomplish. Believe me, trying to fight your way along an improvised climbing rope to a ship under way is not an easy thing to do.

Two things occurred to me at that point. The first was, I didn't want *Báltaí* slipping away at night. Keeping up with her would be hard enough on the open sea. I didn't want to have to worry about losing her in darkness or, more to the point, fog. Night vision does not help you if your target is enshrouded in fog. And so, we'd have to come up with some ploy to keep *Báltaí* in port overnight. I didn't want *Báltaí* disabled for more than a few hours—just enough to keep her around until midday of Day Twelve. I put Rotten Randy Michaels, Nigel, Digger, and Goober on the problem and gave 'em a 1400 cutoff.

Second, I wanted some idea of what *Báltaí's* target was going to be. That way I'd know generally in which direction she was going to head.

Obviously, we're talking a maritime target here. And so, what I needed to know was which vessels would be within range—range being between tomorrow, Day Eleven, and Day Sixteen.

1100. Mick and I started working the phones. But without much result. It's hard to hit up people for intel when you've been labeled too hot to handle, even if national security is involved and lives are at stake. After I smacked snout-first into a series of dead ends, I decided that maybe we could develop the intelligence we needed ourselves, using OSINT—Open Source INTelligence.

1210. We jury-rigged Nod's laptop to his cell phone, and he logged onto the Net. By 1350, he'd come up with five possible tango targets. Two were cruise ships that were scheduled to visit Madeira, which lies southeast of the Azores, about four hundred miles off the African coast. I discounted them: the passengers were mostly French, Spanish, and Scandinavian.

There was a small task force of U.S. Naval vessels heading from Norfolk into the Mediterranean. I crossed them off, too: the Kelleys had already targeted the American Embassy in BA. No: the objective here would be British. Which left two Brit-flagged supertankers carrying North Sea crude to South America, and Cunard Lines *Queen Elizabeth 2*, on the final leg—Lisbon to Southampton—of a round-the-world cruise. The tankers gave me pause. I mean, just think of the mess a couple of million gallons of crude oil could make if it was spread in a huge slick that covered more than a thousand square miles of ocean. And believe me, it wouldn't take more than one Exocet per supertanker to do that kind of damage.

The *QE2* was certainly another possible. It was the flagship of the British commercial fleet. According to one of the unofficial *QE2* Web sites we browsed, it was currently carrying more than two thousand passengers and crew. Sinking her would definitely thrust the Kelleys into the Abu Nidal class of international terrorists. But then, so would breaking apart two supertankers and causing the largest oil spill in history. The two tankers were currently sailing southward, heading toward the mid-Atlantic from the North Sea. The *QE2* was currently en route from Senegal to Funchal, Madeira, where it would overnight. From Funchal, it would head to Lisbon, and thence to its home port at Southampton.

I left Nod to see what he could find while I listened to Rotten's plan for keeping the Kelleys bottled up in port until Day Twelve. Given my druthers, I wanted *Báltaí* to leave Horta sometime after 1200—noon to you civilians out there. There was still daylight until 1730 or so. We'd have to track the ship until it was at least sixty miles from Faial, which would put it over very deep water. We'd overtake *Báltaí* in semidarkness, board from the stern, neutralize the crew, disable the missiles, and then scuttle the sumbitch in eight-nine-ten-thousand-plus feet of water. Once the sea cocks were opened and *Báltaí* was sinking, we'd slip back into our Zodiac and skedaddle back to Horta, using our battery-operated Magellan GPS to show us the way.

You are probably asking yourself why I didn't plan to take *Báltaí* down and then sail her back myself, with the crew, the Kelleys. And Brendan O'Donnell in handcuffs so we could put 'em all on trial. Well, the answer is complex. And the first portion of it has to do with my feelings about how terrorists should be dealt with.

Which is terminally. A dead tango cannot tie up your legal system with a series of appeals. A dead tango cannot make himself/herself a victim instead of a murderer by spinning his/her story in the press. No: I wanted to put an END to the Kelleys and their brand of terrorism. These people were killers. They had caused the death of one of my Warriors. I wanted them and their vessel simply to disappear. It would be neat, and above all, it would be FINAL.

Second, there was a lot at stake here. Eamon the Demon was after my scalp. So were any number of other admirals, generals, and assorted senior government apparatchiks. By sinking *Báltaí* I gave myself deniability. After all, we had traveled under French documents. We had paid for all our tickets in cash. And neither Gunny Jarriel, nor Robert Evers, nor Rae Lloyd was going to talk about where we'd been or what we'd done while we were on their turf. With *Báltaí* in twenty-five hundred fathoms of water, there'd be no evidence of what the current Pentagon crowd thinks of as unfair gamesmanship. So: sinking the Kelleys' yacht protected me, and Mick, and most important, it protected my men from all those politically correct assholes who believe that Warriors aren't necessary anymore, that WAR is reprehensible, and that we can deal with our enemies more effectively by reasoning with them than we can by killing them.

Besides, the whole op was so KISS that it would probably be no more than a POC (look it up in the damn glossary), right? Oh, yeah. Just a simple hop & pop. And if you believe *that* I have some nice real estate to sell you at a bargain price. It's in the Ukraine, and the property glows in the dark.

• • •

1422. Rotten said the best way to keep *Báltaí* around for a few hours would indeed be to tie the cocksucker up. Literally. But in a way that didn't betray the fact that it was an act of sabotage. The consensus was that as soon as it got dark, we should slip into the water, work our way over to where *Báltaí* was berthed, and wrap her prop and shaft with fish netting into which we'd slipped a metal cleat or two. When they powered up, the resulting damage would be severe enough to keep *Báltaí* around for eight or nine additional hours, because they'd be unable to attempt any repairs until daylight. That would give us the WOO[66] I'd told Randy we needed. Rotten had a wide grin on his big, round face when he finished detailing the op-plan. "We kept it simple, stupid, didn't we, Skipper?"

• • •

Day Eleven: 1925. Darkness had come early. The temperature had dropped into the high forties by midafternoon, accompanied by westerly winds and ash-colored clouds carrying rain squalls. It was lousy weather for tourists, which made it perfect for SEALs. Since we weren't carrying skin-blackening cammo cream, we'd improvised with liquid shoe polish. You'd be surprised how much light your skin attracts at night, and I wasn't about to give the opposition the chance to spot us. The shoe polish stung like hell when we applied it. And I knew it probably wasn't gonna do my complexion any good. But I never joined the Navy to become a fashion model either.

Goober, Digger, and I slipped out of our jeans, revealing the shortie wet suits underneath. Shit—they weren't gonna keep us warm. But they were all we fucking had. The water temperature was forty-three. That meant we had about twenty-eight minutes before hypothermia would begin taking its toll on our bodies and our minds.

Mick focused a small pair of binoculars on *Báltaí*, sitting 150 or so yards away. "I see Gerry and Gwilliam in the main saloon," he whispered. "They're talking to someone—looks like the captain judging from the uniform."

"Lookouts?"

He shifted from binoculars to our night-vision device, holding it in place with his left hand. "Two of them in front of the wheelhouse," he stage-whispered, "and one more at the stern."

We'd manage. "See you soon. Don't catch pneumonia sitting

---

[66] Window Of Opportunity.

here." I slipped across the street, the thirty-foot length of mesh fish net slung over my shoulder, made my way to the edge of the quay, and dropped over the side into the dark water, disturbing it as little as possible.

Oh shit, but it was scrotum-shriveling cold. But cold doesn't matter. That's one of the first things you learn during BUD/S. Cold can be handled through SHEER WILL AND SHEER DETER-MINATION—not to mention keeping careful track of the time. So, I swiveled the bezel of the diving watch on my left wrist to mark our immersion time, ducked my head under to wet myself completely, surfaced, spat in my mask and washed it out, then fitted the soft rubber flange to my face and made sure the strap was tight. I passed the net off to Digger and took charge of one of the two cleats we'd weave into it. Damn, it was heavy.

0:02:21. I sidestroked clumsily, the weight of the cleat weighing on my bottom arm, toward the piers to my left. Goober and Digger followed, stroking quietly but determinedly in my wake.

We swam under the first pier, made our way between a pair of fishing boats, and then stroked across twenty yards of open water to the next pier. I waited, the cold water gnawing at my toes and fingers, for my combat swimmers to catch up with me. Digger wasn't more than ten seconds behind. But we waited more than a minute for Goober to show. And when he did, he was obviously in agony. I used my hands to ask what the matter was. He signaled back that it was a leg cramp.

The sumbitch was not going to be any use to me in that condition. I ordered him to go back. He gave me the finger. His hands told me that he would complete the mission.

I understood his drive. He'd had a buddy killed at the hands of these assholes, and there was nothing in the world that would keep him from evening up the score.

0:05:55. I surfaced between a pair of twin-masted barks moored opposite *Báltaí*. I could hear music playing on the big yacht. Keeping the sailing craft between me and *Báltaí* so I wouldn't get caught in the ambient light, I swam toward the end of the dock, and went under it. Digger caught up with me, and my hands told him what I wanted us to do. When Goober finally appeared, I was firm: either he would wait here for us, or go back. I wasn't about to risk his drawing attention.

His expression told me that he didn't like what I'd ordered him to do—but he would comply.

I mouthed, "Good boy." Digger relieved him of the cleat he was swimming with and passed it to me. I tried to hold the pair of heavy metal cleats one-handed. No fucking way. This was not gonna be any fun at all. But I was in no position to complain. I grabbed a big lungful of air, gauged our position, and dove.

It was black and it was cold. I swam—if you could call it that— carefully, shielding the metal cleats against my body—I didn't want to strike *Báltaí*'s hull and alert anyone—moving along the muddy bottom until I'd kicked the twenty-three kicks that I'd guesstimated would bring me past the big yacht.

I eased upward, my right elbow probing ahead of me. It touched the metal of the hull. I moved up, up, up, alongside the big vessel, and surfaced exactly where I'd wanted to: right under the fantail. It was a protected area that couldn't be seen unless someone climbed over the stern rail and leaned way, way out.

0:09:33. My hands were now numb up to the elbows. There was pressure on my chest. I felt a little light-headed, all of which told me that hypothermia was beginning to affect me. I caught a breath of the cold, wet air and waited for Digger. And waited. And waited.

Finally, he came around the starboard side, swimming carefully so as not to disturb the water. He'd gotten turned around completely and ended up under the bow. But then, Eddie's a city boy who has trouble finding his way without street signs.

He unhitched the netting from around my neck and we unfurled it right there to make our job easier once we'd gone below the surface, where we'd be working in Braille. Then I worked the two cleats into the net as securely as I could. I didn't want Mister Murphy pulling 'em free when we attached it to the prop.

0:11:11. I felt my way under the stern, eased below the surface, and, lacking any way to pull myself along the hull, kicked down toward where I thought the prop and shaft would be.

Big fucking mistake. I smacked my head on the goddamn propeller blade. Instinctively, I reached up—and knocked my face mask askew. This was not going well.

I surfaced as quietly as I could, drained and adjusted the mask, and slipped it back over my head. Now I realized that the vision in my right eye was blurred. I was washing my face off when Digger surfaced close by. He examined me up close.

"You're cut," he mouthed, and touched my forehead, two inches above my right eye.

I shrugged. I couldn't feel a fucking thing—the cold, I guessed—and so I wiped at my face, fixed the mask strap, and eased below the surface once again.

0:12:55. This time I managed to stay away from the prop blade. Digger's hand found mine, and we managed to bring the fishnet over and around the big prop and shaft before we had to surface and suck a fresh supply of air.

0:16:48. I slipped up to the surface, grabbed a fresh lungful of air, and went back to work. I used my knife to cut the netting so I could wind it around the shaft and tangle it up in the variable-pitch prop. Except, it was hard to manipulate the knife in the darkness. I kept losing my grip, and the fucking thing would drop out of my hand, and I'd have to retrieve it using the lanyard, then identify the piece of net I'd been cutting by feel, and start all over again.

By which time I'd run out of air and have to surface, breathe, and descend once again.

0:21:20. I was now numb way past my shoulders. I couldn't feel my legs. The water was so cold that it burned. But we kept at it, working as quickly as we could without making a sound. Finally, we were able to position the netting so that when the screw began to turn, the cleats would ding the fouled prop.

0: 22:49. We surfaced. Digger's eyes told me that he was operating way beyond his capabilities right now. Well, so was I. But that didn't matter. Warriors GET THE FUCKING JOB DONE NO MATTER WHAT IT TAKES. And we had to check the fucking net one more time. I wasn't about to allow Mister Murphy to screw with this op—now, or later. It was way too critical.

And so, unmindful of the pain and the cold we dove one more time into the blackness, and we ran our numbed hands over the netting, and made absofuckinglutely sure that the cleats were secured tight and firm and were well positioned to do just enough damage to keep *Báltaí* around for a few critical hours, but not cause any permanent damage. And then, when we had done all of that, which took us three separate dives, we broke the water's surface, frozen and breathless and exhausted, and lay, our heads lolling in the water under *Báltaí*'s stern. We were totally spent. We were physically and mentally gone. Lights out, no one home. I felt . . . drowsy. My thoughts began to wander. Not good. I forced myself to check my watch, laboring to focus on the E-Z read luminous dial. I tried to put words to what I saw but found myself dumbly incapable of doing so. But I struggled on, my eyes and brain trying to synchronize, and finally decided that our elapsed time was 0:31:33. Didn't that mean we were operating in the red zone? Didn't that mean we'd lose muscle control? Somewhere, in the back of my frost-coated mind, a warning light went off, and I knew that if I didn't fight against it, we'd be in real danger of drowning. And we still had to make it back across a wide expanse of cold, dirty water.

I pounded on Digger's shoulder. "Gotta move," I croaked. And then I started swimming.

• • •

We were back in the hotel by 2040. Since the human body cools down twenty-five times faster when subjected to cold water than it does when subjected to cold air, my body temperature had dropped to 94.6 during the thirty five and a half minutes I'd been in the harbor doing God's work under *Báltaí.*

I stood under a hot shower trying to get my body above ninety-seven degrees. It wasn't easy. I'd been as thoroughly chilled down as a shipping carton of Perdue Oven Stuffer Roasters when I climbed out of the water. If it hadn't been for Mick's support I probably wouldn't have made it back to the hotel. Lemme tell you the unvarnished truth about Warriordom: it is tough work, and it is hard on the ol' Rogue bod. In point of fact, Warriordom is an occupation most well suited to youngsters, whose bodies can more easily absorb the bumps, humps, lumps, jolts, dents, and dings that come with the job. Once you start the inevitable slide toward middle age, the body needs more time to recover from the sort of abuse people like me tend to heap upon it.

And so, slapped, zapped, whapped, and tapped out, I stood under the hot water for about three-quarters of an hour until I stopped shivering. Then I stood there another fifteen minutes until I could actually feel my fingers and toes. Then I toweled off, applied a piece of tape to the inch-and-three-quarter laceration on my forehead, wrapped myself in a pile of blankets, and since no one was offering me what I really wanted, which was a beaker of Dr. Bombay Sapphire and a long, long soak between a pair of warm thighs, I threw myself on the bed for a quick combat nap. I figured about half an hour would do me, because I wanted to be up and running in time to see the results of my labors over in the marina. I set my never-fail mental alarm clock, lay back on the mattress, and closed my aching eyelids.

CHAPTER

19

I ROLLED OVER AND PEERED AT THE DIGITAL READOUT ON THE CLOCK-radio sitting on the bedside table. The bright blue numerals told me it was 0735. Oh, shit. Oh, fuck. Oh, shitfuck. Oh, fuckshit. I sat upright and fumbled for the light switch, then blinked when the lamp came on. The room was empty; the shades and drapes pulled tight over the small pair of windows. I rolled out of the sack, stood up, and lurched toward the bathroom. Why the hell hadn't somebody come to get me?

• • •

Day Twelve: 0812. Boomerang, Timex, and Digger were working on plates of ham and eggs and cheese in the hotel's dining room. I picked up a cup of coffee from the bottomless buffet, and dropped into an adjacent chair. I nudged Boomerang's shoulder as I sat down. "Thanks for waking me."

Boomerang shrugged. "Hey, *Pibe*, FYVM. You looked like you needed your beauty rest, so we let you sleep. Besides, there wasn't much to do."

"How's Goober?"

"Sore as hell. He's gone for a run to stretch out his leg."

"What about *Báltaí*?"

"Seems as if *Báltaí* fouled a fishnet, Skipper," Digger O'Toole grinned. "Nicked a prop blade, too. They'll be here until about thirteen hundred."

I looked at Digger. He certainly didn't seem much the worse for wear. "How do *you* feel?"

"Fuckin' great, Skipper," Digger said. He leaned over toward me and whispered conspiratorially, "Except, by the time we got back to the hotel, I couldn't feel the end of my dick anymore. So I went looking for someplace hot and wet to keep it until the feeling came back. Call me fuckin' lucky, because I found me a nice pair of warm thighs and big tits right here at the hotel bar. Man, I gotta tell you: these Portuguese women are something else. They know some tricks . . . whoo-eee."

I do so hate youth. I gave Digger a dirty look. "I really appreciate your sharing that with us all, Edwin," I said.

I sipped at my coffee. Timex continued: "So there's no need to rush, Skipper. We have all morning. Why not grab a decent breakfast?"

I looked over at Timex's two plates, which he'd piled high with slices of yellow Portuguese cheese, sliced tomatoes, smoked ham, and scrambled eggs. Another held popovers, the last half of a sweet roll, and half a dozen slices of well-buttered white toast. "I see you're not shy."

"Heck, Skipper, it's all included in the price of the room. Why let it go to waste?"

The kid actually had a point. In our trade, you never know if you're going to get the chance to eat. So, I picked a fresh plate off the table and started toward the buffet.

As I rose, Timex handed me his bread plate. "Please, sir, as long as you're up, could I have some more?"

Oh, great: my crew of merry marauders now included Priapismic O'Toole and Oliver fucking Twist. I guess that made me Mister Bumble. Actually, that's not far from the mark. Mister Bumble, you'll remember, was . . . an undertaker.

0920. Mick and Hugo had the watch. It wasn't especially onerous duty, as they'd ensconced themselves at the rear table of a small outdoor café facing the marina. But it wasn't downtime either. Occasionally, Mick would sneak a peek at *Báltaí* through his binoculars. That way he'd get a feel for what was where, because once we were aboard, there'd be no time for any landlubbing hide-and-seek.

The rest of us began the load out. Digger and Nigel filled the red plastic jerry cans with gas and tied them down in the stern of the Zodiac. I'd already topped off the little boat's internal tanks. On a whim I bought another two-and-a-half-gallon container of gas. I'd use it to top off the tank just before we left. The small can could be jettisoned at sea. Boomerang and Rotten stowed the two shotguns (which Nod had neatly sawed off to sixteen-inch barrels), the pistols, the magazines, and the ammo in the locker below the double bench seat. Goober made sure that we carried extra batteries for the Magellan in a watertight Baggie. Timex stowed our fishnet, which we'd use as an assault ladder, and our climbing rope, with its improvised hook, in the Zodiac's forward stowage compartment. Nod worked the laptop, scrambling to get us additional intel on the prospective target.

The Zodiac had no windscreen, so I packed all the face masks in case the seas got rough. Uniform of the day would be dark clothes: jeans and sweatshirts, covered by nylon anoraks. Underneath, we'd wear our shortie wet suits. I knew from the previous night's experience that they wouldn't do us much good if it turned real cold. But then, I didn't plan to be out at sea for more than a few hours.

1017. We moored the Zodiac at the end of a pier at the outer edge of the harbor. I called Mick on the cell phone. "What's up?"

"They're making progress," Mick answered in his thick Welsh accent. "They cleared the net about two hours ago. There's a crew of divers still working on the prop, but they're almost finished."

"Any sign of our boys?"

"Oh, yeah. They're in the wheelhouse, bitching to the captain and the chief boatswain's mate."

"How can you tell?"

"Gerry's body language, Mate. Gerry's body language."

"Whaddya mean?"

He handed me the glasses. "See for yourself."

I focused until I could see Gerry. He had one of the crewmen backed up against the bulkhead, bitch-slapping him. Gerry turned away, took a step or two as if to leave, then whirled and came back with a vicious kick. The crewman went down like the proverbial *sac de merde*. Gerry looked at his brother. I could make out Gwilliam's happily malevolent smile clearly through the long lenses.

I handed the binoculars back to Mick. "Nice pieces of work, our Kelley boys."

Mick grunted. "I guess—if you like malicious wankers."

• • •

1054. Mick reported that *Báltaí* had cast off from the dock and was backing slowly into the channel. I told him to get his ass over to our position ASAP. We still had no confirmation of their target. But actually, the target was unimportant, because it would become apparent as soon as they reached open water. If *Báltaí* went north, they'd be heading for the supertankers. If it went southwest, they'd be going after the *QE2*, on the Funchal/Lisbon leg.

1100. Nod jumped into the Zodiac, the laptop under his arm. "It's *QE2*," he said breathlessly.

"How do you know?"

"Because," he said, "the last two legs of this trip are a theme cruise."

"A theme cruise."

"They have VIP speakers. The VIPs get a free first-class cruise in return for a lecture. And their names draw a crowd. This one's about politics in the new century. Lady Thatcher's aboard. So is General Sir Michael Rose. So is Senator George Mitchell."

Margaret Thatcher is, of course, the former prime minister who turned Britain around in the 1970s and 1980s. Mike Rose was an old colleague of Mick Owen's. He'd led 22 SAS Regiment, then gone on to head British forces in the former Yugoslavia. He'd been knighted a few years back. And George Mitchell? He was the former American senator who'd been the main architect of the peace agreement in Northern Ireland that's known as the Good Friday Accord.

Two Exocets were sufficient to sink the *QE2*. And the water north of Madeira was deep: twenty-five hundred fathoms, which translates into almost three miles. Oh, QE2 had sufficient lifeboats to ensure that most of the passengers would get off before she went down. And the crew had emergency procedures training. But the mere fact that Gerry and Gwilliam could hit and sink the centerpiece of the British commercial fleet would cause incredible political repercussions.

Not that they'd get away with it, of course. Because to get to *QE2*, they'd have to go through *MOI*.

1128. *Báltai* eased out of the harbor at Horta, then turned in a northerly direction, skirting the coast of Pico. I gave the con to Boomerang. We followed about two nautical miles behind the big yacht, keeping to its inshore side. The Zodiac didn't give off any more of a radar signature than a small whale. But even so, we zigged and zagged so as not to attract attention.

1228. *Báltai* picked up a little speed. It was now moving at about twenty-five knots. We shadowed it through the strait between São Jorge and Pico, and out into the open sea that would lead us past the island of São Miguel. For them, it was an easy sail. For us, things were not so pleasant. The day had clouded over, and the wind had picked up. It was hard work to hold the little Zodiac steady, and after about an hour and a half, Boomerang relinquished the con to Goober so he could rest his arms and shoulders, which had taken quite a pounding.

So had we all. The Zodiac is not a craft built for comfort, or long-haul trips. It is a short-range boat, built for speed and maneuverability. On the open sea, after a couple of hours in a two-foot chop, your kidneys feel as if they are being worked over by Mike Tyson while the two of you are riding a roller coaster. And then there is the Wet Factor. We shipped a fair amount of water—not enough to overload the twin automatic bailers, but enough to make 'em work hard. But between the spray and the shipped water, we all got wet—which meant we were getting colder by the minute because we were generating wind chill, running as we were at thirty knots.

But as you will recall, hypothermia when submerged is twenty-five times more potent than in cold air. I looked over at Mick, who is not used to this sort of maritime punishment. His jaw was tight, his face dripping seawater. He grunted with each bone-jarring shock. But he rode it out just like the rest of us—gritting his chattering teeth, and keepin' on keepin' on.

1635. By my guesstimation, we were now just northeast of the big island of São Miguel. Guesstimation, you ask? What about the Magellan GPS you ask? Well, lemme tell you about Magellan GPS units—especially first-generation Magellan GPS units. They were not built for this kind of abuse. And so, the readouts we got were sporadic. And interpreting them was being made difficult by the fact that we had to keep the unit inside a plastic Baggie to keep it dry. By 1630, the Magellan wasn't working at all. Was it the moisture? Was it a battery problem? Who knew—and more important, who cared. All I knew was that we were running on sheer guts—and Randy's Silva compass—right now.

I knew that we were heading in a northeasterly direction. I knew our speed, and according to the chart Boomerang had bought, I could dead-recon our position. But where we were vis-à-vis São Miguel, I had absolutely no precise idea. And that wasn't the only thing. The skies had started to darken and the wind had picked up, which meant that the lovely foot-and-a-half chop had turned into a menacing three-and-a-half-foot chop. Now, we had only intermittent sightings of *Báltaí*. Oh, Fuck me. Bad weather is one of your more nasty Murphy factors. Sure, it was something that I had included in my mental list of SNAFU, TARFU, and FUBAR mission possibilities, but since there isn't anything you can do about the weather, there was nothing to do about it. Here and now, however, the weather was going to impact on our ability to continue the pursuit. The Zodiac is a tremendously seaworthy craft. But it's not built for the kinds of seas you may have seen in *The Perfect Storm*.

Moreover, the rougher the seas became, the more gasoline we would have to consume to keep ourselves on course. *Báltaí* was running at about twenty-eight knots. We were doing thirty-two, because it was harder for us to fight against the water and current than it was for the Kelleys' huge yacht. Plus, we'd already run about 130 miles—using more than half of our fuel supply. If *Báltaí* picked up even more speed—kicked up to thirty-eight or forty knots, for example—we could conceivably run dry before we caught up with them, given the waves, the current, and the wind.

1642. I smacked Goober on the shoulder, relieved him, and took the con. Time—and daylight—were slipping away fast. I didn't give a shit where we were, or whether we'd passed the ledge where the bottom dropped from nine hundred meters to thirty-five hundred meters. It was time to ease us up behind *Báltaí*, board her, and take these assholes down. I stood up from the double bench seat so that Nod could break out the weapons, and he and Digger could load mags. Mick and Hugo rummaged through the bow locker to extract our climbing rope and boarding net.

I moved the throttle forward. The little RIB shot ahead, cutting through the chop. With the increased speed, waves were now breaking over the bow. That meant we were shipping a little more water than I would have liked, but the bailers were working okay, so I nudged the throttle a little bit and we picked up some more speed. I didn't want to lose sight of *Báltaí*, which was about fifteen, maybe sixteen hundred yards ahead of us, slightly off to our port side. Even in the growing darkness I could still make out her underway lights. They were faint but visible when the swells worked in our favor. And so, I steered toward those lights, trying to close as much distance as I could before we lost 'em in the dark.

1656. Except I wasn't making any damn progress. In fact, *Báltaí* was putting more and more distance between us. The mother-fuckers had increased their speed. Had they seen us? Had their radar picked us out? It was unlikely, but not altogether impossible. But frankly, it didn't fucking matter. All that fucking mattered was that I had to catch the goddamn Kelleys and do it soon. Before they disappeared into the night and we were left adrift, out of fuel and way past the point of no return.

We were all completely soaked through now—and cold. *Cold?* Oh, that is an understatement. My previously Rogue-size balls had shrunk to the size of marbles and were trying to climb back inside my body. It was so cold that Digger's dick had probably shriveled up to eight or nine inches.

And yes, I'd factored the cold and the wet into the mission's EEIs.[67] But lemme tell you, friends, it's an apples-and-oranges kind of thing to war-game something into an op-plan or tactical scenario when you're sitting in a dry hotel room, and experience said selfsame factors when you are wet and cold and your kidneys are being pulverized by the smack-smack-smack of wind-driven waves against the hull of a small boat out in the open sea who-the-fuck knows how far from the closest haven.

It is one thing to noodle the time-distance-temperature graphs for hypothermia on a legal pad or hotel message sheet with CNN droning on in the background and a nice cuppa java at your elbow. It is another to sit in a fucking RIB and be physically unable to speak because your teeth are chattering too goddamn hard.

---

[67] EEIS are Essential Elements of Information; the info-bits necessary to critical mission planning. In a seaborne attack, EEIs may include (but are not limited to): the sea's state and currents; the weather and visibility; the enemy's sensor capabilities—radar, IR, night vision, etc.—as well as the moon's phase and its set and rise times.

But all of the above did not matter now. Because either we were going to: (A) catch up with the fucking *Báltai,* or we were going to: (B) die trying.

Those were the only two choices. Frankly, I was a lot more interested in pursuing choice "A" than I was in pursuing choice "B."

And so, I screamed "Everybody hang the fuck on!" into the wind, grabbed my face mask from Timex, slipped it over my head, and pulled the strap tight. Then, as soon as my Warriors hunkered down and grabbed onto the safety lines, I slammed the fucking throttle into the firewall,[68] the Zodiac stood on its ass, and we mythic Warrior heroes shot forward into the emergent darkness. It was like, "Hi-Ho, Silver Bullet, *awaaaay."*

Awaaaay for all of about fifteen fucking seconds, that is. At which point the big, powerful, 120-horsepower Yamaha outboard *ca-ca-cough, ca-ca-ca-cough-cough* died, the Zodiac's bow slapped down into the water, and we began to wash dangerously to-and-fro in the swells, vulnerable to swamping and other nasty oceanic possibilities.

---

[68] No, the Zodiac Pro-II does not have a literal firewall. The model we were sailing had a steering console, to which the outboard's remote throttle was attached on the starboard side, and a stainless steel grab handle. I am simply being figurative here. Call it Roguish literary license.

CHAPTER

20

OH DAMN, OH SHIT, OH DOOM ON DICKIE. I HIT THE STARTER, BUT all I got was the kind of halfhearted cough I give out when the friendly dicksmith is (squeeze-squeeze) testing me for hernia. Meanwhile, the Zodiac was being turned broadside by the arrhythmic waves, and we started shipping water, making us vulnerable and pushing me straight into the BOHICA zone. I mean, there was no fucking *ventilateur* in sight, so what the fuck had I done to deserve this *merde*?

And then, I understood. And I realized WTFIW,[69] was that Timex either hadn't been paying attention, or he'd been distracted by Mister Murphy, who'd obviously snuck aboard. Timex, you see, was the fuel guy on this little exercise. And it was obvious (ca-ca-*cough* . . . *sp-sp-sp-sputter* . . .) that he'd let the fucking tank run dry. Being the captain of this pint-size vessel and therefore IN CHARGE, I drew his attention to his nasty faux pas by using command-language RUT.[70]

I wasn't the only one, either—the kid received a fair amount of

---

[69] What The Fuck It Was.
[70] Roguishly Unvarnished Terms.

four-letter abuse from his shipmates. But, to be fair, Timex didn't waste a second once he realized that he'd screwed up and put the mission in jeopardy. He unlashed a six-gallon fuel can, found a funnel, and poured the gas quickly into the Zodiac's double tank. As he finished, Boomerang unlashed a second gas canister and handed it to him. Six more gallons went into the tank. Then six more. Mick stowed the empties and lashed them down securely.

I tried the starter once again. Nothing—and I wasn't about to kill the goddamn battery right now. So I gave the fucking system thirty seconds to reset itself. And then I hit the switch one more time. There was a slight hesitation, and then the big Yamaha growled just the way it should. I made sure everybody was secure, and that the gas cans had been stowed properly, and then I pushed the throttle forward once again, turned the Zodiac into the wind, and we were off.

1701. Rotten's compass got us back on track, even though we couldn't see *Báltaí*'s lights yet. Yes, there was the risk that the big ship had changed course, we were charging ahead on an incorrect heading, and we were about to be fucked. But I didn't think so. First of all, *Báltaí* had been steaming a steady course since she'd left Horta. Second, it made sense that *Báltaí* was heading toward a specific point in the sea—the position from which she would launch her missiles against the *QE2*—and that she'd steam straight to it, instead of zigzagging.

1704. We crested a swell, and there, about a thousand yards ahead and off to port, way out in the darkness, I was able to eyeball *Báltaí*. There wasn't much: I saw a quick flash of red running light, and then it all disappeared in a trough. But I'd *seen* it. And now *Báltaí*, her crew of Kraut kockbreaths, Gwilliam and Gerry Kelley, and Brendan O'Donnell—all of them—were *MINE*. How far ahead *Báltaí* may have been I didn't care. Here's what: *it was time to catch up with her and get the job DONE.*

Oh, yes. We had nautical miles to go before we'd sleep, and we had Roguish promises to keep. We had scores to settle, too: comeuppance for all the murder victims who had been slaughtered by these assholes. Payback for lives lost and peace squandered.

But the most important debt to be paid, so far as I was concerned, was for the death of my shipmate, Butch Wells. "Death," a poet once wrote, "is a debt; a debt on demand."[71] *Well, by fire and by blood would Butch's death debt be paid tonight.* **It would be fucking paid in full by his shipmates who were the final piece of what was in reality a debt/death <u>triad</u>: DET Bravo.** Only then would the Mystical Circle be complete and our mission be fulfilled.

The cold had disappeared. It didn't fucking count anymore. It wasn't a factor because my rage kept me white-hot. I didn't need to see *Báltaí's* running lights, either. I knew exactly, to the meter, where *she* was; where *they* were, and I'd fucking take us there— now—just as if I were a fucking Exocet missile. Instincts keener than any goddamn radar guidance system, I homed in on *Báltaí*, pushed the throttle to the limit, stood the Zodiac on its ass, and we cut through the water at flank speed.

In the dim and fading light, I checked the windblown, water-dripping faces of my men. They were Warriors all. You could see it radiating from every molecule of their being. They had Warriors' expressions: RESOLUTE; FIRM; STEADFAST; UNCOMPROMIS-ING; DETERMINED. They knew the risks and were willing to take them because they lived by the Warrior's Code. They understood that they had no limits; that they were capable of achieving victory

---

[71] The words come from the libretto of John Gay's 1728 hit *The Beggar's Opera*. They were sung by the original London Rogue, a cutthroat named Macheath—aka Mack the Knife. And here's an interesting sidebar: the phrase is actually a pun, because in the eighteenth century, the words *death* and *debt* were pronounced similarly. That makes them all the more relevant to us Warriors from DET Bravo. Did ya Get It? And by "It" I mean the significance of the title of this book now?

Hey, just because I use the F-word a lot, don't think I'm must another hairy-assed, sloppin' hoppin', screw-cap poppin' philistine. 'Cause I ain't. I know this shit. I can do the literary stuff like puns and metaphors and similes, too. You gotta understand, I got *culture*.

over immense odds. They understood death and could accept it, even though they preferred life.

The fact that I was here and now, and about to go to WAR almost made me tear up. Look—this is and always has been an emotional thing for me. You have to understand how much I loved these men and respected their capabilities; their skills; and their commitment. I would kill for any of them, just as they would kill for me. That makes for an incredible bond among men. In many ways it is a closer relationship even than marriage. It is more lasting than life itself.

Let me go even more touchy-feely for just a minute and open up to you. One of the most fortunate aspects of my life and my career is that I have always been blessed by being able to lead Warriors like these. Indeed, I have always believed that the greatest gift the God of WAR can bestow on someone like me is to give to him a group of WARRIORS; Warriors just like these men here, so that I can lead them into a great battle and we can share the absolute danger of risk, followed by the absolute joy of victory.

• • •

1719. Suddenly, we disappeared into a patch of surface fog. It just came on us, and we went into it before I could react. One second, there was wind and rain and you could see the ocean around you. And the next, everything disappeared. It was like somebody had blindfolded me. It wouldn't take much to disorient us if the fucking thing didn't lift soon. You lose all sense of direction, time, and space when you can't see. That's what happened to John Kennedy Jr. the night he put his plane into the ocean. He'd entered a whiteout zone, and tried to follow his instincts instead of his instruments. And that decision killed him.

I wasn't about to follow in his footsteps. *"Rotten—"*

That was all I had to say. Rotten Randy already had his Silva compass out, squinting at it in the dark; calling my heading every fifteen seconds as we charged through the opaque mist, working to keep our course straight so I could keep our speed constant. I never wavered, holding the throttle all the way to FULL as the Zodiac bounced inexorably onward in the dark.

1723. Wisp by wisp the fog evaporated. Now we were back to mere rain and wind. But we were drawing ever closer—I could almost taste it. And then, and then . . . all the hair on the back of my neck suddenly stood up. Mick sensed something, too: I saw him go tense. And it was not more than five seconds after that, that *we saw her.* She was no more than six hundred yards out, about twenty degrees to port, moving on a parallel track, her wake visible even in the darkness and the chop.

I looked over at Rotten and said, simply, "Thank you, Rotten."

His look told me I hadn't needed to say anything, but that he was perceptibly happy I had done so.

As we edged closer, the guys started making ready. They positioned themselves so as to allow the Zodiac the most freedom of movement. They had their War Faces on now; their expressions were absolute masks.

1725. I shifted our course, bringing us about four hundred yards directly astern of *Báltaí.* There was something about the ship I haven't really mentioned, something that hadn't quite registered before: she was fucking *huge.*

Yes, I've told you *Báltaí* was a big yacht. Two hundred and ninety-three feet, in fact, from stem to stern—seven feet shorter than a football field. Its beam was probably thirty three or thirty-four feet, maybe more. That is bigger than many of the Navy's surface warships. Certainly, she was more than a hundred feet longer than one of the PC (Patrol Coastal) vessels assigned to NavSpecWar (and tonight, more lethal, too). But only from the water can you truly sense the size and power and energy of a vessel. Oh, to be sure, an aircraft carrier is impressive when it's tied up: a huge, hulking gray city afloat. But out on the open sea, when approached in a small boat, it becomes even more gargantuan, massive, colossal, because it *moves,* and it also radiates huge amounts of energy—energy that you can actually feel as you get closer and closer.

Here, too, as we drew inexorably nearer and nearer, the same thing happened. Even with the wind, and the rain, and the cold, I could feel the power of this big ship; sense the change in the water caused by her big screw, exhaust, and pumps. The Zodiac began to handle differently as we gained on *Báltaí*. It was affected by her wake and her bulk, just the way a single-engine plane taking off right after a 747 has cleared the runway is affected by the air currents and heat left behind by the jumbo jet.

1733. I brought us to within a hundred yards of *Báltaí*, then eased off the throttle just a bit. The big yacht had slowed down, cruising at what appeared to me to be about twenty knots. That certainly would make boarding her a lot easier. You do not want to board a big ship running at flank speed. The variables are bad enough when it is moving below ten knots. I can recall a 6.5-knot boarding exercise in the South China Sea a few years back that almost killed me.

There are the currents that run alongside the ship's hull, which you have to fight as you bring your small craft alongside. The water wants to push you off; you have to hold your craft tight. But the wind buffets you, as does the wave chop. It is therefore possible, when you are riding in a small raiding craft like the Zodiac we were in, to go up, down, forward, and backward all at the same time.

You say what I have just described breaks all the rules of physics. Lemme tell you something that I have learned through nasty, real-world experience: in situations like this one, the rules of physics don't necessarily fucking apply.

1735. I eased us closer, then turned the con over to Nod, who was the most experienced coxswain in this group of shooter-looters. While he got the feel of the Zodiac, I retrieved one of the Berettas from Mick, checked to see that it was loaded and had a cartridge in the chamber, double-checked that the safety was on, then stowed an additional pair of loaded 15-round mags in the rear pockets of my jeans. I ran a three-foot length of light nylon line through the lanyard loop on the Beretta's butt, secured it tight, and attached the opposite end to my belt. No way was Mister Murphy going to make me lose my weapon tonight.

1738. Nod brought us to within twenty yards of *Báltaí's* fantail. We could feel the temperature of the water rise now, and the little SEAL was having a hell of a time keeping the Zodiac steady in *Báltaí's* wake. But he managed, using the Yamaha's 120 horses to muscle us where we had to be.

Every man knew his assignment: Nod would remain in the Zodiac until we were all aboard *Báltaí*. Then he would toss Nigel a line so the RIB could be towed by the big yacht until we needed it for our exfil. We had only six firearms: four pistols and two shotguns. I had one of the pistols. Boomerang, Randy, and Mick had the others. Goober and Digger had the shotguns. Which left Hugo, Timex, Nod, and Nigel unarmed except for their sheath knives. They would have to improvise.

That was the downside. The upside was that I did not expect more than a few of the crew to be carrying arms. They were out in the middle of the fucking ocean and didn't expect guests. What we had to do, therefore, was to overwhelm them in the first few seconds of our assault. Tonight, the most vulnerable point of the mission would occur just as we attempted to board *Báltaí*. Our force would be split, and the objective held by a pitiful few of my Warriors. If we were discovered coming over the rail, we could be repulsed easily. But once we put a nucleus of armed people on board the yacht, we could use speed, surprise, and violence of action to achieve victory within a few short minutes.

1742. Mick wedged himself into the Zodiac's bow to play security guard. Nod brought us up to the fantail of the big yacht and eased us alongside the starboard side of the eighteen-inch wide diving platform, which was stored upright, flat against *Báltaí's* stern during transit, and latched to the transom of the big yacht by two stainless steel dead bolts. Above it, shielding us from being seen, was *Báltaí's* launch, suspended from two huge davits. The launch swung like a pendulum in the swells.

It wouldn't be easy. *Báltaí* was moving at twenty knots. The kinetic energy the ship caused made it almost impossible for us to sidle up behind it. The slipstream alone was sufficient to blow us backward and sideways simultaneously. But now we had an additional problem: *Báltaí's* wake. It was enough to push the Zodiac's seaworthiness to the limit. The centrifugal force caused by the displaced water knocked the little craft askew every time Nod made an approach.

I pointed to starboard and Nod backed us off twenty yards. My hands told him what I wanted him to do, and he did it: he gunned the Zodiac straight across *Báltaí's* stern, transversing the deadly wake. As we passed the starboard bolt, I stood up, with Goober and Rotten holding on to keep me from going overboard. Nod caught a swell that elevated the Zodiac by a yard and a half. I reached up as high as I could and unbolted the starboard side of the diving platform. Then Nod pushed the little craft forward, turned, and repeated the move from the port side, so that Mick, buttressed by Timex and Nigel, could reach up and unhitch the other dead bolt.

Mick missed on his first try, almost pitching into the water before Timex yanked him back. Nod circled and brought the RIB up close once again, and Mick, straining, managed to flick the dead bolt upward as the RIB caught a big swell. The diving platform dropped on its long hinge. Somehow, Mick managed to catch it so the fucking thing didn't hit smack hard and break off. Then, with the platform down, it was time to get moving.

The only way to lead is to lead. I moved to the Zodiac's bow. Nod whipped the little craft around. As he shot past *Báltaí's* stern, I pulled myself across the Zodiac's gunwale, gripped at the wood lattice of the diving platform, which was only about a foot or so above my head, and started to pull myself across and onto it. Which is when all those laws of physics shattered into the old Irish term for bits & pieces—smithereens—and the Zodiac shifted, rising in a sudden crosscurrent, or wave, or wind shear, or whatever the hell it was, and I was suddenly stretched between the Zodiac and *Báltaí* like some fucking cartoon character made of rubber.

My feet were wedged in the safety line on the Zodiac's gunwale. My fingers were caught in the thick, teak lattice of the diving platform. And I was being stretched as if I were a recalcitrant Marrano on one of Torquemada's racks. This was no fucking way to achieve victory. This was the way to achieve PAIN.

And then, the goddamn Zodiac pulled away. Which left me dragging in the fucking water behind *Báltaí,* my legs churning, my fingers losing their precarious grasp on the diving platform. Below me, *Báltaí's* huge prop was churning the water relentlessly. If I dropped, I'd be ground into Rogue Sausage. I was buffeted by nasty crosswinds. The dark water sucked at my legs. The wet wood of the diving platform caused my grip to slip. I tried to claw forward. I fucking couldn't do it. I lost ground. And then, finally, I managed to thrust three of my fingers through the latticework— and I held on, twisting as I dropped closer and closer to the fucking prop. The pain was incredible. I hurt right down to the soggy cuticles on my toes. All I could hear in my head was the inexorable, throaty invitation of *Báltaí's* prop. It was saying, *"Cmon, asshole—let go. Give up. Drop. You belong to me."*

But was I gonna let go, give up, drop? No fucking way, José. I'd come too fucking far. I'd suffered too fucking much. I was too fucking filled with white-hot rage. I wanted to collect the fucking DET Bravo death debt I was fucking owed by these fucking assholes.

And so, my feet kicking, I used MY WARRIOR'S WILL to pull myself against the water and the current and the slipstream, and inch by fucking inch I gained the distance I'd lost, until I finally muscled my fingers/hands/wrists/forearms/elbows onto the diving platform, reached across and grabbed a ladder rung, and slowly, slowly, slowly, pulled my sore and hyperextended body onto *Báltaí.*

I raised myself onto my hands and knees, my lungs burning, my shoulders telling the rest of my body that I was very much alive. Oh, yeah, I was exhausted. But I didn't have time for exhaustion. We were fucking vulnerable, and we had to act—NOW. And so, we went to Scenario B. Boomerang and Goober tossed me the fishing net, which I secured to the diving platform. Now, there was something across which we could clamber, no matter how much the Zodiac rose or fell relative to the *Báltaí*.

Digger came across first. He flung himself onto the net and pulled himself across onto the diving platform. He was followed by Boomerang's long frame. Now there were three of us—and it was time to go over the rail. I went up the ladder first, one-handed, the pistol in my big right paw. I held just below the rail until Boomerang had wedged himself close behind me. When he tapped my butt, I sprang up, rolled over the stern rail onto the fantail, and went into an offensive crouch, scanning and breathing as the muzzle of my pistol swept the empty deck.

Boomerang came next, followed by Digger. We moved forward to give the rest of the assault team space. You never want to stop-and-go in situations like this one. Like Ranger Randy says, just FIDO—fuck it, and drive on.

1743. Nod crabbed across the net, then from the safety of the diving platform, he untethered the net and tossed it back onto the little RIB. He pulled the line taught, until the RIB was right under *Báltaí*'s white launch. Then he scrambled up and over the rail, pulled the diving platform into its vertical position, and secured it.

1744. The boarding party was complete. The Zodiac was tethered securely to *Báltaí*, but invisible unless you actually hung over the side, because it was now obscured by the stern davit arms and *Báltaí*'s launch.

And so far, we had achieved complete surprise. In a way, that was to be expected. It was now completely dark. The weather was bad. On a night like this, unless you are at Threatcon Charlie, you button your vessel up and retreat to your bunk for a quiet night of pud-pulling over a *Playboy* or a *Penthouse* magazine. But that didn't mean there weren't going to be hostiles on the prowl.

1745. Sheltered by the overhang of the quarterdeck, we broke into our prearranged working groups. We'd committed Nigel's diagrams to memory, so we knew where we were going and (more or less) how we'd get there.

Mick's Delta squad headed to port, with Mick on point, followed by Rotten Randy. Hugo and Nigel, unarmed, came next. Goober was Delta's rear security. Their assignment was to swarm the crew quarters, galley, and engine room.

My Bravo squad went starboard. I took point, followed by Boomerang. Nod and Timex, both unarmed, brought up the middle, and Digger, with his shotgun, was rear security. Our target was the upper deck area—quarterdeck and above—which included the radio shack and wheelhouse, the main saloon, and of course the staterooms housing the Kelley boys and TIRA scumbag Brendan O'Donnell. Oh, I wanted to pay 'em all a room-service call *bad.*

But there was work to be done before I'd be able to have my fun for the night. My first objective was to disable all of *Báltaí's* comms. I wanted no distress messages sent out. Then I'd shut down the engines. Once the ship was mine, I could get on with the real business of the evening: dispatching tangos.

CHAPTER

21

1746. USING THE BULKHEAD TO MASK OUR MOVEMENTS, I MADE MY way amidships, to the crew hatchway that would bring us to ladders leading up past the quarterdeck and the saloon deck to the upper deck. That's where the bridge and the communications shed were located.

We came up to the hatch, and stacked opposite the hinge side, tight against the bulkhead and careful to keep our heads below the thick double-paned glass of the hatch's port. With my pistol locked in my right hand and held close to my body, I eased my left hand along the cold metal, and grasped the handle firmly so I could e-a-s-e it gently open.

The fucking handle moved on its own. I jerked my hand back just as the door swung open.

He came through the hatchway, a cigarette in his left hand. Obviously, he was no sailor, because his focus was straight down, looking down toward his feet, moving ever so carefully so as to clear the hatch combing without tripping, or losing his balance as the ship rolled in the swells.

Mr. Landlubber didn't see me until it was too late because: his gaze was elsewhere, he hadn't expected to come upon anyone, and his eyes were accustomed to the bright fluorescent interior lighting, and it was dark on deck. When he did see me he dropped the cigarette and opened his mouth in panic, as if to scream.

But it was too late. I'd shifted my grip on the Beretta even as he'd opened the door, and using all my energy, I hit him squarely upside the temple with the side of the pistol, breaking as many bones in his face as I could with the sucker punch. Mr. Landlubber went down, and as Boomerang slid behind me and eased the hatch closed I dropped on top of the sumbitch, pounding his face with the butt of the pistol until he stopped moving. I caught my breath, wiped the bloody weapon on his clothes, then stuck it in my belt. Then, still straddling the crewman, I broke his neck, just to make sure he wasn't going to make any more noise.

I rolled off him. Quickly, Nod and Timex searched him. He carried no weapon—that was a good sign—or identification. That made sense, too. What the hell do you need a wallet for in the middle of the fucking ocean? The two SEALs lifted Mr. Landlubber's body off the deck, carried it to the side, and rolled it over the railing into the roiling sea.

Now the clock really was ticking, because sooner or later—and the weight was certainly on the "sooner" part of the equation—somebody was going to miss the asshole we'd just tossed overboard. I silent-signaled. We stacked again, I drew my pistol and then eased the hatch open.

1748. *Show Time.* I cut the pie and made entry. The passage was deserted. There were two ladderways, one leading up, the other going down. Mick's port-side crew was descending—going to hell in a handbasket if the situation went bad. Me, I was the eternal optimist: I knew we were heaven-bound.

Pistol at low ready in a two-handed grip, I led the way up the narrow ladder, moving deliberately tread by tread, trying to keep my wet running shoes from squishing audibly as I climbed. My head poked above the landing on the saloon deck. On the forward-most part of this deck were the masters' cabins: two-room suites each, with private baths for Gerry and Gwilliam.

Brendan O'Donnell's quarters had to be somewhere on this deck, although we didn't have a clear picture of where. It didn't matter: I'd come back and find out as soon as we'd neutralized the rest of the ship. Meanwhile, I followed the sketch in my head and located the ladderway to the upper deck.

1749. Scan and breathe. Scan and breathe. I could feel the tension in my upper body as I took the first three treads of the ladder. Tight behind me, Boomerang's pistol covered the field of fire mine did not. We moved in a balletic syncopation, the choreography having been worked through years of working as a team. Unlike the goatfuck op that opened this book, we were now a well-oiled unit, operating with the cool efficiency of a killing machine. We knew one another's body language; we'd taken fire together—and returned it. We had stood shoulder to shoulder, and back to back, against formidable odds, and we'd won every battle.

Tonight was no different. Oh, sure, my breathing was shallow, and there was a slight feeling of nausea in the pit of my stomach. But that is always the case when a Warrior goes into battle. Show me a man who has no sense of fear, and I'll show you a man I do not want working with me. Show me a man who can handle his fear, whose fear gives him the edge in battle, and I'll show you a man I want as a part of my unit.

1750. Upper deck. Still no sign of opposition. The radio shack was forward, between the bridge and the captain's quarters. Since you never bypass an unsecured area during a takedown, we'd shift positions: Nod and I would deal with the captain's bunk room; Boomerang, Timex, and Digger would go on to the radio shack. With luck, I'd catch up in time to join them and take down the bridge.

I was six feet from the spar-varnished oak door to the captain's cabin when we heard the first gunshots, coming from below. Three hammers—those are double taps—followed by two shotgun blasts. So much for surprise. No need to be stealthy anymore. I hit the cabin door with my foot, smashing it inward. I went in crouched, moving fast, taking territory as I went. My pistol was in low ready. I was scanning and breathing, scanning and breathing, searching for threats. On the starboard side of the small cabin, a gray-haired man of about fifty was reaching for a small automatic pistol that hung in a scabbard holster off the headboard of his single bunk.

I used my Command Voice. "Drop the fucking gun."

He hesitated. Good. My pistol came up. I got a good sight picture, and as the sumbitch realized what I was doing and started back for his weapon, I shot him once-twice-thrice. No, I didn't quite make all three center mass shots. One of 'em hit him in the upper leg. The second caught him in the belly, and the third in the shoulder.

He screamed at me in Kraut. But he didn't stop thrashing around, trying to get his weapon out. The fucking ball ammo—full-metal-jacket—wasn't worth jackshit. I heard more gunfire. His face turned toward the noise. I rushed him, my pistol up and my sight picture improving by the millisecond, and shot him twice in the head. *That* quieted him down.

I sensed something behind me. I whirled, Beretta up, and saw Nod's face in the doorway. "Radio shack secure."

"Good." I jerked my thumb toward the corpse. "Grab his gun. Check this place for intel and paper. Then catch up with us."

Nod didn't have to be told what to do twice. "Aye-aye, Skipper."

I backed out of the captain's cabin, turned to port, and kept going. I looked into the radio shack as I continued toward the bridge. A single crewman sat, sprawled facedown, atop a desk crammed with commo gear. Like the captain, he wasn't going to be going anyplace soon—except overboard.

I ran onto the bridge, saw that the wheelhouse was secure, and waved at Digger. "Follow me."

I reversed course. I charged down the passageway to the ladder leading down to the saloon deck, Digger following at my heels, his sawed-off shotgun at port arms.

I turned, and started down the ladder. At the bottom, a dark-skinned crewman brought the muzzle of his submachine gun up.

"*Gun—*" I threw myself back as he pressed the trigger and hosed the ladderway. He must have caught a 240-volt line with a couple of shots, because the ceiling of the ladderway started to spark. I rolled away from the bullets. But not quickly enough: a ricochet caught the side of my neck. Shit, that hurt. I hoped it hadn't nicked an artery.

Digger lunged past me, his shotgun arm extended down the ladderway. One-handed, he fired twice blindly. The shotgun blasts were answered by a scream. I rolled to the head of the ladderway and peeked around. I saw the subgun lying at the bottom of the stairwell. No time to lose. I scrambled to my feet and dropped down the steep, narrow flight of stairs, landing so hard at the bottom that I heard the tendons in my ankle pop.

Oh, fuck, I didn't need to be crippled. Not now. Not ever. I kicked the subgun toward the bulkhead, turned, and tried to find a target. A trail of blood led down the carpeted passageway, toward the stern. From below, I heard more sporadic gunfire.

Nod, a Walther in his hand, dropped down the ladderway. I handed him the submachine gun—an old Uzi mini in 9-mm—and continued forward, and jerked my thumb toward the blood trail.

"You take him down. Digger and I are going forward."

1754. Carefully, I pushed at the handle of the doorway that led to the Kelleys' suites. There was no reaction, so I eased the thick metal door open, cut the pie, and visually checked the corridor.

It was empty. It was short, not more than twenty feet long. There were two doorways at the far end, one facing the other. Those would lead to the master suites. A second pair of facing doors were at my end of the passage. Those were the "honored guest" staterooms.

Time to pay a social call. I kicked in the port-side door. The cabin was dark. I reached in and switched on the light. The stateroom appeared to be empty. But I wasn't about to assume anything. As Digger covered me I did a quick search and came up dry.

I turned and kicked in the opposite doorway. The second stateroom was just as dark as the first. If this had been a normal op I would have tossed a flashbang, or better, a concussion grenade, and then gone in to pick up the pieces. But we didn't have any grenades, which meant I was going to have to do this the hard way. And so my hand moved toward the light switch. But then, my nose twitched with the scent of aftershave, and the hair on the back of my neck stood straight up. And we all know what those sensory signals mean.

I flung myself onto the deck, the Beretta extended in both hands, just as a volley of gunfire erupted from the darkness. I tracked the muzzle blast and fired at it from my prone position. There was a scream. I started to scramble to my feet, but Digger smacked me back onto the deck, firing both barrels of his O/U, then quick-reloading. "He's still moving," he shouted, and fired again.

An Irish-accented male voice screamed "Oh, fuck" from the darkness of the room. I didn't give a shit what Brendan O'Donnell was doing. I wanted my hands around his murdering throat. This was one of the TIRA scumbags who'd taken children hostage and killed my shipmate.

"Hit the fucking lights."

They flashed on. I blinked, then found my target. He was on his knees behind the bed, trying to unjam his pistol. I churned my feet and lurched forward, threw myself over the bed, and landed on top of the sumbitch, sending him onto his back, writhing. He was tall and broad shouldered, with longish hair and pale white skin, and the sort of defined muscles that come from regular sessions on the weight pile. There was also blood on the front of his dark T-shirt. Good—that meant Digger or I had hurt him.

But we obviously hadn't done our jobs well enough, because the cockbreath still wasn't down for the count. First things first: I knocked his pistol away. It went skittering across the rug. His hands free, he came back at me, raking at my eyes, then smashing the heel of his hand into my jaw, hard enough to knock it out of alignment.

Oh, geezus that *hurt.* But I didn't stop. I wrapped him up, my elbows and knees doing a job on whatever parts of his body they could find. My fingers worked his face, trying to rip his eyes out. We rolled around for a while, each of us fighting for the advantage. And then, and then, suddenly, *I had him.* I could feel it in the pit of my gut.

Oh, he was strong—jailhouse strong—but he didn't have staying power. That's what real-life training is all about. That's what Warriordom is all about. It's more than a matter of pumping iron and doing reps. It's about keepin' on keepin' on, no matter what the odds, no matter what your condition.

I rolled on top of him, got my face close to his ear, bit it— hard—and then whispered into what was left of it that he was going to die—*soon.* He spat in my face and tried to bite my nose off. I replied by head butting him, sending him *smack* back onto the deck. That shook him up. He dropped his hands, giving me a small opening, and I clapped both his ears between my hands. He tried to wriggle away, but there was no way I was going to let go of him now. I straddled his shoulders and got my hands around his neck, my thumbs just below his Adam's apple—and then I applied pressure and broke his windpipe. I mashed down as hard as I could. I told him: "Butch Wells died because of your fucking pals—now it's your fucking turn." I applied terminal pressure and watched his eyes cloud over and roll back into his head.

And when he'd stopped moving, I took my pistol and put a round in his head, just to make sure he wasn't going to ever get up again. No sense taking chances, right?

• • •

I looked down at my watch. It was 1756. Time for the Kelley brothers to die.

Timex and Goober appeared in the passageway. "Engine room's secure, Skipper," Goober reported. "Six tangos down and out."

Timex said: "Bridge is secure, too. We bagged a total of seven, including the one we tossed overboard."

Mental calculation: six, plus seven gave me a baker's dozen. "Any survivors?"

The satisfied grins on my men's faces told me everything I had to know.

"Anybody hurt?"

Goober reported that Mick had a cut on his face—a ricochet. Nothing serious. And Boomerang's team was undinged.

Then it was Show Time again. "Okay, assholes, let's go to work."

We stacked in two two-man teams. Timex had picked up an Uzi somewhere in his travels. He took point on the port-side door, with Goober backing him up; Digger and I stacked outside the starboard suite.

"Go—" I stood back and kicked the fucking door in. It splintered inward, knocked off its hinges.

Pistol up, I made entry. The suite was as lavish as its pictures in the *Observer* Sunday magazine. All done in polished wood, brass, and chrome. I swept into the living room. It was empty. To my left—looking toward the bow—was a cracked doorway. I approached the door carefully, eased it open, making sure no one was concealed behind it, reached for the light switch, and flipped the lever up.

Lights on. I made entry into what was one of the Kelleys' bedrooms. There was a king-size bed—rumpled. And a serving tray, with a half-eaten sandwich and a pint glass half-filled with beer.

I searched the bedroom and adjoining bath carefully. One Kelley was gone—probably trying to hide somewhere.

But the other one was In Custody, as they say on the *America's Most Wanted*. I could hear him screaming obscenities. Obviously, from what he was saying, he didn't think much of Goober's mother. Which wasn't going to do him a lot of good in the personal well-being department, because Goober was quite devoted to his mother.

Yup—the bitching stopped in midsqueal. I walked across the hallway and found Goober standing atop Gwilliam Kelley, who was on the deck, moaning. From the way Gwilliam's nose was bleeding onto the five-hundred-quid a square yard pastel Aubusson, Goober had given the asshole a whole new nasal passage or two.

I looked approvingly at my two SEALs. "Bring him up top to the bridge. I'm gonna look for Gerry."

1804. Gerry wasn't hard to find. Not at all. He was on the stern, trying to figure out how to lower the launch. He wasn't having very much luck. He may have been a software genius, but as a sailor he was mechanically challenged.

I came up behind him. He whirled toward me. His face went through a kaleidoscopic range of expressions. And then he said, "*You!*"

I gave him my War Face. "Remember what I told you, Gerry? We talked about retribution. Well, it's time to do the Old Testament thing."

He gave me the fancy-ass dojo moves again. His hands did all the fucking Oriental shit that hands can do. Claw. Hammer. Whip. Sword. Axe—all that intricate stuff, with the accompanying whoops and screeches and hai-karate, kung-phooey horse puckey. He was a real Bruce Lee wannabe.

And then he came at me—*whoop-whoop.* I let him get close, and then I stepped aside, smacking his face with my open palm as he went by.

He looked at me incredulous, a puddle of drool moving down his chin.

"Yo, Gerry, you losin' it already?"

He gritted his teeth and came at me again. I gave him an elbow in the back of the neck that staggered him against the stern rail.

"I am the only son of the God of War," I told him. "The Old

315

Testament God. The God of the desert. The Nameless Name." I advanced on him. He came at me. Feinted left, then right, then left again, and then struck.

It was a decent hit—his fist caught me in the solar plexus hard enough to take my breath away. But as you know, I do a thousand sit-ups every day, and my stomach is about as taut as a fucking fifty-five-gallon oil drum. So, he dinged me, but he didn't hurt me.

I raised my arms in a tolerable imitation of a bar punk egging an opponent on in the parking lot of Danny's Dew Drop Inn or similar establishment. "Hey, Gerry, whatsa matter? You hit like a girl."

Oh, that riled him. He came at me again. This time I simply sucker-punched him. He never saw it coming because he was tunneling. All he saw was my face—which is what he was aiming at.

Y'know, I wondered how many thousands of pounds sterling he had spent on his martial arts training. Probably a lot of them. But here is the thing: all the dojos in the world and all the wisdom of all the karate masters will not train you for a real life encounter with someone who wants to kill you, and will do whatever they have to do to achieve that objective.

The real world is not the mat in a gym. The real world is not *The Karate Kid Part Six*. The real world is concrete pavement, or gravel, or cold water. The real world is nasty and tough and bloodthirsty. I know—because I AM the REAL WORLD.

I dragged Gerry Kelley along the deck by his legs. "You paid to have one of my men killed," I said as I pulled him up a ladderway toward the wheelhouse. His head kept bumping on the treads. Too bad for him. I wanted him to learn from this experience, and you know what they say: "No pain, no gain."

We'd gotten about halfway to the bridge when Gerry wriggled and kicked out of my grasp. He was woozy, but he struggled to his feet and came at me again. I guess it was desperation because he knew I was going to kill him.

Here is a basic rule of survival, friends: always frisk a suspect. I say that because Gerry obviously had a folding knife in his pocket, but I didn't see it until he had retrieved it, opened it with a flourish, brought it up and across his chest in a whiplike motion, and was slicing at me.

I jumped away. But not soon enough. The very tip of the blade caught my shirt and cut through it, through the shortie wet suit underneath, and through about an eighth of an inch into my chest. That fucking wound was gonna need stitches.

But not right now. Right now, what I had to do was get the fucking weapon away from him. He waved the tip of the blade at me. I put distance between us, put my spine against the bulkhead, and waited.

He had probably been taught blade work by the same assholes who'd taught him martial arts, because he didn't know shit. He backed off, went into the approved stance, and then came at me, feet spread apart, his knife arm low, the blade headed for my belly.

It was a textbook attack. I countered his thrust with my left arm, sweeping the knife away from me. As I did, I stepped toward him, using the bulkhead to give me support, and used my legs, thighs, and hips to power a single blow that caught him right in the throat.

If he hadn't lowered his jaw I would have broken his windpipe. As it was, I probably broke his fucking jaw. He dropped where he was, the knife skittering off onto the deck. I picked it up. It was an Emerson CQC-7—that's top of the line when it comes to combat folders. I know, because I own the seventh CQC-7 Ernie Emerson ever made. I slipped the clip of Gerry's knife over the seam of my right-hand trouser pocket and settled it in place. Now I owned two.

Gerry started crawling toward me. Oh, fuck. I picked him up by the belt and the collar of his shirt, slammed him into the metal bulkhead to quiet him down, and then, exhausted and bleeding, resumed my trek to the bridge, dragging the now-unconscious cockbreath behind me.

CHAPTER

22

1822. WE SECURED GERRY AND GWILLIAM TO A PAIR OF CAPTAIN'S chairs on the bridge. Since they were native English speakers, Hugo and Nigel stood guard and traded insults with the two assholes. Then the rest of us set about our work.

Nod and Randy dragged Mick and me down to the galley, where they found the first aid equipment, and stitched us up. Mick's face looked as if he'd been shaving with a big straight razor and had sneezed just as he began the downstroke on his left cheek. There'd been a lot of blood, but the wound wasn't deep. Nod closed it with tape. Fucking Gerry's blade had cut clean across my chest. It was superficial, too, but I was gonna look like fucking Frankenstein's monster when the scar healed. I looked down approvingly as Rotten covered Nod's rough stitching with bandages and surgical tape. At least the wound wasn't gonna get infected before I could get some more medical attention. Hell—I probably needed a healthy dose of Dr. Bombay Sapphire more than I needed to see some sawbones.

I sent Nod back to the bridge with a bottle of painkillers for Gerry, who was caterwauling as best he could with his broken jaw, and Gwilliam, who had trouble breathing through his much-abused honker. Hey—I may be tough, but I'm not gratuitously cruel. I leave that quality to tangos like Gerry and Gwilliam.

Next, we disabled the missiles, ripping their electronics apart, smashing the internal computer boards into the well-known smithereens and dumping them overboard. Working very, very carefully, Boomerang cumshawed some of the high explosive out of the warheads, and with the help of Rotten Randy Michaels, he made a quartet of small IEDs—Improvised Explosive Devices—which they set strategically. I wanted a backup system in place in case the sea cocks didn't work and the ship didn't scuttle properly.

Then we rigged a block and tackle off the rear of the upper deck and dumped what was left of the Exocets over the side. I didn't want 'em anywhere near *Báltaí* when it went down. Goober, Digger, Mick, and Timex destroyed all the sensitive elements of the missile guidance system and threw the pieces over the rail. Then they unbolted the launch package and, after suitable heaving and huffing, jettisoned that, too, into twelve thousand feet of water. The plastic dome cover was cut up and stowed below. The white plastic would have floated—providing easily seen evidence of *Báltaí*'s final position.

As the men were disassembling the missile package, I pondered from the bridge about whether the Exocets would actually have been launchable from *Báltaí*. From what I could see, the unit had been professionally installed (the Iranians no doubt). The wiring was correct. The guidance units were assembled by the book. The fuses on the warheads were preset accurately.

My conclusion: the system would have worked. And its target? Just as Nod had predicted, the Kelleys were going after the *QE2*. At least, that's the way I read the charts and notes in the captain's cabin, as well as the Cunard Lines schedule the Iranians had tacked up in their crew quarters below decks. The verdict: guilty as charged. You already know what the sentence is.

2030. I sent Timex and Nod back to bring the Zodiac up to the accommodation ladder. They did, and tied it off. Then I throttled

Báltaí back to two and half knots, set a course that would take the vessel due north, and lashed the wheel. I am, of course, being facetious here. On yachts that cost more than thirty million pounds, you don't have to lash the wheel to keep the fucking ship on course. All I really had to do was set the ship's autopilot.

Gerry and Gwilliam were getting a little nervous by now. They were writhing in their chairs, because they understood that *Báltaí* was about to go down—and they'd go down with it. Gwilliam actually got so nervous he pissed on himself.

"Hey," I said disapprovingly, "that's expensive fabric in them there trousers."

He looked up at me with a psychopathic glare.

I put my War Face on, put it close to his, and mimed tweaking his broken nose. "Problem with you, Gwilliam, is you got no sense of humor."

2045. I checked the ship's charts. We were way outside the shipping lanes, heading north, into the five-mile-deep deep waters of the Iberian Basin. That's how the Kelleys had planned it. *Báltaí*'s port of destination had officially been listed as Rabat. That was good: anyone looking for the ship would focus their search eight hundred-plus miles southeast of our current location.

I took a look at the big GPS screen in the wheelhouse to double-check our position. I'd taken another Magellan—a brand-new one still in its box—from the captain's cabin. It was *le bec fin,*[72] as they say in Paris: a third-generation, waterproof, shockproof, Murphy-resistant, long-life battery unit, as well as a spare battery. It hadn't been on the market for more than a month. But that's Krauts for you: only the best. From what the color readout told me, we had a nine-hour sail back to the Azores.

Hugo and Digger filled the jerry cans with gas from the tank used to supply *Báltaí*'s launch. There were a pair of five-gallon

---

[72] The latest thing.

containers in the launch itself, and I took those, too. That gave us forty gallons over what was in the Zodiac's topped-off tanks— enough to get us back to Señor Pereira's warehouse on Pico even if Mister Murphy stowed away. Then I used the weather radio to check on climatic conditions over the next day or so.

The good news was that the front we'd obviously come through on our way out had passed. That meant the winds were dying down, and we'd have an easy transit back to the Azores.

Easy? In an open boat filled with gasoline and two more passengers than it was rated for? Well, let me put that differently. We'd get back without killing ourselves.

2200. I shut down *Báltai*'s engines. Digger, Timex, and Goober went below and opened her sea cocks. Boomerang set the explosive charges. We had about eighteen minutes to get off *Báltai* before she went down. If she didn't scuttle properly, the explosives would do the job. And because of the way they'd been rigged and the way we'd stowed what was aboard, there wouldn't be a lot of flotsam. The fuses were set for twenty-five minutes. We'd stick around long enough to make sure she sank.

"Okay—let's saddle up." I looked at Gerry and Gwilliam. "Untie 'em, stow 'em in the RIB, and secure 'em."

You should have seen the looks on their faces. It was like I was a god—a merciful and compassionate and beneficent god. Yeah— *right.*

2212. We loaded out. *Báltai* was already so low in the water that the accommodation ladder was almost level with the deck. Aboard the Zodiac, the fuel was lashed down and so were the Kelleys. We trimmed the little craft with our own weight, I made sure that everything was shipshape, and then we cast off. I looked up. The skies were finally clearing out. I could see a few first-magnitude stars through gaps in the cloud cover. By 0300 hours we'd be sailing under a canopy of constellations.

2217. *Báltai* slipped under the surface. She was a big vessel, but she died in silence, easing slowly out of sight with the majestic, wounded vulnerability that only a sinking ship can muster. She settled into the swells, then rolled slightly to the starboard, and *then . . . she . . . was . . . gone,* leaving nothing behind but a slight foam that dissipated quickly in the wintry chop.

I eased the throttle forward, leaned into the steering wheel, and the RIB moved away from the yacht's gravesite, cutting through the swells, heading south and west, toward the Azores. We hadn't even gone eight hundred yards when we sensed the shock from the explosions. *Báltaí* had blown apart underwater. The pieces would be scattered five miles below the surface. The ship would never be found. I felt as if a huge weight had been lifted off my body.

2330. The skies had cleared out some more. I could see clusters of stars now. It was cold, but we could handle the cold, because we had completed out mission. Well, almost. I eased the throttle back. The Zodiac slowed down, then stopped. We sat in silence, the only sounds were the sea and the idling Yamaha. I reveled in this moment, bobbing in the swells, becoming a part of the sea, and the sea becoming a part of me.

I looked over at Gerry and Gwilliam, hunkered down, miserable and cold. How many people had they killed? The answer was none, if you are speaking literally. They never pulled the trigger. They never, as I have, stared into the eyes of their enemy, and then snuffed out a life. They did it the new-fangled way. They paid others to do it for them: the tangos from TIRA; the narcoterrorist *pelotudos.* They bought can't-cunts like Greasy Leather Boy from the Irish People's Army, or dumbshits from the Irish Brotherhood. The Green Hand Defenders was nothing more than a front. It was Kelley money at work. Well, it was time for the check-writing to stop.

I flipped out Gerry's former Emerson CQC-7 folder and cut through their bonds.

"I've been thinking about it," I said. "I'm going to let you go."

"Huh?" Gwilliam was confused. "What do you mean," he mumbled through his broken nose.

I looked at him the way you look at a disbelieving child. "I mean you can go. I'm letting you off."

"You're going to set us free?"

Mick Owen nodded. "Precisely."

Gerry frowned. He was having a hard time talking, so I think he said, "Thank you." It was either that, or "Fuck you." With his broken jaw I really couldn't tell.

But since I am an optimist, I lifted my hands like a traffic cop. "No need to thank us. Just be on your way."

Gwilliam looked at me. He looked at the boat. "I don't understand."

Sometimes, people are really dense. Like he didn't know what I was saying? So I gave it to them one more once. "You're free to go. Skedaddle. Vamoose. Get lost. Beat it. Amscray. Sod off. I don't give a shit how you say it, just *leave*."

That's when Gerry—I guess he was the bright one—*Got It*. I think he *Got It*, at least, because he hunkered down and held on to the safety line with both of his hands, whimpering nonsense syllables and whining, *"No-no-no-no."*

I pried his fingers off, one by one. Yes, I admit to breaking a couple of them as I did so. But it couldn't be helped—really. And once I'd gotten his hands off the safety line, I took him by the seat of his pants and the scruff of his neck, and I threw him overboard. He splashed around, spitting water. Mick grabbed Gwilliam and tossed Kelley the younger after Kelley the elder. The two of 'em thrashed around in the cold water like shark bait.

"Yo, chum," I said, pointing toward the east. "Spain's over there." I thought about it. "No it's not. But Portugal is. You can reach it in a couple of weeks if the currents are friendly."

Mick started to say something. Maybe he was going to remind them about not exerting themselves. The water temperature was about forty-five degrees, and if they conserved their energies, they might survive as long as three hours before they succumbed to hypothermia. Then Mick shook his head. There are times to give advice, and Mick, quite correctly, realized that now wasn't one of 'em. Besides, this whole episode had not been a time for words. It had been a time for action. And Mick and I had *acted*. We had—independently of each other—made what is known in the trade as a command decision about the Kelleys' fate. And I was pretty fucking happy with it, too.

Now, I know that a few of the more panty-waisted readers among you are thinking that what I've done is wrong. That I've just caused cruel and unusual punishment, and that I am morally misguided for acting the way I have.

You are grossly mistaken. My job is to kill people and break things. That's why SEALs were created by Roy Boehm. Not as cops, or social workers. Not as do-gooders, or Boy Scouts. And certainly, not to spend time pondering the moral consequences of their actions. No: Roy created SEALs to shoot and to loot. He created us to **wage fucking war without mercy or compassion.** He created us to **kill as many of the enemy as we could, any way we could.** Just like the Ninth Commandment of SpecWar instructs: we will kill our enemies by any means available. And that is precisely what we had just done.

And therefore, dear readers, my conscience was clear. So was Mick's. And frankly, we'd solved a hell of a political problem for the folks back in London and Washington, whether they'd ever realize it or not (and believe me *we* weren't about to tell 'em). I mean, whenever you take assholes like Gwilliam and Gerry and put 'em on trial, a couple of things can happen. First, folks like the Kelleys can afford the very best of legal assistance. So it was altogether possible that they'd pull an O. J. Simpson on us and get off scott free. Second, even if they didn't—if the evidence was airtight and the case was unassailable—they would still be heroes and martyrs to *other* tangos, who'd go out and kill more innocent victims in order to emulate their "heroes."

Moreover, I knew that this particular op would never come back to bite us on the ass. Mick and I had used false IDs to rent the

Zodiac. My men had what's known in the intel trade as complete deniability. Certainly, Mick and I weren't going to own up to what had gone down. In fact, in my mind's eye I could right this minute see myself reporting to Eamon the Demon (whenever we got back to London). *"Admiral, as soon as I hear anything about the Kelley brothers and the Green Hand Defenders, you'll be the first to know. I promise."* I'd say it with a perfectly straight face, too.

No, it would be better for everyone if Gwilliam and Gerry Kelley simply . . . disappeared. Vanished. Evaporated. Without a trace. Which is why I thrust the Zodiac's throttle to the limit, spun the wheel, and we charged off toward the southwest, and the Azores. Within a minute, the Kelleys had disappeared, vanished, and evaporated. Without a trace.

0022. We were heading west-southwest now. According to the brand-new waterproof series three Magellan GPS, we were right on course. I signaled for the guys to dump all the weapons, ammo, and mags overboard. Then I throttled back to thirty knots and stowed the GPS unit securely. After another five minutes or so I eased up on the throttle, slowing us until the Zodiac rocked gently in the swells. Above us, the skies had cleared out. There was a new moon, and so the stars were especially bright. I lay back and looked for some of the constellations the ancient mariners used to guide themselves across these vast, trackless oceans. I saw Pegasus, and Aries. I picked out Taurus, and the Pleiades, and, low in the sky, Orion's belt. I followed the line from the front edge of the Big Dipper to the very end of the tail of Ursa Minor—the end of the Little Dipper's handle. *That* was the North Star. It was the key to all navigation.

My eyes shifted back to the Big Dipper. Free association: there was gonna be one Big Dipperful of trouble to handle when we got back. Mick's star was gonna be on the line. So were my stripes. But if that's the way it would go, well, so be it. Frankly, neither of us gave a shit about our careers. All that mattered to Mick and to me—all that has *ever* mattered to Warriors like Mick and me—

were our men, and their welfare, and getting the job done, no matter what.

I dropped my gaze, and surreptitiously looked upon my magnificent Warriors. They were Warriors in my own image; Warriors with whom I'd willingly go to the ends of the earth. Men I would not hesitate to die for. I snuck a look at Mick. He was also looking skyward, and then his gaze, too, fell, and he slyly peeked at the men in the boat. The expression on his face told me he'd been thinking the exact same thoughts I'd been thinking. That's why we were—and always would be—closer than mere fraternal brothers. *We* were brothers-in-blood. *We* were brothers-in-arms.

Mick shifted his eyes, focusing on me, a craggy, satisfied smile unfolding across his face. "Dick, me lad," he said in his thick Welsh accent, "S*oo*mehow, I feel like dancin'. So let's go home and face the f*oo*kin' music."

There was no need for more words. And so, I swung the boat around, found my heading like all the generations of sailors who'd come before me by checking the stars, and firewalled the throttle. My brother Mick was right. It *was* time to go home.

GLOSSARY

A²: aforementioned asshole.

ANF2A: Absofuckinglutely No Fun At All.

AODW: All Over and Done With.

BAW: Big Asshole Windbag.

BDUs: Battle Dress Uniforms. Now that's an oxymoron if I ever heard one.

BFD: Big Fuckin' Deal.

BFH: Big Fucking Help.

BIQ (Pronounced *beak*): Bitch-in-Question.

BOHICA: Bend Over—Here It Comes Again!

BTDT: Been There, Done That.

BUPERS: Naval BUreau of PERSonnel.

C-4: plastic explosive. You can mold it like clay. You can even use it to light your fires. Just don't stamp on it.

C₂CO: Can't-Cunt Commanding Officer. Too many of these in Navy SpecWar today. They won't support their men or take chances because they're afraid it'll ruin their chances for promotion.

Camuflaje (Spanish): camouflage.

cannon fodder: See FNG.

CC&B: Creeping, Crawling, and Bleeding.

Christians in Action: SpecWar slang for the Central Intelligence Agency.

CINC: Commander-IN-Chief.

CINCUSNAVEUR: Commander IN Chief, U.S. Naval forces, EURope.

CNO: Chief of Naval Operations.

cockbreath: SEAL term of endearment used for those who pay lip service, i.e., presidential squeeze Monica Lewinsky.

CONUS: CONtinental United States.

CQC: Close-Quarters Combat—i.e., killing that's up close and personal.

CT: CounterTerrorism.

DAC: Divide And Conquer.

DADT: Don't Ask, Don't Tell.

DEFCON: DEFense CONdition.

DEVGRP: Naval Special Warfare DEVelopment GRouP. Current U.S. Navy appellation for SEAL Team Six.

DIA: Defense Intelligence Agency. Spook heaven based in Arlington, Va., and Bolling Air Force Base.

diplo-dink: no-load fudge-cutting, cookie-pushing diplomat.

DIPSEC: DIPlomatic SECurity. SEAL shorthand for the Diplomatic Security Service, the Department of State's special agent shoot-and-looters.

dipshit: can't-cunt pencil-dicked asshole.

DIQ (pronounced *dick*): Document-In-Question. You can have sensitive DIQs, big, thick DIQs, or even tiny, penciled DIQs. And if you drop your DIQ into a puddle of water, you'll probably end up with a limp DIQ.

Do-ma-nhieu (Vietnamese): Go fuck yourself (See: DOOM ON YOU).

doom on you: American version of Vietnamese for *go fuck yourself.*

DT: Deserving Twat. No-load, shit-for-brains asshole.

dweeb: no-load shit-for-brains geeky asshole, usually shackled to a computer.

EEI: Essential Element of Information. The info-nuggets on which a mission is planned and executed.

EEO: Equal Employment Opportunity (The Rogue always treats 'em all alike—just like shit).

ELINT: ELectronic INTelligence.
EOD: Explosive Ordnance Disposal.

F2T: Full Fucking Ton.
FIDO: Army Ranger shorthand for Fuck It, Drive On. *Hoo-Ah!*
flashbang: disorientation device used by hostage rescue teams.
FLFC: Fucking Loud and Fucking Clear.
FLIR: Forward Looking InfraRed.
FNG: Fucking New Guy. See: CANNON FODDER.
Four-striper: Captain. All too often, a C²CO.
FUBAR: Fucked Up Beyond All Repair.

Glock: Reliable 9-mm pistols made by Glock in Austria. They're great for SEALs because they don't require as much care as Sig Sauers.
GNBN: Good News/Bad News.
goatfuck: What the Navy likes to do to the Rogue Warrior (See: FUBAR).
GSG-9: Grenzchutzgruppe-9. Top German CT unit.

HAHO: High-Altitude, High-Opening parachute jump.
HALO: High-Altitude, Low-Opening parachute jump.
HICs: Head-In-Cement syndrome. Condition common to high-ranking officers. Symptoms include pigheadedness and inability to change opinions when presented with new information.
HK: Reliable pistols, assault rifles, or submachine guns made by Heckler & Koch. SEALs use H&K MP5 submachine guns in various configurations, as well as 9-mm or .45-Cal. semiautomatic pistols.
HKTB: Hot knife Through Butter.
HUMINT: HUMan INTelligence.
humongous: Marcinko dick.

IED: Improvised Explosive Device.

Jarheads: Marines. The Corps. Formally, USMC (Uncle Sam's Misguided Children).

KATN: Kick Ass and Take Names. Roguish avocation.
KISS: Keep It Simple, Stupid. The basic premise for all special operations.

klik: Verbal shorthand for kilometer. One klik equals six-tenths of a mile.

KSO: KISS Step One.

KST: KISS Step Two.

LANTFLT: atLANTic FLeeT.

LTWS: Lower than whale shit.

M³: Massively motivated motherfuckers.

Mark-I Mod-0: basic unit.

MILCRAFT: Pentagonese for MILitary airCRAFT.

NAVAIR: NAVy AIR Command.

NAVSEA: NAVy SEA Command.

NAVSPECWARGRU: NAVal SPECial WARfare GRoUp.

Navyspeak: redundant, bureaucratic naval nomenclature, either in written nonoral, or nonwritten oral modes, indecipherable by non-military (conventional) or military (unconventional) individuals during normal interfacing configuration conformations.

NIS: Naval Investigative Service Command, also known as the Admirals' Gestapo (See: SHIT-FOR-BRAINS).

NMN: No Middle Name.

NRO: National Reconnaissance Office. Established 25 August 1960 to administer and coordinate satellite development and operations for U.S. intelligence community. Very spooky place.

NSA: National Security Agency, known within the SpecWar community as No Such Agency.

NSD: National Security Directive.

NYL: nubile young lovely.

OPSEC: OPerational SECurity

P⁴: pricked, pierced, punctured, and perforated.

PDMP: Pretty Dangerous Motherfucking People.

PEO: President's Eyes Only.

PIC: pissed, irritated, and confused.

PIQ: (pronounced *pick*): Pussy In Question.

plano (Spanish): street plan; map.

POC: piece o' cake.

Póg mo thón (Gaelic): kiss my ass.

QOO (Pronounced *KOO*): Quick Once-Over.

RDL: real dirty look.

RPG: Rocket-Propelled Grenade.

RSO: Regional Security Officer. State Department's diplomat with a gun.

R²D²: ritualistic, rehearsed, disciplined drills.

RUMINT: RUMor INTelligence. Urinal gossip.

S¹: Square one.

S²: Sit the fuck down and Shut the fuck up.

S³: Shower, Shit, and Shave.

SAS: Special Air Service. Britain's top CT unit.

SATCOM: SATellite COMmunications.

SCIF: Sensitive Compartmented Information Facility. A bug-proof room.

Semtex: Czechoslovakian C-4 plastique explosive. Can be used to cancel Czechs.

SES: Shit-eating smile.

shit-for-brains: any no-load, pus-nutted, pencil-dicked asshole.

SIGINT: SIGnals INTelligence.

SNAFU: Situation Normal—All Fucked Up.

SNAILS: Slow, Nerdy Assholes In Ludicrous Shoes.

SpecWarrior: One who gives a fuck.

SUC: Smart, Unpredictable, and Cunning.

SWAT: Special Weapons And Tactics. Commonly refers to police tactical teams. All too often they do not train enough, and thus become SQUAT teams.

sympathy: The word found in the SEAL dictionary between *shit* and *syphilis.*

TAD: Temporary Additional Duty (SEALs refer to it as Traveling Around Drunk).

Tailhook: the convention of weenie-waggers, gropesters, and pressed-ham-on-glass devotees that put air brakes on NAVAIR.

TARFU: Things Are Really Fucked Up.
TECHINT: TECHnical **INT**elligence.
TFB: Too fucking bad.
THREATCON: THREAT CONdition.
TIQ: Tango-In-Question
TTS: Tap 'em, Tie 'em, and Stash 'em.

U2: Ugly and unfamiliar.
UNODIR: UNless Otherwise **DIR**ected. That's how the Rogue operates when he's surrounded by can't-cunts.
USSOCOM: United States Special Operations COMmand, located at MacDill AFB, Tampa, Florida.

VERB (noun): Vacant-Eyed Rich Bitch.
VTVE: Very Thorough Visual Exam.

Wanna-bes: The sorts of folks you meet at *Soldier of Fortune* conventions.
Weenies: Pussy-ass can't-cunts and no-loads.
Whiskey Numbers: NSA compartment designator for intercepts that go to the very highest levels of the government.
WHUTA: Wild Hair Up The Ass.
WOO: Window Of Opportunity.
WTF: What The Fuck.
WTFIW: What The Fuck It Was.

YAA: Yet Another Asshole.

Zulu: Universal Military Time (formerly Greenwich Mean Time or GMT). Designator used in military communications.

INDEX

All entries preceded by an asterisk (*) are pseudonyms.

INDEX

INDEX

INDEX

INDEX

RIB (Rigid Inflatable Boat), 257, 259,
    260, 291, 292, 302, 304, 322, 323
Richardson, Bill, 225
Rio de la Plata, 115, 131, 169, 178,
    181–82
Río Lujan, 129, 173–80
river crossings, 173–75, 176–80
Roger (Special Branch intel dweeb),
    10, 16, 20, 25, 26
Rogue Warrior®, 26, 111, 146, 164,
    175, 182, 207, 259
  First Law of Self Preservation, 81
Rogue's First Rule of Conversation, 88
Rogue's First Law of Physics, 99,
    159, 214
Rose, Sir Michael, 288–89

SAS, 35, 36, 232
  Pagoda Troop, 34
SAS shooters, 13, 31, 34, 44
  joint CT op with, 116
school takeover, 32–37, 39–51, 53–54,
    59, 75, 92, 114
SCIF (Sensitive, Compartmented
    Information Facility), 105, 108, 110
Scotland Yard, 7, 8, 13, 21, 31, 65
  Special Branch, 7, 10, 13, 14, 112
Scowcroft, Brent, 132
SDR (Surveillance Detection Route),
    169, 242
sea-borne tactical assault, 257–58
SEAL Team Six, 152, 208
SEAL tie tack, 156, 160–62
SEAL trident, 160, 161, 162, 163
SEALs, 5, 6, 7, 14, 15, 20, 33, 35, 43,
    65, 67, 108, 112, 116, 160, 161,
    162, 175, 177
  equipment, 257–58
  failure unacceptable to, 211
  Marcinko as, 260
  pistols for, 170
  purpose of, 325
  rule(s) of thumb, 176
  in Vietnam, 175

weather for, 279
SIS (Secret Intelligence Service),
    235
SO-19, 7, 13, 14, 35, 65, 70–71
  in hostage rescue, 41, 44
Somalia, 89, 108, 153
South America, 77, 186, 243
surveillance, 5, 17, 73, 134, 135,
    140–43, 273

Tai Li'ang, General, 65, 81, 131
Tanzania, 131, 158
targets
  American embassy Buenos Aires,
    221–22, 276
  Americans and Brits, 6–7, 62, 70,
    107, 110, 113, 131, 222
  of *Báltaí*, 276–77
  of Kelley operation, 226, 276–77,
    288, 320
TEAM (concept), 96–97
Ten Downing Street, 72, 75, 84*n*, 111,
    112
terrorist operations, 70, 110, 192
terrorists, 6, 59, 64, 68, 92, 227, 230,
    240, 277–78, 323
Thatcher, Margaret, 70, 91, 288
Timex (Terry Devine), 34, 285, 286
  and assault on *Báltaí*, 287, 293,
    295–96, 301, 302, 305, 308, 309,
    314, 320, 322
  in Buenos Aires, 123, 130, 135, 136,
    137, 139
  in hostage rescue, 44, 45
  intelligence gathering, 65, 69, 71–72,
    73
  investigation of/attack on Kelley
    villa, 193, 201, 202, 206–07, 209,
    210, 211, 222
  in investigation of *Patricia Desens*,
    172, 173, 174, 177, 178, 179
  and preparation for assault on
    Báltaí, 260, 266, 269
  trip to Buenos Aires, 116

341